Luma jumped, and the city propelled her into the air. She grazed the dripping crystals of the great hall's chandeliers, leaving them rocking and tinkling. Breathing deep, she braced for the coming landing.

Her outstretched feet struck Noole in the back. She rolled, hitting the pedestal of a statue to a long-dead contralto. She made her way up, watching Noole as he rose and drew a rapier. Her own weapon lay on the rug a few feet away; she'd dropped it to avoid cutting herself as she landed. Feigning dismay, she let him come at her midsection. The thin sword jabbed skillfully at her. With equal aplomb, she evaded the thrust. Continuing the motion, she snatched up her sickle and dove at her opponent. He kept her at bay with a feint of his blade. They circled one another, Luma leaving ghostings of flour wherever she stepped.

"I can't guess what you want with me," the gnome said, "but I want nothing to do with you."

"Drop your weapon and I'll explain," Luma answered.

He held it out as if ready to let it go, then lunged. The blade caught Luma on the side of the neck. It hurt, but she could tell the wound was only superficial. She swiped at his legs with her sickle; he hopped back with flamboyant ease. Adopting a perfect fencing stance, he waited for her to come at him.

His moves so far revealed one fighting style disguised as another. Noole added flourishes to what was, at its core, a cautious waiting game of precisely timed blows. He was waiting for Luma to make a mistake he could capitalize on. In this, and in his general deftness and quick reactions, he favored an approach to combat that was also Luma's. One patient, calculating scrapper faced another.

This could go on all day

The Pathfinder Tales Library

Blood of the City

Robin D. Laws

paizo
PUBLISHING

Cover art by Adam Danger Cook.
Cover design by Andrew Vallas.
Map by Robert Lazzaretti.

Paizo Publishing, LLC
7120 185th Ave NE, Ste 120
Redmond, WA 98052
paizo.com

ISBN 978-1-60125-456-6 (mass market paperback)
ISBN 978-1-60125-457-3 (ebook)

Publisher's Cataloging-In-Publication Data
(Prepared by The Donohue Group, Inc.)

Laws, Robin D.
  Blood of the city / Robin D. Laws.

    p. ; cm. -- (Pathfinder tales)

  Set in the world of the role-playing game, Pathfinder.
  Issued also as an ebook.
  ISBN: 978-1-60125-456-6 (mass market pbk.)

  1. Druids and druidism--Fiction. 2. Balance of power--Fiction. 3. Imaginary places--Fiction. 4. Betrayal--Fiction. 5. Good and evil--Fiction. 6. Fantasy fiction. 7. Adventure stories. I. Title. II. Title: Pathfinder adventure path. III. Series: Pathfinder tales library.

PS3612.A87 B56 2012
813/.6

First printing August 2012.

Printed in the United States of America.

With glaive-guisarmes raised
in memory of
Dave Arneson & E. Gary Gygax

MAGNIMAR

Nirodin
House

ALABASTER DISTRICT

Triodea

Derexhi
House

CAPITAL DISTRICT

NAOS

Pediment
Building

Cenotaph

Irespan

Seacleft

Bazaar
of
Sails

DOCKWAY

LOWCLEFT

Celwynvian
Charge

KEYSTONE

BEACON'S
POINT

Bent Rib
Alley

Z

ORDELLIA

Chapter One
Shadow

Crouched over broken cobblestones, her siblings hidden nearby, Luma opened herself to the citysong. Its melody, perceptible only to a special few, played on all five senses.

Overhead hung the ruined expanse of the Irespan. From this angle, the bridge's cracked basalt canopy blotted out the sky, casting the shadow that gave the district its name.

Luma heard the wind rattling across it. The city, building from these simple notes, rushed in on her. She felt the first light of dawn strike the Seacleft, the great cliff that divided the city into its two halves: the Summit above and the Shore below.

Atop the reaching tower that was the Arvensoar, a watchman coughed. The cries of peddlers and hawkers chorused in, echoing from marbled walls. Galleons laden with trade goods groaned in the harbor. Foreign tongues counterpointed on the piers. In the temples incense wafted, pungent with prayers to a dozen gods. Rich men of the Summit snored on velvet beds; in their kitchens rose the smell of flour and lard as servants kneaded bread for their breakfasts.

Heat from these distant stoves, carried to her by the citysong, warmed Luma's bones. She felt the aching muscles of Bridgeward quarrymen as they picked up chisel and hammer to stumble to yet another day of labor. In a shop of the high-moneyed Vista district, the scent of citrus and cloves escaped from a toppled perfume bottle. For an instant, Luma burned with the shame of the shopgirl who knocked it over. The flash of emotion disappeared back into the pulsating citysong, one story among thousands. Other glimpses fleeted by: despair and a rattling chain in the depths of the Hells, a hookah-smoked hangover in a Lowcleft brothel, a face soothed in the pure waters of the Seerspring, and by the loamy reek of its surrounding garden.

The city sang the greed of thieves, the hunger of beggars, the frustration of actors, the waywardness of husbands, and the determination of wives. Luma flapped as a crow across slate-roofed warehouses, scuttled as a rat through trash-strewn gutters, and whickered as a horse stabled near the Bazaar of Sails. Together, these parts—people, places, animals, and the workings of nature, ever present and ever persistent—formed a greater whole, which was the spirit of the city. And from this spirit, Magnimar in its essence and entirety, flowed Luma's power. Such as it was.

Few in the city of Magnimar, or for that matter in all of Golarion, could tell you about cobblestone druids—or citywalkers, or streetcallers, or whatever one chose to call them. Those few who felt qualified to speak might say that each city boasted its own celestial guardian—if not a god, something akin to one—from whom the citywalker gained divine magic. Luma herself did not much understand it, but as far as she could tell, there was no city god. Not for her, at least. Instead there was the song. To draw on it was not to pray, but to listen.

Though thirty years old, Luma was frequently mistaken for a girl of half that age. Her father, and others inclined toward kindness, attributed this to her elven blood. The smoothness of her pale skin, her blue and slightly over-sized eyes, and her small, pursed lips combined to convey a falsely callow first impression, they said. That was not all there was to it, though. Even as she hunched down in a district of troublemakers and thieves, sickle in hand, ready to fight, Luma held herself with a child's diffidence. A gust tousled at her wild tangle of bright red hair. A strand fell across her face. Unaware of the gesture, she wrapped it pensively around a forefinger, then chewed on it.

Luma shook off her apprehension to focus on the objective at hand. A boarded-up hovel, its decaying timber scourged by salty air, stood kitty-corner from her position. Assuming their informant had his scuttlebutt straight, they'd find their quarry and his kidnappers inside. Luma ran through the situation again. Once inside, any tiny detail could tip the balance between victory and humiliation.

The adversaries were Shoanti extortionists. Luma had heard fashionable people speak of the Shoanti with admiration—always making it clear they meant only those who dwelt far away, and not their degenerate city-dwelling cousins.

On the plains of Varisia, particularly the uplands of the Storval Plateau, Shoanti existed as wild men, surviving off the fruits of the faraway land. Tales of their hunting, foraging, and occasional raids fed the city-bound imagination.

Stories about Shoanti gangs in Magnimar, however, recounted incidents of vicious mayhem, many of them mostly true. People called them savages, fiends, headchoppers. The trades they plied brought trouble out of proportion to their meager numbers. In gangs of their own, or in service to local criminals, they lived by ransom, theft, and extortion. To them, the city Luma loved was just another wilderness. This was what her brother Ontor liked to call an ironic reversal.

Luma had a simpler observation: in a fight, Shoanti were tough, unrelenting opponents.

Even a conversation with one bore a constant potential for sudden violence. Prone to offense, they bore some improbable grievance against the ruling Magnimarian people—people like Luma and her family—and loved to go on about it. To Luma, who shied from any hint of politics, the prospect of arguing with Shoanti was almost as bad as having to fight them.

The objective of the raid was a prisoner, Alam Scarnetti. His father, Gradon, oversaw a timber empire from a tomb-like manor squarely in the Summit's dearest quarters. The younger Scarnetti could blame his predicament on a taste for wagering. He owed money to gamblers, who sold his debt to the Shoanti, who took him hostage, demanding a payout with considerable penalties. The older Scarnetti, it turned out, would rather hire private enforcers, risking his son's life, than hand over the ransom. Luma, who never met with clients, gathered that Scarnetti senior was not much fonder of his son than he was of extortionists.

This introduced a dangerous ambiguity: Alam could be an accomplice in the scheme. It wouldn't be the first time a wastrel scion had teamed with shady creditors to squeeze a higher allowance from a reluctant family. She'd be careful not to turn her back to him.

Whatever motivated Gradon, it wasn't parsimony. Of all the squads her father hired out, the services of the family team warranted by far the highest fees.

Luma's siblings had considered and discarded various complicated plans, leaving as their best option the old smash and grab. They'd launch a sudden assault from all sides. If it worked, one of them would spot the target and separate him from the extortionists before they could slash his throat. If it didn't, they wouldn't be paid.

Members of her family, the Derexhi, had been paid for missions like this for generations, starting back when the city was nothing but a collection of wagons and shacks atop the big cliff. Luma wasn't worried that they'd fail to save their man. What plagued her instead was the thought of another mistake, like last month with the half-orc squatters. They'd won then, and been handsomely paid, but that didn't stop the scolding afterward.

Beside the one-story hovel teetered a higher tenement, also deteriorating. Ontor rose from its roof. He took a few seconds to survey the state of the tenement wall, then clambered down, gripping free-handed its rotting plank facing. Ontor wore supple black leather armor, shorn of ornament and modified for ease of movement. While on the job, he kept his flowing black hair tied in a topknot. A proud smirk animated his elongated features. Its swagger cast a favorable light on his beakish nose and pointed chin, which in another man could have seemed homely.

Ontor landed soundlessly on the hovel roof. Pressing himself flat, he shimmied to its edge. He withdrew a flat chisel from his belt and found a gap between the hovel's roof and wall. His efforts revealed it as predictably ill-constructed: in this case, the planks had been nailed directly into the side of the roof. One plank at a time, he set to work widening the gap. When he'd pried a plank away to his satisfaction, he reached down to tug free its nails. He then let the plank fall back into place, turning the poorly fashioned wall into a false front.

A voice, languorous and sibilant, spoke into Luma's ear. "Be ready. They may waken, or have a sentinel posted." It was Luma's sister, Iskola, magically watching from a hiding place inside yet another nearby tenement. Her wizardry would be carrying the same words to the others as well.

Ontor raised a beckoning hand. Luma crept from her corner position. The others emerged from their hiding spots.

Broad-shouldered Arrus cricked his thick neck from side to side, as was his habit before battle. Shafts of sunlight, which shone below the bridge for an hour each morning, highlighted the red in his close-cropped hair and beard.

Mouthing a silent dedication to his god, Eibadon produced a bulbous mace. The family priest closely resembled Arrus, save for the good looks. Though the younger of the two, Eibadon appeared older. His clerical tonsure did little to flatter him, instead emphasizing the roundness of his jowls and double chin.

Ulisa, her shaven head adding to an overall impression of skeletal gauntness, gathered her saffron robe about her, expression turning inward. She neither carried nor needed a weapon.

Arrus unsheathed his longsword, giving the signal.

Ontor lowered himself onto the roof. He lay on his back and kicked, knocking down the planks he'd loosened. The hovel's front face collapsed, leaving only the odd board in place. Luma let Arrus take point, then followed, with Eidabon and Ulisa keeping pace.

Inside the hovel, Shoanti brawlers scrambled from their sleeping mats. They seized axes, clubs, and daggers.

Ontor swung from the roof into their midst, planting a knife between the shoulder blades of his closest opponent. The thug dropped to his knees, flailing behind him to grab the hilt, then went still.

The Shoanti howled in wordless rage.

Arrus entered the hovel, swinging his sword. It struck true, and another rebel collapsed, clutching his throat.

Nearing the now-gaping threshold, Luma spotted the prisoner lashed to a bench in a darkened corner, thick seafarer's rope coiled around him.

With the deftness of a woman used to pressing through city crowds, she dodged the swipe of an incoming axe. Her sickle returned the blow, slashing her enemy's wrist. His axe clattered to the floor. As he came for it, Luma waved her weapon at him. Something about the ropes holding Alam Scarnetti tugged at her attention. Distracted, she failed to keep her enemy at bay; he snatched up the axe and plunged at her.

Ulisa stepped in, seizing his other arm and folding it neatly behind his back. The axe man contorted in pain. The manipulated arm fell limp at his side. He came at Ulisa, but the injury had thrown off his balance. Easily ducking his blow, she snatched his axe from his hand. In a single movement, she bashed its butt into his glottis and hurled the axe into a support beam, where it stuck, quivering.

Shoanti reinforcements boiled into the hovel. Luma paid them no heed, intent on the prisoner. Something was amiss.

Ontor slid behind a rebel to stab him in the spine, then lunged to free their target.

"No!" Luma shouted.

Shoanti had a way with simple but ingenious traps, and with toxins. In this they were scarcely alone; the Magnimarian passion for poisoning ran deep. Luma reached into the citysong, calling on the dark part of it that reveled in venoms, blights, and corruptions. Its tune altered, bubbling with the whispers of crooked apothecaries, clinking with bottles and jars, crunching with the grinding of pestles. The citysong reverberated at her from a spot amid the ropes: a long, thin needle jutted through the coils, a nearly invisible lacquer covering its tip. The lacquer joined the citysong. *I am poison*, it sang, at a frequency only Luma could hear.

She pointed to it. "Poisoned," she told Ontor.

The needle had been positioned so that any careless attempt to untie Alam Scarnetti would plunge its tip into him, his rescuer, or one and then the other.

"Don't move," Ontor told Scarnetti.

The prisoner barely managed to speak. "I won't."

A burly figure, easily a foot taller than Arrus and elaborately muscled, burst toward them. He seized Luma by the shoulders and hurled her into a wall. Before she could right herself, he was on her, kicking and punching. Each blow landed with bruising intensity. She scrambled for her sickle; it lay on the floor, out of reach. He kicked her again, then bent over her, seizing her by her leather cuirass. His head was hairless save for a greasy ponytail which dangled into her face. On his forehead was a tattooed Shoanti emblem: a two headed-snake wrapped around a pair of jutting axes.

"Now the weakblood moneybelts send their pale daughters to fight me?" His roar flecked Luma's face with spittle. "To fight Priza, they send children?"

He spun her around, wrapping his left arm around her neck. In his right he held a curved, serrated dagger, set to rasp across her jugular vein.

Arrus approached; the Derexhi closed formation around him. Behind him, the Shoanti dragged off their wounded. New additions swelled their ranks.

"You insult me," Priza growled, "by sending such as this against me."

Arrus essayed an icy smile. "You'd rather fight me, then?"

"You will leave, or this one dies. Later, you will receive our ransom demand for her. And Scarnetti's ransom will double."

"There is no negotiating with kidnappers," said Arrus.

"Who's negotiating?" Priza snorted.

Sweat pilled on Priza's bare arms. Luma waited for the instant of maximum adjustment, then used it as a lubricant to slip free. As she'd trained herself to do, she used her slight stature to advantage. To grab her, he'd overbalanced himself. She pulled him forward, then stepped to the side. Priza stumbled into the reach of Arrus's sword. Arrus chose a cleaving blow. Dropping the knife he'd held at Luma's throat, the Shoanti warrior expertly turned, taking the strike on a well-armored shoulder. His knees buckled, but he recovered, pulling loose his axe. He pushed at Arrus, forcing him back.

The two sides stood as if mesmerized, watching the two men fight. A flurry of parrying and swinging left both Arrus and Priza gasping. They joined in an instant's pause, then flung themselves against one another again.

Certain of the other rebels leapt back into the fray, engaging Ulisa, Ontor, and Eibadon. Luma rushed to the prisoner's side. Ontor's burglary kit still lay beside him. Luma grabbed a pair of long-nosed pliers. "Stay still," she told the Scarnetti.

"I will," he whispered.

She grasped the poisoned needle and jerked it loose from the rope. Then she started in on the complicated knot, the heavy rope abrading her hands. Gradually the rope loosened and fell. Shame contorted the prisoner's face: a ripe ordure smell wafted from his body.

The fight lost the adrenaline intensity of its first clashes, giving way to exhaustion and wary circling. More thugs lay dead or groaning in a circle around Ontor,

Ulisa, and Eibadon. Arrus and Priza bashed away at one another with declining energy and increasing fury.

A slight, ebony-clad figure stepped into view from the street. It was Iskola, Arrus's twin. A high forehead and hawkish nose offered variations on the basic Derexhi facial features. She took in the scene with wide, protruding eyes. As was her habit in combat situations, she'd left her intricate hairpiece at home, leaving instead a bowl of glossy black hair flattened to her scalp. A high, latticed collar of black lace and a pair of laced, fingerless gloves lent her the outre aspect Magnimarian society expected of an accomplished wizard.

Iskola raised a finger, paused to calculate, and sent a blaze of blue energy through the room. The results showed the perfection of her angle: the electricity blasted through nearly every Shoanti, while leaving the Derexhi unscathed.

She'd left Priza out of the spell's trajectory. Arrus stepped back, giving the man room to withdraw.

Iskola saw that Alam Scarnetti was free. She addressed Priza. "This confrontation has reached its natural end."

"I can take him," said Arrus.

Priza bared gleaming white teeth.

"Taking him is not the mission," Iskola said. "Priza, is it?"

Priza nodded his acknowledgment.

"You might be able to fight all day, but your men are done. Your prisoner is loosed from his bonds; your odds of keeping him, poor. Need I enumerate further?"

Priza fumed, then raised his axe to point in turn at each of the rescuers. "Take him and go."

Chapter Two
Bridgeward

The Derexhi siblings escorted the Scarnetti scion from the Shadow district into Bridgeward. There, at a tavern called the Hammer and Stone, factotums of his father's household awaited his return.

Here the citysong rang with the sounds of stonework, of smithy ovens and firing kilns. Bridgeward was Magnimar's neighborhood of artisans. Their pooled intentions permeated the citysong. In it, Luma heard their pursuit of perfection, their lust for fine materials, the heat of their desire to outshine rivals. The magics they used to throw their pots and cast their jewelry and color their glass ran through her hair and sparkled across the backs of her hands.

A wind caught furls of marble dust; it drifted over the group as they made for the pub. Alam Scarnetti batted it as if it were a cloud of gnats. "I'm so ashamed," he said.

"Your men will purchase new clothes for you before you return home," answered Iskola. "If those barbarians refused you the use of a chamberpot, you cannot be blamed for it."

Alam made a clucking sound. "That's an embarrass-ment, to be sure," he said. "But the entire affair—it started with a simple game of cards. Then the fights at Tessik's, which I'm reasonably certain are rigged—"

"Oh, Tessik's fights are rigged, all right," said Ontor.

"I thought those people were my friends, but they led me down the golden path to debt, and then they sold me to those—those savages . . ."

"This is Magnimar," said Ontor. "If they're not family, don't trust them."

Luma wasn't sure she trusted Alam. There was still the chance he was in on it. She hung back a step or two to listen to the citysong. The city understood people. The tens of thousands of folk who had lived and died here over the decades had thought all the thoughts it was possible to think. They might be gone, but their echoes had joined the citysong. As a consequence of this phenomenon, one attuned to Magnimar's collective essence could peer into minds, at least to find the simple, obvious ruminations floating around on top.

The father was the real client. If Alam had been betraying him, working with the Shoanti to bleed his fortune, he deserved to know.

She found the strain of citysong, woven from the thought patterns of its citizens, that separated truth and falsehood as the Seacleft divided rich and poor. At first she caught a whirl of meaningless words— undecipherable fragments of thoughts current and past, from the living and the dead. Luma let this mental flotsam wash past her, and concentrated on Alam.

Father will be insufferable now he'll never let me live this down he wants me to be like him but I can't I've tried and I can't I don't care about timber or ledgers there has to be

*more to life than leasing forests and cutting down trees just
because we've always done it so they're truly all brothers
and sisters how does that work because the mousy one
looks like she's got elf blood in her I suppose her father
got a little faerie dust on him before settling down with
humankind she doesn't dress herself or comb her hair but
maybe she'd be up for a tumble though I suppose in my
state of humiliation I'd have a better chance of couching
with the goddess Shelyn than bedding her . . .*

Flushing, Luma erased the laneway she'd created
between his mind and the citysong. All manner of
nonsense filled Alam Scarnetti's head, but none of
it spoke to a guilty conscience. He was merely as his
father saw him: reckless and gullible.

Still, when they reached the Hammer and Stone, and
she saw the disapproving faces of the Scarnetti family
retainers—gray men in gray cloaks, savoring the chance
to sorrowfully shake their heads—she couldn't help a
pang of sympathy for him. Alam's body language, as he
followed Iskola to their side, reminded her of a scolded
puppy. She wanted to see him hold onto at least a scrap
of dignity. The smallest gesture would have done—a
sheepish grin, an insouciant shrug. Instead he shuddered, as if on the verge of bawling. Stiffening in disgust,
the retainers wrapped a blanket around his shoulders.

After an exchange of curt nods, Iskola withdrew. In
a manner befitting the dignity of the client, payment
would be separately arranged.

Luma swallowed. Soon it would begin.

Ontor jumped in before Arrus could introduce the
obvious subject. "I wouldn't like to be him, when he
gets home," he said.

"A foolish man was foolishly raised," said Ulisa, her
robe flapping in the breeze.

"It won't help that his father has to pay our fee," said Ontor.

Iskola brushed marble dust from her ebony raiment. "We'll be paid in a currency dearer than coin."

"Is that so?"

As was his habit before making a pronouncement, Eibadon cleared his throat. His voice, like the rest of him, had prematurely aged. "As is said in the Proverbs of the First Vault, there is nothing one finds in a strongbox that is worth either more or less than gold."

Ontor laughed. "Is there a meaning I should take away from that, Eibadon?"

"Meditate upon it and what must be revealed, shall be."

"You can bet that I will give it full consideration, the next time I meditate." Ontor untied his top-knot, allowing his silken hair to spill across his shoulders. "Does Father need us all back?"

Arrus examined a bruise spreading across his forearm. "Why do you ask?"

"The fire of battle still floods my veins. It might likewise flood some of yours, those of you who have them. A stop at a tavern might cool our nerves."

"I'd join you," said Arrus, "but the sun has barely crept above the horizon."

"Any time of day when a Shoanti tries and fails to take your head off is suitable for the hoisting of flagons."

"Then raise a second one for me. Father will be anxious for his report."

"Suit yourself. Anyone else?" Ontor asked.

"So, Luma," said Arrus.

"What?"

"I suppose I have no choice but to mention that you got yourself taken hostage."

"Tell him what happened," Luma shrugged.

"She got herself free," said Ontor.

"And if she hadn't?" Arrus failed to keep the enjoyment entirely out of his tone.

"Unless I took a hit to the head and have completely taken leave of my recollections, I'm certain that she did," said Ontor. "As are the rest of us." He looked to the others, but none of them spoke. "Abadar's kidneys, Arrus. You're more of a pain by the day."

"Between the pain of an unpleasant discussion, and that of death by enemy hands, which should we choose? Luma?"

Luma wanted to leap onto an alleyway wall and climb away like a scuttling spider. This was no metaphor, but a real trick the city had taught her. But later she would have to come back, her shame redoubled. "You're right, Arrus. It was a misstep. I can do better, and I will."

Ontor's fists clenched. "Any of us could have been caught out like that. It was a fight, Arrus. Bad moments happen. And don't forget, she's the one spotted the poison needle. Without her, our rescued wastrel would be a corpse. Maybe one of us along with him."

Arrus clapped him on the shoulder. Ontor winced; he'd taken a hard blow there. "Don't mind me, little brother. You're right. The heat of battle lingers in the blood. You slake your fight-nerves with Fort Indros Ale. I gnaw over the report, seeking improvement. I daresay your method is the healthier. Yet as Eibadon can't help spouting proverbs, and Luma can't stop herself slouching, I can't restrain myself." Ontor evaded a second shoulder-clap, circuiting out of range.

Thwarted, Arrus came up behind Luma and bear-hugged her off the ground. Feet flailing, she tried to slip from his grasp, as she had Priza's, but he'd placed a grip surer than the barbarian's. He ran his fingers through her tangled hair, carelessly pulling it. He roughly rubbed her scalp. "Our half-sister knows we love her. Don't you, Luma?" He made to let her down, then hauled her up into the air again. "Don't you?"

"Of course!" she yelled. Immediately she regretted her volume. Workmen hauling worked stone in a barrow stopped to stare.

Belly-laughing, Arrus released her.

"Arrus, you're not twelve anymore," Ontor groaned.

Arrus wiped sweat from his brow. "I haven't offended you, have I now, Luma?"

"No," she insisted.

"See, Ontor? She's not the delicate vine you think she is. She may be half elf, but the other half of her is Derexhi. She can take it."

"I'm not the one calling her a . . . oh, never mind," said Ontor.

"A strong leader's tread," Eibadon quoted, "may flatten some wheat."

Luma jolted to attention; the citysong had shifted its pitch. She sensed that the source of the disturbance was nearby. Her head turned just in time to see a shape ducking out of sight on a rooftop across the way.

"What is it?" Iskola asked.

"Nothing," said Luma. The song had returned to normalcy.

She'd had this feeling before. Once, early on, she'd alerted the group to imminent attack. But then, as always, the moment passed. She couldn't pin it down. There was imbalance in it, and observation, too. But whether it was a menace yet to come, or one of the thousand random occurrences of a bustling city, she could never be sure. Maybe it was the citysong itself testing her, a premonition of secrets it would soon reveal. Sometimes she felt funny, then realized shortly afterward that Magnimar had been adding new magics to her repertoire.

"Are you certain?" Iskola asked.

"A false alarm," said Luma. "A bird or somesuch."

They walked without comment for a while, wending past workshops and warehouses.

Arrus broke the silence. "Luma understands if I'm overprotective of her. Don't you?"

Luma couldn't tell if this was remorse for crossing the line before, or a prelude to another round. "We all have to watch each other's backs."

"After all, not everyone has a cobblestone druid with them, do they?" It was not clear who Arrus was addressing—perhaps himself. "Our little Luma, if we keep her alive, may someday surpass us all. She'll walk on air, like it was as solid as this street beneath our heels. Bring the dead to life in new bodies. You'll be of great use to us then, won't you?"

"She's of use to us now," said Ontor.

"That's what I said. But those would be great workings, wouldn't they? The stuff of legend, eh, Luma?"

The group rounded a corner. At the end of the street clanked a party of men, encased in armor both flamboyant and menacing. Each suit, dull as slate and as dark as iron, was ornamented in the extreme. Flanges, spikes, and crests rose from or surrounded the helmets. Spikes fared from shoulder-plates. The fingers of their metal gloves were shaped like claws, either straight or curved. The knee-guards alone outweighed an ordinary soldier's helmet: they took on the stylized forms of ram's heads, or gargoyles, or glowering suns. More outlandish still were the sculpted breastplates, each in the shape of a voracious, diabolical face. One warrior paraded about in a toothy skull; another wore a reptilian visage. The man to his left sported a beetle's face, outfitted with articulated, clacking mandibles. The effect was irresistible: one always looked into the face on the breastplate, ignoring the helmeted head above.

"Nothing improves a morning," said Ontor, "like a squad of Hellknights."

The armored men, previously walking in loose formation, stopped and spread out, blocking the street.

Dimples appeared on Arrus's face. "They wish to test the family resolve." He marched toward them; Luma and the others kept pace, a step back.

Hands hovering over sword hilts, the Hellknights braced themselves.

Arrus dropped into a saunter. When he reached earshot, he faked out a salute, which at the last minute became a dismissive wave. "Rather early for you boys to be up and about, isn't it?"

The man with the reptilian breastplate spoke for the others. "What business brings you to Bridgeward?"

"Whom do I address behind that black helmet?"

"I am Maralictor Perest Sere Maximete, and I will brook no insolence from hired law-enforcers."

"The Derexhi enforced law in this city long before your kind arrived."

"Yet we were invited by the Justice Council."

"Not everyone can afford our services. It is good to have those willing to serve the wretched."

"Your ilk lacks severity."

"Our methods contrast, it is true. Rather than emulate devils and their torture racks, we Derexhi find inspiration in human values."

A scoffing noise echoed in the maralictor's helmet.

"Now that we have compared our ways," continued Arrus, "you'll of course step aside and allow us to pass."

"My question has gone unanswered."

"We have no business in Bridgeward, except to pass through it. We did have a task to perform in Shadow, but you have arrived much too late to watch us perform it."

"You are insolent," Maximete said.

"You are merely guests here. We are Derexhi."

"You will tell me what you were hired to do."

Arrus scratched at his beard. "There is no great secret. Shoanti kept a man hostage over a debt. We liberated him."

"Who led them?"

"Priza, I believe his name was."

"This man poses a grave threat to public order. If you knew his whereabouts, you were obliged to inform us."

"This city has few laws, and that is not among them."

Maximete's clawed glove came to rest on the pommel of his sword. "I speak of higher law."

"A quaint notion."

The hellknight's fingers wrapped around his sword-hilt.

Arrus breathed in deep, expanding his chest to its full dimensions. "If you're planning to use that weapon, Maralictor Perest Sere Maximete, I would have to say you show scant grasp of local politics."

Iskola stepped in. "Gentlemen, our interest in this Priza creature has come to an end. We'll gladly direct you to his hiding place. He'll be gone from there, naturally. But perhaps you'll find a way of tracking him to his next lair."

"This is what you should have said immediately."

Iskola replied with an ambiguous bow, then beckoned Luma. In a few swift strokes, on a scrap of vellum produced by the Hellknights, she drew them a map. When she was finished, Maximete snatched it from her hands. Without farewell, they clanked off, headed for the Shadow and Priza's hovel.

Ontor watched them until they turned a corner and disappeared from sight. "In a fight between them and the Shoanti, I'm rooting for neither."

"They can think of only one way to ask a question," said Iskola. "And do you know what that means?"

"No," said Luma. "What?"

"They will always be pawns."

Chapter Three
Derexhi House

Luma sat in the salon of the family manor. Lined with books and appointed in oak, with stuffed furniture the color of spring leaves, it was her favorite of the many rooms that composed her drafty home. She'd wedged herself into a corner of a large loveseat; not an inch of her could be seen through the room's arch from the adjacent hallway. She read a leather-bound volume of journals by the explorer and venture-captain Vrenn, who visited the land before either of its main cities, Magnimar and Korvosa, had been imagined. The book described in flat detail the author's peregrinations among the Shoanti, and among another, more numerous vagabond people—the sensual Varisians. It was a recent addition to the library, whose books she'd all read from cover to cover, even the boring ones. She'd bought it with her own allowance down in the bazaar. The bookseller tried to pass it off as a rarity, until she quoted his own thoughts back to him.

Luma did not like the idea of a land without citysong. But in the wild magic of the primeval woods, she found touches of awe akin to her own experiences amid Magnimar's streets and monuments.

Vrenn's prose sprang to life only for a single topic: his epicurean adventures. His delirious account of a boar-roast set Luma's stomach to rumbling. She abandoned her book, carefully laying a crimson ribbon between the pages, and padded off to the kitchen.

Returning with a goblet of wine and a bowl of cut apples sprinkled with curds, she passed Iskola and an unfamiliar older woman leaving the meeting room where clients were entertained. The woman's bejeweled, old-fashioned garb revealed her as a patrician among patricians. She smelled of talc and lavender and spoke in a formal accent that was now disappearing even from the Summit's loftiest heights. The woman smiled at Iskola, as she might at a child, and took the liberty of caressing the wizard's face. Though the woman noticed nothing, Luma could see Iskola suppress a squirm. Iskola escorted the woman to the front foyer, where her liveried servants came to attention.

Luma drifted back to the library. Iskola's shadow fell across the pages of her book. She reached into Luma's bowl, snatching up a curd and a slice of apple and popping it into her mouth.

"Who was that?" Luma asked.

Iskola chewed pensively, as if apples were somehow unknown to her. "Our real client."

"From this morning?"

"Alam Scarnetti's grandmother." She spotted the goblet. "What have you opened?"

"It was open already."

Iskola removed the goblet from Luma's hand and took a cautious sip. "Syrinelle?" she said, asking from which grape the wine was made.

"From Riverspire."

"I'll have some, too." Iskola drifted from the room.

Moments later, a familiar musk, of spice and sweat and old slippers, drifted in. Luma bounced from her chair. Her father, Randred, took a seat opposite hers. He placed a ledger book on an adjacent side table, letting it land with a thunk. "Was your sister just here?"

"Iskola? She'll be back in a moment."

Luma had always thought of Randred as the template for all other Derexhi. His head was squarish, his jaw prominent, his eyes dark and well-spaced under a brow now creased with parallel lines. Lately, to the chagrin of Luma's stepmother, he'd granted permission for his white hair to grow out and his beard to flirt with untidiness. He puffed and rubbed at his joints; the effort of lowering his oft-wounded body into the chair gave him pause. A burgundy robe, collared and cuffed in the white fur of the northern bear, draped over his still-wide shoulders. He played with a bulky golden ring, inset with a fat diamond, twirling it absently on his fingers.

The gesture prompted Luma to realize that she'd been chewing at her hair again. She brushed it away with what she hoped would be a concealing gesture.

"That was Urtilia Scarnetti Iskola was meeting with?" her father asked her.

"If that's the name of Alam Scarnetti's grandmother, yes."

He nodded at the clear significance of this.

Iskola returned with the rest of the bottle and two goblets. "I thought I heard you up," she said. She set the glasses on the side table and poured. "I won't tell Mother if you don't."

As Iskola passed him the goblet, Randred momentarily brightened. He drank deep and let his eyes flutter shut. "A fine vintage. And we got the case for a song. The wineseller had no idea of its true worth."

31

Iskola held up her goblet. "To another assignment, well closed." Luma and Randred joined in the toast.

"That's what I meant to talk to you about," said Randred. "It's not true, is it, that you waived payment for this morning's rescue?"

Iskola stiffened. "That I did, Father." She glanced at Luma, as if willing her to leave the room.

Luma savored a curd.

Randred shifted forward. "You of all people, Iskola, should understand the state of our finances. This household bleeds money. Yet we cannot allow ourselves to curtail outward fripperies, as we would lose standing with the other houses, who purchase our services."

Iskola sighed and settled into a chair. Luma felt sorry for her; when her father took it upon himself to lecture, there was no interrupting, even if everyone in the room had the speech committed to memory.

"You must not underestimate the value of the top squad. The rest of our business—the sentinels, the bodyguards, the rumor-gatherers—for these our margins are slim, because of the competition. It is you—Luma, and you, and the others—who offer what our rivals cannot. You comprise this concern's premium inventory. Your magic, your swords, your reputation and resourcefulness . . . No one in Magnimar can do what you do. For this we must charge a remorseless mark-up. You simply cannot use the team's time as an incentive for other business. Do you think that Urtilia Scarnetti will hire a dozen more guards than she needs, now that you've scooped up her scapegrace grandson?"

Iskola jumped on the question. "Of course not, Father. I didn't give her a gift. I put her in my debt. When was the last time you took your council seat?"

Randred shifted his weight back into the chair. "Pah. The ceremonial occasions are bad enough. I can no longer sit for all that wrangling."

"In that wrangling lies our future. You haven't been paying attention, but Urtilia Scarnetti has been amassing allies on the council. She's a faction unto herself—"

"Until Amarai Burda decides to reel her in, you mean."

"Amarai Burda hasn't left her bedchambers in months. She isn't expected to live out the year. It's Urtilia now. This is why you should cede your seat to Arrus, so someone who wants to protect our interests can do so."

"Pfft!" Randred finished the contents of his goblet. "Arrus would sooner wrestle a fire giant. What about Luma? She's the eldest."

"Be serious, Father."

Luma's ears burned. She told herself not to be offended. She didn't want the family council seat. Certainly she did not expect it. And Iskola's brusqueness was not aimed at her, in particular. It was her way. Still, the ease of her disregard rankled. Luma retreated further into the corner of her chair.

"Arrus wishes to politick now?" Randred asked.

"He's better at it than you imagine."

"His capacity I don't doubt. He's handsome, charming, with a touch of the bully about him—the perfect combination. He could go far, were our lord-mayor not unassailably ensconced." Puffing with the effort, he turned his chair to face the side table. Iskola moved to help; he waved her off. "What I question about his new hobby—or yours—is the price." He licked a finger and paged through the ledger. "Is this why you've been giving the squad's services away? Politics?" Randred jabbed at an entry. "Kaia Shilba—future considerations. Viokala Jaberyni—future

33

considerations. Lenehti Mintisio—future considerations. All important councilors. Useful to have on our side should trouble come, I grant you. But. Future considerations won't pay our forces. Or our servants, or our vendors." He closed the ledger. "Bank a few favors, Iskola, here and there." Randred stood, chucking Iskola under the chin. "But slow down, my dear."

"Understood, Father."

He pulled her to him, enfolding her in a tight embrace. "Neither he, nor you, will be ready to take over until you learn to worry." Randred released her. "At your age, I was just as rash. More so. It's what allows you to burst through a hovel full of cutthroats and cut them down. The squad needs your impetuosity." He gazed down at his ruined physique. "Don't hurry to become this creaky bag of bones."

Iskola kissed his cheek. "Good night, Father. You have a long time yet to creak." She glided from the room.

Randred leaned over Luma to refill her goblet. "Sunk in melancholy again, I see."

"It's nothing, Father."

He emptied the rest of the bottle into his own vessel and lowered himself into his chair. "Count your blessings on one front, my darling. At least you'll never have to run this house." Randred pulled a candle closer to his account book. "If you'd been born in proper wedlock, you'd have this to look forward to. When I was your age, I dreaded having to do what my father did. And I was right."

"It can't be so bad."

He rubbed his forehead. "It is, but deservedly so. I gave my father as much trouble as they do now. The wheel turns, doesn't it? Sometimes I wish the law were different, and I could make you heir. The rest of us could use a touch of your quiet."

She rose to wrap an arm around his shoulder. "We are who we are."

Randred patted her hand. "There's no greater truth than that." He chuckled. "I could give you the council seat, if you want it. The law says the estate must go to the eldest legitimate male heir. It says nothing about the seat, though people assume otherwise. The pretension of it! As if any in Magnimar are true nobles. The loftiest of us are dirt-shod scrabblers, six generations removed. Now we surround ourselves with marble monuments and call ourselves aristocrats. Nonsense. Would you want it?"

"What?"

He winked at her. "The council seat. That would teach the rest of them a lesson, wouldn't it?"

Luma withdrew. "I don't think that would be a good idea."

"I suppose not. Then I've no choice for the moment than to keep it warm myself."

The next morning, Luma sat at her window, taking in the citysong, when Bhax, the family's white-haired senior butler, knocked on the door. He bore a message from Arrus, summoning her to the squad room. Luma considered pulling a comb through her hair before acknowledging the futility of any attempt. She moved through oak-paneled corridors, passing portraits of her ancestors on her human side. Each head of House Derexhi gazed determinedly from his canvas, swathed in armor and proudly scarred. Randred's portrait hung at the end of the line. Painted a decade ago, it depicted a harder, freer man, his brow unfurrowed. The painted Randred, Luma thought, could not conceive of a problem that would not yield to his stunningly detailed sword.

She found Ontor in the squad room as well. The two brothers competed at a knife-throwing game. Two leather purses sat on the table, promising reward for victory. Ontor would win, of course. But Arrus would come closer than he had the last time he lost, and would fume and fret and accept the pain of the defeat as the cost of doing better next time.

Ontor, pretending to be distracted by her arrival, took a step off balance, breaking his ideal posture. He threw at the wrong time. Yet the knife flew unerringly for the bull's-eye. Ontor could not refrain from a small jump of delight. Arrus's expression tightened. Luma read what it meant: only at this moment was he realizing that Ontor had been holding back, even while consistently beating him. He was much further from catching up than he'd imagined.

Nonetheless, he placed himself at the red line on the squad room floor, knife ready to throw. "Luma, an assignment for you."

"Yes?"

His knife sailed through the air to land in the target ring next to the bull's-eye. He hissed through clenched teeth. "You're needed to shadow Khonderian. You know of him?"

Luma nodded. "The chief of the lord-mayor's bodyguard?"

"The same."

Ontor removed the knife, stepped up to the line, and made a show of concentrating.

"Why?" asked Luma.

"Why what?" answered Arrus.

Neatly maintaining the illusion of a close game, Ontor hurled the knife precisely into the same ring of the target his brother had struck.

"If I'm following the lord-mayor's chief bodyguard, aren't I also following the lord-mayor?"

"No," said Arrus. "He commands the bodyguard but doesn't go out on detail with them. Any man who works with sword or knife and answers to the lord-mayor takes his orders from Khonderian."

"So he's the lord-mayor's dagger, then."

"That's right."

"And why am I trailing him?" asked Luma.

"Can't tell you," Arrus said.

"Oh."

Arrus removed the knife from the target and marched to the line. "You may go about it now."

"What am I looking for, then?" Luma asked.

"Whatever he does, wherever he goes, whoever he talks to. Note it and report back to me."

"Who's the client?"

Arrus sized up his throw. "Had I meant to tell you, I would have."

"You don't trust me to keep my mouth shut?"

He threw the knife. It barely made the target. Arrus swallowed a curse. "I don't need your pestering this morning."

Ontor retrieved the knife from the target, but hung back from the red line.

"Good work comes from good briefings," Luma said.

"Don't quote Father at me," said Arrus. "Just get going."

Luma let the door slam on her way out.

Ontor followed her down the corridor. "Wait, Mouse, wait."

Luma stopped. "What?"

He turned her around. "You know he's always like that when he's losing."

She wouldn't look at him. "Yes, he is always like that. That's why I'm mad."

"I've been meaning to talk to you, Mouse. You can't go slamming doors like that."

"It's my fault?"

"It's not—it's not a matter of *fault*," Ontor searched for words. "There are . . . repercussions. I'm saying this because I care. I see you're unhappy and I don't like that. You understand?"

"Sure."

"It would all be fine if you made an effort to get along more."

"If *I* made—"

"I know, I know, I know . . . it shouldn't be you who has to. You're right. Completely so. But then there's another side to it, too."

"How can there be another side if I'm completely—"

"See?" Ontor said. He pulled her into the armory so their voices wouldn't carry down the hall. "Arguing back like that. It isn't . . . endearing. It would all go so much better for you if you tried to go along a little more."

"When do I not do as they ask?"

"You do it, but you slam, you shuffle, you slump. They want to feel you're one of us. Make them think you respect them."

"I do. When we go into a fight, we depend on each other . . ."

"Of course. Not that kind of respect. I mean, here, around the house. Be charming. It's what you'd do with a witness you wanted something out of, right? Make them feel good."

"Kiss up, you mean?"

"Okay, sure," Ontor said. "Kiss up. The tiniest bit would help."

They could hear Arrus yelling for a resumption of the game.

"I shouldn't have to," Luma said.

"Luma, Luma." Ontor put a hand on each of her shoulders. "Luma, maybe that's true. This is a family. We all love you. But—*but* . . . it would be easier all around if more of us *liked* you."

Chapter Four
Street of Taverns

Luma caught up to Khonderian in the Capital District, as he exited the Pediment Building, where his and the lord-mayor's offices were located. She followed him across the monument-choked Way of Arches into Bridgeward, the artisan's district.

A receding hairline and prominent, chestnut-colored widow's peak extended Khonderian's face. He wore his hair long and scraggly, over a nondescript leather jerkin of an approximately matching shade. Patchy stubble dirtied his chin. At his hip swung a scabbarded longsword. Luma noted knives hidden in each of his boots, and strapped by an armband under his right sleeve. No detail of his dress or equipment suggested a high post. Nor did he project an air of intimidation.

In the quick, casual movements of his head, Luma recognized the constant yet masked awareness of a professional observer. He loped along, moving to avoid knots of people and the threat of conversation. Nonetheless citizens occasionally spotted and hailed him. Each time he waved, breaking into a grin that exposed a bright white overbite, and moved on without slowing.

To evade his gaze, Luma rode the swells and crests of the citysong. When it grew louder, it foretold some hubbub or distraction ahead. Prepared for this, she could take chances, closing the gap between herself and her quarry, sure that his eye would fall on whatever unexpected commotion was about to cross their paths. When it quieted, she hung back so that she would not be caught in a sudden gap, standing out on an otherwise empty street.

As she shadowed him, Luma rehearsed a speech for Arrus. She couldn't help imagining what she might say, even if she wouldn't, in the end, dare voice it. No longer could she work this way, without full knowledge. Whatever she was looking for would be easier to find if she'd been told what it was. Surely they meant her to get close enough to him to pick out his thoughts. Yet Arrus hadn't said so.

Most likely it was a political job. Probing Khonderian for an unexploited weakness that could be used to blackmail him, or force him out. The lord-mayor's dagger would be a useful person to have in one's pocket. Any number of councilors and luminaries doubtless worried that their secrets might be rattling around in his head. Equally likely, their client wanted him to spill those of others.

Shades of pink and orange streaked the clouds. The citysong always changed its pitch at this time of day, when work ended and the people of Magnimar turned to play. The shift just as reliably brightened Luma's mood. She felt the anticipation of laborers headed for taverns, of lovers anxious for reunion, of mothers relieved that their sons and daughters had made it safely through another day.

Khonderian turned onto a street of taverns. Tables spilled onto the streets, forcing those who wished to navigate the lane to wend between them. Brass emblems screwed to their tops identified the borderlines where those belonging to one establishment ended, and another's began. Luma had been here before. More intoxicating than the wines was the song of conviviality that swelled from the assembled drinkers, a drunken harmony only her senses could hear.

Her quarry took a seat at an empty table. Other tipplers converged on it—then, seeing who he was, diverted to another. Khonderian was waiting for someone.

Luma found a stool by a railing—the best compromise between seeing and not being seen. A stooped barmaid took her order for a half-jug of white. She settled in to watch Khonderian while seeming to hold her gaze elsewhere.

For the first time, it struck Luma as odd that Khonderian, well established in a city whose notables proudly sported two if not three names, went by only one. Though presumably he had a given name, she could not recall it and had never heard anyone apply one to him. He was always simply Khonderian. For all she knew, maybe that was his given name, and it was his surname that had fallen away from him.

Two flagons of ale appeared at Khonderian's table. He sipped absently from one of them.

Distraction impinged on her. The citysong, usually jolly here, hummed with an undertone of disquiet.

Two men, both in their middle years, sat down nearby, continuing a loud conversation. One had bits of clay beneath his fingernails. Small burns, likely from the spilled, molten metal of a jeweler's workshop, spotted the other's hands.

"You're not telling me he won't make it?" boomed the potter.

The jeweler waved for service. "I won't say he won't, as I fear to jinx him, but the barber says too much of him is crushed."

"He can't afford the healing?"

"Who can, these days?"

Hoping to drown them out, Luma attuned herself to the citysong. But as the din of laughing drinkers rose, the jeweler and potter compensated, shouting all the louder.

"The guild won't pitch in?"

"Did I say the guild won't pitch in? It'll take a lot of healing, that's all I'm saying. The guild's only got so much coin. They'd sooner spend it to hire golem-fighters."

Now Luma adjusted her position for better eavesdropping. This was beginning to sound like a possible job. If she brought word of it to Randred, and it came to something, it might earn her some credit with the others.

"Hellknights?"

"You don't hire Hellknights."

"They hate disorder, don't they?"

"I'm no expert on what Hellknights do and don't despise."

"Smashing into a shop in broad daylight, fatally beating patrons and wounding the proprietor. Tell me that's not the very definition of disorder."

"There was Hellknights down at the shop. Maybe they'll step in, maybe they won't."

"How many times is this now?"

"Fourth shop in three weeks. Six people dead. Couple more likely to go."

"For the first time, I'm grateful pots ain't as valuable as gold and gems."

"Your wit overwhelms me. I'd close up, but how do I earn a living?"

"You wouldn't think golems would be hard to find," said the potter.

"If that were true, wouldn't someone have found them, then?" asked the jeweler.

"Renegade golems. What's the city coming to?"

"What's the city coming to indeed? It's high time we set up more city guards."

"You know what happens when the moneybelts hire more guards? The taxman comes around. And not to their doors, but to ours."

Their words seemed to fade into the general din as a short-statured figure took a place opposite Khonderian, doffing a feathered, wide-brimmed hat. From behind it took a moment to tell if this new arrival was a gnome or a halfling. Gnome, she concluded. She noted olive skin, delicate fingers, and the disproportionately large head characteristic of gnomekind. Curly raven hair spilling from the hat betrayed the dull regularity of a dye job. As a gnome, he might be covering up an outlandish natural hair color—crimson, or even green. The fripperies of his garb supported that theory, announcing its wearer's strained effort to follow the tastes of local high society. Rich brocades adorned his velvet doublet. Frays marred its edges; grime ringed the cuffs of his flowing shirt.

As they conversed, the two proved a contrast in body language. The gnome flourished his arms, leaned back in his chair, and carried himself as if engaged in a friendly colloquy. He drained his flagon in a single go and gestured for another. Khonderian contained himself, hands folded on the table, avoided gesture, and barely moved his lips when he spoke. Any nearby movement fell under his subtle scrutiny.

Luma counted out the distance between her stool and their table—too far to try to eavesdrop on his thoughts. If she moved closer, she'd move into his sphere of attention.

Khonderian slid an object across the table. The gnome held it up to his ear: it was a purse, and he was theatrically listening to the clank of the coins inside. Khonderian's face twitched in mild amusement. Then he stood, gave the gnome an ironical half-bow, and departed, shoulders hunched.

The gnome stayed seated, finishing his ale. Luma threaded through the tables toward him, taking a moment to commit his features to memory. Along with the big eyes and triangular chin typical of gnomes, she noted a curling, dandyish mustache, and a beauty mark to the right of his nose—possibly painted on.

Pressing on, Luma called on the citysong, finding the notes in it that were the thoughts and feelings of the revelers around her. In their beery symphony, she isolated the instruments—the singular minds of each participant. As she wove toward the gnome, a rich and unusually complicated trilling grew insistent. Luma was sure it was him.

She glanced ahead: though seeming to do no more than amble, Khonderian had already put the obstructing mass of tables behind him. If he turned down a side alley, she'd lose him.

For a moment, as she squeezed past the gnome, a flash of his thoughts came to the fore. Luma was already well through the tables by the time she made retrospective sense of them. He'd been calculating how many roistering days Khonderian's purse would buy him. Near the end glimmered a consideration of the debt he'd racked up at his favorite drinking hole. Luma missed the conclusion, but somehow suspected that no coins would be headed the taverner's way.

Luma dropped into the deceptive body language of the unseen pursuit. She moved with a timidity and uncertain purpose that hid where she was looking and how quickly she covered ground. In shadow, she picked up the pace; when she could not help but step into a pool of lantern light, she slowed. She held herself alert to other's gazes, while remaining herself unnoticed.

She reached the end of the avenue; Khonderian was gone from sight. From a belt of pouches lashed around her waist she withdrew a hawk's feather, harvested from a nest hidden in a pillar of the Irespan bridge. Luma concentrated on the citysong, picking out the cries of Magnimar's birds: pigeons, warblers, crows, grackles and gulls. From this cacophony she plucked the shriek of the hawks that preyed on them. She went inside the hawks to borrow their keenness of vision. Swiveling her head at the intersection, she caught sight of Khonderian, crossing beneath a candlemaker's awning. He cut through an adjacent alley. Save for a huddled beggar or two, the street stood empty. Soft boots betraying neither shuffle nor squeak, she darted down the walkway, closing the distance between them.

Ahead, halfway between her and her target, Luma spotted a flutter of movement from the lip of a recessed doorway. She moved to the alley's other side and pulled her sickle from her belt. As she passed, a hunched, black-clad man pressed himself against the door, hands held submissively up. A sap swung from his wrist. He opened his mouth to speak; Luma held a finger to her lip. The mugger nodded obediently as she passed by. Continuing on, she put a name to his lumpen face: Dunnam, sometimes called Dunnam the Codge. She'd run him down during the Danosko Gor disappearance; he hadn't been in on it directly, but had truck with the culprits. Ulisa had kicked him across the room. Luma had held a dagger to this throat and plundered his terrified thoughts.

Such were the advantages of the family reputation. Few who tangled with the Derexhi were eager to repeat the experience.

Hitting the end of the alley, Khonderian turned to the left. Luma slowed her pace; when shadowing, edging too close to one's quarry could prove as disastrous as losing him. She stopped; his footfalls had ceased. Luma ducked into another doorway, like the one Dunnam had lurked in. She recalled the melody of the citysong on chill mornings, when fog pooled above the cobblestones. Her connection brought into being a cloud of mist; it swirled around her. For a touch of realism, she kicked at it, sending tendrils of fog out into the alley.

Khonderian came back to peer around. Luma was sure she hadn't done anything to alert him. But then, he was an experienced watcher. He might be reacting from a well-honed instinct, or with the aid of the magical charms and gewgaws a man of his resources inevitably carried.

Ready to draw his sword, Khonderian took several steps back down into the alley. His head made a choppy series of contained, near-imperceptible movements as he took the scene in, detail by detail. The spill of fog across the street caught his notice for a moment. He then broke and went on his way, faster than before.

He hadn't seen her, but now traveled as if shaking off pursuit. As he made his way back to the Capital District, he made periodic, abrupt stops, meant to expose anyone on his trail. A less able shadow might have been caught out. Luma, with her knack for people and the way they flowed through the city, studied his walk and the giveaways hidden within it. Soon she could predict his stops, perhaps even before he had quite decided to make them.

Without this rhythmic anticipation of Khonderian's moves, she might have been unprepared for the angle at which he jaunted across the Way of Arches. She lost sight of him amid the white, spanning monuments lining the avenue—but not of the shadow he threw against them. Scurrying across, she found herself surrounded by trees. He'd ducked into the park west of the Founders' Archive. Swaying branches, caught in lantern light from the avenue, cast confusing shadows. Luma slipped from tree to tree, pausing with her back against each trunk. Were she the pursued in this situation, this is where she would come suddenly at her pursuer, knives out.

No attack came. Now deep in the park, she'd realized that she'd let herself get turned around. Reaching into the part of the citysong that was all angles and planes, she found north, and oriented herself.

Khonderian had shaken her off. But a map of Magnimar's streets, more accurate than any sold in a cartographer's shop, ran through Luma as surely as her veins and arteries. She called the area to mind, envisioning the park and the streets that bordered it. As if seeing a red line tracking a hypothetical Khonderian's progress through the map, she imagined the best route back to his most likely destination—the Pediment, from whence he had come.

The most obvious route would be exactly the one a savvy man like Khonderian would never take. On the other hand, few mortal minds could plot a genuinely unpredictable route between two fixed points. People liked to get where they were going efficiently, an instinct they broke only with concentrated effort. Habit led them to well-trod routes and kept them from the unfamiliar. Khonderian, unless somehow blessed with superhuman intelligence, would pick one of the two second-shortest paths to his destination, and think himself quite clever for it.

The red line through the map in Luma's head faded. Two new lines appeared, branching through the park: a green one snaking directly east, and a blue one that arrived at its destination after a confusing circuit south. The lines filled in, moving at speed to the Pediment. Which would he choose?

Several times on his way to the street of taverns, Luma had seen Khonderian favor the roundabout route over the straight. He might give this up now that he'd reached his home ground, but Luma deemed it unlikely. People tended to stick with one habit of movement, changing it only when a new condition intervened. Khonderian had trained himself to walk a crooked path, and Luma should anticipate accordingly.

The green line on Luma's imagined map faded, leaving only the blue.

Khonderian loomed back into view on Settlement Street. A muck-encrusted scrounger hailed him. Luma looked for a hiding spot, anticipating a second meeting, like that with the gnome. Khonderian waved at the man and swept on by.

Luma trailed Khonderian all the way to the Pediment. To her disappointment, he slipped inside without further incident. She staked it out from across the street for a few more hours before heading home, gaining no more intelligence to take back to her siblings.

Chapter Five
Gnome Trail

Arrus sat fletching an arrow in the squad room, a deteriorating wooden chair creaking beneath him. His afternoon's handiwork lay stacked in a neat pile on the room's great table. A few discarded shafts formed a smaller, disarranged stack on the other end of the table, as if exiled for their imperfections. He plucked a goose feather from a pile, checking to see if the dyeing process had damaged it. Arrus's taste in arrow feather colors had recently changed, from red to violet.

"Why didn't you follow the gnome?" he asked Luma.

She had neither been offered a seat, nor taken one. "You told me to follow Khonderian."

"I understand that." Finding the feather unsuitable, Arrus added it to the cast-offs. "What I'm asking is why you didn't show greater initiative. Obviously the gnome was the greater unknown. And doubtless lived somewhere easier to sneak into than the Pediment."

"If you want me to use my judgment, you have to tell me what's going on. What I'm looking for."

"What we are always looking for. Malfeasance. The unusual. The gnome should have stood out to you as a blinding beacon of the second. And likely the first."

Luma stifled a sigh. "And if I'd followed him, and left Khonderian to go gods-know-where, would you not now be upbraiding me for that?"

Arrus stood. "You think this is a scolding?"

"What am I meant to take it for?"

He sorted through the unused feathers, tossing aside one, then another. "We need better from you, Luma."

"I did what you asked."

"You are Derexhi. You must do more than is asked." Arrus returned his attention to his arrows.

Luma felt a familiar, betraying sensation rise through her. Her skin burned; she knew she'd gone as red as a cock's comb. Her chin wobbled. She forced it straight, but by then Arrus had seen the loss of composure.

Contempt flitted across his face.

She left, ducking into the empty library. She banged her fists into her thighs. Again. She'd done it again. No wonder they despised her. Or regarded her with their various individual mixtures of pity and indifference. In the field, she feared no one.

Well, that wasn't quite the way to put it. She controlled and used her fear. Shaped it, to make herself seem hard. Fed on it, to propel her into danger with sickle outstretched. Luma's intense acquaintanceship with her fear alerted her to trouble. It gave her insight into the fears of others, which she exploited when leaning on targets and witnesses.

It was only at home, with them, that her defenses crumbled, that paralysis gripped her, that her tongue forbade her from fully defending herself.

She might be the eldest, but when the first of the half-siblings arrived, they'd closed ranks. They made themselves the true children of Randred, and Luma the footnote. Even as they lay in their cradles, long before they could speak, Luma felt their hostility. Maybe it was her elven blood they sensed. When she picked one up, no matter which twin it was, Arrus or Iskola, the howling started. And then the other one joined in, too. They possessed that link that sometimes grows between twins. If she tried to play with Arrus in the nursery when Iskola was out on the lawn, the one's furious keening would trigger the other's. With their mother, with Randred, they were as angelic as babes are supposed to be. Whenever she crept near, they transformed themselves into squalling furies.

As soon as they could talk, they learned to slight her with their words. As their brothers and sisters arrived, spaced close together by their mother's clockwork fertility, they took command and walled her off. They trained the others to see Luma as they did: The interloper. The odd duck. The not-quite-them.

They'd sharpened their claws on her. Sped themselves to adulthood by keeping her a child.

Worst of all, Randred had never seen it. Hiding it required little effort. He did not want to see.

No, that wasn't the worst of all.

The worst of all was that she loved them, each and every unyielding one of them, because they were her family, and she had no other.

It was like a pinched nerve which, whenever struck, sent shocks of pain through the body. Any slight, no matter how minor, or how reflexively given, returned her to this childish helplessness. Sent the snot running from her nose and the tears gushing down her stupid face. Reminded her of every other slight.

She had to stop blaming them. It was her fault for letting them get to her.

But there was the matter of the squad. The family depended on it. Until Randred's talk with Iskola, she hadn't realized quite how much. And if whatever lay between them interfered with their missions, Randred had to be made to understand. Better to have an air-clearing row than to wind up with one of them lying dead after a raid because they'd lost their trust in one another.

Her father would ask her why she hadn't spoken up, and she'd have no answer. She should have done this years ago.

It would get worse before it improved, but she had to finally speak up. Maybe it would give her the kick in the ass she needed to overcome this.

Maybe they'd sort it out, all of them, and remember they were all Derexhi, aligned together against the world.

And if that happened, she'd find out why she was chasing Khonderian, and what the gnome meant, and whom their client might be.

Luma dried her eyes and blew her nose and breathed in and out and in and out. She was a thirty-year-old woman. This had to stop. Straightening her shoulders, she stalked from the library.

Randred wasn't in his counting room, so she ascended the great winding stairs, carved from rare Mwangi mahogany and chased with floatwood, headed for his bedchamber. She found her stepmother, Yandine, exiting the room.

Yandine projected a beauty neither of her daughters quite laid claim to. Carefully cultivated ringlets of ink-black hair descended to sharp, rosy shoulders. Her tight bow of a mouth bore a red gloss, impeccably applied. Yandine had plucked her eyebrows into thin, ironic lines. Her bodice displayed her decolletage to intimidating effect.

Luma could tell you little about clothing, but had overheard that Yandine's revealing neckline and voluminous skirt would have been all the rage in the city of Korvosa a generation ago. Yandine's conception of elegant attire had evidently frozen at the time of her courtship with Randred. On a day when she was trying to be charitable to her stepmother, Luma might reckon that her father wanted her to look like she did when they fell in love. The rest of the time, she figured Yandine still felt like a Korvosan, even after living in Varisia's other great city for more than a quarter century.

This brought Luma to consider another of her own character flaws. As a citywalker, forever bathed in its song, Luma was a part of Magnimar, and it was a part of her. She had no choice but chauvinistic pride in her city, and a wary distaste for its rivals. If Korvosa had a trait that Magnimar did not share, Luma disdained it. Or perhaps the disdain arose from the citysong, and Luma merely absorbed it. Korvosa had kings and queens; Magnimar, the Council of Ushers and a lord-mayor. Therefore, Luma disliked monarchies and all of their trappings. In Korvosa, the old families styled themselves as nobles; here they acted like nobles but mostly shrank from the term itself. For this reason, aristocratic affections rankled Luma, even as she granted the thinness of the distinction between one custom and the other. Most of all, Korvosans ached to reassemble the shattered Chelish empire, from its harsh justice to its new devil-worshiping faith.

Therefore a revulsion for the empire and a loathing of devils were etched in Luma's soul.

All of this tainted her view of Yandine. Luma conceived of her as queenly, autocratic, devilish. How much of this was fair and how much prejudice she could no longer tell. The question was all tangled up in her magic now. She tried to remember what she thought of Yandine before the city called to her. The recollections were of distance, of those lacquered eyebrows forever raised, of unflattering comparisons to her blood children.

Then again, though Luma had always told herself she should embrace Yandine as an ally, she had never truly tried. The time for an attempt, she decided, was now.

Luma made for the door handle. Yandine reached out, and with smooth, cool fingers, gently removed her hand from it.

"Your father is sleeping, dear."

"It's important."

A hint of smile drifted across Yandine's lips. "It always is, isn't it? Come with me to my room. I'll pour you tea."

Luma summoned the image of someone comfortable in the world of etiquette. She settled on Byrillia Laxander, a woman of about her age who would always come to the balls and masques that Yandine threw. When at a loss for what to do, she would imagine Byrillia talking to Yandine, and do as she would. As she slipped down the hallway to Yandine's room, she also tried to see herself from Yandine's vantage. She was a wild, half-elven creature, incapable of grooming, hostile to fashion, unwilling to raise herself from a slouch. A walking, shambling ambiguity, neither woman nor child. A nervous wretch, bristling whenever Yandine mentioned her beloved Korvosa.

Maybe they were right to dislike her.

With a shudder, Luma recoiled. That was precisely what they wished her to think. They'd planted their collective mocking voice in her head. It said crueler things than the real siblings ever did.

A wave of perfume buffeted her as she followed Yandine into her chamber. Luma unwrinkled her nose, but it was too late—her stepmother had already seen it. Up went the eyebrow. The left one, this time. There was a code to it, a hierarchy of disapproval, but Luma had never succeeded in cracking it. The left might be the worst of the two, or might not.

On an iron-topped side table rested a Senaran heatstone. Yandine poured water from a ceramic jug into a kettle incised with the paired swords of the Chelish imperial seal. "You are aware of your father's illness?" she said.

"Yes."

Struggling with the weight of it, Yandine placed the filled kettle on the stone. "The news is worse than your father and I have let on." She spoke the stone's word of invocation.

Luma tried to tell herself it was not a call to Asmodeus, King of Hell. She'd read of Senara, a place deep in the empire where the line between man and devil had blurred. "What do you mean?"

"Your father forbade me to tell any of you what the physicks have been saying. But a waste has appeared deep in his organs. It devours him from within. We've consulted priest after priest, but they say his natural allotment of years has run out."

"That can't be. He's too young."

Yandine waved to a high-backed chair opposite her bed. She sat on her mattress, hands folded in her lap. "That is what I keep saying. The priests reply that each man has his number of years, as laid out by fate and known only to Pharasma, goddess of graves. That number may vary. And when it is short, it seems an injustice. Yet on such imbalances the worlds and planes are founded." Her hand tightened around a hank of silk bedsheet. "When I hear their fatuous platitudes, I want to tear at their faces. Yet we have had many healers in and they all say the same. He must prepare for his soul journey. And we must all together ease his mind in the days we have left with him."

"Days?"

"I hope it is months. Or years. Perhaps if you pray to the city. *Do* you pray to the city?"

"Yes and no. It's hard to put into words."

Yandine cocked her head. The gesture reminded Luma of the fishing eagles that perched on the seawalls of Dockway. "I have not taken the time to understand you, have I?" Yandine asked.

Luma did not know how to answer this.

The kettle shrieked. Yandine rose, pouring its contents into a ceramic teapot fashioned in the shape of a dolphin. She opened the lid of a shallow ebony box, revealing its compartmentalized contents. After a moment's contemplation, she selected a tea and, with an ornate silver spoon, filled a perforated metal ball attached to a delicate chain. With one hand, she clipped the end of the chain to the opening atop the teapot. With the other, she overturned a sand timer of brightly colored blown glass. Pink grains tumbled through the narrow opening between the upper and lower bulbs.

"Why has Father kept his condition from us?" Luma asked.

A sad chuckle caught in Yandine's throat. "Would you expect anything else?"

"He's too stubborn to show us."

"He has been husbanding his strength," Yandine said. "You must help ease his path, Luma. And your brother's as well. It will be a great loss to Arrus, to be deprived of his father's counsel so young. Iskola plans well, but cannot replace your father's wisdom, which comes from having lived. It is unfair that Arrus should have to fill Randred's boots so soon. He underestimates you, does he not?"

"Who?"

"Well, your father has also, but I refer to Arrus. My son fails to see you as you are."

Luma hesitated. "Often I am kept in the dark," she offered. "On missions. And then called on the carpet when I improvise wrong. If he were more forthcoming during briefings . . . and Iskola, too."

Yandine poured the tea. "The right move depends on correct information." She passed a cup to Luma, then took one herself.

Luma took in the tea's aroma. "Do the others know?"

"Arrus and Iskola only. I should perhaps have told you first, as you are the eldest, but it is Arrus who will inherit the house and its council seat. It is he who must prepare himself. And as what goes in Arrus's left ear comes out Iskola's right, there was no point in telling one and not the other."

"And now you'll inform the others." Luma tried the tea; it was still too hot for her.

Yandine gulped it down, though. "Your father would fall into apoplexy if he realized I'd disobeyed him. He thinks he can will the sickness from his bones, with none the wiser. The less said aloud, the better. I'd hate for him to overhear."

Luma watched bubbles chase each other on the surface of her tea. "And you'll speak to Arrus for me?"

"And advise him to trust you better?"

Luma nodded. "And Iskola. As you say, they are front and back cover of the same book."

Yandine wrapped chill fingers around Luma's free wrist. "Leave it to me, my dear." Her voice dropped. "I have ill-treated you, haven't I?"

Luma stammered.

"That was a terrible question to put to you, wasn't it? You must excuse me. My mother drilled me from an early age in the principles of verbal combat. In a Korvosan ballroom, one must be prepared with every utterance to put one's interlocutor on her heels. It is as difficult to break as any habit. So let me say it straight out. I have wronged you, by omission. There is no love blinder than a mother's for her children. In my zeal for them, I let you roam about untutored. In those days I was a frightened girl in a woman's gown, anxious for my position and for theirs. Fear makes one a fool. Yet as it ebbed and I came into myself, I still permitted you to be treated as an inferior in your own house. I come to you asking for your filial duty, but how have I discharged my maternal obligations? Indifferently at best."

"It's not as bad as all that," Luma heard herself saying.

Yandine retook her perch on the mattress. "It is kind, of cours,e for you to say so. The truth is that you needed a mother, as much as any of them. More so. Yet I was too silly to be that for you." A quaver distorted her speech. "My brood eats fire and spits pride. And that is good. But you should not have been excluded. "

"I should have stood up for myself sooner."

"We could all blame ourselves. Your father, too. But now is not the time. I'll talk to them."

"If we have it in for Khonderian, I need to understand why."

Yandine tapped absently at the handle of her cup. "That would be squad business. I can't ask directly."

"I'm sorry," said Luma.

Yandine shook her head. "You apologize too much. And for my part in that, it is I who am sorry. They are adults now, too. All of us must prepare to change our long-held ways. In the meantime, I beg you, be easy around your father."

"I will."

"And do not let on that I have told you."

"I won't."

Yandine stood. "Let's be as Randred, and adopt a stoic mien."

Luma and Ontor went out together to find the gnome. As they cut through the Marble District on their way to Bridgeward, a guilty urge to confide pushed aside all other thought. Ontor deserved, as much as Arrus, Iskola, or she did, to know that their father was dying. Then again, whatever her misgivings, she'd given her word. If Yandine did mean to help her with the others, Luma couldn't very well go back on that. But how would Ontor—or, for that matter, Ulisa or Eibadon—respond when they learned that she'd been in on the deception? It set her head to spinning. The teeming complexity of the citysong, arising from thousands of minds, plus places and traditions and animals and climactic conditions, she understood. By comparison, the interrelations of a mere eight persons seemed impossibly elusive.

Luma couldn't stand it. She would touch on the matter without giving herself away. "How stands it with you and Father these days?" she asked.

Ontor kept his gaze on those moving alongside them: a stooped man leading a mule; a soot-stained pair of laughing urchins; a covey of penitents, masked and robed. "Why do you ask?"

Already she wished she hadn't said anything. "Sometimes it is good between you, sometimes not."

"Yes, but why do you ask?"

She groped for a suitable lie. "You said I should watch my step with Arrus."

"I didn't say it like that."

"Maybe the problem is that I'm selfish. Do I ever ask how the rest of you are doing?"

Ontor adjusted the collar of his leather cuirass. "So this is you showing you care?"

"I suppose."

"Maybe one way to do that would be leaving well enough alone."

The two passed a trio of Randred's employees on their way to guard duty at one of the grand manors. In lieu of salute, the men tipped the bills of their helmets. Ontor waved in silent reply. After they'd gone, Luma realized that she ought to have done the same.

"So that means it's not good?" Luma said.

Ontor sighed. "Take a hint, will you? I suppose it could be worse. The same old."

"The same old what?"

"You know Father. He wanted a footpad in the squad. He's not so sure he likes one in the family."

"Did you have words?"

"Lately we communicate by dirty looks. What's this about?"

"He doesn't really mean it."

"Neither do I. He's a father, I'm a son." Ontor shrugged. "It's how it goes."

She tried to think how she might nudge him in the needed direction without giving away Yandine's secret.

Ontor had to patch it up with him, and urgently. Father could slip away unexpectedly. If that happened before Ontor had a chance to reconcile with him, it would be her fault. He'd never forgive her—and he'd be right.

Luma detached from her surroundings to let the meeting with her stepmother spool through her head. How had she let Yandine maneuver her into that promise? She should have seen its consequences, but hadn't. Sometimes she had no idea why she did what she did.

Ontor appeared grateful for the lapse into silence. They reached their destination, the street of sprawling taverns. Tables and benches stood piled in front of their alehouses, awaiting nightfall, when they'd be placed out in the street. Luma spotted the barmaid who'd served Khonderian and his guest. The server applied soapy water to one of the stacks, a rag in her hand and a bucket at her feet. Ontor assumed a genial expression.

"I'll handle this one," he said. He walked past the barmaid, then stopped himself short, as if noticing her only in retrospect. Turning on his heels, he doffed his sheep's-hide cap to her.

With the instinctive caution of a woman who deflected approaches all night long, the barmaid drew back.

From her unobtrusive corner, Luma kept a lookout for signs of her unknown observer. She did this reflexively, without thought, as she watched Ontor work the barmaid.

He subtly adjusted his posture, adopting a body language that was for a moment conciliatory, then more subtly forward. He flashed a smile at her. He essayed a comic half-step back.

Before long, her resistance melted. She looked away from him, then coyly back. Adjusted her hair. Fussed with her neckline.

Luma couldn't decide whether to admire her brother's skill, or deplore the barmaid's poor showing on behalf of womankind. The two positions, she decided, were entirely compatible.

Ontor chatted with her for a while before flattening his hand and holding it up at roughly the height of a gnome. The barmaid flushed. Vigorous gesticulations followed. Luma could tell that Ontor's inquiries had come up positive: assuming they had the same gnome, she knew him all too well.

The conversation drifted back into flirtation. Ontor let it go on for a polite long while before finally breaking it off. As he left, the barmaid reached out to brush his wrist with her fingers. Rather than return to Luma straightaway, Ontor kept on in his original, feigned direction. Luma slipped off down a back lane. A few minutes later, according to the squad's well-ingrained protocol for surreptitious, coordinated foot travel, they reunited. They lingered over a table of items for sale outside a candle shop and pretended to be interested in the merchandise.

"She liked you," Luma said.

"They always do. It's sad, when you think about it."

"You're melancholy these days."

Ontor said nothing. Luma changed the subject. "The fellow we're looking for is called Noole. He's a regular there. Not to mention a hundred other drinking establishments."

"So he likely asked Khonderian to meet him there, instead of the other way around."

"Possibly," Ontor allowed.

"Did Arrus tell you why we're poking into Khonderian's affairs?"

"Unlike you, I'm only as curious as I have to be."

They moved on to the next stall, this one featuring candlesticks of pewter or brass. Many took the forms of Magnimarian landmarks and monuments: Twin's Gate, the Guardians, the Battle of Charda. The vendor, a round, florid-faced man, roused himself for a moment, then lapsed back into a nap.

"Noole's a poet," Ontor said, "and apparently a popular one, at least with those with a taste for sonnets and quatrains. He gives readings in the smartest Summit salons, and gulps down rotgut in the worst Rag's End dives."

"Meaning he could be anywhere in the city."

"Indeed."

"And that he'd be a superb spy," Luma mused, "able to infiltrate any crowd." They moved off to a third table, heaped with stacks of cheap candles, sold by weight. "Khonderian gave him money. It must have been for information."

Ontor frowned. "Spy implies concerted effort. He might simply be selling some tall tale he ran across."

"Likely so. But until we can say otherwise, let's not underestimate him. Did your barmaid name any specific haunts?"

"Several. The closest's a drinking shack down by the bazaar. The No-Horn. Heard of it?"

Luma shook her head.

"Then I say we head there and ask around."

Chapter Six
Bazaar of Sails

Even before its flapping pennants hove into view, Luma heard in the citysong the strain of commerce distinctive to Magnimar's bazaar. It vibrated with clinking coins, barker's cries, and the chuff of scoops into bags of spice. In its harmonies, greed, hope, and wonder intermingled. The luffing of tents, rattled by stiff gusts from the sea, percussed themselves into a drumbeat of buying and selling. Foreign undertones joined in: wisps of citysongs from the world over, brought here in the memories and longings of its traders. From a chaos of clashing civilizations they came into sync with Magnimar's marble echoes.

Ontor let Luma lead as they penetrated the first, least glorious ring of tents and stalls. These formed the territory of the food vendors. Smells of grilling sardines, simmering fish stock, and soured skillet grease rose to meet them.

Beyond these lay steadily grander, sturdier stalls, which in turn would taper off near the piers, where the pattern reversed and the selection grew dodgier once more. From the barmaid's sniffing description, the No-Horn Tavern would be found amid the bazaar's dicier precincts, either near or directly next to the docks.

Along the way, Luma glimpsed a cloaked figure whom she thought might have been her mysterious watcher, the one that so often pricked at her senses. On a second look, however, she identified him as a person of lesser mystery: a priest of Desna, clad as a layman, furtively ducking into a backstreet whorehouse.

Enveloped in clouds of steam from a stall selling crab soup stood one of Luma's odder contacts. The cargo-handler V'kka belonged to the reptilian race known as the lizardfolk. She held a soup bowl up to her snout, gurgling its contents into her gullet past a row of dagger-shaped teeth. Hot liquid, interspersed with flakes of crab meat, dribbled down the green scales of her arm. Her long tail whipped from side to side in pleasure, her head-spines quivering in a complementary rhythm.

V'kka indicated her desire for seconds by slamming her bowl down on the soup stall's rail. The gray-faced vendor sighed, as if the lizard-woman's brusque manners were a matter of morning routine, and ladled her another serving. Luma announced her presence with a cough.

The stevedore wheeled on her, then lapsed into a state of wary recognition. "Luma!" she hissed. She took note of Ontor. "You must be her brother, Arrus."

"Her brother Ontor," he corrected.

"Ah yes, he is the better-known one, isn't he?"

Ontor faked a smile. "He is the eldest, yes."

V'kka pointed to Luma. "This one aided me, when alchemists stole our egg-kin."

"I worked that case as well," Ontor said.

She subjected him to a blank, reptilian stare. "It is her I trust."

"V'kka," said Luma, "we're looking for a—"

"You are here to investigate the assassinations. The others won't listen to me, but you will agree that it has to be the Red Mantis."

Since the apprehension of the alchemists, Luma had learned to depend on V'kka only for the simplest pieces of information. The lizard-woman collected wild tales of conspiracy as children gather shells on the seashore. The last time they had spoken, V'kka had convinced herself of an imminent invasion by the atheists of arid Rahadoum. Before then, she saw in every ill omen the frost-bitten hands of Irriseni witches. Whatever alarmed her now, it would not involve the dreaded assassin cult.

"We pursue an unrelated matter," Luma said.

"You can't catch the Red Mantis killers themselves," breathed V'kka, "They disguise themselves in stolen faces, and walk in summoned shadows. But those who hired them, those you can pursue. The question is, who benefits?"

It would be easier to humor her than to change the subject. "From what?"

"The deaths of our guild leaders. It can only be the shippers, who wish to break us, and bully down our fees."

"How many have died?"

"First Balold, and then, not two months later, his successor, Fustolt."

"And were either felled by a sniper's arrow, or had their throats cut by a sawtoothed blade, so that they drowned in their own blood?" The latter was the infamous signature weapon of the Red Mantis cult throughout the world. Those of Magnimar showed an equal predilection for the perfectly aimed bow shot—if, that is, the terrified whispers about them held any truth.

V'kka extended her head-fins. "Balold supposedly died of a bad oyster. That can only mean poisoning. Fustolt stood where a pile of crates fell, and was crushed. But who tipped them over?"

"If the guild believes itself threatened, send them to Derexhi House. We will charge our usual fair fee, and get to the bottom of it."

"Those fools attribute it all to coincidence!" V'kka snorted.

"About our other matter. We're looking for a tavern called the No-Horn. Where might we find it?"

V'kka's long, pink tongue thrust itself from between her teeth, then retreated back into the cavern of her mouth. "Your drinking spots are all the same to me. I do not frequent them."

After an awkward farewell, Luma and Ontor went on their way, moving farther down the lane of food stalls.

Ontor grimaced. "We're not going to have to stop and chat with every eccentric of the bazaar, are we?"

"I thought she might know the place. People here have good reason not to talk to us. V'kka owes us, so I thought she might help."

"More help like that, and we'll be here all day."

Luma set off for the stall of a weathered crone. The woman shrank back. Luma held out a trio of coppers, the price of a barley pie.

"Hello, Tlina," Luma said.

The crone looked through her.

Luma added a few more coppers.

The vendor gritted her toothless gums and snatched them up. "Spicy or mild?" she demanded.

"Mild." Luma pulled out a handkerchief to hold the hot pie, which the crone served up with a pair of crooked tongs.

"I can't be seen talking to you no more," Tlina mumbled. "Princess says no more snitching. And to the city guard, no talking at'all."

"The Derexhi aren't the city guard."

"Next thing to it. I'm not running afoul of no Princess."

The title of Princess was self-anointed, currently claimed by a woman named Sabriyya Kalmeram. Because Luma had no idea what this business with Khonderian was, she couldn't say for sure that it wouldn't involve the locally popular gang lord. But it was best to say that it wouldn't. Here, as elsewhere in the city, people made as much of their own law as they thought necessary. The family's dealings with Kalmeram's people had always been touchy.

"Asking for directions isn't snitching, is it? We're looking for the No-Horn Tavern."

"Tavern? There's a place called No-Horn's, but tavern's too flattering a term." She pointed a quavering arm over to the south.

"And incidentally, are you acquainted with a gnome named Noole?"

Tlina spat, her trajectory missing her own tray of merchandise by the slimmest of margins. "Happens that I'm not and wouldn't tell you if I was."

Luma waved Ontor over; they followed Tlina's directions, dodging, in sequence, a stumbling beggar, a two-child team of apprentice cutpurses, and an extravagantly puking gutter-wretch. This last bazaar denizen suggested that they had reached the desired radius. Indeed, they soon caught sight of a leaning black structure constructed from discarded pieces of ship's hull. A tavern sign hung askew over its curtained archway. It depicted a unicorn chained and tormented by hopping devils. Each danced about holding a bottle of spirits. The largest of the devils held aloft the creature's severed horn.

"Auspicious," said Ontor, parting the curtain.

Shafts of sunlight, admitted by gaps between ill-fitting planks, jabbed into the drinking hole's gloomy interior. Stacked barrels butted against its sturdiest wall. A dirty rope, tied to wobbly wooden stanchions, performed the duties of a bar counter, separating kegs from patrons. Leaking wine and beer filled the room with the odor of evaporated alcohol. Drinkers huddled at uneven tables, holding tight to their flagons so they wouldn't slide off. They numbered a dozen, give or take. All were men, no two of them outfitted in the same manner. Whether sailor or longshoreman, vendor or carter, their clothes clung to them, damp and sweat-stained.

Behind the rope, on a leather chair that leaked yellowed stuffing, hunched the barman. At first glance, Luma took him for some unidentifiable hybrid of man and hobgoblin. As she drew closer, and her elven vision adjusted to the darkness, she saw that he was fully human, but terribly disfigured. She studied him without appearing to stare. His ears had been lopped off, and his flesh deeply scourged. Mottled patches of skin marked the boundaries of a less-than-complete divine healing.

His sniff resounded with suspicion. "Yeah?" Neither she nor Ontor were soiled enough to fit in here.

Ontor tossed him a golden coin. It spun through the air; the barman fumbled to catch it.

"A round for the house," he said. "Keep the rest."

The drinkers responded with a grudging murmur. They stood, flagons in hand, and queued up to have them filled. Heaving himself to an upright position, the barman seized the first of the flagons and waddled to the nearest spigot.

"When he said a round for the house," said a patchily bearded patron, "he meant your best stuff."

"That I did," Ontor said.

Grumbling, the taverner reached for a higher spigot. "So what do you want of us, then?"

One man, Luma noted, had refrained from joining the line. He'd positioned himself at the smallest of the bar's tables, wedged into a corner. She angled herself to better take his measure. Wide shoulders and a barrel chest gave way to a disproportionately narrow hips and a pair of spindly legs. Sooty robes, worn loosely, exposed gaunt pectorals. Dark tattoos writhed across his olive skin, giving him a mottled appearance. They encircled and overran patches of shiny flesh—burn scars. An uninitiated viewer might take the tattoos for mere decorative designs. Luma recognized them as letters written in arcane script.

Something in the man's stillness tweaked her caution. It was unnatural to him, she intuited—a dam about to burst. As Ontor interviewed the barman, Luma stepped away. She thrust her hand into a pouch at her waist, feeling the milled edges of a glass prism. She called on the citysong, drawing it through the object. It chorused in her mind's ear: pages turning at the library, the drone of lecturing voices at the school of the arcane, the key turning in the lock of the museum's forbidden collection, the hollering of raggedy charlatans down in Dockway. The tattoos on the man's face, chest, and arms shimmered into intelligibility. His ink marks rendered into written form the primordial speech of an elemental plane. The man wore the language of fire.

Luma shifted awareness, back to the exchange between Ontor and the barman.

"You're Derexhi, ain't you?" the barman said.

Ontor kept his smile pleasant. "He's owed money; we're to make arrangements for payment."

To the impatience of the next man in line, the barman stopped pouring. "Not just Derexhi. *The* Derexhi."

Ontor doffed his cap. "It's on behalf of a friend of his. Our client has come unexpectedly into money and wishes to discharge his many debts."

The barman snorted. "The question ain't if we give a fig about Noole. The question is, if we help you run him down, what's our cut?"

"Another gold piece," Ontor said.

"He gets around, that Noole does. For all the locations he might be, a gold sail barely covers it."

The man with the fire magic tattoos started muttering.

"If you can't narrow it down, that argues not for a hefty payment, but against it," Ontor said.

"Try down at the Triodea," suggested the sailor.

"Don't just out and tell 'im!" the barman cried.

The tattooed man finally spoke out loud. "Don't say anything."

"Or Grand Arch," pitched in a snaggletoothed drinker. "He's taken a squat there."

"Idiots!" said the barman.

"If he's handing out coins, I want mine," snaggletooth retorted.

The tattooed man stood, upending his table. "Noole is our friend!"

The barman addressed him with the exasperation of a governess saddled with an unmanageable child. "Calm yourself, Hendregan."

Hendregan giggled. Then, as quickly as it had vanished, his anger returned. "You're betrayers."

Luma saw that he rubbed a ball of putty-like material between thumb and forefinger. She cried out Ontor's name and leapt across the room, knocking him onto its hard dirt floor.

With a practiced overhand throw, Hendregan threw a tiny projectile of burning light. It landed on the barman and blossomed out into a ball of orange-red flame. With a whoosh, it met the alcohol hanging in the air and sitting in half-opened casks.

The walls blew apart. The roof caved in and dropped on the drinking hole's inhabitants. As they fell, planks caught fire, or were incinerated instantly.

The blast of heat pulled the air from Luma's lungs. She lay across her brother's back, less than a foot from the fireball's dissipating edge. Her cloak caught fire; she rolled and put it out. Ontor gasped beneath her.

They rose, staggering out of the wreckage and taking in the blast's aftermath. A black cloud bubbled from the former site of No-Horn's. Blazing barrels disgorged beer and wine. Their contents washed over the barman's blackened corpse. Others of his clientele lay motionless around him, charred flesh falling from exposed bone.

Hendregan stood unharmed in the wreckage. Flame licked at the sleeve of his robe. He scooped at the fire, flicking his wrist, sculpting it into the shape of a dragon, which then dissipated. The sound of a belly-laugh boomed from his unmoving lips. He spotted Luma and Ontor and advanced on them.

Ontor reached for his throwing knives. Luma pulled him down. A second blast of flame—this one straighter, more keenly directed—roared through the air above them.

"Let's go," Luma said.

Ontor showed his agreement with a running crouch toward a refuse heap. Luma forked her path away from Ontor's, so they'd be two targets instead of one.

Hendregan stomped at them, intoning an incantation. As he prepared to loose another blazing orb, Ontor popped up to hurl a knife at him. The wizard—or sorcerer, or whatever he was—ducked back, his spell-speech interrupted. Flame fizzled and popped around him.

Wind carried ashes from the ruined bar onto nearby tents and the awnings of freestanding shops. Proprietors spilled from them. When they saw Hendregan, confusion turned to rage. They scrabbled for rocks and chunks of debris. Hendregan ignored their first peltings, stalking toward the garbage heap where Ontor had found cover. As the rain of stones intensified, he whirled on his tormentors.

Luma peered out from behind a bale of nautical rope taller than she was. Hendegran had rashly opened himself to this comeuppance. Spell-hurlers needed others to cover them so they could perform their precise gesticulations undisturbed. With no one to shield him from the mob's improvised missiles, Hendregan had no choice but to flee. Once he turned to run, the bystanders showed little appetite for the chase.

Ontor rejoined his half-sister. "Do we want to chase him?"

"Do *you* want to chase him?"

In unison, they shook their heads. Luma picked her way across still-smoldering floorboards, between the prone victims. She found the man who'd mentioned Grand Arch. Though badly burned, he had survived the attack. Luma knelt beside him. "If you can tell me more of Noole's place, I'll heal you."

The drinker moaned his assent. "He mentioned a statue . . ."

He shrank back as Luma placed her hand on his shoulder. She called on the city's spirit of renewal. Magnimar sang to her of buildings rebuilt, of streets resurfaced. The song stole into the temples of the gods and collected fragments of their healing powers, as a wind picks up leaves of dust and whirls them down a laneway.

Black sheets of crackled skin absorbed themselves into the man's flesh. It burned in reverse: blood slipped back into veins and wounds closed up. Were Luma a healer-priest, she might muster the power to grant him full recovery. Instead, the weaker healing magic of a citywalker would have to suffice. He would live, and had been accelerated instantly through the worst months of physical torment.

A commotion grew from the lane to the west.

"Hasten this," Ontor said.

"I need a street name," Luma told her patient.

The man marveled at his restored hands. "Not sure . . . Wheatman's Lane, or Barley Way . . . it had the name of a grain in it."

"Describe his squat."

"He said it had a fine statue outside, one the owners could not know the value of, or they'd have sold it. A horse of pink marble, rearing up."

Luma stood, following Ontor's gaze to an approaching assembly of baton-wielding toughs. The princess's men.

It was time to get scarce.

Chapter Seven
Grand Arch

Together Luma and Ontor returned to the Summit. Once there, they headed south to Grand Arch, a district abutting the city's southern wall. In this district clustered the homes of international traders, many of whom dwelt in Magnimar only during the warm months. The trading season had not yet reached its peak. Early arrivers might be reopening their houses now, but it would be a month or so before the area returned fully to life. The habit of leaving lush manses unoccupied for long stretches gave license to squatters. Pennywise traders who refused to foot the bill for year-round guardians sometimes came back from travels elsewhere to find locks broken and larders raided. Those more cautious than thrifty hired sentinels from the Derexhi or their competitors.

Luma reviewed her mental map of the city for streets that took their names from grains, or might be misremembered as such, and that stood largely abandoned in the off-season. She came up with six and ranked them from closest to farthest. If she and Ontor were lucky, they'd find Noole at Wheatman's Lane, just as the burned man had said.

To Luma this part of town posed a nagging paradox. It was made up of foreign bits and pieces which together one might regard as an imposition on Magnimar's character. Here, structures of various styles jostled promiscuously up against one another, proclaiming not the unity of the monument city, but the variety of builders' homelands. Through roofing styles the traders blazoned their affiliations. On one street alone, the roofs recalled the pagodas of Jalmeray, the tropical counting houses of the Shackles, and the high spires of legend-ridden Absalom. Yet if each structure sang of its own distant origin, their discordant harmony joined to form a distinctive whole unique to Luma's city.

As a hedge against robbery that had proven more hopeful than practical, the streets here went unmarked. Luma, who could recite the name of every laneway, alley, and crescent in any order specified, had no trouble finding the ones they sought.

The moment they turned down Wheatman's Lane, they spotted a pair of guardians in Derexhi livery. At languid attention, the two protected the stone wall of a black house gabled in the style of haunted Ustalav. Ontor greeted them by name: Chenward and Derovia.

"Much trouble with squatters this year?" he asked.

"No, sir, not hereabouts." Chenward, a weedy man with a shovel-flat face, appointed himself spokesman for the two of them. "Too many Derexhi guards here on Wheatman. Though, as your father commanded, we've taken note of them what haven't hired us and have had trouble with prowlers as a result."

"Good to hear it," said Ontor. "We'll not rest till we've signed up the whole street."

"Is there a place along here with a horse statue out front?" Luma asked. "Made of pink stone?"

"No ma'am," Chenward answered.

"I seen one like that on Brewer's Dale, when I was stationed there last year," said Derovia, a strand of chestnut hair escaping her well-polished helmet.

Ontor thanked them and they made their way to Brewer's Dale.

"It's not named for a grain," said Ontor.

"But you need grain for brewing," said Luma, "so you can see why he'd get the association mixed up."

"We'll see soon enough."

After a few minutes of quiet walking, Luma added, "I bet when we do find it, it'll be the street with the fewest of our guardians assigned to it."

"I suppose."

"Our sentinels won't intervene to protect a house they aren't paid to, but robbers think otherwise. They take us for city guards. At the very least, they reckon our retainers will testify against them."

"You're coming to a point of some kind. I can sense it."

Luma sighed. "If we were better briefed on our own family business, we'd both be able to rattle off every assignment in the district. We could have started our search with the least-guarded streets. Every piece of information counts. And we aren't even versed in our own doings."

"Back to that old hobbyhorse."

"Doesn't it bother you—expected to be a genius in the field, and treated like a subordinate at home?"

"Doing what you're told is agreeably simple. You should try it sometime."

"I have been. That's the problem."

"Just remember what I said, all right?"

Luma lapsed back into silence. After a while, Ontor brought up a new subject: the likely guests at an upcoming ball over at Paleankari House, especially those of the young and female variety. As best she could manage, she indulged his chatter. The world of romantic conquest lay beyond both her interest and her understanding. One day she'd work it out, but likely not from Ontor's observations. He liked girls pretty and insipid, and Luma had no idea how to be either.

When they reached Brewer's Dale, the house with the horse out front was waiting for them just around a bend. As Luma had guessed, few of the manors here kept sentinels out front. A few posted the crest of a rival firm, but none of its retainers were in evidence.

Ontor and Luma hopped the locked gate and marched past the stone horse like they'd been paid to be there. Copper minarets fixed to the roof heralded the absent owner's connection to sand-swept Qadira. The building's shutters were closed and locked. The two Derexhi slipped around to the side, where they found the servants' entrance. Ontor produced his burglary kit and knelt to jimmy the lock, opening it without leaving a mark.

The door opened into the kitchen. The pantry door swung wide. Dirtied plates teetered on a side table; flies buzzed around a pile of chicken bones.

"Someone's certainly been living here uninvited," Luma said.

Weapons ready, they prowled the manor, stepping into each room in turn. Whoever had been here was no longer present.

In the master bedroom, Luma got down on hands and knees to peer under the bed. A ball of crumpled vellum rewarded her hunch. After straightening it flat, she scanned the contents: fourteen lines of verse, marred by scratch-throughs and inkblots. She read for a while, then set it aside, flushing.

"He's flown the coop, but there was a poet here."

Ontor picked up the poem and whistled. "Racy stuff," he said, folding it carefully and putting it in his pouch.

"From the state of the kitchen, I'd say he hasn't been here in weeks," Luma said. "Or longer."

Ontor nodded. "A dead end, then. Where else did they say he favors? The Triodea?"

Luma threw open the shutters and looked for the sun's position in the sky. "It's getting late. We'll have to scour the opera houses and coffee shops tomorrow."

"Singers and actresses. My favorite quarter!"

The window afforded a view of the manor across the way. Furtive figures—Luma counted at least five of them—darted from ill-tended hedges into its main house. They were variously armored, with swords swinging from their belts. Luma called Ontor over, but by the time he reached the window, they were gone.

"Another argument for Derexhi security," he said, after she'd described them.

"Do we go for a look?"

"Were they gnomes?"

"No, humans. Or close enough."

"Are we getting paid to nose in?"

"Right. Nothing more to see here."

Alert for signs of the lurkers across the street, they departed the Qadiran trader's manor. Luma waited until they were well away from Brewer's Dale before musing aloud. "So this is how I think it puzzles together."

"We report, Luma. We don't puzzle."

"Brewer's Dale is awash with squatters. I bet that's what's going on. This Noole character scouts out abandoned manors whose owners are too mingy to protect their homes and belongings. He either reports to Khonderian, or buys him off—no, it's Khonderian

83

paying him, so the lord-mayor's man, or maybe the lord-mayor's office, is making money on the side renting out places they don't own. Noole doesn't seem to have looted his temporary roost, but who's to say the others aren't?"

Ontor fiddled with a loose button dangling from his doublet. "So assuming this is our affair, who's paying Father to have us look into this?"

"The traders? The lord-mayor, wondering what his man is up to? A rival to the lord-mayor, aiming to dirty him up? Iskola's been cozying up to plenty of important councilors lately."

"I have to hand it to you, Mouse."

"How so?"

"That's a great many leaps to arrive at the dullest conspiracy ever contemplated."

Chapter Eight
The Hells

Dusk edged into night as the two strode through the Marble District, rounding the sweeping curve of Dachari Avenue onto Avalos Lane. Servants of the various houses, as if in clockwork coordination, lit lanterns affixed to iron poles near their manor gates.

Ahead, near Derexhi Gate, Luma spotted a low black carriage. Around it milled an assortment of armed men. She discerned a carved and painted wooden plaque on the back of the carriage: the mayoral crest.

Ontor tensed. "I don't like the look of this."

Their sister Ulisa dropped into lockstep with them, her stride suggesting that she'd been there all along. She had secreted herself, Luma guessed, behind a hedge of chirping rustflowers. A single petal, the color of dried blood, clung to the temple of her shaven head. "You're not to run," she told Luma.

"Why would I run?"

She took Luma by the elbow. "You'll be protected."

"From what?"

"Yes, from what?" Ontor asked.

"We'll find out."

Luma hesitated.

"You are Derexhi," Ulisa told her. "Project inner strength."

Luma quickened her step and did her best to straighten her spine. She brushed her hair from her face, though the wind blew it immediately back. As she approached the carriage, she saw the rest of the family arrayed on the other side of Derexhi Gate. They'd arranged themselves in a rough V formation, with Randred at its point and Yandine at his side. It would take a close observer to see that he was leaning against her. Arrus and Iskola flanked them, with Eibadon hanging back, swinging the chain of his clerical medallion.

The lord-mayor's men parted as she approached, then closed ranks, encircling her. She went to her father. "What's happening here?"

"They won't tell us." His hand shook as he reached out for her. She clasped her slim fingers around his thick ones, hiding his quavering from the mayoral guards.

It had to concern the Khonderian business. Whatever that might be.

With parade ground formality, the guardsman with the most braids on his uniform stepped forward. "Luma Arcadios Derexhi?" he asked.

"That is me," she answered.

"By the authority of Lord-Mayor Haldemeer Grobaras, I place you under arrest."

Luma breathed in deep. "What are the charges?"

"You will be informed of the charges against you in accordance with proper protocol."

The arresting officer moved toward her, then froze, stalled by Randred's imperious gaze. True nobles or not, the gap in status between the head of a founding house and a mere bodyguard yawned like a chasm.

Randred leaned in to whisper in Luma's ear. "It's politics. We'll get you out."

Arrus spoke in her other ear. "Say absolutely nothing."

Luma imagined what either of them would do in her place. They would command the situation. She turned, imitating the way father and son each squared their shoulders when pressed. Head held high, she said, "I will go with you." Though an unwelcome vibration marred her tone, Luma saw she had acquitted herself well: the officer bowed without quite realizing it. His gesture as he beckoned her to enter the carriage was that of a butler ushering one of his master's guests into a ballroom. She swept past him.

"Mademoiselle," he prompted. "Your weapons."

"Of course." Drawing out the process, both to avoid sudden movements and to maintain the superiority she wished to assert, she handed over her sickle, then her darts, then her sling and its handful of bullets, the dagger at her hip, and the one hidden in her boot. She considered holding out the last item, but if they found it, as they likely would, she'd be surrendering her place on the high horse.

The officer pointed to the leather pouch tied to her belt. "And your ingredients."

"Naturally," said Luma. She handed over the purse containing her prism, feathers, copper coins, and trio of vials respectively containing soot, insect legs, and a live spider. Their confiscation impeded her chances of escape far more than the loss of her weapons. There were still magics she could pluck from the citysong without them, but the most directly useful ones were now taken from her.

A female guard, a buxom woman with a bent nose, patted her down, checking both boots. She did her job thoroughly; Luma was glad she hadn't tried a hold-out.

The search complete, Luma breezed into the carriage. The last sight she caught on the way in were Arrus and Iskola, exchanging what she presumed were doubtful whispers.

The coach rattled down cobbled avenues, the commanding officer and the female guardsman sitting across from her. Their demeanors discouraged conversation. The carriage took a hard turn from Avalos onto Dachari. As it fishtailed, Luma caught a flutter of dark motion behind one of the avenue's many marble statues.

It was her distant watcher. She was as sure of this as of the number of fingers on her hand. A chill ran through her. Was he the one who had engineered this trap, and now watched as it was sprung?

The carriage wheeled onto the Way of Arches, and from there into the heart of the Capital District. As it caromed toward the Pediment Building, Luma's confidence ebbed. In its proximity, the citysong darkened. Its percussion resolved into the slam of cell doors and the rattling of chains. Sharps and flats counterpointed into a duet between implacable lawkeepers and despairing prisoners.

Now she could see the structure through the carriage window. Its gray, unadorned surface thrust up into the sky. In contrast to the city's other official buildings, it strove for neither grandeur nor beauty. The visible part of the building comprised only the top half of it. From the ground floor up, the Pediment housed the offices of the city guard and lord-mayor's forces. As many stories lay concealed below the surface in the Hells, the warren of cells and interrogation chambers for the imprisonment of wrongdoers and the extraction of their confessions. Luma heard their contribution to the citysong whenever she drew near the building, but had never been inside. Now she'd be an inmate.

The carriage rounded the building, entering the compound through a back gate. The wail of the citysong grew ever louder in Luma's mind. She tried to shut it out, but couldn't. When she was distraught, her oneness with the city overrode her. The wretches of the Hells wished to be heard.

When the carriage came to a stop, mayoral guards hopped to, pulling the doors open.

"Off with the armor," the female guard ordered. Luma complied; the exercise left her in an under-tunic, linen breeches, and her boots.

The arresting officer gestured for her to exit first. He followed her, producing a set of shackles.

"That gate," said the female bodyguard, "was where your special treatment ended."

Luma thrust out her hands. The guard clipped one set of shackles around her wrists and placed another on her ankles. The woman and another guard stood to either side of her; the arresting officer led the procession, its speed limited by Luma's ankle restraints, from the carriage into the building. Her captors took her through a forbidding iron door, scored with flecks of red paint. Inside, a ruddy-faced jailer sat at a high desk, its pine face painted with the crest of Magnimar. He belonged to the diminutive, broad-footed halfling race, a relative rarity among the city's peoples. Because the desk had not been modified for his shorter stature, its edge met him at the mid-chest. He jutted his fat-swaddled chin at Luma as if daring her to smirk at the awkwardness of his position.

Quill pen in hand, he barked out questions, scratching away as Luma confirmed her name, age, and place of residence. Luma thought she detected an unease between the halfling and her escort, perhaps because he was regular city guard and they were of the quasi-official mayoral corps. The encroachment of the lord-mayor's swords into law enforcement was an innovation of the current regime, one that still rankled the regulars. This tension might be leveraged to her advantage.

The halfling reached a new entry on his form.

"Crime?" he asked her.

"I am innocent," Luma said.

The clerk assembled his face into an expression of unutterable boredom. "What crime are you accused of?"

"Never mind that," the officer said, moving the procession along. They departed to the sound of the halfling's pointed paper-shufflings.

A fetor assailed her as they entered the cells proper. It combined vomit, blood, rotting food, and generations of foul perspiration. Prisoners rose from their benches to scream unintelligible obscenities. The procession altered course as a stream of urine hit the corridor floor. The buxom guard struck out with her baton, catching a random set of fingers thrust through cell bars. Luma heard the crunch of fracturing bone. The victim howled; his fellow inmates bellowed in glee.

Two sets of stairs and a series of snaking corridors took them to their destination: a holding cell about thirty feet wide and fifteen deep. Seven other women huddled inside. As one of her partners unlocked the barred door, the female guard unlocked Luma's shackles.

"We'll see how long you stay the little princess," she said, shoving Luma into the cell and thudding its door shut behind her. The arresting officer was already halfway out of sight.

"When do I learn what I'm accused of?" Luma called. No one answered. The remainder of the bodyguards departed, leaving Luma alone with her cellmates.

Hunger gnawed at her. They'd arrested her right before dinner. To ask for a meal would only make her look weak, and therefore stupid. Surely there'd be no food till breakfast. She shrugged it off, as her father would have done, when he was hale enough to stand it. As Arrus or Ulisa or any of the others would do, if they'd been the ones thrown in here.

The Hells' lamenting version of the citysong crashed in on her. She chose to embrace it, to sift it for clues. As feared as the place was, escapes were hardly unknown. Its stones and mortar and bars and barriers were as much a part of the city as any other structure. If she answered its song in the right way, it might reply to her, giving up its secrets.

"What are you, hazed on flayleaf?" a harsh voice demanded. It was one of the other prisoners, who came abruptly for her. Luma ducked her shove, but another of them had positioned herself behind her. She pushed Luma into the first woman, who shouldered her back. Judging from their thick brows and jutting teeth, both of her attackers had a little orc in them. Each was half again Luma's size.

"You're small," observed the first.

"You'll be fun to play with," said the second.

From the way they carried themselves it was plain that they had more than bulk going for them. These were seasoned brawlers. Luma could use some of the unarmed techniques Ulisa had taught her, but there were two of them, and she had little room to maneuver.

"You two." The gruff statement issued from a small woman wedged between wall and bench. Without it, Luma would have sworn she was sleeping. Her short stature and barrel construction gave her away as a dwarf. Beyond that, a tightly wrapped blanket concealed any distinguishing features. "Don't make me open my eyes. Because if I have to do that, we're having another go-round."

"Thaubnis . . ." the first orc-blood whined.

"She's under my protection," said Thaubnis.

The orc-bloods backed away like scolded hounds. They settled in the corner of the cell opposite Thaubnis.

Luma wandered tentatively toward the dwarf. She'd heard enough about the Hells to understand that certain offers of protection were dangerous to accept. This dwarf might be ally or exploiter; she could not afford to mistake one for the other. "Thank you," she said.

"Shut up and let me sleep," said Thaubnis.

Luma lowered herself to the cell floor, exhaustion falling over her. She rested without truly going under, a part of her remaining alert for sudden assault. The hours swam by as a fitful drifting.

The clank of the key in the cell door lock returned her to full awareness. Her first thought was that the guards had come for her. Instead, they summoned the orc-bloods. The two of them exited the cells, shoulders slumped in dread.

Though the cell admitted no light, Luma could tell it was morning by listening to the music of the city, pushing through the pain and fury of the Hells' inhabitants to the birds outside.

Soon another guard showed up to push metal bowls of a porridge-like substance across the cell floor.

Thaubnis finally stirred, hopping up to grab the fullest bowl. No utensils accompanied the gruel; the dwarf ate by shoving her bony fingers into the concoction and licking them off. Luma tried to eat, but the smell of spoilage overwhelmed her hunger. She shoved the rest over to the dwarf.

"You sure?" Thaubnis asked.

"I might regret it later, but I'm sure for now."

"Midday meal's worse, and dinner more unspeakable still." The dwarf clearly spoke not out of a spirit of persuasion, but of general information: she had already dug into the second bowl. Oat fragments spattered her prominent jaw and clung to the deep creases in her face. Red splotches flared around her pitch-black irises. Empty perforations ran up the outer rims of both prominent ears; presumably, she'd been stripped of her jewelry before they threw her in here. From her head tufted kinky gray hair. As Thaubnis ate, Luma noted that she turned her left arm to conceal a raised area on the inside of her forearm, just above the elbow. She guessed that it had been made by a brand, but could not make out the shape without making her observation obvious.

Neither could she place the dwarf's accent, except that it originated outside Magnimar.

"I thank you again for intervening with the orc-bloods," Luma ventured.

"If I let them beat you, they might get to thinking someone other than me was in charge," Thaubnis said.

"I can arrange for my family to help you."

Thaubnis licked her fingers clean. "This might surprise you, but I don't need your help."

"You have friends who can get you out of here?"

"Friends? That's a laugh."

"Then what do you have?"

Thaubnis took a good stare at her new cellmate. "Nosy one, aren't you?"

Luma shrugged and backed away.

Thaubnis scooted closer. "What I got is what gets everybody out of here. Everybody who gets out, that is. Information. There's an entire network of poisoners I can squeal on." She tapped her temple. "Names, locations, who bought the poisons, who ingested them. That cancels out whatever nonsense they might have on me."

"And what nonsense do they have on you?"

"I broke the wrong jaw—allegedly. It's piffle. I'll be drinking in the Basilisk's Eye before moonrise."

Luma cocked an eyebrow. "Truly? It seems like you've been here a while."

The dwarf crossed her arms. "I didn't say which moonrise. Soon as they come for me, I'll tattle my head off, and that'll be that."

One of their remaining cellmates, a corpulent woman still savoring her rancid porridge, muttered something about informants.

"Don't make me come over there, Quaali," Thaubnis said.

"I've heard they get rough down here," said Luma. "What if they decide to beat it out of you, this information you have?"

"Rough? That's also a laugh."

"What do you mean?"

"I mean, I can tell you about rough, and around here they're amateurs."

"I don't follow you."

"You're not meant to," said Thaubnis.

Quaali chipped in. "Thaubnis is a torturer by trade," she sniped.

"You shut up."

Quaali made a grumping noise.

Thaubnis turned to Luma. "Not a torturer. An inquisitor. Two very different vocations."

Quaali squinched up her face, then blurted: "An inquisitor's just a torturer for the gods, ain't it?"

Thaubnis leapt up, ran over to her, and slapped her. Quaali yowled in protest. Thaubnis menaced her a while, then came back to sit cross-legged next to Luma. "Used to be. Used to be an inquisitor."

"Until they let you down?" Luma asked.

"Who?"

"Those friends you mentioned."

"Let's just say this. When you're an inquisitor, you talk to a lot of heretics."

"Talk," scoffed Quaali. "Ha!"

"You have to be careful," Thaubnis continued, "that you don't start agreeing with them."

"Your colleagues turned on you," Luma said.

"They gave me this." In response, Thaubnis turned her arm to show Luma her brand. It was the symbol of Magrim, a dwarven god so obscure even Luma had read little about him.

A door banged open. Luma's arresting officer came to the bars with the female bodyguard and a jailer. He ordered the jailer to open the cell, and waved Luma out. "You're coming with us," he said.

They moved from corridors she'd seen on the way in to another set of passageways. Under her breath, Luma hummed her invocation to the citysong. Her imagined map of the city shifted in her mind's eye. She beheld the Capital District and the Pediment. Now the view altered, revealing the building's interior as she had seen it so far. Corridors flowed out as she walked them, committing them to memory, adding them to her map. A compass rose manifested, showing her where north was. The orientation might prove invaluable, should she have to attempt escape.

Luma perceived an alteration in her captors' mood. The day before, they'd comported themselves with crisp professionalism, even deference. Now they gave off a cold rage. What had changed? She wished she'd been able to scrounge up a copper piece to replace the one they'd taken from her. With it as a focus, she could try her thought-reading trick.

As they turned a corner, the woman shoved Luma into it. She timed the attack so that it did no good to anticipate it. Pain radiated through Luma's arm and shoulder.

"We found out what you did," the woman hissed.

They moved her up from the Hells into upper stories, the Pediment itself. Exposed stone gave way to flocked surfaces and gilded ornamentation. The awful smell receded into a faint soapy odor. Functionaries' chatter replaced the groans of the jailed.

For a moment, Luma thought she sensed the presence of her distant watcher. Then she was in the lord-mayor's office.

Chapter Nine
The Pediment

With a heavy silver pincer, Haldemeer Grobaras cracked into a six-inch lobster claw. The enormous creature splayed before him on a serving plate of translucent aquamarine glass, surrounded by lemon wedges and a lake of melted butter. Also overspread across his desk, on dishware of matching splendor, were a shank of mutton, thick slices of honeyed ham, a bowl of boiled eggs, and an entire deep-fried eel, cut up into bite-sized morsels and arranged in a meandering version of its original shape. Side dishes spilled from pewter bowls: steamed cabbage, roast leeks, and a salad of dandelion leaves and gangava fronds. A half-full bottle of Molthuni wine sat by the lord-mayor's elbow. Two emptied predecessors had been pushed to the desk's outer edge, exiled alongside a pen, an inkwell, and a sheaf of stray documents.

He hunched over his food, supported by a reinforced chair in the heavy Old Grodhian style. Leering from its high back was not the mayoral seal, but a needlepoint rendition of Haldemeer's personal crest: a pelican, its beak gaping, fishtails lolling from its pouch.

Grobaras had pushed up the sleeves of his doublet and white tunic, but did not wear a bib or have a napkin in his lap. A glamor on the doublet caused it to sparkle brilliantly, independent of lighting conditions. Sapphire beads lined his cuffs and topped his laces. Intertwined snakes patterned his hose. On his head he wore a pillbox hat of red and gold, topped by a trio of pluming jadebird feathers. Each finger displayed a jeweled ring; no gemstone appeared twice. Medallions hung across his chest, dragging now and then across the food.

An assortment of tapestries, all recently loomed and garishly colored, hid the room's gray walls. A chunk of myrrh smoldered in a censer. Attendants, some in the drab garb of city functionaries, others wearing gaudy Grobaras livery, lined the back wall, ready for orders. When Grobaras needed a plate pushed toward him, the closest of the latter sprang into action. The bureaucrats, Luma could only presume, waited to fulfill more official duties, should any arise. Yet a third group, this one well-armed, watched with affected nonchalance from an adjacent chamber. From where Luma stood, she could clearly see a handful of them. The angle of the wall hid at least one or two others.

Grobaras ran gobbets of lobster meat through the butter slurry and stuffed them into his mouth. A line of juice dripped down his recessed lips and out onto the first of his three protuberant chins. A servant stepped up to dab it from him before droplets struck his tunic; the lord-mayor elbowed him away. He clutched his wine goblet, held it under his cleft nose, sniffed deep, and drank. A rivulet of sweat emerged from his spikes of sand-white hair, tumbling down his shiny forehead. This he permitted his servant to wipe away. He speared a forkful of cabbage and sucked it into his mouth. Still chewing, he said, "Under ordinary circumstances I do not involve myself in the affairs of the city guard."

He left a pause, either to graze on the leeks or to allow Luma to respond. She could think of nothing worth saying.

Wiping his mouth on the crook of his arm, the lord-mayor continued. "In fact, it has always been my contention that a city thrives best when governed inattentively. So you can understand my dismay when the action of certain citizens interrupts my affairs, forcing me to trundle down to this, my secondary office, what with its paltry furnishings and insalubrious atmosphere. At certain moments, it seems to me that suffering from the Hells below rises up, like vapor from an alchemist's alembic, to suffuse the entire structure. Veritably palpable, wouldn't you say?"

"I would," Luma said.

"It is good to begin a discussion with a point of agreement." Grobaras gulped down more wine; an attendant already worked a screw into the cork of a fourth bottle. "Pleasantries thus achieved, let us plunge to the marrow of the thing. Who put you up to it? The paterfamilias, I hear, is unwell. Yet he can still give orders, can he not?"

"I don't understand your questions."

"Do you feign ignorance, or am I merely over-eloquent?" Luma shifted her weight. "What am I accused of?"

Grobaras's laugh loosed a spray of egg fragments. "Let us proceed as if all tiresome denials have been already issued, shall we? I speak lightly, but your offense is vast. Khonderian was a good and useful man. I felt an affection for him. That you will die for your crime is a given. That you shall pay reparations on the torture slab is likewise foreordained. The only question before us today is to what degree you care to minimize the duration and extent of your scourging before you are borne to the gibbet."

"You're saying Khonderian is dead?"

The lord-mayor banged the table, rattling the silverware. "Tediousness! You know it better than any! It is by your hand that his throat was sliced."

"You're wrong."

Grobaras's face went from flushed to erubescent. "We have dispensed with that. Who ordered it? You are the weak link. Oh yes, I've had you looked into, Luma Arcadios Derexhi. It wasn't your idea. Your father commanded it—or your brother Arrus, who seems to give the orders in his place. Or perhaps your wizard of a sister, who is the whisper behind the curtain."

"If you had evidence you'd have us all in chains."

"Evidence? You were seen trailing him."

Luma said nothing.

Grobaras waved a piece of eel at her. "You deny it?"

"My family has friends. This is all bluster."

Grobaras stood. "You were merely the instrument. The Derexhis may be an old family, more pedigreed than mine certainly. But underneath the family seal and the grand balls and the airs you assume, you are hirelings and have always been so. I will know who paid you to kill my man. Who struck this blow against me."

"We are not assassins. You confuse us with the Red Mantis, perhaps."

Trailing his sleeve across the food-strewn desktop, Grobaras pushed several of the bowls and plates together, creating a space on its corner. From a drawer, he produced Luma's spell bag, spilling its contents on the desk. The live spider scurried frantically as its vial rolled, coming to a stop against the base of a wine glass. "Tell me the purpose of these objects," said Grobaras. "Which sorceries do they conjure?"

"No sorcery," said Luma.

The lord-mayor's face dimpled. "Technically correct, when the term is finely construed. You spellcasters and your narrow distinctions. You think you Derexhi own the only library in the city?" A bureaucrat stepped forward in response to Grobaras's backhand wave. He held a book, which he opened to a marked page and held out in front of his boss. Grobaras scanned for the relevant passage. "Your kind isn't too common, hey?"

Luma forced herself to stand straighter. "Your Honor speaks elliptically."

"We found accounts of others like you. You're a street witch, are you not?"

"I'm not familiar with the term."

Grobaras glanced back at the book. "Or do you call yourself a cobblestone druid? Streetseer? Or is it citywalker? Ah, that's the one you answer to."

Luma wondered how she'd given herself away. It must have been one of her flinches. Grobaras was as she had heard him described—damnably skilled at reading people. An oaf he might be, but far from a fool. Thus his dozen years and counting of unassailable power, and his long line of vanquished rivals.

He continued: "You talk to the city, and the city talks to you. Is that it?"

"My capacities are modest."

"So you wish others to believe, with that hangdog demeanor and shuffling gait." The lord-mayor's hand drifted over to the ham. He visibly restrained himself from snatching up another piece. "By what leave do you suckle from my city's teat?"

"By what leave?"

He picked up a carving knife. "Magnimar is mine, girl. I tolerate no rival suitors." When she did not rebut him, he went on: "Several explorers write of street witches in the *Pathfinder Chronicles*. Tell me, can you ask the city to lift you on its vapors, allowing you to walk on air?"

"If I have asked that, it has never been granted."

"*If,*" Grobaras growled, tapping the spider vial. "And do you use this to climb like a spider, or become one?"

"Perhaps that answer is also in your library."

"Whether you climbed *as* a spider, or climbed *like* a spider, you could have easily entered Khonderian's high apartment undetected. As you could have if you ascended on steps of wind."

"I have never walked on air."

He pointed the knife at the book. "Here it says that there was a street druid of Katapesh who could reach into that city's memories, and pluck from them a new face for any occasion. How many faces do you wear, girl? Which one did you present to the world when you slipped away from Khonderian's quarters? An anonymous servant? A grubby urchin?"

"I wear only one face." Luma had not heard of this particular gift. Her magic was mysterious to her. Every now and then she would get a hunch, sense that the city was ready to show her a fresh trick. She'd try it and it would happen. Sometimes it would be a spell, sometimes both like a spell and not. None of the few descriptions she found written in books exactly matched the way it was for her. Maybe every citywalker felt it differently, just as every city possessed its own distinct soul.

"I can't help feeling," said Grobaras, "that I lack your full attention."

"You are right. You spoke just now, but my thoughts went elsewhere."

Luma would not have thought it possible for the lord-mayor's face to grow any redder, but it did. He called into the other room: "Send it in."

Luma noticed that the cornice at the apex of the door's archway had been removed.

A hissing noise erupted from the adjoining chamber. A cacophony of clicking and ratcheting followed. From an initial chaos it resolved itself into a tick-tick-ticking sound. The floor shuddered under a weighty tread. With ungainly steps, a figure passed into the archway.

The unseen member of the lord-mayor's bodyguard was at once a creature and a machine. Its top-heavy design collected copper tubes and globes into a crudely parodied human form. A riveted globe composed its torso. Its hips and pelvis were a wheeled, jointed contraption, from which two thin tubes protruded. Spindly knees connected them to asymmetrical blobs of molded metal that served as its calves. They terminated in a clawed system of pegs, which looked too narrow to support its obvious weight. Its shoulders were wheels within wheels, wrapped in a gear-like frill. A second set of tubes, even thinner than the legs, protruded from them. Comically enlarged conical forearms flared out from the articulated elbow joints. Their end pieces had been molded into the form of clenched fists. A ball-like head rotated on top of the torso piece. Incised to resembled a helmet, it leaked green alchemical steam.

Luma recognized the construct immediately. Golems were the city's most outlandishly notable export. Her mind flashed to the conversation she overheard while trailing Khonderian, about the so-called golem rebellion.

Khonderian commanded the lord-mayor's bodyguard.

One of his bodyguards was a golem.

These were pieces of something, all right, but she didn't have enough to fit them together.

They might not relate at all. It was a curse of the citysong—the hearer perceived the mystical interconnectedness of the innumerable elements that made up Magnimar. But mystical kinships were not the same as literal ones. She couldn't let herself confuse the two.

An insight hovered on the brink of her understanding. This particular sort of golem had been chosen for a special property, the details of which she strove to recall. She plumbed the depths of memory for whatever offhanded conversation had touched on the lord-mayor and his whirring bodyguard. She maybe remembered someone mentioning the lord-mayor acquiring such a thing, but could dredge up nothing more specific than that.

Luma had seen all sorts of golems before, and read about the rest. She pictured herself in the library, studying its various volumes on golems and their manufacture. No, not the big one with the red cover. It was all lovely diagrams and blatant falsehoods. The smaller folio, with the list of golems, the history of their creators, the dry enumeration of their various properties . . .

Now she had it. This was a clockwork golem. The diagrams she'd seen had given them triangular heads and curved forearm and thigh tubes, but the ticking gave it away. Those fists didn't just punch. They opened up, revealing whirring saw blades that cut flesh and sawed bone. A useful and intimidating property in a bodyguard.

On the other hand, you never wanted to fight alongside such a device. Or against it in close quarters, if you were the one to drop it. Luma remembered the relevant passage.

"You have a clockwork bodyguard," Luma said.

Grobaras's features contorted in annoyance. Clearly he'd meant to intimidate her with the thing. By giving her a puzzle to chew on, he'd calmed her.

She pushed his irritation, moving closer to the golem. Its head tick-tick-swiveled, tracking her progress.

"You have it as a deterrent against close-up attacks. When dealt a decisive blow, a clockwork golem explodes. Red-hot shrapnel and flying blades fill the air. To get at you, attackers have to drop it—at which point it blows, and kills everyone nearby. Though I assume the others are meant to drag you out of the radius before that happens. If all goes according to plan, that is."

"Reading books doesn't make you clever, girl."

"You must also have a measure against missile fire, yes?"

Grobaras turned his back on her. He took a drink, popped an egg into his mouth, chewed it down, drank again, and faced her, his composure regained. Luma took the flustered reaction as confirmation.

"It's true," he said, "that I'm not much of an interrogator." He picked up a spoon and idly tapped it against his palm. "Khonderian would do a much better job of this. If you hadn't murdered him. You see . . ." He patted his gut. "You wouldn't think it, but I've a weak stomach. Can't stand the sight of blood. After a heavy meal, especially."

"It would have gone better for you, girl, if you'd let yourself be intimidated. Save face, then reveal the truth. Now you'll still tell us, but at what cost?" He tapped the golem's torso; it rang hollow. "Will you break after he takes your right hand? Or both of them? With the legs, we might have to do it in sections. Take the feet first, then perhaps halfway up the calf . . . I'm not a bloodthirsty man, but don't doubt my determination."

Voices rose in the hall outside. The lord-mayor's human bodyguards swarmed to the main entrance. Luma heard a muffled conversation at the door, which eventually opened. In swept Councilor Urtilia Scarnetti, whose grandson they'd rescued. Her small entourage included several other councilors and Iskola, who acknowledged Luma with a curt tilt of the head.

Luma found the lord-mayor's response surprisingly moderate. He corrected his posture, strolled to the desk, and picked up the wine bottle. A servant produced another glass, which Grobaras then filled to the halfway point. He held it out to Urtilia.

"I'll abstain," Urtilia said.

"Fair enough." Grobaras drained his glass, then the one he'd poured for her.

Urtilia held out a folded piece of vellum. A bureaucrat intervened, taking it from her and passing it to Grobaras, who glanced at it and let it drop to the floor.

"By order of the lord justice," Urtilia said.

"I can read, Urtilia," replied the lord-mayor.

"You've exceeded your authority. For years your bodyguard has encroached on the duties of the city watch. To think that you could seize a member of a great family, bypassing the Justice Court. We have rules in this city, Grobaras. Rules which will remain in effect long after your gout-ridden carcass pollutes a grave in the Cenotaph."

Grobaras smiled. "You continue to elevate our rhetorical discourse."

"Don't condescend to me, you fat bag of offal. If you've enough evidence against this woman to charge her with a crime, refer the case to the court. If not—and I gather you don't—release her posthaste."

Grobaras picked up the lobster tail and peeled a strip of meat from it. "We'll keep her, pending the filing. Given her family's stature, she'll be spared forcible questioning, until the lord justice approves the writ."

Urtilia Scarnetti twitched in disgust. "Long have you profited from disunity among the Council of Ushers. You wish to bring us together, Grobaras? Defy a direct order of the court. Then see what happens."

He stepped to her. "That supercilious look will fade when I prove that the Derexhi killed my chief bodyguard. Then you'll have to explain why you stood up for them."

Urtilia hesitated.

Iskola moved to her side. "His Honor has already conceded the point. My sister is free to go, correct? And when we have been cleared of this false suspicion, the lord-mayor will admit that anger blunted his judgment. A lapse we shall graciously forgive." She took Luma by the arm and led her from the lord-mayor's office.

Chapter Ten
Triodea

Arrus had been sitting on the grand staircase's lower steps, and jumped to his feet as Bhax and another of the servants hauled open the foyer doors. For a moment, Luma thought he might come down to wrap his arms around her. When he reached her, stopped short, and put his hands on hips, she saw the absurdity of her assumption.

"What are you smiling at?" he asked.

"I'm not," Luma answered, realizing that she was, a little. Trying not to smirk made it worse.

Iskola tried to steer her around him. "Let it rest, Arrus . . ."

"Rest? We can hash this out here, or in the squad room, but we have to— Luma, what did you tell him?"

"Nothing."

"Did you genuinely say nothing, or did you banter with him and trip yourself up?"

"There was nothing to say. He thinks one of you ordered me to murder Khonderian, and that I did so, on behest of a client."

"So you didn't do as I told you."

"When we got there," said Iskola, "we found Grobaras on the verge of apoplexy. From that, I judge Luma's performance more than adequate. Now let her wash up."

Arrus paced. "So did you succeed in drawing him out?"

"Someone saw me following Khonderian," said Luma. "That's all he has."

"And how did you let yourself be seen?"

"Can't say," Luma shrugged. "It's tough enough doing a one-person tail and not having your target see you. I don't recall being made, but then I wouldn't, would I?"

"You're awfully impertinent, given the cost of this failure."

"Maybe compared to the threat of a golem sawing my limbs off, being second-guessed by you isn't so terrifying."

Arrus stopped pacing. "What's that supposed to mean?"

"The mouse has a point," Iskola said.

Arrus wheeled on her. "You're her defender now?"

"Arrus, calm yourself."

"I don't need to be defended," Luma blurted. "I didn't fail. An operation threw a wheel. Happens all the time. To each and every one of us. It's how you recover that counts. And I recovered fine."

"Don't shriek at us, Luma," Arrus said.

"No, I'm going to say this and you're going to listen. I resign as family scapegoat. No longer will I accept this."

"Accept what?"

"You know very well. I comported myself perfectly in there. Same as you would have. I even have a lead."

"A lead?" Arrus asked.

"This thing, it has something to do with golems."

"What do you mean?"

"I don't know yet, I sense it . . . the lord-mayor has a golem bodyguard, there's a golem uprising in Bridgeward . . . it hasn't come together yet in my head, but it's all part of the same complex melody . . ."

Arrus threw up his hands. "I'm sure that will hold up at the Justice Court. You hear the city sing to you . . ."

Luma pointed at Iskola. "My magic is as real as hers. That's exactly what I mean. You're constantly denigrating me. All of you, but you more than everyone, Arrus. Because I let you. Well, this is my notice to the lot of you. Starting today, it stops."

Arrus turned to Iskola. "And I'm the one who has to calm himself?"

"Let's all of us pause for breath," Iskola responded. "This is what Grobaras wants. For us to turn on each other."

"Who hired us to track Khonderian?" Luma asked her.

Iskola passed her outer cloak to Bhax, who bore it away to the garderobe. "As soon as it's possible, I'll tell you. You have my word."

Luma pursued her out of the foyer and into the ballroom. The floor squeaked under her feet. "That's not good enough."

"It will have to be," Iskola answered.

Luma grabbed her and pulled her around. "I'm the one they're fixing to stick up on the gibbet!"

Iskola pulled her arm away. "I'll talk to the client. It will take some persuading."

"I don't care what you tell the client."

"Certain of our patrons find you an uneasy presence."

"What's that supposed to mean?"

"You're spooky. You lurk. You think the city talks to you."

"It does."

"And nobody likes a girl who can steal their thoughts."

Luma stormed up the steps, headed for her father's room. This time, Yandine was nowhere in sight. Silently she turned the latch and peeked in. Her father sat propped against the head of his bed, a ledger in his lap. With a jittering finger he followed its entries. If he'd heard the argument through his chamber's thick walls, he betrayed no sign of it.

She slipped inside. "Father," she said.

Randred's features lit up. "You're back," he said. His expression clouded. "They mistreated you."

Shaking her head, Luma sat on the mattress' edge and wrapped her arms around him. He smelled of camphor. "Iskola showed up with political reinforcements before that could happen."

"Then that unpaid mission I upbraided Iskola for has more than justified itself," he said. "I owe her an apology."

"I am grateful for it," Luma said.

Before she could go on, Randred insisted on knowing all that had happened: in the coach, at the prison, before Grobaras. Luma's efforts to quickly summarize events fell before his frequent interjections. She gave him every detail.

"We've won the merest respite," he said, when he had wrung it all from her. "Grobaras believes he has you. He has always disliked us, as he does any force in the city outside of his control. Only the true killer, delivered to him on a platter, will move him from his assumption. No one will do this for us."

"Indeed," Luma said.

"But you must confine yourself here and let the others take point. Anything you do might be construed as cause to seize you again. And then all the Urtilia Scarnettis in Magnimar won't save you from the torturer's slab."

"Father, Grobaras doesn't just want me. It's all of us. He kept asking whether it was you who ordered Khonderian's murder, or Iskola. Whichever of us goes out will be exposed."

"But you most of all, Mouse."

"We need someone who can sneak, who can pry open loose lips. Ontor can't do it alone."

"Then I'll pull in dirt-sorters from other squads." He clutched his side.

"You're unwell," she said.

"It's nothing."

She considered telling him that she knew. And she would, soon. One battle at a time, she told herself. "I would never question your authority, Father."

He gave her a wan smile. "Which means you're about to."

Luma clutched his hand. It was cold. "I've come to a decision. If I'm belittled around here, it's my doing. I'm a Derexhi, and an adult. Older than them. As capable as any of them. The only way to earn their respect is by standing up to them. Starting now."

"Starting with what?"

"Iskola wants me off the streets, too. I'll be defying that order. If it means defying yours, too . . ."

Randred dropped the ledger to the floor and held her. "Belay what I just said. I was talking nonsense. I've been suffering a touch of the rheum and it's fuddled my head. Of course you must act. Whatever the others say. This is Magnimar. No one here will give you respect if you fear to seize it."

Luma broke the embrace. "It is also Derexhi House. Where the same maxim applies."

Informing no one, Luma left early in the morning for the Triodea. She walked along the Avenue of Hours, where the warm winds of early spring came out to greet her. Gulls circled overhead; she felt their hunger and greed. Thinning clouds skidded through the sky, transforming it from gray to blue. In these signs—well, except for the gulls, gulls were a constant and didn't mean anything— she chose to find an omen. Her standing up for herself, and behaving like a woman instead of a girl, would be good for all. They would kick and complain; to adjust one's thinking is never pleasant or easy. When all the fuss was over, they would see the advantage in adding a full, equal partner to the squad. They would trust her better, and she, them. To fight without trust is to invite defeat.

As she trekked on, the sun rose higher. Traffic trickled on the avenue, then grew thicker. She passed ox-sellers, laborers, gilded carriages, bird-catchers, chimney sweeps, and a flag-draped cart carrying a troupe of traveling players. She ducked a wandering fortune-teller, warned a carter that a wheel was coming off, and stole a pickpocket's purse when he tried to take hers. Its contents she doled out to child beggars and blind men.

By the time the Avenue of Hours opened into the plaza housing the Triodea, the citysong had reached a peak, high and clear. Nowhere to Luma's senses was its sublimity purer than here. Mid-morning sun shone on the tripartite structure. It intensified on the long, white hangar of the Grand Stage and dulled on the gray surface of the adjoining concert hall. Bright-breasted birds gathered atop the reaching awning of the rooftop stage. The plaza, called the Starsilver, glittered beneath

Luma's feet. In place of cobblestones, it was surfaced by tiles inlaid with pieces of reflective abalone shell. A well-scrubbed work crew took its unhurried time searching out broken tiles. When they found one in need of replacement, they gathered around in murmured colloquy. After prolonged contemplation, the crew leader nodded to an aide, who dipped a brush into a pot of soluble red paint, hunched down, and encircled the offending tile.

She strode over to them, greeting the crew captain by name: "Mordh!"

"Luma," he answered.

Luma passed around the last of the coins she'd taken from the pickpocket, which the tilemen pocketed without comment.

"Aren't you s'posed to be in the Hells?" Mordh asked.

"I like to think otherwise." She kept up with the crew as it resumed its hunt for faulty tiles. Luma spotted a cracked one before they did. They gathered around to peer at it. "You know a gnome named Noole? He frequents the performance halls. Fancies himself a poet."

"I never asked him his name," said Mordh, "but a fellow matching that description comes 'round now and again, to practice his quatrains on us."

"And cadge coins," added another of the tilemen, a tall man who wore his thinning hair close to the scalp.

"That too," said Mordh. "I prefer that to the verses."

"No," argued a gaunt third tileman, "the poems is good."

"Seen him lately?"

Mordh pointed across the plaza, to the doorway of one of the taverns installed in the Grand Stage's right flank. "Went in there an hour ago, thereabouts."

Luma left them with a wave of thanks. The gaunt tileman squatted to paint a red circle around the tile she'd pointed out. She wended her unobtrusive way through the plaza's sprawling foot traffic. At the tavern entrance, she held herself so that she seemed to be gazing up at the rooftop stage. In fact, she spotted Noole at a corner table, a flagon at his left elbow and a piece of vellum stretched out before him. He held his pen at an abstracted angle. She eased into the tavern.

The gnome spotted her and bolted. His table toppled, taking tankard, inkwell, pen, and poem with it. He dashed for the kitchen entrance. Luma followed. As she passed through the swinging doors, a jar hurtled at her head. She ducked; it hit the wall behind her, shattering. A cloud of flour puffed out from it. Now coated in white powder, Luma sprinted for Noole, who dove out a service door into the Grand Hall. The tavern's cook, swearing in the dwarven language, hurtled at her, waving his butcher's knife. She drew her sickle and smacked it out of his hand. The knife flew end over end before splashing into a pot of hot oil. Scalding droplets rained on the cook; Luma was already through the door.

Noole fled with surprising speed through the concert hall's plush lobby. He'd knocked a lantern from its sconce; panicked servants rushed to douse its flames before they spread. Luma sped past them. Her hand thrust into her pouch of spell objects, now replenished. Each of the vial tops had its own distinct texture, allowing her to quickly find the one with the cricket leg. She reached into the citysong for the sound of the chirping, jumping bugs, and pilfered a touch of their magic.

Luma jumped, and the city propelled her into the air. She grazed the dripping crystals of the great hall's chandeliers, leaving them rocking and tinkling. Breathing deep, she braced for the coming landing.

Her outstretched feet struck Noole in the back. She rolled, hitting the pedestal of a statue to a long-dead contralto. She made her way up, watching Noole as he rose and drew a rapier. Her own weapon lay on the rug a few feet away; she'd dropped it to avoid cutting herself as she landed. Feigning dismay, she let him come at her midsection. The thin sword jabbed skillfully at her. With equal aplomb, she evaded the thrust. Continuing the motion, she snatched up her sickle and dove at her opponent. He kept her at bay with a feint of his blade. They circled one another, Luma leaving ghostings of flour wherever she stepped.

"I can't guess what you want with me," the gnome said, "but I want nothing to do with you."

"Drop your weapon and I'll explain," Luma answered.

He held it out as if ready to let it go, then lunged. The blade caught Luma on the side of the neck. It hurt, but she could tell the wound was only superficial. She swiped at his legs with her sickle; he hopped back with flamboyant ease. Adopting a perfect fencing stance, he waited for her to come at him.

His moves so far revealed one fighting style disguised as another. Noole added flourishes to what was, at its core, a cautious waiting game of precisely timed blows. He was waiting for Luma to make a mistake he could capitalize on. In this, and in his general deftness and quick reactions, he favored an approach to combat that was also Luma's. One patient, calculating scrapper faced another.

This could go on all day.

"What was your business with Khonderian?" Luma asked.

"That name is naught but a distant wisp of fading recollection."

She faked a strike; he didn't fall for it. "Set aside your perfumed words, poet."

"It reflects ill on you, to say 'poet' like it's an insult." He faked a strike; she didn't fall for it.

"I saw him pay you off in Bridgeward, on the street of taverns. What for?"

"Surely you've mistaken me for another gnome of equal handsomeness."

White light filled the lobby. Luma glanced back to see what had changed, at the same time anticipating and deflecting an expected blow. She caught the gnome's rapier in the crook of her sickle and twisted it from his hand.

Workmen had opened one of the large entry doors to toss out the still-smoking rug. Luma decided on a stratagem. She shouted with inarticulate, feigned bloodlust and came at the gnome with apparent recklessness. Noole sidestepped her; she pretended to trip and fall into the wall, her sickle lodging in its flocked surface.

If the gnome turned out to be more interested in finishing her than in escaping, this would prove a terrible error.

But Luma was right: he took the opportunity not to strike at her, but to scoop up his rapier and sprint for the open doors.

This gave her the time and distance she needed to call on another of the city's boons. She attuned herself to the crunch of pebbles and grains of sand underfoot. She called to bits of gravel strewn on rooftops and trapped in their eaves. Through the citysong she plucked stones from the soles of boots. All of these she gathered together in an enfolding, spiraling wind.

As Noole reached the threshold, a thick hail of stone and gravel did too. It struck him in the chest and face, sending him back on his heels. Stunned, he tottered and fell. Luma, who was already running, jumped on him, a foot on his emptied sword-hand and the curve of her sickle around his throat.

"I can kill you, or buy you a drink," she said. "Which will it be?"

He twitched his mustache at her. "It's not yet noon. So I'll stick to ale."

The daytime house manager, kitted in a uniform of rich green and velvet, hovered warily nearby. Luma handed him Noole's sword, daggers, and throwing knives. "You're going to hold on to these while the gentleman and I repair for private conversation," she told the manager, who gulped in frightened assent. She removed Noole's ensorceled rings, which substituted for armor, and handed those over, too.

To her surprise, she found no burglar's kit on his person. From his way of fighting, she'd pegged him as a footpad. Judging from his accoutrements, the gnome was instead a swordsman—plain, though hardly simple.

"We'll return for these shortly," she told the manager. "If all goes well." Later she'd return to the tavern where her chase had wreaked havoc and arrange for payment of damages. For the moment, she escorted Noole across the plaza to a rival establishment, the Sock and Buskin. Around a central table, actors half-heartedly recited lines, committing them to memory.

Noole winced. "Not *The Inconstant Nymph* again! What a chestnut!" He cupped his hand theatrically to the side of his mouth and shouted, "Stage something new for once!"

The eldest of the actors, who held himself with an impresario's authority, stood up. "Cleave to your sonnets, hack!"

Noole wandered toward their table. "You're not playing Donatio, surely. That part is thirty years too young for you."

The impresario threw Noole the tines. Luma took Noole by the arm and led him to a corner table.

Luma took the bench, leaving Noole the chair, where his back would be exposed to the room. The gnome settled in. "A hail of stones. Never seen that one before."

"Need I repeat the question?"

"You're not the one they say murdered old Khonderian, are you?"

Luma felt herself bridle.

Noole's eyes glittered. "You are, you are. Well, I daresay you don't seem the murdering type. Else you'd have opened my throat too."

The barmaid, whose blasé demeanor and overly painted face led Luma to think of her as a disappointed ex-actress, ambled to their table.

"I'll have a pint of Old Asmodeus, and so will she," said Noole. "And your cured meat plate, and your cheese plate, and shall we say the pickle assortment?" He cracked his fingers together.

"No drink for me," said Luma.

"Have you had the Old Asmodeus?" Noole asked.

"No."

"Then she'll take the half-pint and at least taste it," Noole told the barmaid, who shuffled off.

Luma leaned in. "I suppose I should ask if you killed Khonderian."

"Me? Why would I?"

"What was he paying you for?"

Noole sighed. "The life of a versifier can be at times a chancy one. Yet for all its material deprivations, I am blessed with the chance to ascend and descend the social ladder. Oft times in the same afternoon. Along the way, one picks up scraps—sometimes a fine duck rillette, sometimes a pregnant rumor. "

"You were his informant."

"I prefer gossip. The other sounds impersonal."

"And what intelligence earned you that clinking purse the other night?"

The barmaid made her way over, carrying the first of the food plates. Noole rubbed his hands together. "I am no gentleman poet. To keep a roof over my head, I must at times resort to the unconventional."

"You were squatting in a Qadiran trader's house in Grand Arch."

He popped a chunk of blue cheese into his mouth. "If only I had a critic who followed me as avidly as you, my peach." He frowned. "Don't blush, child. I mean nothing by it."

"Don't call me child."

"At Grand Arch, did you happen to notice any skulky characters about?"

"Across the way from you."

"Yes. A small troop of highly armed men and women, their every furtive glance broadcasting ill intent. I crept over there one night, as I am wont to do. They spoke with Korvosan accents. Alas, I heard little of their discourse. They did have a map of the city up on the wall. Stuck there with a dagger. A breach of squatter's etiquette, I must say."

Luma nibbled absently on a piece of cured boar. "And that's all you told Khonderian?"

"He wanted me to do some more creeping about. I left that open as a possibility."

"But never followed through?"

"The muse led me elsewhere." He shoved the tankard, which she hadn't touched, toward her. "Try it. Strongly hopped, with a hint of persimmon."

She took a grudging sip. "Why go to the head of the lord-mayor's bodyguard? Why not the lord justice?"

"My tittle-tattle is of a political nature, chiefly, and of little interest to the law." He drained the last of his ale. "Also, Khonderian paid well. The city guard can scarcely afford blade polish."

"And you have no guess as to why Khonderian was killed?"

He gestured to the barmaid for another Old Asmodeus. "It can't have anything to do with me. Speaking of which, his departure leaves a gaping void in my future earnings. Surely you Derexhi could stand to enlarge your network of informants."

"We cultivate unpaid sources."

"Then I venture to say you're missing a trick." With one swipe he cleared the meat plate of its olives. "Let's talk advance."

Luma stood. "Let's go get your weapons back to you."

"My second tankard hasn't arrived. Listen, I hate to argue from need. I can impose on dear old Lady Khedre for a week or so in her servant's quarters, but do so hesitantly. Ours is an association that wilts under the heat of prolonged proximity. Khonderian's payment was not so generous as you may have assumed . . ."

Luma paid the barmaid. "Drink up, gnome. I'll tell the manager he's free to give you your sword when you come to ask for it."

Chapter Eleven
The Lost Workshop

Korvosan squatters . . ." Arrus mused, distractedly drumming on the squad room table. Iskola sat at his side, fingers intertwined, in her standard state of glacial serenity.

"Does that have anything to do with our client?" Luma asked.

"I'm not sure. Iskola has already sent word, asking to meet."

Iskola broke from her contemplation. "I meant to seek permission to reveal to you, and our other siblings, the name of the client and the general objective of the mission. Now I will add this other question. It is possible that our patron has been withholding information from all of us. If so, I will express our displeasure in the strongest terms. No matter how lucrative the contract, our first priority must be defending you against the lord-mayor's false charges. Should we be forced to breach it and refund our advance, so be it."

"Yet," added Arrus, "it is a sizable sum, so it would be preferable not to."

"I understand," said Luma.

Iskola shifted uncomfortably. "It was short-sighted of me to agree to so confining a secrecy requirement. I should have anticipated that you and the others would find it difficult to perform your duties under its strictures. On reflection, I cannot but concede that I erred."

"Clients are trouble," Arrus said. "Sometimes they insist on measures meant to trip us up so they can haggle the price down when the job is done."

"Next time," said Iskola, "I will take you along with me, to see the tricks they play."

"I would like that," Luma said.

Arrus produced a scroll case. "The squatters might play a role in this, or could mean nothing. Nonetheless, you did good work, and showed initiative by tracking down the gnome."

"If you'd come to us first, we might have tried to stop you," said Iskola, "Yesterday we exchanged harsh words. Afterward, we reflected on what you said and saw the justice in it."

What to make of this? Luma expected to wage a long war for their contrition, and here it suddenly was. It should please her, but didn't. Then she realized why. Her father. Would he tell her to stand up for herself, and then go straight to Arrus and Iskola to plead her case for her? Absolutely he would. She could see the entire scene unfold before her: their initial denials, then the full force of his logic, followed by a flare of his temper, topped off with a soothing helping of self-deprecating humor. It was what she'd wanted, when she went to him, but now that she had it, it felt hollow. He meant to help, and she couldn't blame him for it, but he had taken her chance to win this on her own.

Still, given a choice between an unearned victory and none at all, she'd settle for the former. "If I spoke harshly, it was only in the heat of argument," she said.

"We pushed you to it," Iskola said. "If we are to lead, we must learn to listen better." She rose and embraced Luma. "You are our sister." Both held themselves awkwardly. By mutual, unspoken impulse, they quickly disengaged.

A moment of collective chagrin hung in the air. Arrus cleared his throat.

The door swung open; it was Ontor. "We found it, all right," he said. Ulisa and Eibadon came in behind him.

"Found what?" asked Luma.

"To defend you, we must work on several fronts," said Iskola. "Foremost, we must learn who killed Khonderian. But that will go for naught if we can't convince others that it's true."

"She means politics," said Arrus.

Iskola nodded. "I've spent the day lining up support for you in the Council of Ushers."

"Which costs money," added Ontor.

Iskola crossed her elegant arms. "Father has good friends on the council. But a gift never goes awry."

"So," said Ontor, "I followed up on that possible job you mentioned—the golem attacks in Bridgeward. First of all, the idea that magical constructs have acquired intelligence and an agenda has to be nonsense."

"No boat dreams of shore," Eibadon intoned.

"If golems are attacking jewel and gem stores, that's not a rebellion, that's robbery. And where there's robbers, there's a hideout—and loot to be retrieved. So I went to the Jewelers' Guild, and the Goldsmiths as well. Between them, they're willing to spring for an acceptable up-front fee. Should we find the lair where whoever it is has stashed their golems, we earn a substantial reward. As a further bonus, if there's merchandise to be recovered, we keep half, free and clear."

"Well negotiated," said Iskola.

"Politicians elude me," said Ontor, "but merchants I understand."

"Very well," said Luma, "how do we find them?"

"Already done," said Ontor. "Hand me that map, Arrus." His brother passed him the scroll case, from which he unfurled a detail map of Bridgeward. "The golems storm in suddenly and escape just as fast. A group of gigantic constructs doesn't stomp from neighborhood to neighborhood unnoticed. That means the hideout has to be near the shops they raided." Ontor stuck pins into the map. "Those shops are here, here, and here. Wizards have been building golems nearby for generations. So I had Eibadon check the library for mentions of laboratories that might not exist any longer."

A wormy smell suffused the room as Eibadon opened a copy of the city chronicles. "Thirty years ago, or thereabouts, the workshop of Laurdin Iket, subsequently called Laurdin the Mad, was consumed by living green fire. The account hints that devils visited the catastrophe on Laurdin for failing to meet unspecified obligations. The laboratory, and he and his automatons, are described as having fallen into the earth itself."

"So," said Ontor, "I'm reckoning someone dug down and found Laurdin's old workshop, now a subterranean chamber."

Luma reached for the book. "The golems raiding the shops were built by Laurdin the Mad?"

"And only now rediscovered by our robbers, or so I'm surmising. No one would create golems just to steal from stores," said Ontor.

"They're too expensive to build," said Iskola.

"That's right," said Ontor. "The value of the loot would pale in comparison."

"This is not to say that these robbers are clever," Iskola said. "If they've found Laurdin's laboratory, there a chance they've also stumbled across an item of great value. One worth far more than the gems and jewels their golems have taken from the good guildsmen of Bridgeward."

Ontor grinned. "This item—it would buy us a lot of politics, I take it."

"Precisely so." Iskola rolled up one of her sleeves, which had fallen out of place. "The dampening ring of Laurdin Iket. The annals describe it variously, but from the name we can reckon its shape. It is likely a construction of precious metals, worked together with rivets and joins."

"And it controls golems?"

Iskola nodded. "A singed remnant of the wizard's own journal, held in the library's Forbidden Collection, describes its use against errant golems one might accidentally create during the experimentation process."

"A hazard of the profession, I suppose."

In sour acknowledgment of her brother's banter, Iskola crinkled her lip. "When placed on the golem's torso, the device instantly drains it of all animation."

"So it's not a ring, as in a piece of jewelry," Luma ventured.

"No," said Iskola. "Look for a hoop-like affair, perhaps six inches in diameter. I believe it affixes itself to the golem by a form of magnetism."

Luma leaned forward. "In other words, if we find ourselves fighting golems, and we catch sight of the device, we should toss it onto the nearest or toughest automaton, and hope that it stops where it stands."

"Throw it to me first," said Iskola. "It may require activation. I've studied accounts of the item, and may be able to do that."

"And what are the odds we'll find it?" Luma asked.

"Let's not count on it," Iskola said. "But if there's truly an iron golem with them, as the robbed merchants report, it would be good to have. Such creations often exhale poisonous fumes, which are not readily countered."

Ontor reached for the chronicles. "The history doesn't give a location for the workshop at all. But it does say that, after the green fire and the collapse, the other laboratories moved west to avoid contamination. Only a few streets sit both east of the current golemworks and close to the targeted shops. So Ulisa and I went out combing them for cellar doors and other entryways that might lead to a once-buried and now-recovered wizard's lab. I found a good candidate—a metal trapdoor, secured by a fresh new lock. I wanted to poke my nose in, but Ulisa talked me out of it."

"If there are golems in there," Ulisa said, "all six of us must face them together."

Luma examined the map. "Where did you find this door?"

Ontor took another pin and jabbed it into the spot.

"The map is wrong," Luma said, pointing to a laneway. "This has been blocked off for years and is impassable. If it goes sideways and we have to flee back up to the street, we must all head south. These buildings have been torn down and replaced by two others. Now there's a space between them, too narrow to call itself an alleyway. That's our escape route; we can squeeze through it, where golems can't."

"A good plan," said Ontor, "but let's hope it doesn't come to that."

"It will be a tough fight," said Arrus. "Worse than Shoanti wildmen. Are we all agreed?"

"We need gold to shield Luma from the gibbet," Iskola said, "and right away. Has anyone else found a better source of it?"

No one answered.

"Then I say we must do it," Iskola said.

"I agree," said Arrus. "Ontor?"

"I want to see what's down there."

"It is the only course," said Ulisa.

"A city may not thrive," said Eibadon, "when disorder reigns."

Arrus massaged his sword hand. "You have the most to lose here, Luma. What say you?"

"I say let's go," she said.

Ontor led them to the Street of White Dust, a deserted avenue near the majestic ruins of the Irespan. Shore birds flapped above it, diving and fighting for prime spots to perch. Luma heard the flatulent growls of pelicans and the death-rattle cry of the speckled turnstone. A pair of Varisian children, olive-skinned and raggedy, crept up on the birds, carrying frayed loops of rope to use as snares.

The Derexhi took scant notice of them. Wherever there was a margin or a cranny in the city, members of that vagabond people could be found scrabbling for a living or winkling out a main chance. When most people thought of Varisians, they thought of the roaming caravans of tinkers and dancers that had given the region its name. In Magnimar, however, most Varisians were of the settled sort, working laborers who scratched out lives the best they could, and had for generations. In a very real sense, Luma knew,

Magnimar's land had been theirs first. Yet compared to the Chelish explorers who built Magnimar, they'd done little with it—or so Arrus was fond of saying.

On another mission, the team might have waited as Ontor braced the Varisian children for scuttlebutt, offering them a copper or two in return. Instead, he kept on going, past a series of deserted but locked and well-kept warehouses. He counted the buildings as he went, until they reached the one where he'd found the trapdoor. It was as he'd described it: patently new, fashioned from a metal sheet, and secured by a padlock.

Luma heard the citysong: beneath the avian shrieking and the crash of waves against coastline hid a drumbeat of metallic clanks. She ducked down to the trapdoor, alongside Ontor. The clanks, she realized, were audible to any ear. They came from below.

"Open the lock," she said, "and I'll go in and get the lay of the place."

"Are you certain?" Ontor asked.

"There could be any number of golems down there," Luma answered.

"All the more reason to go in together," Ontor said.

"There might be too many to go in at all," she said.

"Let her," said Iskola.

Ontor laid out his burglary kit, withdrew a shim, and wiggled it into the lock mechanism. The padlock clicked; he pulled it open and set it aside.

Luma pulled from her pouch a chunk of desiccated gray material. She pushed through the bird cries of White Dust Street to an under-chorus that scratched and scuttled everywhere in Magnimar: the all-but-silent prowlings and spinnings of its spider population. Cities gave shelter to spiders of all kinds. Those she sought lurked in crevices of the nearby cliff face, where they preyed on birds in their nests. By rustling mottled gray legs together, they sang to her of primal hunger, of scavenging curiosity.

Clothing, armor, gear and all, Luma vanished. An enormous crab spider, about the size of a mastiff, reared up in her place. It tested its fearsome mandibles and twitched its spinnerets. Sunlight illuminated its layer of coarse, downy hairs. Stray red tufts rose from the top of its head.

"Hideous," Arrus shuddered.

"You want her to be able to see without a light source, don't you?" Ontor said. "And it's the perfect cover. The basements and underground chambers around here veritably crawl with the things."

Arrus over-enunciated his annoyance: "I understand why she's doing it."

"A little disgust never hurt anyone," Ontor said. An odd note had entered his voice. From below, with senses altered, Luma couldn't judge his expression.

"Shut up, you prattling . . ." Arrus caught himself short. "Let's get this over with."

Ontor raised the trapdoor. Luma lowered her boneless spider body to squeeze through. She passed from light into darkness, which through arachnid eyes was not so great an adjustment.

Her eight legs adhering to surfaces vertical and horizontal, Luma found her footing. It had not been so long since she'd learned this strange trick of the city, and the sensation of being inside another body, one so different from her own, still filled her with freakish wonder. Her searching forefeet sought out a wooden beam. She ran upside down, clinging to the beam, adjusting to her spider's view of the world. Objects swirled and pooled before converging into the colorless gaze of an alien hunter. Her six eyes—two above, four arrayed below—combined to create a single ever-fluid image, with blurs at the edges and sharpness in the middle. Below her she detected a lattice shape. She stopped, skittered her way down, reached out with her front four limbs until she touched the rough stone-and-soil surface of the chamber wall. A false ceiling of steel mesh overhung the chamber. Luma eased herself onto it, then moved across the metal lattice with a stalker's deliberation. It comprised a series of panels, most of which had presumably been damaged when the lab had collapsed into its basement so many years ago. About one in three had fallen away entirely; others had partially detached and now dangled down into the room. A rare few were merely bent, as if they had softened under a terrible heat and then hardened again. These Luma traversed in a series of stops and starts, surveying the chamber and its inhabitants as best she could.

The place, she saw, might better be called an excavation than a room. All four of its walls were hewn unevenly from the earth, sloping above floor level into debris piles composed of stone, earth, and scrap metal. Makeshift wood-beam supports leaned against their soft spots, fixed to platforms which had in turn been spiked into the gravelly floor. Additional beams reached across the floor at uneven intervals, keeping the ceiling in place. Crude sconces held oil lanterns which cast intersecting pools of soft yellow light across the chamber floor.

An assortment of figures stood frozen in odd positions about the chamber, as if ordered to halt in mid-movement. Two were human-sized and made of wood. The rest towered above them, their sculpted heads nearly grazing the latticed drop ceiling.

One was fashioned from iron, another from glass. Another seemed to have been carved from a block of the ubiquitous marble seen in so many of the city's monuments. In the corner leaned the last of them: a bizarre assemblage of struts and cylinders, periodically interrupted by glass tubes and globes. The largest orb sat atop its metallic torso, containing a bubbling liquid and a lump of gray, wrinkled matter.

A long wooden table, legs shimmed against the floor's unevenness, occupied the chamber's northeast quadrant. Upon it lay piles of junk: the remnants of countless other golems, now in the midst of a sorting effort. Luma spotted a stone hand, buckets of glass, lengths of copper wire, various rusted fittings, and a tumble of bones. A thick tome splayed open in one corner. Though her spider vision made only a dark mush of its contents, Luma reckoned it for a manual outlining the arcane procedures of golem construction.

In the pile lay a hoop-shaped object fitting the uncertain description of Laurdin's dampening ring. From its position in the heap of assorted parts, Luma wondered if the excavators had mistaken its purpose.

The only movement came from three men, draped in filthy smocks. Gauze veils clipped to pillbox hats covered their faces. Steel sabatons, as would normally be worn with a set of full plate armor, protected their feet. Flexible leggings of a scale-like metal mesh shone dully between smock and sabaton.

One of the men stood at a remove and issued orders, the other two poking and probing at a complex device of rusted steel and pebbled iron, which occupied fully a quarter of the space, next to the long table. From its position, Luma reasoned that it had fallen onto its side during the collapse of Laurdin Iket's workshop. It jutted from the wall, still partially buried under bricks, marble slabs, and dirt.

What was once its back was now its top. Along its exposed side jutted a lever as long as an ax-handle, surrounded by a network of cogs and belts.

The workers jabbed a wood-handled brush into an assembly of interlocked saws and teeth, about ten feet in width. With nervous gestures they removed filings, shredded metal, and clumps of soil. They stepped back from it as their boss stepped to the lever. The clanking sound Luma had heard from above resounded through her exoskeleton.

A worker looked up at her. She froze. He twitched in revulsion, much as Arrus had, and returned his attention to the machine. His casual reaction suggested that Luma wasn't his first giant spider he'd seen crawling around down here. She congratulated herself on her clever choice.

The boss reached for the table, seizing a crumpled copper mask which might once have served as a golem's face. All three men gave the device a wide berth as he tossed the mask into the grinding teeth. It chewed through the mask, spitting it out as a fine dust from a chute located below the lever. The machine thrashed to a halt, sputtering acrid smoke.

This, Luma deduced, would have been part of the original workshop—a device to reduce failed experiments back to metal dust for later reforging.

After standing before the device in consternation, hands on hips, the boss reached over to the side of the device, sliding a large button in the shape of a mocking jester's face along a short track. The chewing saws reversed themselves, spitting curls of copper at the worker's feet.

As tantalizing as the mystery of the device might be, Luma could not let it distract her from less remarkable details of possible tactical use. The wooden staircase leading down from the trapdoor bore inspection, to see if it was sound or rotten. It was, she noted, newly installed and strongly reinforced, as it would have to be to allow the golems out. It could more than support the weight of the entire team.

She crept across the false ceiling, transferred over to the beam, and crawled to the spot below the opening. Ontor had propped it open a crack with a loose cobblestone, allowing Luma to squeeze up through.

"Well?" said Ontor.

Luma cut the tie she'd made to the part of the citysong that spun webs and ate bugs, instantly resuming human form. She pulled a scrap of paper and a pencil from her pack to sketch out the chamber's details, which she described in detail. "I counted six golems and three men, all of whom might be wizards. Or alchemists, maybe. None of the golems were moving. Some might be inactive altogether, but we can't count on that."

"Did you see any loot?" Ontor asked.

"No, but who leaves that out in plain sight?"

Iskola pointed a lacquered nail at the map. "What's that?"

Luma shivered away a few lingering spidery perceptions. "Their table of salvaged parts. I don't think they have the wherewithal to build new golems. They're just discovering, repairing, and awakening those created by Laurdin the Mad."

"Did you see the dampening ring?"

"I think so. On the table. If they don't know what they've got, I bet I can guess why: they think it's a part they haven't yet pieced onto its golem."

"We need reinforcements," said Ontor.

"Nonsense," said Iskola.

"Together we're a match for the iron golem by itself," said Ontor. "On a good day. Am I right, Luma?"

"Yes," said Luma. "But Iskola has the same idea I do."

The wizard nodded. "Golems act without independent volition. Depending on the wording of their instructions, they may well return to dormancy if we take out the three men."

"How depending is 'depending'?" Ontor asked.

"If the salvagers said, 'kill anyone but us who comes into this room,'" Luma said, "we're in trouble. If, as is more likely, they said, 'protect us if we are attacked,' they will stop as soon as the attack does—even if it ceases with their deaths."

"Golems are a literal-minded lot, then?"

"They lack minds of any sort," said Iskola. "They are magical devices and thus follow the laws of magic. These bend inexorably toward the smallest possible expenditure of arcane energy into the realm of matter. Thus, any instructive statement is carried out according to its narrowest interpretation."

"Pretending I understood that," said Ontor, "what happens if these clowns gave the golems the wrong set of orders?"

"If the constructs keep on going after the men are dead," Iskola answered, "we stage a retreat as orderly as it is immediate."

"And what if they said, 'pursue anyone who kills us to the end of time'?"

"Too metaphorical, too open-ended, and otherwise unlikely. Have you any further queries, Ontor?"

His posture crumpled. "Waiting won't make this easier . . ."

Arrus stepped up to outline the plan. "Iskola and Ontor will sneak in first and, crouching on the false ceiling, fire down at the salvagers. Between Ontor's arrow and a well-placed fork of lightning, we might finish them all without the golems activating at all."

Luma shook her head. "Too great a risk. The false ceiling is insecurely anchored. It might not bear your weight. And if it does, and you fail to slay all three men in a single volley, the golems can simply reach up and tear the ceiling loose. The two of you will plummet to the floor, ripe for the stomping."

"What do you suggest, then?" Arrus asked.

"Better Iskola and Ontor open fire from the stairs, then step aside for Arrus, Eibadon, and Ulisa to run in and engage the salvagers while they're still in disarray. The rest of us try to disrupt or hold off the golems and hope our close fighters make short work of the salvagers."

"Anything else?" said Arrus.

"Yes," she said, pointing to the map. "Don't let them lure you near this grinder device. If you catch a cuff or sleeve in it, we'll be burying you in liquid form."

"Sound points." Arrus turned to the others. "Never mind my plan. We'll do as Luma advises. Are we ready?"

By drawing their weapons, they agreed that they were.

Arrus lifted the trapdoor. Ontor and Iskola entered, rushing down the wooden stairs. Luma heard the thwang of Ontor's bow-string and the stentorian rhythm of her sister's incantation. Flashes of light came from below as Iskola triggered her invocation. As if in a single movement, Ulisa, Arrus, and Eibadon poured themselves into the hole. Luma followed, hard on Eibadon's heels.

By the time she got down there, the golems had already stirred into lifeless motion. One of the salvagers lay dead on the floor, a smoking scorch mark over his heart. The remaining pair had taken cover behind the table, which they strained to upend. An arrow pierced the boss' upper arm, drenching his smock with blood.

Only four golems shuddered toward them, the rest still frozen in place. One of the wooden constructs, plus those of iron and glass and the strange assemblage of tubes and struts, moved to shield the salvagers. Now that Luma could see normally again, she confirmed what she'd suspected about the indescribable golem: in the translucent globe that composed its head sloshed a gray human brain.

Arrus ducked the iron golem's blow, launching himself over the table to engage his living opponents.

The unknown golem threw a green globe; it struck the bottom of the stairs and exploded. Ontor and Iskola fled the damaged steps. Luma fell, planks giving way beneath her. She staggered up, disoriented and cut all over. Her belt hung loose, cut through by a chunk of wood. Beneath it, blood spread through her tunic. Not daring to test the wound, she secured the flapping belt by tying its end around one of the straps holding her leather hauberk in place.

Smoke from the golem's alchemical projectile obscured her vision. The scene before her registered as a series of disconnected flashes, glimpsed between greasy clouds. The wooden golem caught fire—Iskola's doing, undoubtedly. Ulisa spun through the air, saffron robes fluttering, and delivered a kick that sent the thing staggering.

Luma lost track of her position. A figure came charging through the smoke at her: the glass golem. Luma drew her sickle and landed a solid strike against its knee. The energy of the blow glanced off the construct and vibrated painfully up her own arm.

The wood golem, already charring to cinders, toppled into one of the support beams near the grinder device.

The beam slid several feet, then held. The golem continued its caroming fall, landing on the device's lever and activating the machine. Its gears thumped and clanked, straining to mesh together.

Luma retreated from a wave of searing heat. Was it a spell, directed at her? She hadn't time to guess. The great glass figure pounded toward her. To evade its punch, she had to wheel back. Luma saw what it was doing: herding her toward the now-churning grinder.

She dropped her center of gravity, making herself a tempting target for a kick. The glass golem swung its leg at her. She pivoted, beckoning the citysong. Her mind went to the piers of Dockway, to the ships in the harbor, to the ropes on which cargo was lifted ashore, and then from these great ropes to a slim length of cord wrapped around her waist. With a flick of her wrist, she pulled the cord free. A few twists made it a snare, which she flung through the air, wrapping around the construct's legs. She pulled it tight.

The golem overbalanced, falling into the jaws of the shredding machine. Scooting back to avoid breathing in the inevitable cloud of pulverized glass, Luma watched as the device devoured her opponent. The machine's spout vomited a spray of glass shards.

Eibadon, fighting over by the table, saw it coming and raised his shield.

His opponent, the salvager leader, bore the brunt of the spray. Fragments blasted into his torso. He staggered to the table, where he groped for a stand containing a half-dozen glass vials. There was only one reason to do such a thing mid-fight—one or more of them had to contain some form of healing elixir.

With a mace strike to the back of the head, Eibadon put a stop to that plan. The salvager collapsed, gasping for air, lines of blood trickling from mouth and nose. The stand of vials fell onto its side next to the hoop-shaped object Luma hoped was the dampening ring.

The iron golem took a step back. With ticking head movements, it calculated the positions of its enemies. It opened its jaws. Luma remembered what Iskola had said—these constructs could breathe clouds of toxic gas.

"Eibadon!" she yelled, shouting above the thumping of the grinder machine. Pulverizing the glass golem had taken a toll on the device, and a burning haze issued from it, filling the chamber. "Eibadon!" she shouted again. "The ring!"

The priest threw himself across the table, grabbing the device and flinging it to Luma. She caught it and ran at the iron golem, leaping up to slap the metal circle onto its chest.

The ring hissed and sparked; the iron golem froze, its jaw still gaping.

Across the room, the weird golem readied itself to stab Iskola with its needle fingers. Arrus saw and dashed for the downed salvager leader, who lay groaning near the table. He raised his sword, ready to deliver the helpless man a death blow, but before he could, the salvager expired, sparing him the necessity.

The remaining golems stopped in mid-strike, as surely as if they'd been frozen by the dampening ring of Laurdin Iket. The condition governing their locomotion had ended, returning them to the status of inanimate objects. Luma and Iskola had been correct: the instructions impelling the golems to fight applied only while a salvager still lived.

A rain of glass continued to spout from the grinder mechanism. Shards pelted the wooden support beams. Three of them shifted by inches. One snapped in two.

Another responded to the growing pressure by popping loose. It flew across the room, straight for Ontor and Iskola. He pulled her down, and the beam continued on its way, crashing into another, blasting it from its moorings. The ceiling groaned overhead. Cracks rippled along its surface, bleeding streams of grit and gravel.

Unabated, the flow of glass struck another beam.

Luma ran for the lever. She felt a snap, and a loosening—her belt had untwisted itself from the strap she'd tucked it into. The end of the leather flew into the grinder's jaws, pulling her toward it. Even as she jerked back, she hooked her sickle around the lever, yanking it back into its original position.

Ontor stepped a wary circle around the now-still golems. Behind him, Iskola sorted through the jumble of components around the upended table.

The grinder teeth slowed, but did not completely cease their chatter. Luma's belt tightened, and she fumbled with the strap. Her hauberk twisted behind her, hauling the belt out of reach.

She gesticulated to Ontor. "The lever! It's not all the way off." She looked into the jaws: a sizable block of glass had lodged itself in the overtaxed grinding mechanism. It was stuck off to the side, but if she shifted it, she might jam the jaws entirely. Or it might chew through the block, and then her, too.

Instinct told her to chance it. As Ontor reached for the lever, she hooked the crescent of her sickle around the block of glass, pulling it into the center of the jaws. A sulfurous vapor belched from the device. Black ichor, sluggish as blood, pooled out from below the machine. The machine jerked, working to chew up the glass block. At any moment, it might buzz through the momentary obstacle, clearing the jam. "The lever!" Luma shouted.

Inexplicably, Ontor had stepped back from it. Luma pulled at her belt, finally freeing herself. She gasped in relief and fell to all fours, crawling across the chamber's rough surface as Ulisa and Eibadon approached.

An odd inflection crept into Ontor's voice. "You hurt?"

"A close call, but I'm fine," Luma answered. She was still dizzy from her brush with death. "Why the hell didn't you pull the lever?"

Ontor held himself in confused hesitation, as if torn between two possible actions. Gathered in a staggered rank behind Ontor, her other siblings looked to one another, as if each waited for one of the others to act, or to reveal to her some dire fact. For an instant, she wondered if she'd been dealt a mortal blow, and had yet to realize it. She looked down at her abdomen, half expecting to see a spreading wound or an impaling blade. As far as she could see, she was unharmed.

Shifting stone rumbled overhead. A section of catwalk dislodged itself from the wall and swung down behind them. Chunks of rock clattered onto the machine. Eibadon held up his shield to deflect a debris chunk bigger than his head.

"We've got to get out of here," Luma said. She dashed for the exit.

His words drowned out by the sounds of the dropping rubble, Arrus signaled to Ulisa and Eibadon. They blocked Luma's path.

"What are you doing?" she shouted, attempting to push through them.

Ulisa laid swift hands upon her, and before Luma could react she was caught in a hold, her sister's fingers jabbing a pressure point she didn't know she had. Eibadon seized her by the other hand. Together the monk and cleric marched her back toward the machine, avoiding her wild kicks.

Luma cried out in panic and confusion. Her brother and sister neither acknowledged her or showed a hint of emotion. She twisted around to see Iskola removing the dampening ring from the iron golem, as unperturbed as if she were pulling a book from a library shelf. Ulisa dug her fingers harder into the pressure point, forcing Luma to relax into her hold and abandon her resistance.

Arrus now stood by the lever. With a jabbing thumb, he signaled Ulisa and Eibadon. As he pulled the lever, they picked Luma up and hurled her back into the jaws of the machine.

Her legs went in first. A moment of white agony gave way to nothingness as her body closed off her sense of pain. By fits and starts, the dying machine drew her into its jaws. Though spared direct sensation, she could hear the wet tearing of her flesh and the crunching of bones. She thrust her arms out, pleading words she herself could not hear.

Eibadon bent down to inspect her condition, then spoke in Arrus's ear. Luma wondered what maxim he'd be using, to say that she was good as dead.

The machine coughed again, pulling her in further. It had her up to her pelvis now. She tried not to see her gushing blood as it coated the front of the machine, intermixing with the ichor.

The room shook as a chunk of ceiling came down, burying a quarter of the room and loosing an advancing cloud of dirt and dust.

Her siblings sprinted for the stairs, dodging showers of rubble. Only Ontor remained, his gaze shifting back and forth between the exit, the crumbling ceiling, and Luma.

Maybe he still meant to save her, and was waiting until the others were out of sight.

Another lurch of the machine pulled her in further. Its jammed blades had lost the capacity to slice her apart; now it simply crushed her.

A shaking Ontor crouched before her, head turned as far to the side as he could manage, clutching and unclutching his fingers. Dust caked his features. Behind him, another section of the catwalk crumpled to the floor.

She tried to speak, to beg him to stop the machine. Time remained to get out, to regroup, to understand whatever madness had gripped Arrus and the others. Her lungs refused to draw air.

Ontor spoke, sobs swallowing his words: he repeated the same phrase over and over. Dimly Luma realized what he was saying.

"I'm sorry I'm sorry I'm sorry . . ."

He summoned a measure of composure and rose to his feet. He still couldn't look at her. "I'm sorry," he said, "that it had to come to this." His head swiveled as a tumble of stones landed on the steps, breaking several of them. If he waited any longer, he'd be trapped, too. "This wasn't supposed to have to be me." Still barely looking at her, he plucked a dagger from its scabbard. "None of us wanted to have to do it. We were hoping . . . I warned you, again and again. But you wouldn't understand." He took a step toward her. The blade rose.

Luma shut her eyes and slumped, playing dead. It was her only chance. Ontor didn't want to do it. Were he truly ready to pull the knife across her jugular, she had no way to stop him.

A heavy object crashed onto the machine.

Ontor bolted, reaching the stairs moments before another tumble of rocks dashed them into a heap of broken boards. Luma heard the trapdoor slam shut.

She was alone.

Inch by inch, movement by movement, Luma pulled herself toward the lever side of the device. Now the pain washed in, her body screaming its alarm as blood vessels ruptured and muscle separated from bone. Consciousness wavered; she willed herself to remain awake. She groaned as her fingertips brushed the corner of the machine. She felt for the button that would reverse the mechanism. It was still out of reach. Luma twisted; a terrible report of breaking bone sounded from her lower limbs. Her hand found a raised round shape about the size of a saucer. Which way had the salvager slid it? From left to right, or the other way? Luma called to mind the colorless, blur-edged visual memories of her spider form. She would have to slide it farther away from her. Even now she might not achieve the needed reach. Driblets of commingled blood and sweat dripped from her brow. Clamping top and bottom teeth together, swallowing a cry of torment, Luma shoved herself over just a little more.

The button yielded, jolting the machine to life. The teeth on either side of her whirred at top speed as the mechanism reversed. They caught the sleeve of her reaching arm and shredded it. She pulled it away before it could do the same to her forearm. Where the device's jaws pressed down on her, the teeth moved in halting stages, pushing her out piece by piece. More fluid spilled from the machine. It screamed and gnashed. Clouds of arcane vapor, black interspersed with flashes of green, belched from the jaws each time they found purchase.

Now Luma prayed for unconsciousness, even for a moment. Desperate for distraction, she tried to tap into the citysong. All she could reach was that part of Magnimar that suffered and despaired. Her death throes joined a chorus of others: a man expiring from his stab wounds in a Dockway tavern, a woman dying during childbirth down in Rag's End, a fever victim thrashing on a Naos sickbed.

Finally the machine expelled her. Luma lay panting in the black-red muck. She feared to look back at herself. From the waist and below, all sense of having a body, of being able to move or control her limbs, was gone. Had she lost them entirely? In the end she couldn't stop herself from checking. Her legs were shattered, crooked, pulverized, but still attached. They were one big wound, leaking gouts of blood. If she couldn't staunch the flow, she had but minutes to live.

As she slipped in and out of awareness, the rhythm of falling wreckage slowed and finally stopped.

The pain gave way to shock, the blessed severance of sensation that accompanies grave injury. Luma knew this both from books and from experience. It had happened to Ontor once, when he fell from a rooftop onto a spiked fence, impaling himself through the abdomen. She'd clutched his hand as they waited for Ulisa to summon Eibadon to perform the healing. Ontor had regarded her with serene bafflement: "I don't feel hurt."

Now the situation was reversed, except that Ontor and the others were responsible for what had happened to her. And if Eibadon should happen to return, it would be to bash her skull in.

She pushed away thoughts of betrayal and protest. They wouldn't help her survive, not in this moment, and so she could not afford them. Luma imagined her grievances, her countless questions, as a physical manifestation—a red and swirling cloud. She pictured her numbness as a chamber, much like this one, deep underground, sealed with a trapdoor. In her delirious inner vision, the swirl, representing her anger, her sorrow, her need for answers, flew into the cavern. The door clanged shut, and a lock clicked around its latch. If she made her way out of here, she would unlock the door, and ask herself what she had done to provoke this from her own brothers and sisters. She would find out what had turned them into murderers. How they aimed to profit by this.

But that was if she made it out, a task for which distraction was the enemy.

Luma reached into the city to pilfer a sliver of loose healing magic, as she had done for the burned man at No-Horn's. Though the working exerted no visible effect on her shattered body, she felt the closing dark of unconsciousness halt and recede. That was all she'd expected, and was better than dying.

Plunging her fingers into the yielding ground, wending around stock-still golems, she crawled to the table where the wounded salvager had fumbled for a vial. Several of the glass containers had been smashed by falling stone, but two remained in the toppled stand. They might contain nothing more useful to her than alchemical fluids. But since the salvager had been reaching for one of them in the middle of a fight, the odds were better than even that she'd find a healing draught here. If not, the contents might do something absurd, like grow her to giant size or cover her body with a granite carapace. A potion's color revealed nothing consistent of its purpose, but Luma could usually tell by smell. She popped the cork on the first vial; a whiff of ammonia rose from it. It fell from Luma's weakening fingers. This was it. She was going to die right here, right next to this bandit. Her vision narrowing once more, she managed to get the second vial open. It smelled of camphor, cloudberries, and lemon—like certain arcane medicines she'd had occasion to down in the past. Without it, she was grave dust. Making silent prayer to Abadar, god of streets, cities, and her former family, she opened her mouth and gulped it down.

A soft heat permeated her, bringing with it a second glimmer of strength. Steam rose from the wounds on her legs as they cauterized into a network of scars. Broken bones still protruded from her flesh, but the skin had sealed around them, stopping the bleeding.

The healing draught had been of some use. But it wasn't nearly enough. Under any pressure whatsoever, some or all of those wounds would tear back open.

With her legs crushed, that was a more than probable event. Nearly any strenuous movement might reinjure her.

She turned her attention to the extent of the cave-in. It had reduced the size of the chamber by more than half. A treacherous wall of rock, cement, marble, and cobblestone cut her off from the exit. She'd spotted no second way out during her reconnaissance. If it had existed, there was a good chance it was now buried, too.

She looked up; the collapse had opened fissures in the ceiling. Through them Luma saw filtering daylight. She dragged herself back to the mouth of the machine. Her bag of spell ingredients, lost when her belt snapped, lay nearby. With trembling fingers, she sorted through it, hoping the item she sought had not been damaged. Though its vial was cracked, the component, a living spider, appeared stunned but intact.

The spell, which she'd used more times than she could count, required a healthy pair of arms. The legs, however, could perhaps dangle loose. She would hurt them, again and again, but it was her only way out.

Again she dragged herself, this time to the portion of the rubble pile closest, by vertical distance, to the ceiling's widest fissure.

To attune to the citysong took all of her hazy concentration. This time she sought out not the great hound-sized spiders of the cliffs, but the humble spinning spiders that lived in the dark corners of hovels and manors alike. She did not want to become a spider—that magic was spent—but rather to borrow their means of locomotion.

Their jittery energy filled her arms. She placed hands on the rubble wall and felt them adhere to the surface, just as they had done while in spider form.

The effect wouldn't last forever. There was no time to rest and prepare herself. She had to find the strength to pull herself up the wall, reach the fissure, and crawl through—and she had to do it now. She placed her hands as far as they would go without having to bear the dead weight of her body below the waist. Then she breathed deep and heaved herself up.

A river of agony washed over her before subsiding back into shock. Each instant an eternity, she pulled herself up farther. Jolts of pain broke through with each heave, as her useless, malformed legs banged against the rocks.

She sucked in a startled breath as a stone dislodged itself under her spidery grip. By reflex alone she reached out and seized a firmer handhold. The rock tumbled down, striking her shattered knee on its way to the chamber floor.

She made the mistake of looking down and saw wounds reopening across her ruined legs. Nausea rippled through her. Now fresh reservoirs of pain opened up, in her shoulders and arms. Her arms straining in their sockets, she moved herself up to the ceiling.

As she did, her perspective shifted. Luma beheld herself from a higher vantage, as if floating above her own body, above the chamber itself. She regarded the poor climbing wretch with pity. Why couldn't she just give up and move on to whatever the next realm held for her?

That's you down there, Luma realized. Either her soul was detaching from her body, as it supposedly did at the moment of death, or she'd fallen into a delirium of pain and hallucinated this vision of her own wracked body. She felt tugged from above. Was this the pull of the celestial planes?

If so, it was too soon. Luma thought of her family, and what she had to do. Luma had to live. To understand. She had to. She would will herself to do it.

Luma fought the pull until it let up, releasing her back into her physical form. All other matters would have to wait. Only the effort of moving up the wall could save her.

She reached the ceiling as the climbing magic ebbed. A chunk of ancient beam, exposed by the collapse, jutted toward her. In a series of tiny, aching movements, she turned herself around. She launched herself at the beam.

It might easily detach, sending her dropping to the floor and landing on her to boot. But the beam was part of the city, her beloved Magnimar, and Luma had no choice but to trust that it would not betray her, as her siblings had. She held her breath.

The beam held. Eyes watering, Luma pulled herself along it until she reached the hole.

A woman's hand, pale and thin, thrust down, waiting for her to grab hold.

Chapter Twelve
Between

Awareness came in bursts. She was being lifted up, borne somewhere. Carried in a pair of strong, stick-thin arms.

There was a place she should have recognized but could not quite bring to mind.

At times she thought she had died and gone beyond, but this place between places was neither up nor down.

Luma could feel but not see. A blindfold, or perhaps a sleep mask, lay upon her face. She tried to pull it off but her arms were restrained at the wrist.

She was in a bed—a pillow under her head, blankets weighing down on her legs. Which didn't move and maybe weren't there anymore.

The pain grew worse, into a steady throb that would not leave her.

Someone came periodically to spoon salty broth into her mouth, or to pour water onto her tongue and lips. Occasionally the liquid was neither of these things, but tasted like the healing draught she'd taken down in the golem room.

She submitted wordlessly to these ministrations. The impulse to speak had left her. As had the ability to measure time. Eventually she heard herself talk: "Ontor?"

If it was Ontor, he didn't answer.

Her dreams took on a seeming reality, convoluted and menacing. A gray-bearded man with part of his upper lip missing told her that her father had been fatally poisoned. She woke up trapped on an island, alone in a trackless sea. She looked at herself in a mirror; reflected back at her was the strange golem figure of struts and tubes. The brain bubbling in its central globe was all that was left of her.

Most of the time she wandered through streets that resembled those of Magnimar just enough to confuse her. She had the entire place imprinted in her, yet now its avenues and byways went on forever without ever taking her anywhere familiar.

In one dream she wandered into a place that was and wasn't Grand Arch. She hopped a white stone gate to drift toward an alabaster palace. Looking down, she realized she had no legs, but this did not impede her progress. Through carpeted, perfumed rooms she swept, until she came to a courtyard. There, on a throne of marble, skulls, and gold ingots, lounged a lovely woman, her neck swanlike, her eyes green and cruel. The woman beckoned her, holding out a stone plate heaped with figs.

Behind her Luma spotted a coffin. Columned and ornamented, it resembled the palace she stood in.

"Who are you?" Luma asked the woman.

"Ask that about yourself," said the woman.

"No," said Luma, "I must know who you are."

"You already do."

"You are Magnimar," Luma said.

A golden ringlet dropped from the city's coiffure to swing elegantly over its pale forehead.

"I always pictured you as a man," Luma said.

The city smiled. "All the thrusting pillars?"

"Well, yes."

Magnimar shook its head. "All within my confines— all my children—they are born, they live, and they die . . . taken from me. Yet the city goes on. It remains strong, and survives. No, I can only be a woman."

"I see," said Luma.

"Do you?"

Then Luma stood beside the coffin. "Whose is it?" she asked.

Magnimar stood beside her, skin fragrant with allspice and olives. "Who do you think?"

Luma frowned. When she spoke to the city in her usual way, through its song, she received better answers than this. She opened the coffin—or rather it was then open, because she had wanted it so.

Luma gazed on her own corpse, broken and doll-like. Though it had been cleaned and strewn with lilac petals, her injuries could not be hidden. "Am I dead, then?"

The city caressed her cheek. "Do you choose to be?"

"No. I have a task to perform. A series of tasks."

Magnimar peeled a fig. "What you seek to do, I require. Your blood is blood. My blood is order. To ensure order, one must be prepared to mete out punishment. Are you?"

Before Luma could answer, the dream ended. She came to, the mask gone from her face, her wrists no longer restrained. A single small candle illuminated the unadorned room, no more than a quarter the size of her bedchamber back home.

A woman approached her. For an instant, Luma mistook her for the figure from her dream. "Magnimar?" she asked.

"Where else?" the woman snorted. She held herself in a hunch and had bundled herself in layers of coat and blanket, all various shades of brown. A kerchief wrapped over her head hid her hair and shadowed her face. Wrinkled, liver-spotted hands held a bowl of soup. She thrust it, along with a wooden spoon, toward Luma. "Reckon you can scoop your own broth now," she said.

Luma took the soup and ate. Orange beads of fat swam its surface, tantalizing her senses. There was pork in it, and barley, and spices she could not quite place. She dropped the spoon on the bedsheets and slurped directly from the bowl.

"The worst of it is over," said the woman. "Reckon you'll still hurt bad for a good long while. Still, better than dead, hey?"

Luma tried to identify her accent. It was a quite good Rag's End lilt, but underneath it was another note, perhaps from outside the city. Or she'd come here as a child and lived in Rag's End for most of her life. "Who are you?"

The old woman shook her head. "Don't trouble yourself."

Luma lifted up the covers. Her legs were still there, all right, and intact, with bones straight as ever. Under a cross-hatching of scars, the muscles had atrophied. She had become a spindly replica of her former self. Luma inspected her arms: those too had lost their sinew.

"How long have I been here?"

"Long as you needed to be," the woman said, as if offended.

"Months?"

"Weeks." She studied Luma's expression. "You're wondering how you lost all your conditioning so quick. They gave me only so many healing draughts. The rest of your recovery your body has had to do on its own. Like I said, preferable to the alternative, hey?"

"I must refer to you somehow," Luma said.

The woman cocked her head. "Then call me Melune."

Luma swung her spavined legs out over the edge of the mattress. The effort dizzied her. She placed her bare feet on the stone floor. The woman moved to her side, her impassive expression undisturbed. Luma waved her off. "The divine philtres needed to restore me. They would be expensive."

"I wouldn't know about that," Melune said.

Luma wove to her feet. Numbness needled through her legs, her arms, and the area around her mouth. Melune offered her an elbow, which she refused. She took a step across the floor, then another, and another. Melune kicked a pair of slippers her way; she stepped uncertainly into them and went on. She made it to a wooden support beam in the middle of the room and leaned herself on it.

Melune threw open the wooden door, revealing a larger chamber beyond. Weapons covered the wall, among them a sickle of Luma's preferred weight and size. Mats lined the floor; a stuffed sparring figure cast a shadow across them. "We're reckoning you'll want a regimen."

"Who's *we?*"

"To get back to how you were before." Melune waddled into the room, taking down the sickle and handing it to her.

A different weapon drew Luma's attention. This, too, was a sickle, but like none she'd ever seen before. It was long and crescent-shaped, its blade almost like that of a scythe, but jagged and barbed. She took it from the wall and tested it by swiping it through the air. "I won't be who I was before," she said.

Over the weeks that followed, Luma retrained, drilling herself with the new weapon, lifting weights to recover her strength. She persisted in her questions of Melune—for whom did she work? Why did they save her? How did they find her? Where were they, and when would she meet them? The woman clung to her silence like a barnacle to a hull. As her muscles blossomed and tightened, Luma began to suspect that she hadn't been asking the right questions.

She asked herself why she hadn't tried to escape the bounds of Melune's hideout. In principle, the existence of unidentified benefactors ought to give her pause. In Magnimar, apparently selfless acts were to be viewed with utmost skepticism. A favor granted was a debt incurred. Yet for reasons she couldn't divine, intuition told her she was safe here.

A greater unease attended the floor-to-ceiling mirror that hung at the far end of her sparring room. Luma hadn't examined her reflection since she was hurt. It wasn't only her legs that were scarred. Whenever she brushed her face with her fingertips she felt raised lines and depressions on her cheeks, chin, and neck. These had puzzled her at first, until she remembered how she'd been caught in a shower of wood splinters when the bottom steps exploded.

Finally she steeled herself. She would put fear behind her, along with so much else. Grabbing her new sickle, she ventured to the mirror and struck a pose.

A strange woman blinked back at her. Yes, scars broke the smooth lines of her face. But it was harder in other ways, too. The healing magic hadn't changed her; the alteration was all in the way she held herself. Her chin looked stronger. Retraining had sculpted away her old slumping posture. Most of all, there was the chill in her eyes.

She remembered the mental image she'd used to maintain focus and stay alive during her escape from the collapsed golem chamber. Into a mental replica of the chamber she'd sent all of her fury, and all of her questions about why her siblings had done what they had done, and who, if anyone, she was without them. Over the long weeks of retraining, the anger had leached back out again. So cut off was she from her own thoughts that it had gone elsewhere without her noticing. It had traveled to her face, and was now incised in the grim visage glaring back at her from the mirror.

Why had they done it?

That remained to be seen. She would gather the facts, and then she could say. To speculate without information was stupid.

Who was she now?

Another foolish question. She was an arm holding a blade, and a mind that heard the song of Magnimar. They had killed all the rest of her, all the parts of her that were useless—her doubts, her knack for shrinking away, her deference.

And yes, her way of thinking about her problems instead of solving them.

All of this was stupid. That Luma was dead. Emotions could stay in that dark chamber. Even the rage would be sheathed, a weapon drawn only when needed.

Luma was dead, and that was good. Any further moaning about it was idiocy, and that was that.

Melune shuffled in. From the citysong, Luma had determined that the woman's hideout rested below street level, and near a place of reverence. It was about time for her to discover precisely where, one way or another.

"You're strong enough now, hey?" Melune croaked.

"That's right. Who do I owe for this?"

"I've booked you passage on a ship to Absalom."

"Why would I want to go there?"

"From there you can go anywhere. Leave Varisia. Start life anew."

"I'm not going anywhere."

Melune's shoulders sank. "Reckoned you'd say that. Well, you can't stay here."

"I reckoned you'd say that," Luma replied.

Chapter Thirteen
The Celwynvian Charge

After one more futile attempt to coax the identity of her benefactors from the old woman, Luma asked to be led to the exit. She ascended a spiral staircase, which led to a ceiling and stopped. There she found a circular trapdoor. She popped it open and crawled up, finding herself near a familiar monument.

A gift to the city from its elven population, the branches of the Celwynvian Charge stretched nearly thirty feet into the air. White wood and crystal intertwined in imitation of a legendary tree. Through a trick of natural mathematics, the sculpture looked symmetrical from any angle. Only by closely studying it did the onlooker realize that this was at no point the case. Through a permanent glamor, the branches grew real leaves, which budded, unfolded, turned color, shriveled and died in cadence with the seasons. During her time in Melune's redoubt, Luma had missed the budding of the leaves, which were now full and green.

Luma replaced the trapdoor, seeing how tightly it fit: from this side, the door was invisible even to close scrutiny. She turned to drink in the sights of the city.

The citysong, muted since the incident, rushed back in on her in all its tumult. In it she heard the wail of babes, the determination of weeds to seed themselves in gaps between stones, and the whetting of blades.

To the west stretched the stone cottages and creaking tenements of the quiet and the humble, the folk whose virtues the politicians extolled and whose needs they ignored. Smoke wafted from brick chimneys to be caught on the salt-damp winds and dispersed south over the city walls. To the east pulsed the excitement of Lowcleft: strolling hawkers touting their wares, minstrels banging tambourines and bawds hooting for business.

She navigated the citysong, pushing past all strains save for those generated by the city's thinking inhabitants. When only their hopes, fears and petty distractions hummed in her mind's ear, she further narrowed her attention, calling to her those notes associated with the Derexhi. Her family occupied a measurable territory of Magnimar's collective memory. They'd taken part in its founding. Today their retainers ranged throughout it, and lent its people an impression of order and protection. The Derexhi had, in short, become an idea, one that Luma could hear as a pulsation of brassy notes, underpinned by brisk reports on a snare drum.

Following these notes, she wove deeper into spiced and perfumed Lowcleft. Though the day was not yet old, foot traffic already swelled lanes. Foreign travelers prowled in search of early revels; locals estimated the weight of their purses. Luma forged through the assembled marks and sharpers, changing direction when the harmonies she homed in on grew louder and doubling back when they faded. They led her past stooped water-carriers, hollering teamsters, and stumbling drunks. Where before the betrayal she might have slipped in and around people on the street, now she walked a straight line, impelling those in her path to step aside. Her passing quelled a fight between prostitutes and turned a mugger on his heels.

On the Street of Strays, the Derexhi melody intensified, while at the same time acquiring an undertone of melancholy. Its brass gave way to strings of faded nostalgia, leading her into a musty tavern. The design swinging on a sign over its doorway announced it as the Old Sword, or maybe the Rusty or Notched Sword.

It was a place for old men. They sat along a counter nursing cups of brandy, backs bent, knuckles arthritic, faces sagging. Broken noses, missing fingers, and rivers of scars testified to lives spent in the fighting professions. A face from the past glanced at Luma as she entered. Its owner sat alone at a table, listening halfheartedly to the well-polished war stories and hoary grudges emanating from the bar. A flowing yellow-white beard, tied near the end with a ribbon, countered the baldness of his wrinkled pate. On his doublet he still wore the Derexhi emblem, though with the violet border that indicated retired status.

He squinted in thwarted recognition as Luma took the seat opposite him. "Garatz," she said.

The old man leaned back, blinking. "Luma? That isn't you, is it?"

"It is," she said. Only after signaling the taverner, pointing at Garatz's near-empty brandy cup, did she pause to check her purse. A fistful of spotless silvers clinked inside it. "Though my face is perhaps not as rosy as it was when you taught me to throw a knife."

He drained the remnants of his cup and set it down with a plunk. "Much rosier than expected, given the event I attended not weeks ago."

"Event?"

"Your funeral, milady. Haven't you heard? You're supposed to be dead."

The barman brought a second brandy for Luma, though she had not meant to ask for one. She let him withdraw before speaking further. "For the moment, at least, may I ask you to keep my survival between the two of us? Certain persons may be surprised to learn otherwise, and I wouldn't want to see them discomfited."

Garatz raised his cup in a toast to her. "As you wish." He took note of her intimidating new sickle. "If you've come hoping for help in killing, I'm sorry to say I'm willing but unable." He held out his sword-arm to show her that the hand had withered into a frozen claw.

"I've been away a while, and seek only an account of the time I missed. How did I die?"

"Gloriously, ending the menace of the golem rebels. It was an iron golem that got you."

"As good a way to go as any. Mourners filed past a closed coffin, I presume."

"Your injuries were terrible, they said."

"And the tears—did they flow?"

"Yours was a stoic affair, rich in dignity, if naught else. As I said to old Daillidh, it was a poor thing to see so few invited, with the deceased a Derexhi by blood. They said it was out of concern for the health of your poor father." With his good hand Garatz suddenly clutched her wrist. "You must go to him quick, milady. If it is not already too late. Lord Randred has gone to his deathbed. Everyone knows."

Luma him quickly and left the Old Sword, making her way up the sloping road called the Ascent and onto the precipice of the great cliff that bisected the city. She cut through the fine shops of the Vista district, and, as the sun slipped toward the horizon, through the Capital.

Sprinting around the corner of a drab-faced counting house, she nearly collided with a contingent of city guards who leaned against its wall, munching hardtack as they leered at passing serving girls. Luma corrected her pace, heading away from them on a diagonal.

The burliest of them handed off his biscuit and followed her. "You there!"

Consulting her mental map of the city, Luma found scant avenues of escape. She stopped and waited. "Yes, guardsman?"

"That's some weapon you have there."

"Thank you."

A wee triangle of facial hair atop the guardsman's fat chin quivered in annoyance. "That's not what I meant. I meant, where are you going with that?"

"Are blades now prohibited in Magnimar?" Luma watched the other guardsmen as they crowded in to join their comrade.

"What I meant is, I don't like the way you have about you."

"I have done nothing to warrant your attention, constable."

Another of the guardsmen, this one skinny and spotted with pimples, peered at her. "Ain't you the Derexhi girl?"

So much for keeping her survival a secret.

"She's dead, ain't she?" asked a third guardsman.

Luma readied herself.

The pimpled guardsman pointed at her. "That's her right there. The one who killed Khonderian."

Luma spun, whirling her sickle in a wide arc, intended not to strike but to put them off balance. She darted for the nearest side street, then turned again. Pressing herself against a wall, she reached into her trickbag, her fingers finding the telltale ridges of her spider vial. As she did so, she remembered that it had been weeks since she last attended to it. She needed a live creature to conjure the magic around, and expected to find a black, dried-up ball. Instead, a brown spider twitched inside. Melune had replenished the vial with a fresh specimen.

The city granted Luma's muttered request for aid, animating her limbs with insect-like motion. She skittered up the side of the building and onto its slate roof. There she dropped prone, observing the guardsmen as they milled about, wondering where she'd hidden herself. She waited till they broke away, then jumped to the roof of an adjacent building, whose stonework offered an easier way down. Luma climbed to the lip of a first-floor balcony and jumped the rest of the way, landing with ease. Seeking out quiet streets, she made speed past the Avenue of Hours, through the statue-dotted manor lawns of Naos, and into the Marble District.

Under a moonless sky she crept onto the grounds of the estate adjoining theirs. She hugged the outer contours of its hedge, then made a dash for a vine-strewn border wall. Though the family had never bothered with guards before, deeming their own presence safeguard against attack, Luma paused to ensure that Iskola hadn't changed the policy now. Seeing no one, she vaulted the wall and, with long, quick strides, made it to the house. As she'd done without a second thought since the age of six, she scaled her way up to her father's balcony.

Through its windowed double door, Luma saw her father unconscious in his bed. He seemed to have aged two decades since she had seen him last. Loose, yellow skin drooped from his bones. His hair had thinned and his beard grown patchy.

She tested the balcony door and, for the first time, found it locked. Luma ducked down to work on the latch with the tip of her dagger. Its simple mechanism resisted her less-than-expert touch. Instead she dug at the grout around the pane of glass nearest to the latch. When she had peeled away as much of it as she could get at, she tapped the pane with the dagger's pommel. It came partway loose, allowing her to stick her hand in and turn the latch to the open position.

Luma went to Randred's side. The outline of his body under the bedclothes was a shrunken memory of his former self. A dull wheeze rattled in his throat. She took his hand in hers, hoping in vain to wake him. Abandoning the effort, she placed her thumbs on his eyelids and, in turn, delicately raised them. The whites had gone sallow; in his brown irises floated strange purple flecks.

This was no ordinary malady.

A nauseating thought gripped her. If her siblings had been willing to kill her to mask whatever plot they were hatching, surely they'd have to do the same to Randred. He was the sharpest of them all—and if he stumbled onto their mysterious scheme, he'd find a way to stop it. Unless they removed him from the equation, too.

Luma inspected the contents of a clay water jug which rested on a side table. She sniffed the water, then poured a few drops of it onto her palm and tasted it.

Moving back to Randred's bed, she began her invocation to the city's long history of poisoners and poisonings. It wailed of Red Mantis assassins, of murderous business partners, of wives who dripped doses into the ears of brutal husbands.

The liquid's toxicity buzzed in her palm. Concentrating, she tried to discern its type. No further answer presented itself. That fact itself was revealing: the poison was rare.

She deepened her connection to the city, reaching for a magic of greater power. She could fix this. With the power of the citysong, she could convert the poison in his body to an inert liquid, something that could then pass harmlessly through his system. She dug into her trickbag and found a lump of charcoal, then raised it over her father's chest, entreating Magnimar to aid her.

Luma held her breath as the energy gathered from the city flowed from her, through the little lump of cinder and into her father.

He stirred not at all.

Luma clenched her teeth so hard her jaw ached. It was worse than she'd thought. They'd clearly been dosing him in small amounts over many days or weeks—perhaps since he first began to physically falter. Nullifying the small quantity currently polluting his blood would do nothing to reverse the damage he'd already suffered. That kind of healing lay beyond her gifts.

The door popped open, revealing Yandine in a robe of violet silk, her hair piled in a net atop her head. A plum dropped from her hand, rolling across the rug to stop at Luma's feet.

Luma tilted her head, indicating the sickle at her hip. "Step into the room," she said.

Yandine froze. "You."

"Step into the room."

"You're dead."

"It would be the worse for you, were I deceased and standing here giving you orders."

"Don't hurt him," Yandine said.

"Why would I do that?"

"You haven't tried to wake him, have you?" She shuffled on slippered feet past Luma, to Randred's bedside. "He's so much worse than when you saw him before. Clinging to life." Yandine's gaze darted from husband to stepdaughter. "Dear. How did you . . . ?"

"Survive being stomped by an iron golem?"

Yandine shrank from her. "Something's not right with you."

"Lower your voice, Yandine."

"Get away from me!" she shrieked.

Luma bowled at her, spinning her around, clamping a hand on her mouth. Yandine went limp in her arms.

With a bang, the door flew wide. In a saffron blur, Ulisa flowed into the room, hands held like twin bird beaks.

Luma grabbed her sickle in time to keep her at bay. "You were asking how I survived, Yandine. It's a good question, because your daughter here, and the others, did their best to murder me."

Ulisa kicked at her; Luma turned aside from the blow, blunting its impact.

"Not in here!" Yandine cried.

With a table behind her, the wall to one side, and the bed to the other, Luma was hemmed in. She rebalanced her sickle, leaving it to Ulisa to take the next shot. "Is that news to you, Yandine? And if it is, what do you think they've done to your husband?"

Ulisa feinted right, then came at her from the left, whirling around her. Unfazed by the lack of maneuvering room, she directed a hard kick to Luma's breastbone. Luma staggered back, striking the side table and knocking the jug to the floor.

Luma swung her crescent blade at Ulisa; her sister flowed easily out of range, then back in. As they traded ineffective blows, Yandine sank to her knees, covered her face, and sobbed.

"What do you have to say for yourself, Ulisa?" Luma punctuated the question with a swipe of her blade. It caught Ulisa's sleeve, tearing it and tracing a superficial cut along the line of her ulna. "Nothing, as usual?""

Ulisa ducked low and, while Luma was still open, barraged quick, bent-knuckle punches at her kidney. Luma stepped back, pressing against the foot of the bed. Then she fell to the side, pulling Ulisa down with her, so that her shaved head smacked into one of the wooden globes that topped the bed's posts. As Ulisa scrambled back, Luma caught hold of her sickle and pulled the weapon to her. She brought it up, ready for a downstrike.

Yandine howled.

Ulisa's hand snaked up, slapping the blow aside, and Luma's blade cut a gouge across the face of a lacquered changing screen. Ulisa rippled to her feet, punching through the reach of Luma's weapon. The blow caught Luma square in the nose. She felt blood gush from her nostrils.

From the hallway came the sound of footsteps.

Luma positioned herself in front of the double doors and let Ulisa come at her. Her half-sister launched herself into the air, right foot outstretched. Luma flew back into the double doors, her falling body throwing them open. She swung wide with her sickle, nicking Ulisa's leg. As Ulisa struggled for balance, Luma shouldered into her, knocking her down, then kicked her in the face.

A pair of angled beams supported the balcony from below. Luma swung over its lip, then onto one of the beams.

She heard Arrus: "Where is she?"

Then Ulisa: "She hit an artery."

"Get Eibadon to seal it up, then."

Luma heard her brother's breathing as he stepped out onto the balcony. It soon receded. "We need Ontor! Where in the name of Abadar's pesthole is Ontor?"

Whispering a call to the city, Luma asked it to shroud her steps from trackers. A song of skulking feet and dull, fluttering moth wings chorused its agreement. Luma waited until all went quiet, then dropped onto the grass. Light spilled by swinging lanterns angled across the grounds. Elven heritage gave her the advantage: she could see without giving herself away like that. She dodged through the garden, staying clear of the moving light pools, and thus out of sight. A quick dive over the wall led to a sprint to her neighbor's gazebo, where she regained her breath and waited out the effort to find her.

Chapter Fourteen
Alabaster

Noole stood before a mirror, trimming his eyebrows with silver scissors, clad in a brocaded robe and a pair of thick wool socks. He thrust the fingers of his right hand into his armpit and then sniffed them. Wrinkling his nose in disapproval, he reached for the first of several ornate perfume bottles atop a dresser. He spritzed a cloud of honeyed vapor into the air, rejected it, and chose another bottle. This he used to generously douse his armpits and points below. He leaned forward to assess the state of his mustache. From an amethyst jar he swiped up a dab of wax, applying it with laborious care.

The room around him announced its owner's predilection for fussy excess. Velvet curtains fringed in gold swaddled the windows. Antique jars and vases, many in the fluted Hermean style that touched off a collector's craze a decade back, jostled for space on overfilled shelves. On the new Qadiran rug beneath Noole's feet, intricately rendered roses battled one another for supremacy.

"I need your help," said Luma, climbing through the window.

Noole leapt into the air, reaching for a sword he wasn't wearing. His belt and scabbard hung on the back of a chair.

Luma fixed her gaze at a point above his shoulder. "Your robe . . ."

The flustered gnome reached down and tied it shut. "What the hell are you doing here?"

"As I said, I require help, and thought of you."

Noole drifted indirectly toward his weapon. "Me? Why? You've got to get out of here. How did you find me?"

"You mentioned your lady admirer by name. I came to her manor to inquire about your whereabouts. Then I spied you through the window, saving me the trouble of asking."

"You stay away from Khedre." Noole stepped to the guest room door and locked it. "Her taste for danger is strictly of the aesthetic variety. Wait, aren't you dead?"

"How dead do I look?"

He cupped his hand around his chin. "You're different. But not in an animated corpse sort of way. But to the point: why should I agree to help you?"

"One, so I'll depart with haste, leaving you to enjoy the ample charms of your Alabaster District matron, safe from interruption or scandal."

Noole crossed his arms. "And two?"

"You are a poet, are you not?"

"Quite a good one, as a matter of fact."

"What I pursue is poetic to the bone. I invite you to witness firsthand as this grand theme plays out on life's true stage."

"In exchange for my assistance?" Noole asked.

"Naturally so."

"So that I might find inspiration in it?"

"Should you wish," said Luma.

"Usually when the muse reveals herself to me, she is not carrying a sickle."

"I don't offer you the usual," Luma said.

"You've a flair for understatement, Luma Derexhi. Very well. I'll ask. What is it you pursue?"

"Vengeance."

A line of modest shops and eating houses adjoined the city wall, across from the ostentatious manors of Grand Arch. Here servants ate cheap lunches and bought workaday supplies for their Summit masters. Butlers and cooks filled themselves on darkbread and ale at an open-air cantina, the Rag and Garter. They sat under the hot noon sun, griping about their masters. Luma sat at the end of a communal table, waiting for Noole. He showed himself a quarter-hour after their appointed rendezvous, patting down mussed and unruly hair. He took ale with his bread; Luma ordered sardines with hers. She began to recount in full detail the tale of her betrayal, but stopped when the tables filled. They rushed their food and departed, taking the slow way through the district so that she could tell the story unheard by other ears. Her account drew to a close as they neared Brewer's Dale, where Noole had found his squat.

"Wait," said Noole, "I have a question."

"Spit it out."

The gnome watched a fetching Varisian woman, her elegant figure betrayed by a dowdy servant's uniform, sway past. "First, the practical. If your siblings wanted you out of the way, why didn't they leave you to rot in the Hells?"

"Not sure," said Luma. "My guess? It left too many factors to chance. Under torture, I might reveal something that could sour their plan, whether I understood its significance or not. Although . . ."

"Don't go silent on me now, Derexhi."

"It was only after the Hells that I put my foot down. Demanded to know what was going on, with the whole Khonderian business. And said that if they didn't tell me, I'd find out. I can't shake the feeling that they hadn't quite decided to do me in at that point. At least, not all of them had. Not until then. By standing up for myself, I tipped the balance."

"In favor of your own execution, you mean."

"That is what I mean."

"This won't do," said Noole.

"What?"

Noole slowed his pace. "You precisely enumerated every detail, from the layout of the room to the specifications of the unusual golem. But you left out any part of the tale that might interest a poet. That is the quid pro quo, is it not?"

"What did I leave out?"

"Your heart, Luma Derexhi. How you responded to each moment. Poetry is not just about the color of a sky or the ineffable beauty of a sylvan glade. Without emotion, a poem dies on the page."

"Perhaps I will have call to read some, one day."

Noole laughed. "Every page you've ever read has been a treatise—or worse, from the journals of cretinous Pathfinders. Hasn't it?"

Luma shrugged.

"Even when you tell me," said Noole, "of your beloved family heaving you into that device, willing to see you suffer the most excruciating demise imaginable rather than personally strike the killing blow, your words remain tactical, detached. If I am to continue on, you must say what you felt."

"Pain."

"That's not what I mean."

Luma hefted her sickle. "Follow me, gnome, and you'll see what I feel."

Arriving at Noole's old squat, they saw that its master had reoccupied the premises. A lissome girl in a maid's uniform beat at a rug, dust pluming from its surface. Footmen touched up a carriage, applying a fresh layer of gilded paint to its carven clamshells and curlicues.

No such signs of activity attended the manor across the road. To the disinterest of the Qadiran merchant's servants, Luma hopped its low wall, followed by Noole.

"And what do you hope to find here?" he asked.

"Why did my siblings try to dispose of me? They must be planning something they thought I'd try to spoil. Maybe they thought Khonderian was trying to spoil it, too."

"You believe they killed him?"

"I have no better theory." They reached the manor's back steps. Luma peered in a window. "Your suspicious squatters have decamped," she said. She tested the servants' entrance door. "Are you any good with locks?"

Noole straightened his shoulders. "What do you take me for?"

She bent down to probe the keyhole with her dagger tip. "I only asked."

"It's painters who are thieves, not poets. Should you need someone stuck with a rapier, I'm your fellow."

Luma set aside the dagger in favor of a throwing knife and its thinner blade.

Noole turned to keep watch. "And what makes you think my squatters have anything to do with this? Whatever 'this' is."

"They might or might not, but it's a place to start. It's what Khonderian was inquiring into when he was murdered."

"He was likely looking into a dozen matters," said Noole.

"Did he react with any special interest when you told him about these squatters?"

"Possibly. Not unlike you, Khonderian was a hard read."

"Blast it," said Luma. She set the knife down, stepped back, and kicked the door in.

The squatters had left little trace of their presence. Luma ran her finger along a mantel; it came up clean. "As unwanted guests go, they were oddly tidy. It looks like they even dusted the place."

"Overfascination with cleanliness is the first sign of a diseased mind," said Noole, stepping into the kitchen. "Here's something," he called.

Spots of red and blue paint dotted the kitchen table. As Luma watched, Noole knelt to gather plaster fragments swept beneath the legs of a raised larder cabinet. Taking them to the table, he assembled them into a whole.

It was a medallion, as one might attach to an armband or shield. Against a blue field were marked seven simple symbols, arranged in a circle: a moon, a spire, an axe, the sun, a skull, the head of a hawk, and a swirl.

"The Shoanti gang emblem," Luma said. "Each marking represents one of the seven great wild clans. The citified barbarians here in Magnimar array all of their emblems together, symbolizing their unity against us."

"The squatters didn't look Shoanti," said Noole.

"We have to be sure."

"I don't suppose you maintain contacts among the savages?"

Luma wrapped the plaster fragments in a handkerchief and placed the resulting bundle in her trickbag. "I had recent dealings with them, let's say."

"That doesn't sound good."

"The meeting may be difficult," she said. "I'll go, and meet up with you later."

Noole surveyed the contents of the larder. "Now you're mistaking me for a dancer. No true poet is a coward."

"Very well."

"But if we are to swagger into a den of cutthroats, I suggest we reinforce our numbers."

"There's no one else I can call on."

Noole twitched his mustache. "You may be friendless, but I'm not. A recent acquaintance may tip the odds our way. He calls for careful handling, but we may need what he can do."

"I don't like the sound of that."

"In fact, the two of you may have already met."

Luma kept watch for city guards as she and Noole headed up the western spur of the Avenue of Sails. Clicking abacus sounds joined the citysong as they approached the carpeted shops of the Vista district. Noole called a halt before they got there, stopping before the grounds of the Iomedaean temple. A procession of old soldiers slow-marched through the warrior goddess's martial columns, banners flapping and trumpets blaring. Noole directed Luma to a landmark opposite: the Founder's Flame. A pedestal rose from a bronze bowl filled with green oil. A nimbus of fire enveloped the pedestal, changing shape according to an arcane rhythm. Occasionally the entire bowl ignited, or the flames changed color, cycling rapidly from yellow to orange to violet to blue. A ring of marble benches, set at a safe distance from the heat, allowed citizens to sit and contemplate the display. Noole beckoned for Luma to take a seat.

"He comes here most days, about this time," Noole said. "Unless you're in haste to confront the Shoanti . . ."

"Allay my doubts again."

Noole plunked himself down. "There are two of us, against the five in your squad alone. Each of them famed for his or her fearsome prowess. Then there are Shoanti barbarians, and, oh yes, the lord-mayor's men and the city guards are after you, too. Have I left any enemies out?"

"Allies require trust."

"And you have no more of that to give? Understandable." Noole held out his hands, basking in the heat given off by the flame fountain. "Though you're trusting me, for a reason both slender and compelling: you need someone. As that someone, I'd be derelict if I didn't say that you need more than one sword behind you."

Luma took a spot on the bench. "I need time to think. This all fits together, I just have to assemble the pieces . . ."

"In that case, I'll take a few nods," said the gnome, doffing his cloak and rolling it up. He placed it under his head as a pillow and lay sideways on the bench, knees tucked up to his chest. "Last night presented me with few occasions for sleep."

Luma's thoughts were soon accompanied by the gnome's snoring. She counted a dozen of the fire fountain's cycles, then another, before a bandy-legged, barrel-chested figure stepped over the bench across from her. As the fountain reached its height, he threw off his ragged, undone tunic and exposed his tattooed chest to it. He moved close enough for its flames to lick at him. His flesh burned, sizzling and popping, but healed just as quickly.

Catching sight of Luma, and then Noole, he advanced, head bobbing like a pigeon's. A globe of flame sprang up around his right hand. Luma vaulted the bench, putting it between her and the fire magician, and readied her sickle. "Noole!" he called. "What has she done to you?"

Noole jolted awake. "No, no, she's with us."

The magician squinted doubtfully at Noole, then at Luma. With a whoosh, the aureole of flame around his hand disappeared. "She was snooping into your business, before."

Noole patted him on the back. "A misunderstanding, my friend. All has been resolved."

"What do you want with me?" The magician drifted back toward the flame.

"You were saying before, Hendregan, that you hear a voice that tells you to burn people. That when you do not satisfy it, it grows louder and louder, until you are fit to explode."

"I said that?"

"You did, my friend." Noole tried to move his way, but faltered in the rippling heat. "You also said that you do not like to burn just anyone. That they must deserve it."

Hendregan rubbed his ink-stained head. The tattoos appeared to undulate in response to the movement. "That is the sort of thing I would say . . ."

"Well, my friend, we may have found people who do deserve your wrath. Very much."

"What did they do?"

Noole gestured to Luma. "Her half-brothers and half-sisters tried to murder her. She wishes to find out why, to see who else might have put them up to it. And then . . ."

The tips of Hendregan's jester-like shoes bobbled as he walked over to her. "They did that to you?"

"And came near to succeeding," Luma said.

"Your family?" Hendregan asked.

"Yes."

Hendregan sat down next to her, knees pointed skyward. "My family is also strange. But they wouldn't do that."

Noole touched his shoulder. "Before we confront them, we must understand what they're up to. If we are to give you this chance, you must make us a promise. Yes, Hendregan?"

"What promise?"

"You mustn't sent anyone on fire until we ask it of you."

Hendregan rubbed his fingers together. "I'll try to keep that promise."

"Good," said Noole.

"I always try to keep that promise."

Luma stood, pulling Noole aside. "You're joking, yes?"

"He's a misfit, to be sure. But pointed at the right target . . ."

The fountain flared; Hendregan cackled, then, in a muttered undertone, seemed to speak to it.

"Luma, my circle includes a number of dangerous men. Of these, Hendregan here is the most reliable."

Luma scratched at one of her facial scars, which had begun to itch. "How so?"

"Of all of their various goals and intentions, his is the simplest. In case you should forget it, it's written on his face."

"At No-Horn's, he callously killed a half-dozen men."

"Then let's make sure his next rage vents itself at the guilty."

"I can't believe I'm entertaining this."

"Look at it the other way. With your enemies, who would be so reckless as to place his trust in you, save for fringe-dwellers and madmen?"

Luma set her jaw and approached the magician. "Are you wizard or sorcerer?"

"Yes," Hendregan answered.

Luma cut short a sigh. "You must not only *try* not to burn people until we ask. You must succeed. Do you understand that?"

"I do. I should tell you this, though: some tell me I'm insane."

"I told you that," said Noole.

"Well then," said Hendregan. "Where are we going?"

Chapter Fifteen
Rag's End

Luma set off alone, heading down into Lowcleft. She ducked past jugglers, drummers, a storyteller declaiming an old yarn about the Red Mantis cult, and a blind illusionist's display of dancing lights. The sight of a Hellknight squad gave her pause; when she saw they were busy harassing a troupe of Varisian mummers, she breezed boldly past them. She found Garatz at the Old Sword and beckoned him to a quiet corner. He stood and instead ushered her out of the tavern. He turned a corner and leaned against a wall, winded.

"You can't poke your head in there no more," he said.

"Someone came around asking," said Luma.

"Ulisa. She was tight-lipped as ever, not quite coming out and saying it, but it was you she was after. And any of us who had helped you."

"I won't endanger you further." Luma walked away.

He hobbled after her. "I never said I was afraid," he growled. "I never got the full account from you before. You're in trouble with the squad, aren't you?"

"You could say that."

"Your sister's manner, I didn't like it. You see your father?"

"Thank you for telling me to go to him."

"I'd never open my mouth about this. Not until now. But there's always been a wrongness in them. Your sisters and brothers, I mean. I never could say why. Randred, as far as he was concerned, they could never put a foot wrong, but the rest of us could see different . . . A father's supposed to look on his children with pride, isn't he? You can't fault him for that."

"I don't."

"They haven't hurt him, have they?"

"I can't get him out of there all on my own."

"And you can't go to the city guard when they think you murdered Khonderian."

"I have to figure out all of that before I can move, and hope it's not too late. This is why I've come here. You still hear the scuttlebutt, yes?"

"Sure."

"Any Shoanti sightings? Preferably Priza, but I'll take whatever you've heard."

"Come back in a couple hours," Garatz told her. "No, wait. Here's too hot. Remember the olive press, across from Frehgan's smithy?"

"In Keystone," Luma nodded. "I'll be there."

Luma whiled the time scouting for a hideout. She walked west, into the Marches, home to simple traders and ordinary folk. At its rougher edges, near the city walls, she might find a shack to rent. City guards rarely ventured there: its people were neither rich enough to warrant their protection nor desperate enough to require arresting. In their place, acolytes of various temples did their best to fill the vacuum of authority. The fortunes of House Derexhi would mean nothing to them, nor would the desires of the lord-mayor or his men. If the safety of anonymity awaited her anywhere in Magnimar, it would be here.

She let the citysong guide her to a narrow lane, one she had never seen before. Its name bubbled up from the depths of memory: Bent Rib Alley. It ended in a cul-de-sac, where a pair of corpulent men sweated and cursed, hauling bundles of worn clothing from a teetering hovel. Luma approached them, and before she knew it had rented herself a hideout.

Checking the sun's position, she saw that she'd left herself little time to make the rendezvous with Garatz. The citysong helped her find the fastest route.

"Rag's End," said Garatz. "There's an old storehouse, looks to be abandoned. There's a tunnel dug underneath it. You remember Saian Logos?"

"Father sacked him for extorting extras from clients."

"He's now collecting debts in Rag's End. Says he went in there looking for a scarper and found he'd stepped into a nest of savages. He turned tail, throwing axes whistling past his ears." Garatz produced a scrap of parchment marked with nigh-unintelligible scrawls. "This is the map he drew me."

Luma looked at it, matching the lines to her mental map of the city. "I see where this is," she said. She departed without further word. With Garatz, none was needed.

The storehouse had suffered a collapse of its south-facing wall; its roof sloped down toward the gaping hole. Rats surged over a debris pile and into the structure. A rusted chain looped through the handles of its wooden bay doors. Its lock had been painted black to disguise its newness.

Luma waved Noole and Hendregan closer. She addressed the wizard, or sorcerer, or whatever he was. "I don't suppose you sideline in lockpicking?"

Hendregan wrapped his fingers around one of the handles. They glowed from within, igniting the wood. It charred, turning black and then white. Hendregan brushed the cinders away, lifted the chain, and made as if to toss it aside. Noole took it from him and lowered it soundlessly to the ground.

Luma pushed the door open and ventured in. Her footfall fell on a loose floorboard, levering it up. Gradually reducing the pressure, she brought it back down without a noise. Testing the floorboard next to it, she found it just as loose.

The storehouse consisted of a single room, interspersed by vertical support beams. At its center, about ten yards from the door, a circular railing made from old metal tubes lashed together thrust up from below. This could only be the entrance to the tunnel Saian Logos's story described.

Its inhabitants had clearly removed the nails from some or all of the floorboards, turning them into a simple yet effective alarm. Perhaps they left a path for themselves, leaving a few of the boards selectively in place. More likely they banged across it each time they entered the tunnel. If they came in this way at all: there could be another way in that Luma hadn't spotted.

"There's no way across without making noise," she said, her voice low. "Let's go." She ran, with Noole deftly following. Hendregan waited till the two of them had knocked boards out of place, then picked his way across the floor, stepping on the uneven ground they exposed.

Two shaggy heads popped up from the tunnel entrance. Arrows flew at the intruders. "Move aside!"

Hendregan called. Luma veered to the left; Noole, to the right. A bead of flame grew in Hendregan's hand, then grew to a fist-sized globe. With an overhand hurl, he launched it into the air. It grew as it hurtled toward the railing. The archers ducked out of sight just before the ball enveloped it. The flames kept expanding until they filled half the room. Hot cinders blew everywhere as the fireball consumed the floorboards around the tunnel entrance, leaving a perfect circle of burned matter. Little remained of the railings; the leather straps had burned away, dropping most of the metal pieces into the hole. A few spars, red with absorbed heat, remained.

"We're here to talk, not to fight," Luma called.

A reply in shouted Shoanti instructed her on what she ought to do to herself.

Hendregan stepped nearer the hole. "Hole-dwellers!" he called. "How big is your hole?"

They did not answer.

"My next fireball I'll drop down into your hole. Unless it is very, very big, flame will fill it up, crisping you all. So come out and let's be friends."

Harsh whispers followed. Hendregan loudly began his next incantation.

The barbarian lord Priza rose from the tunnel entrance. "Derexhi!" he spat.

Luma stepped forward. "I've come to ask you questions. If your answers satisfy, we'll leave you in peace."

"Spoken like a true oppressor."

Luma tossed him the emblem, which she'd glued back together. "This is yours, I take it?"

Priza caught it reflexively. As he studied it, his demeanor changed, fury giving way to bafflement. "Mine? This is a fake."

"How so?"

He waved her closer; without hesitation, she stepped up. Priza weighed the emblem in his hand. "First, we don't make our emblems from plaster. Each man carves his own, from wood. Every slip of his knife he infuses with his righteous yen for freedom. This was made from a mold. A copy of a brave man's ardor. It is nothing."

"Why should I believe you?"

"I don't care if you do. True words may enter Chelish ears, but they soon fall out." He turned the emblem in his hands. "You will not believe what a savage tells you. So go to any of the so-called scholars who entomb our ways in their dead and empty books. Ask them about the seven tribal sigils painted here, and why two of them are wrong."

"While I have a fire magician with me, why don't you spare me the trip?"

Snorting, Priza pointed to the swirl representing the wind clan. "The ensign of the Tamir-Quah clan is reversed. No Shoanti would make this mistake." He tapped at the spire emblem. "Not for a dozen years have we of the Magnimar street clan honored the sign of the traitorous monolith-worshipers. The Shundar-Quah we expelled from our ranks, when they tried to sell us out to your fat pig of a lord-mayor."

"Where the lord-mayor is concerned, we share an opinion," said Luma. "You wildmen are as often at war with one another as with us. Can I be sure this didn't come from a rival gang?"

"I tell you, no Shoanti would make this. Where did you get it?"

"At a manor in Grand Arch."

He tossed the emblem back to her. "And what led you there?"

"Suspicious characters were seen there, several weeks ago."

"That is a Chelish answer: it replies to the question, without saying anything."

"Why do you care, Priza?"

"You tell us that we are the victims of another plot, then expect us to shuffle away and mind our place?"

"Victims?"

Priza spat. "Do you play at stupidity, or are you truly blind? Again and again your kind has blamed its crimes on us. Whoever made this left it there deliberately, to lead you to us. You Chelish will believe anything when our names are invoked."

"They didn't leave this for our benefit," Luma said. "They made more than this one emblem. We recovered it, broken and discarded."

"Then there is some greater crime than squatting they mean to pin on us. What is this case of yours, Derexhi?"

"What do I gain by telling you?"

"My axe," Priza said.

"Your axe?"

"You are not here with your vaunted brothers and sisters, are you, Derexhi? Instead you come to me with only a gnome and a lunatic to back you. Your people have cast you out, haven't they? As we cast out the mealy-mouths of the Spire Clan."

"You're guessing all that?"

"We are not so savage that news does not reach us."

"My affairs are none of your concern," said Luma.

"You came here seeking my help, did you not? Why, when I offer more than you ask, do you now refuse it?"

"I distrust your motives."

"It is one thing to be blamed for what we have done. When a warrior conducts an honest raid, reprisals are to be expected."

"Honest raid?" Luma scoffed.

"Honest raid indeed," said Priza, warming up to the subject. An attitude of bemused patience settled on his confederates, as if they were used to indulging his lectures. "This land belonged to us, and to our Varisian friends, before you Chelish came and took it. You slaughtered us, enslaved us—"

Luma set her feet apart. "Maybe the Korvosans did that, but not us."

"Korvosans, Magnimarians—it is all the same. Put your backs against the wall, and you reveal yourselves as the same Chelish devils who slit our throats and dashed our children against the rocks."

"I'm trying to be civil, but I'll not let you call me Korvosan."

Priza laughed, rubbing his shaved scalp and grabbing the base of his ponytail. "Magnimarians are so different, then? After the Korvosans came to murder us—not as honorable raiders, but as exterminators—your ancestors beckoned us. You would shelter us, you said. Protect us from those terrible Korvosans, who were oh so different from you." Priza looked back to his fellows, who laughed obligingly at his mocking impression of a mincing fat-purse. "You wanted our help against them, and were glad to get it. But when we got here, we saw what your generosity meant. We were to stoop and bow, as your dogsbodies, your lackeys, groveling for coppers. When we tried to join your guilds, we were refused. We tried to become you, and were jeered at, spat upon, cast aside. So yes, we resorted to the way of the plains. We took what you would not give. Fought when we were hungry. As justice allows."

"Barbarian justice, you mean."

"If you are civilized, I am proud to be a barbarian. But what I will not be is a scapegoat. When others commit crimes in our name, it is we who face the raids of Hellknights and city guards. Not to mention the accursed Derexhi. And it is our weakest—our women, our children, our old men—who will suffer the force of their blows. Do you deny that?"

"My family has never beaten the helpless."

"Your family," Priza laughed. "Perhaps not. But they aren't your family anymore, are they? About you there is the look of a wounded animal. The scars that adorn you—they were not won when the two of us fought."

"No, they weren't."

"So the Derexhi have made you their enemy. You hate them for it, yes? Do not deny it. You might as well ink it in your skin. All of us here are outcasts."

"That's my business, not yours."

"He who shares my hate is my brother."

"I don't believe that for a moment."

"Then believe this: we will find out who seeks to frame us, with or without you. What would you rather have, Derexhi: my aid, or my interference?"

"You negotiate skillfully, Priza. Are you sure you're not Spire Clan?"

He raised his voice to address Noole. "And what do you say, gnome?"

"She's in charge."

"That's right," said Luma. "Forgive my Magnimarian arrogance, Priza, but I imagine you're the type who helps by taking over."

The barbarian flicked his ponytail. "A war party must have a single leader," he said. "Let us see if you warrant the honor."

"Until you decide otherwise, you mean."

"That is the trouble with your kind. You give voice to what should be left unsaid. Wait while I gather my gear."

Chapter Sixteen
Dockway

The Basilisk's Eye sat in a depression on Sand Rope Way, on the landward fringe of the Dockway district. Luma found a corner table and sat down, assessing the clientele. Warehouses hemmed the place on all sides; as she expected, it catered to the laborers who worked in them. Why this would appeal to a renegade dwarf, she couldn't guess. Maybe that was it: if you were a renegade, you felt at home only among people you had nothing in common with.

A flat-faced matron in a barmaid's apron approached her table, her expression like a gargoyle's. Luma wondered if she was the titular basilisk.

"Double brandy," Luma said.

"You in the right place?" the barmaid asked.

"Good question," said Luma. "Does a dwarf named Thaubnis come here?"

"Oh, her," the barmaid said. "Should be here any time now." She turned and headed for the bar.

In fact, it took Luma several hours of pretending to drink her brandy before Thaubnis swung through the doors. Unbidden, the barmaid poured an ale and dished out a barley stew. Luma came over to pay for the meal and the drink.

"What are you doing here?" Thaubnis asked.

Luma gestured to her table. "Let's talk over there."

"I suppose . . ."

Luma carried the bowl; Thaubnis, the flagon. As Luma sat, Thaubnis lingered near the table's edge. "How did you find me?" the dwarf asked.

"When we met in the Hells," said Luma, "you said you'd be back here before moonrise."

"You got a good memory. You haven't answered my first question."

"So you turned in those poisoners you were talking about?"

"Well," Thaubnis finally took her seat. "Funny, that."

"Care to elaborate?"

"I got out of the Hells thanks to a patron unknown. Someone put a key in the porridge. Since no one gives a fig for my fate but me, I reasoned the key was meant for you."

"Me?"

"Who else in that cell would anyone care about?" Thaubnis reached for the stew and spooned several gobs of it into her mouth. "So I owe you for getting out, and you're here to collect?"

Luma sat back in her chair. "This is the first I've heard of it."

"Your family didn't slip it to you?"

"They got me out by other means."

The dwarf ate with her mouth open. "A back-up plan, then."

"They didn't mention it."

"Maybe I owe someone else then."

Now Luma remembered: while in there, she thought she'd glimpsed her distant watcher. With all that had happened since, she'd let that mystery slip from her mind.

She'd always sensed the watcher as a threat. Was it instead a protector?

Could it have been Melune? Her nurse had scarcely been a figure of furtive grace. But then, she did seem to be a put-on of some kind. A disguise.

Thaubnis snapped her fingers. "It's rude, isn't it? To invite me to sit with you, and then go blank?"

"The poisoners," Luma said.

"Yes?"

"You didn't turn them in, so they're still out there."

"Oh," said the dwarf, as if the situation had finally clarified itself. "Who are you looking to poison?"

"I'm tracking the purchaser of a particular toxin."

"And to find him you have to find the seller."

"That's right."

"Mm," said Thaubnis. "And I'm helping you for what reason?"

"You want that favor off your ledger sheet, don't you?"

"Thought you said the key wasn't meant for you."

"I've just now had a glimmer of who it might be, and yes, you got out using my key."

Thaubnis cleaned porridge from her lips. "Good enough, I suppose. These poisoners, they're no friends of mine. I'll take you to them. But don't expect me to raise a hammer for you when it gets rough."

"Wouldn't dream of it."

"Just so the arrangement is understood."

"I'll gather my forces and meet you. You tell me where."

Thaubnis led them to a wooden tenement on Pacification Boulevard. The three-story structure resembled a crate that had been dropped on its side. Noole counted a dozen apartments and said to Luma, "You were wise to leave the fire magician behind."

"These poisoners will lead us to the conspirators?" Priza asked. "The ones scapegoating us?"

"They might," said Luma. "We can't say till we talk to them." She turned to Thaubnis. "Which apartment?"

The dwarf pointed to the middle window on the third floor. Lantern light shone through its flimsy curtain. "The one with the window glass," Thaubnis said. Oilskin covered the tenement's other windows.

"Ah, vanity," said Noole. "Despoiler of many a hideout."

"Talk plainly, versifier," Priza said.

"Glass panes are too expensive for this neighborhood," Luma explained. "A luxury. Whoever lives there earns more than their neighbors. Like many criminals, they can afford better but prefer the low profile of a shady district."

"But at the same time they like to show the neighbors who they are," Noole said. "Or maybe they simply hate drafts."

"It's a small detail, but also a giveaway to anyone who cares to look," Luma said. "Can anyone else here climb?"

"Of course," said Priza.

"Doors are no longer fashionable?" Noole asked.

"With poisoners," Luma said, "you have to be prepared for traps. A while back we had a case where they rigged the hinges as a trigger mechanism. One of our retainers kicked in the door. A dart hit him and he died on the spot, his throat closed tight."

"Clever," said Priza.

"And a polite approach is out of the question?" Noole asked.

"They're not running a market stall up there," said Thaubnis. "Knock on the door without someone to vouch for you, and you'll be choking on nightmare vapor before you have a chance to unsheathe your blade."

Luma gazed up at the building. "Priza and I go in through the window. The two of you wait outside their door, in the hallway, ready to stop them if they bolt."

Noole and Thaubnis headed off. Luma let the barbarian get halfway up the side of the tenement before reaching into her trickbag. She sacrificed another spider to the magic of the city and skittered up to pass him.

Priza had his shield strapped to his back. When he reached the window, he told Luma to take it. He hung with one arm free, then the other, as she worked him clear of its straps. The barbarian folded himself precariously on the narrow outer sill. He gestured for her to hand him the shield, then used it to smash the window glass. Using it as protection against shards, he jumped into the apartment. By the time Luma was through, he had already landed on one man and was pummeling him viciously. Two others left him behind to flee for the door. Luma lunged for the closer of them, catching at his shoulder, but he spun out of her grasp.

The fleeing men threw open the door, revealing Noole and Thaubnis. The dwarf lurched back, stunned; the door had struck her in the nose. The poisoners drew thin, elongated daggers, and an acrid odor permeated the air. Noole's rapier tip kept his man at bay. The other poisoner shrank from the swings of Thaubnis' hammer, which the close quarters circumscribed. As she dropped the hammer to draw her short sword, the poisoner feinted at her.

It was a trick; he held a second dagger behind his back. She blocked the phony blow with her elbow, leaving her open to a strike with his true hand. Noole kicked his opponent into hers, so that the second poisoner took the blow meant for the dwarf. The stricken poisoner clutched his neck; though only nicked, the wound blackened and hissed.

The man who'd cut him gasped: "Amun!" He dropped his own weapon and thrust his hands into the air. "Please, let me administer the antidote."

Luma came up behind him. "We'll let you, and then you'll talk." She followed him into the apartment, sickle-tip at his shoulder blades. "Try anything and you're gone."

"If I try anything," said the poisoner, "my brother is gone." He rushed to a cabinet.

"Open it slowly," said Luma.

"Please don't delay me," he said, complying. "He has but moments left." He plucked a tiny red bottle from a shelf. Luma let him pass back to the hallway, where he poured the bottle's contents on Amun's neck, arresting the wound's growth. It had already spread enough to leave a gruesome lesion stretching from ear to collarbone. Thaubnis laid her hand on it; blood spurted up through the gaps between fingers. "You'd better be grateful for this." She spat out a terse prayer to her dwarven god. When she lifted the hand, the wound had closed, and a disconcerting smell of steamed mutton drifted through the hallway.

Thaubnis manhandled her patient to a standing position. Noole moved to flank him, blocking him should he decide to make a run for it. The dwarf herded the stumbling poisoner into the apartment. Once inside, she hooked her ankle around his and pushed him onto a couch. He sprawled there, dazed.

"You saved me," Thaubnis said to Noole, as if in disbelief.

"Why, of course," replied Noole.

Luma barked at the uninjured poisoner, who stood before her with hands raised in surrender. "Against the wall." He did as he was told. "What's your name?"

"Nahi Laior Tzarla. My brother is Amun Zerdira Tzarla. That one," he said, indicating the man Priza had beaten, who lay unconscious near the window, "is Bela Zuskoan Gauldor, known also as Gauldor Cut-Freeze." Gauldor's face had been battered into an unrecognizable mess. Priza squatted over him, vigilant for signs of movement.

Luma studied the faces of the two brothers. The Tzarlas were identical twins, distinguishable only by the fact that Amun had gone for a few days without shaving. They wore the same nondescript clothing: green tunics, brown leggings, black boots. Even the rings on their fingers matched.

"I will tell you the symptoms of a poison," Luma told Nahi, "and you will tell me which toxin it is, and who you sold it to. I can hear your thoughts, if I want to. So if you are lying, the two of you will suffer what Gauldor has, and worse. Do you understand?"

"You need not threaten me further," said Nahi.

"This poison mimics the effects of a long illness, leaving few visible traces, save for a sallowing of the eyes, and purple flecks in the iris."

"The flecks give it away. This is known as Hermit's Breath, or sometimes the Kiss of Barbatos, after the archdevil of that name. One uses it when the victim must seem to expire innocently."

Priza rose, apparently satisfied that his vanquished enemy would not try anything, and opened the cabinet containing the poisoners' inventory.

"Don't touch anything in there," Nahi said.

Priza bristled. "You think me a fool?"

"Many men who do not look to be fools nonetheless touch what they ought to leave alone," replied the poisoner.

With thumb and forefinger, Luma pincered Nahi's chin, turning his face back to hers. "And to whom did you sell the Hermit's Breath?"

"It is very rare, and dangerous to handle. We have never stocked it."

"I find that difficult to credit. Thaubnis described you as big fish in the city's venom trade."

Nahi glared at Thaubnis. "We should never have trusted you."

"I never asked you to," the dwarf replied.

"We do our humble best to supply a product many in this city demand," said Nahi. "But Hermit's Breath ill suits our clientele."

"Why is that?" Luma asked.

"Its use requires repeated doses, administered over a period of many weeks. Our customers tend to be in a hurry."

"Who does sell it, then?"

"I hesitate to say."

"Priza," said Luma, "would you please break his brother's legs?"

Priza moved toward the couch.

"Todoban Boria!" Nahi blurted. "If anyone in the city could procure a venom so dear, it's he!"

"And where do I find this Tobodan Boria?"

"He operates a wine shop in Vista. Only the elect know of his special stock. When a grandee or council member dies from poison, it is surely Boria who profited from the transaction."

"Where's this shop?"

"On Lemnius Lane, same as all the other expensive wine sellers. It is not my neighborhood."

Priza returned to the cabinet. "None of these are labeled."

"A precaution against thieves," Nahi sneered. "Take all you wish, Shoanti, and good luck to you."

Priza closed the cabinet and stalked away.

"Is there an antidote?" Luma asked.

"To Hermit's Breath? None that I've heard of," Nahi said. "But then we sell so few antidotes."

"Those in that cabinet are strictly for your own use?" Nahi nodded. "When we have one, we always recommend it, at only a nominal price. Yet so often the buyer balks. We lose more customers that way . . ."

"Perhaps you should supply them gratis," Noole said, "in the interest of keeping your market alive."

The poisoner laughed. "In this business, demand is the only thing that doesn't die."

"Tie them up," Luma said. "So we don't depart in a hail of venomed darts."

"A wise precaution," said the poisoner.

Chapter Seventeen
Vista

Five stewards, each sporting the livery of a separate great house, milled in Todoban Boria's wine shop, exchanging hushed opinions on Kyonin vintages with the taverners of the Silken Bowl and Electrum Steps, and Madame Remeka Abantiir, proprietress of the city's most exclusive brothel. On soft-soled feet a half-dozen of Boria's attendants mingled with them, drawing attention to the rarest bottles. Boria himself stood behind the counter, perched on a widened footstool that lent him a majestic command over the commerce of his shop. A row of dyed spit curls accentuated the roundness of his pitted countenance. Behind him yawned an archway, its wooden frame decorated with carved grapes and vine leaves. It provided a view of a neatly appointed back room, featuring stacks of crates and a staircase leading down below floor level.

Luma entered the shop, followed by the others. The faces of its inhabitants drained, a reaction that took Luma momentarily aback. Then she realized how they must look to these pampered creatures of the elevated serving class: a scarred and sinewy half-elf, a muscled

Shoanti barbarian, a muttering, skeletal man covered in weird tattoos, and a stern dwarf woman dragging a heavy club. The closest her group came to ordinary was a foppish, rapier-toting gnome.

The five stewards, two taverners, and one procurer exited with dignified haste. The attendants, clearly yearning to do the same, hesitated. Luma ordered them out with a curt motion of her head; Todoban Boria signaled for them to obey.

The doors banged shut.

"Hands on the counter," Luma commanded.

Boria placed face-down palms on his counter of polished floatwood. He was framed on one side by a metal rack housing a quintet of bottles, and on the other by a delicate, uncharacteristically decorous ivory figurine of Cayden Cailean, the drunken god. "If this is a robbery," he said, in a voice both whiny and graveled, "I warn you, I am owed favors by many ruthless men."

Luma interlaced her fingers and cracked the joints. "We're not here to steal."

"I cannot guess what other business persons of your ilk would—"

"Shut up," said Luma. "A few months ago, you sold a dose of Hermit's Breath. You will name your client, or my associates will dice to see which one of them earns the right to extract the information."

Boria sweated. "You have mistaken me for—"

"It's been ages," said Thaubnis, "since I last did an interrogation. I hear the knack never leaves you."

"I can tell you little," said Boria.

"You admit you sold a dose of it?" Luma asked.

"If you are aware of my sideline, then surely you understand that a greater discretion attaches to it than the sale of brandies and rieslings."

"Thaubnis, roll your die," Luma said.

Boria showed her his palms. "It is not that I do not wish to cooperate. I am fond of this existence and am skeptical of the pleasures that might await me in the next. But I am unable to identify her for you."

"Leave that aside for the moment. I'll repeat: you did sell a quantity of Hermit's Breath, also known as the Kiss of Barbatos. Correct?"

"Were I rumored to have done so, that rumor might be true."

"Did you also sell its antidote?"

Boria clucked his tongue. "I cannot have done so, for no such mixture exists."

"What if the doses cease?"

"Has the victim passed permanently into a state halfway between sleep and trance?"

"Yes," said Luma.

"Then it is my sad occasion to tell you that this person will not recover."

"Your client was a woman?" Luma asked.

Boria sighed. "She was dressed in black, her features concealed by a silver mask."

Luma felt her scars go hot. "Did she wear her hair in an elaborate pattern?"

"She wore a hood. When my patrons choose to hide themselves, I do not make it my policy to peer too closely."

"Slender build, and tall for a woman? About six feet, two inches, would you say?"

Boria attempted a smile. "Again, you ask for a precision I strive to avoid."

"Were I to find this mask, could you recall its details?"

Perspiration soaked the linen ruffle at his throat. "To you, or the authorities?"

"Both."

"I am sad to say that it was quite plain, as silver masks go."

"She spoke with a local accent?"

Boria tilted his head from side to side. "She did not seem especially foreign."

"And in a cultivated manner? Her words a little clipped, perhaps?"

"To purchase from me, one must have means. As to the duration of her consonants, I might confirm it to you. In confidence."

"Though not at the Pediment."

The poisoner sucked air through his teeth. "Have we not dispensed with this talk of official action?" His hand shot out for the figurine.

An arrow pierced his forearm, nailing it to his side of the counter. Boria screamed.

Hendregan's hand burst into flame; Priza produced his sling and slipped a bullet into it. Luma signaled them to stand down.

A figure both familiar and not emerged from the back room, a fresh arrow pointed at the back of Boria's head. She seemed taller than before, or at least held herself straighter. Her previous bulk was now revealed as padding. The limping gait was gone too, replaced by a still poise. Also absent was the kerchief; now the only adornment she wore on her head was a simple diadem consisting of a thin leather strap, with a clear crystal positioned in the middle of the forehead. The color of her cloak, tunic and leggings, white with a yellow undertone, would blend in perfectly against the city's marble. Her frowsy hair had straightened into a cut of utilitarian simplicity. Though still plain-featured, the woman's wrinkles had vanished, and the heavy brow now proclaimed a daunting confidence. "Stand back," she said, to Luma and the others.

Boria had gone white. The woman pulled the arrow from the counter, and back through his arm. The poisoner's blood spotted her clothing and then vanished, as if glamored away. He lost consciousness and slid out of sight. "Sleep venom," she said. She beckoned Luma to come around the counter.

"Are you going to explain who this is?" Thaubnis asked.

Luma approached the woman, who opened a cupboard door beneath the figurine. Beneath it hung a bellows, attached to a mechanism triggered from within the statuette. "This will be filled with a spore mixture," said the woman, "likely a mixture of lungtaker and green carbuncle."

From this angle, light shone through a dozen tiny drill-holes, positioned before the bellows' tip. Had Boria succeeded in striking the figurine, the spores would have puffed out into the room, forming a cloud around Luma and the others.

The woman kicked at Boria with the pointed toe of a soft gray boot. "He'll have taken small doses of both spores over a period of many years, immunizing himself against its effects. A useful precaution, when you want to kill everyone else in a room." Her accent bore the hushed notes of the Vista district. Underneath it hid something from farther away.

"I repeat my question," Thaubnis said.

"This is Melune," said Luma.

"An old friend?" asked the dwarf.

"Excuse me," said Luma. "The two of us have a matter to discuss." She stalked into the back room, moving behind a stack of crates. Melune came with her. "This time," Luma said, "you must tell me who you serve."

Melune's features betrayed scant emotion. "I will accompany you," she said, "but in exchange you must agree to not ask."

"I'm not asking you to go with us."

"Yet nonetheless I will."

"And why will I agree to that?"

Was there humor in Melune's expression? "For one, you must be tired of trying and failing to open locks."

"You're a burglar?"

"Close enough."

"I thought you were a nurse."

"What it is necessary for me to be, I become. And at the moment, it is necessary that I assist you."

"Necessary to whom?"

"To you, for one. You'd all be dead without me."

"All right. Let's say I want you along. Which I might, since you're another part of this puzzle."

"That is not the way to think of it."

"You must at least tell me what parts of this are your doing, so I can set them to the side. It was you who left a key in the Hells for me, yes?"

"Yes, that you can set to the side."

"Meaning that you've been watching me for a while."

"I can assist from afar, but will be of more use close at hand. Which will it be?"

"I'll need an explanation for the others."

"Lie to them," said Melune.

Luma returned to Boria's show room, where Noole helped himself to a few select bottles. "This is Melune. She brings useful abilities, and will be joining us."

After inspecting a label, Noole snatched up the bottle, swapping it for one already in his pack. "If you trust her," he said, "so do we."

Priza, squatting, studied Boria's spore-spreader. "I trust none of you."

Hendregan chortled.

As they stepped onto the street, heads turned. A ponderous woman in voluminous finery gaped at them, clutching a small black dog closer to her bosom. A courier's bodyguard tightened his stance and interposed himself between them and his charge.

In a pack, they were too conspicuous. "We'll split up, and meet at the place separately," Luma said. The others drifted away. Luma headed past an expensive cobbler's shop, ducking between it and a store selling gilt-thread cloaks. She walked an unpredictable path of alleyways and side streets until she reached the precipice of the Seacleft.

Diffuse clouds wafted up from the city below. When they struck the cliff face, they broke up into remnants, which appeared to scale it. They swirled around the upper entrance of the Arvensoar, the tower garrison for which Magnimar was famed. The barracks began in the lower city, hugging the cliff side for three hundred feet, then rose on their own for another hundred. From the pinnacle watchers scrutinized earth and sky. Flashes of reflected sunlight bounced from their massive, copper-mounted lenses.

Wooden scaffolds clung to the sides of the tower like vines to a wall. Workmen scrubbed and scoured its stone, clearing off decades of salt-crust, stained by the sooty exudations of the Golemworks. Luma vaguely recalled a mayoral initiative to spit-polish the tower's outward surfaces. The anniversary of its construction was imminent, or had been declared to be so. Historians said that Haldemeer Grobaras had jiggered the dates as pretext for a festival. Overruling the objections of pedants, he and his allies would spend city money and reflect the celebration back upon themselves.

Martial drumbeats pervaded the citysong, as they did whenever Luma approached the Arvensoar. Today she took them in, incorporating them into her own determination. She would borrow their relentlessness, use it in pursuit of her goal.

She cut back into Vista, avoiding the open boulevard of the precipice until its last slope drew near. Once deposited in the bazaar, she cut a diagonal across the city, paralleling the Avenue of Sails without exposing herself to its traffic. Dusk settled on the city as she reached the Marches and headed for Bent Rib Alley.

Priza was waiting for her at its mouth, emerging from behind a pile of construction rubble. "Time to relocate," he muttered, stepping into pace alongside her.

"Where are we going?"

"Temporary quarters. Your unexplained friend, Melune, is here; she'll direct the others to it. It wasn't so foolish, to pick a bolthole here, where the law doesn't go."

"But . . . ?"

"But locals left to shift for themselves learn vigilance. As strangers, we stick out like fish in a field."

"What happened?"

"The nightsoil carters here are Varisian, and thus my brothers in oppression," said Priza. "I asked them if they'd seen anything, and they said Hellknights down Bent Rib Alley. Would your family enlist them?"

"A few weeks ago, I'd say never. Now I can only guess."

"Or the lord-mayor went to them, to get you for killing Khonderian."

"I didn't touch Khonderian."

"Where we're going, you should say you did."

"And that would be . . . ?"

"There's places the law doesn't bother itself with. And then there's where it dares not go."

The barbarian took her east, to a spot west of the lower city's gate. There he entered a low-slung tenement, its lobby guarded by a half-sleeping Varisian swaddled in a moth-eaten wool cloak. In what sounded like Shoanti-accented Varisian, Priza issued apparent instructions. When he mimed the height of a gnome and a dwarf, she guessed what they were: Priza was telling him that the others were on their way, and were to be allowed through.

Priza opened what looked to be an apartment door; it instead revealed a square of exposed earth. The room had been gutted from the floorboards up, and a hole dug down into the ground. A precarious brick staircase granted access to a tunnel below. Luma followed Priza down.

Chapter Eighteen
The Woods

The staircase led into a cramped, ill-supported earthen passageway. Luma followed Priza through it and up an equally treacherous set of stairs at its opposite end. They emerged in the midst of a gorse stand. She oriented herself, thorns plucking at her cloak. To the east stood the city gate, with its parapet of sentinels, prepared to challenge comers and goers.

"We tired of bowing and shuffling to them," said Priza.

"So you made your own gate," Luma nodded.

A wooded plain surrounded the city. Priza plunged south, and soon its walls could not be seen for trees.

The citysong dwindled, then fell away entirely. This would have troubled the old Luma. The new one chose to embrace the silence. Her power might or might not withhold itself from her, outside the city's bounds. If it did, and trouble came, she would find some other strength.

Earthly music replaced the singing in her head. Low- and high-pitched drums combined in a complex, twisting rhythm, overridden by discordant fiddles. Nearby flame-light flickered across tree trunks. Priza led her into a hollow, where dozens of Varisians camped.

Tents and wagons circled a central clearing, a bonfire burning at its heart. Men and women sat on blankets, children dashing around them. Among the colorfully garbed Varisians mingled a few dour Shoanti. Some of these wore the standard tunics and leggings of city folk, while others had thrown them off in favor of breechclouts. The wild-garbed men went shirtless, or adorned themselves with ruffs of fur. Their female counterparts covered their breasts with armor pieces, or leather bodices covered in the colorful feathers of ark-ark birds.

A tipsy line of Varisian revelers wove blithely around them. The barbarian presence in their midst concerned them not a jot.

So this, Luma realized, is where the Shoanti gangsters went when the city grew too hot. She and her siblings had wasted more than one fruitless day in pursuit of Shoanti thieves and kidnappers. They'd never thought to search the Varisian camps outside the walls. It made perfect sense, now that she saw it. One disregarded minority would naturally find common cause with the other.

A trio of wrinkled Shoanti, streaks of dye brightening their white beards, saw Priza and gestured for him to halt. "Don't talk yet," he told Luma, and went to meet them. She watched as they exchanged words in the barbarian tongue. One of the elders directed the questioning, with the others interjecting now and then. At length, they departed, arguing among themselves.

"We're unwelcome here?" Luma asked.

Priza watched the old men wander away, splitting up to return to family groupings around the fire. "They can't turn you away. We are as much guests here as you are. If hospitality is to be withdrawn, it's for the Varisian headman to say."

"So what was that all about?"

The barbarian crossed his arms. "Their objections have been heard and overruled. An old warrior may advise, but when his arm is no longer strong enough to strike his enemies, his authority has ended."

"They wonder if I can be trusted."

"I wonder that, too," said Priza. "Come and meet my wife."

A woman sat on a blanket, sharpening a knife against a whetstone. Around her gamboled three children: a boy about eight, a girl a year younger, and another boy, perhaps four years old. The eldest boy had snatched a flute from his sister's hand; the girl chased him as the youngest jumped up and down, clapping. The sister tripped the boy, sending him tumbling into the grass. To the laughter of her younger brother, she grabbed the flute. Her older brother got up, fists balled, ready to leap on her. The woman barked a command; the three children halted in their tracks. The mother and daughter wore bright, tight-fitting shirts over flowing, bangled skirts in the Varisian style. The boys wore next to nothing and had painted themselves as diminutive Shoanti raiders.

Gray streaks accented the woman's flowing hair. Lines of hard living scored her forehead and the area around her mouth. As she caught sight of Priza, her handsome features softened, and her green eyes took on a shocking warmth. She wrapped her arms around him, pushing herself into his chest, as if a fear had been lifted from her. He spoke to her in Varisian, his voice striking Luma as altogether changed.

The children stood by, reining themselves in, until their father acknowledged them. Then they rushed into him, the eldest boy and girl wrapping themselves around his legs. He scooted them momentarily aside to lift the youngest onto his shoulder. They chattered at him, talking over one another, until he decided enough was enough and set the young one down. The children ran a few yards away, then flung themselves onto the ground. They lay on their bellies, chins on hands, drinking in his presence.

A hand on her shoulder, Priza brought the woman to Luma. "Luma Derexhi, this is Zhaana."

Zhaana performed a dancer's bow. In return, Luma tightly nodded.

"There are others coming, too?" Zhaana asked.

"Yes."

Zhaana broke from her, calling out to others among the women. The Varisians readied an impromptu feast, hanging iron spits over the fire. They filled iron pots with water and dangled them from spits. Luma saw lentils, onions, and thumb-sized red root vegetables thrown into the pots. The women softened salted fish in pans of water.

As they worked, Luma noted sharp elbows and sunken cheeks: neither hosts nor guests were well fed. They could ill afford this display of hospitality. Yet no matter what mix of Varisian and Shoanti rules of hospitality applied here, she understood the affront she'd cause if she declined to eat her fill. Nor would it do to offer help.

As Varisians cooked, the younger Shoanti gathered around Priza. Doubtful intonations provided all the translation Luma required. She settled herself cross-legged on a lush tuft of grass near the firepit. Custom supposedly protected guests from harm. Still, she did not let her hand stray far from the grip of her sickle.

The heat soon made her drowsy. She risked lying down, then letting her eyes shut. The various fragments of her situation whirled through her head, refusing to cohere: Hellknights, Hermit's Breath, Khonderian, the lord-mayor.

She had to save her father. The last time, she'd gone to Derexhi House alone, and could only flee. Now she had allies. Granted, they had never run an operation together. Not against serious opposition: the invasion of the poisoners' tenement hardly counted.

These considerations paled against the urgency of her father's condition. Were Boria to be believed, he was as good as dead already.

That didn't matter either. She couldn't stand by and let it happen.

Sitting up, Luma grabbed a stick and sketched out a map of her house in the dirt. Plans of attack formulated themselves, then dissipated. Too many variables applied. It would all turn on how many of her siblings happened to be present when they staged the assault. She ran through scenarios, considering ways of drawing them elsewhere.

Noole made a wary appearance on the encampment's periphery. Luma thought about letting her companions in on the planning. But then, she knew so little of them. Their capabilities were largely unknown to her, their reasons for throwing in with her ambiguous at best. The gnome had come along on a lark. Priza had his own agenda, which might turn Luma into a traitor if she wasn't alert enough to head it off. Melune was lying by omission and served patrons unknown. Thaubnis had been drawn along like a leaf on a stream, by nothing more than inertia, or perhaps the lure of comradeship. And the magician was insane.

Still, when you have only a rock, you fight with a rock. Luma would figure it out, and find a way to use them.

Thaubnis and Hendregan showed up in short succession, about half an hour after the gnome. When the eating began, the drumming stopped. Luma ate as sparingly as she could without rejecting the gift her hosts bestowed. Tight-chested Varisians, clad in bright red vests and voluminous pantaloons gathered at the ankle, passed her bowls of sharp berry wine. As she finished one, then another, she discovered a new capacity for drink. Hendregan passed out early. Her other allies proved themselves prodigious, outlasting Varisian and Shoanti alike.

Noole raised a bowl in toast: "When drinking in earnest, always side with the dwarf and the poet."

Finally unsteady as predawn came, Luma, led by Priza and Zhaana, swerved toward a wagon painted with both a Varisian sigil and the emblem of Priza's Axe Clan. This, she presumed, belonged to his own family. His children already slept under the stars. Luma and Thaubnis arranged themselves on one side of the wagon, a row of pillows separating them from Noole and Hendregan. As sleep enveloped her, Luma realized that Melune hadn't made it to the camp.

A slim hand slid aside the wagon's back curtain, exposing Luma and comrades to the scattered light of an overcast day. Luma stirred; the others grumped and pulled blankets over their faces. She blinked; it was Melune. Once again her appearance struck Luma as altered, though not in a way she could pinpoint.

"Let's go," said Melune.

Luma groaned, a hangover bouncing in her skull. "What?"

"There's somewhere you'll want to be."

Luma shook off her grogginess. "And the others?"

"Just you."

Chapter Nineteen
Cenotaph

Worthies in formal regalia milled by the hundreds on a cobblestone plaza around another of the city's famous monuments. This stone cylinder stretched up for ten stories, dwarfing the structures bordering the square. A frieze of heroic figures struggled and fought their way up its stone surface. From Luma's vantage, atop the roof of a nearby workshop building, the friezes appeared only as a rough, pebbled texture. She'd spent many an hour studying it, though, and could easily call to mind the tale the carved pictures told. They depicted the most popular of Magnimar's founders, Alcaydian Indros. The images cast him as a man stern of jaw and thick of hew, forehead tilted ever upward, gazing to the future. They showed him slaying a dragon with his sword, laying stones at the foot of the Seacleft, and presenting his fellow founders with the city's credo of freedom and opportunity, as represented by a flowing scroll.

Over the years, Luma had come to associate Alcaydian Indros with her brother Arrus—perhaps because he practiced striking those marble stances in the mirror.

Various other founders appeared in a few panels each, though always off to the side and never as large as Indros. A bearded battler, his helmet beaked like a hawk, a falcon on his shoulder and a spear in his hand, showed up as often as any. Randred had always pointed him out when taking Luma there as a child. He was Aitin Aioldo Derexhi, the first of their line.

Luma remembered the words her father spoke, his finger grazing the stone beard of his graven ancestor. "Aitin served as Indros's bodyguard," he'd said. "A dozen times enemies came to kill the paladin— savages, pirates, goblins and giants. The worst were the Korvosans, who had declared us outlaws for daring to start our own city, free of their authority and that of the empire."

Sensations from that day welled up within her: The sharp, cool wind. The warmth of the pastry Randred bought for her and pressed into her hands. The way its greasy flakes clung to her palm. Its smells of honey and cumin. She heard her father's voice: "And each time, at his side was Aitin Aioldo Derexhi. Silent, watchful, and quick to strike when needed. Twelve times the would-be killers of Alcaydian Indros fell and lay dead at Aitin's feet. We must be ready to strike as he did, to protect our clients."

Luma recalled her father bending down to her level, his voice dropping, to tell her the last part. "It ends in sadness. When his warring was done, Indros turned our forebear away. It was a time for making buildings and passing laws, activities for which Aitin lacked patience. His grim visage disturbed the talkers and the planners. So he went into business— our business—doing for money what he once did for friendship.

"No one else knows this but us. When Indros died, it was by treachery. The ones who slew him wanted him out of the way, so they could take power. Aitin learned of this. He tracked them. He did not tire or relent, until he had avenged Alcaydian Indros. That is the part that this column, built with the aid of Indros' killers, does not dare show. This is who our ancestor was."

Melune spoke, breaking Luma from reminiscence. "It arrives," she said.

Into the plaza rolled a high black carriage, draped with the red and silver family colors. In a frame above the coachman's seat hung the Derexhi crest: the falcon rampant, a silver sword clutched in its talon. The coach came to a halt before a platform covered with crimson cloth. Footmen dismounted, opening a door at the rear of the coach.

A second carriage, which Luma had ridden in many times, followed it into the plaza. Yandine stepped from it. Then, in birth order, the siblings: Arrus, Iskola, Eibadon, Ulisa, and Ontor. Under black cloaks and hats, they wore their simplest finery, save for Eibadon, who was clad in his ceremonial robe. The siblings arranged themselves into double ranks and advanced on the back of the coach. With footmen standing by to assist, they removed Randred's coffin and bore it in precise quarter-time to the platform.

Eibadon stepped onto the stage, taking a place beside the casket. A few yards away, the gate to the catacombs below gaped open.

The crowd thronged in to hear, the rich and the mighty elbowing one another for desirable spots. Luma took a head count. At Yandine's side stood the family's latest political patron, Urtilia Scarnetti. Her rival, Verrine Caiteil, spokeswoman of the Ushers'

Council, attracted attention with a glittering black fascinator. Remeria Callinova, who as head of the less powerful Varisian Council supposedly represented native interests in the city, surrounded herself with urbanized Varisians in Chelish-style tunics. Even the criminal lords had come to pay homage to their opposite number: the wrinkled burglar queen Lady Vammiera Symirkova and bazaar extortionist Sabriyya Kalmeram dripped with gems and shot each other acidic glances.

Notable in his absence was the lord-mayor. Lord Justice Bayl Argentine, however, wove to a spot near the two powerful criminals. His impassive mien made it unclear whether he intended to eavesdrop on them, or exchange ironic pleasantries when the ceremony broke up.

Yandine and the rest of her children finished their greetings to those near them in the crowd. With Arrus supporting Yandine from the right and Ontor from the left, they led her up the platform steps. All the family, except for Luma, now clustered on the platform.

Melune took her bow from her pack, placed an arrow, and took aim. "I can take them all now, if you like."

"No," said Luma.

"You're certain?"

"My father must be buried in dignity."

Eibadon commenced his homily. Though out of earshot, Luma could guess its contents: a parable about Abadar, the city god, and how his realms cannot thrive without men to keep the peace. Maxims would pile upon platitudes and jostle with proverbs.

Arrus took over for the eulogy. As he orated, he indeed posed himself in imitation of the founders on the Cenotaph frieze. The wobble in Luma's throat turned to gall as the mourners fell under his spell. When he bowed his head and waved Eibadon back to lead the final prayer, she saw several of the mourners catch themselves on the verge of clapping. Urtilia Scarnetti beamed at him.

When it came time to move the coffin into the catacombs, Luma stopped watching. Instead she studied Melune's demeanor. The woman's knuckles whitened as she gripped the low rooftop wall.

Luma heard an exhalation in the citysong as the catacomb gates swung shut. Yandine and the siblings would observe the interment privately, accompanied only by the Master of Graves and his attendant. A collective sound of hushed conversation billowed from the plaza as the crowd broke into small groups. Urtilia Scarnetti clasped the hands of fellow councilors. Remeria Callinova sought a word with Verrine Caiteil, who evaded her. The Lord Justice Bayl Argentine did, in fact, seek out the criminal lords, one after the other. Lady Symirkova and Princess Kalmeran laughed with him, but not with one another.

Luma turned to Melune, who was trembling. "I know who you are," Luma said.

"No, you don't."

A Derexhi sentinel, a blunt-cheeked bravo named Johail Mahkeiln, gazed up from the plaza, checking each of the overlooking roofs in turn. Luma and Melune ducked down together.

"You're my mother," Luma said.

"Why do you say that?"

"You still loved him." Luma tilted her head toward Mourner's Plaza.

Melune neither moved nor spoke.

"I suspected it from the beginning, but wouldn't let myself credit it," said Luma. "You were dead. I've always been told you were dead. There's no group behind you, is there?"

"Quite the opposite," Melune said.

"No unseen benefactors. No cryptic agenda. Just you. You've been keeping an eye on me, haven't you? All through the years, the feeling someone has been surveilling me from afar. It's been you all along."

Melune's features blurred. As she did, the crystal at the center of her leather diadem pulsed with fleeting light. The brown-haired human disappeared, giving way to the elevated cheekbones, arched eyebrows and pointed ears typical of elvenkind. Straight, silvery hair shimmered around her face. Like any elf, her irises made up the whole of each eye; these were silvery, too. Her frame became slenderer still, and her fingers elongated. Cracked, irregular fingernails melted into perfectly manicured ones.

Luma waited for her to speak, but she didn't. "Does that mean I'm right?" Luma asked.

"I'm breaking an oath just by being here with you."

"Is that the real you?"

Melune nodded.

"Why?" Luma said.

"I'm sorry."

"Why were you gone my whole life? Spying on me from a distance when you could have . . . Why was I told you were dead? I wasn't even told your real name."

"I'm so sorry."

Luma moved toward her; the woman scrabbled back.

Luma stopped. "Don't tell me you're sorry. Tell me who you are."

Melune crept to the rope ladder they'd used to reach the roof. "I'm sorry," she said, "because I can answer none of your questions. I beg you not to ask."

They climbed down together and walked in silence. Luma thought of questions all the way from Bridgeward to the Varisian camp, and kept them all inside.

Led by Noole, in the depths of the night, the six traveled the city, from the Marches up through Lowcleft. They arrived at their destination as the sun rose. The gnome swept out his arm in a gesture of unveiling. The group stood before a crumbling old barracks. Noole ducked through an open window. "This is perfect," he said.

"Perfect?" Priza scoffed. The abandoned garrison lay in the shadow of the Arvensoar. Soldiers drilled in the square at the foot of the great watchtower. "We're a stone's throw from the city guard."

Noole leaned out the window he'd just clambered through. "And are they looking at us?"

"Not at the moment," Priza said.

The soldiers straightened their spines and saluted in response to a pair of approaching officers.

"And they won't," said Noole. "City guards don't look for fugitives here. Here they drill and loaf and arrive late for shift. This is where you'll find them at their laxest."

"Because no one would be fool enough to set up a bolthole within spitting distance of their fortress," Priza said.

"So you too admire my genius," said Noole, disappearing into the structure's large single room. When the others had followed him in, Noole put up a wooden panel; once in place, it mimicked a boarded-up window.

The place smelled like spilled wine and ordure.

"I like it here!" said Hendregan.

Luma started; it was the first intelligible sentence the fire magician had said all day. "Someone else was here before us," she said.

"A troupe of traveling players," Noole answered. "They've found the local demand for High Chelish Devil Opera surprisingly scant. I traded them for your place down in the Marches."

"Their neighbors won't like them."

"They're actors," said Noole. "No neighbor does."

Thaubnis peered out through a hole left by a missing brick. "I don't like this, either. Something's afoot out there."

"A commemoration of some sort," said Noole.

"The anniversary of the Arvensoar's founding," Luma said.

Priza jabbed the gnome's shoulder. "And you tell us this won't attract attention?"

Noole's mustache waggled. "Any place you have to hide is bad. When we find better, we'll scuttle. This is closer to the action, at least, than the woods outside the city."

"That's what worries us," said Thaubnis.

"Noole will keep looking," said Luma. "In the meantime, this beats the camp."

"You did not care for life among the dispossessed?" Priza asked.

"I didn't care to endanger them, if Hellknights came calling."

Priza pulled his cloak around his shoulders and settled down to catch lost sleep. "So heartening, Derexhi, that you suddenly ooze concern for us."

"They don't talk to the law," said Luma. "Right now, that makes them my best friends. What say you, Melune?"

Melune jolted from contemplation. "What?"

"Is this hideout acceptable, for now?"

Finding a clear spot, Melune unpacked her bedroll. "You're in charge."

Noole stood over her. "I must say. Though the import of your physical transformation eludes me, this form is considerably more fetching than your last."

Luma opened her own pack. "Leave her alone, Noole."

She tried for sleep but couldn't stop the questions rolling through her head. Across the room, Melune assumed a meditative posture atop her bedroll. Luma studied her, looking for a physical resemblance. Aside from her generally elven features, they seemed most unalike.

Now that Melune had admitted—tacitly, at any rate—who she was, she seemed more a stranger than ever.

It occurred to Luma that this thought would have sent her old self into teary self-pity. Her present self, the one who had seen her father placed in the catacombs, put there by his murderers, searched for feeling and came up short.

The blood that mattered was between her and her siblings. They'd killed Randred, and tried to kill her, in furtherance of a plan. She still had the one angle of attack: the Khonderian mystery. This woman might be of use, but was not worth burbling over. Questions about her offered only distraction. When Melune wanted to tell her, she would. If she chose not to, she would not. In neither case would this magically transform her into a true mother. That barn had already burned.

At this, Luma dropped into a sleep of dreams. In her dream, she heard the citysong and wandered unfamiliar streets. She was supposed to meet her family in a place she had never heard of. Whenever she took a new turn, she expected to be there, but instead found herself farther away.

Faces came at her, as unrecognizable as the lanes and avenues her sleeping mind laid out before her.

Soon that was all she saw: a field of black, and faces, starting small and coming her way. A leering old man. A handsome youth. A blue-eyed bride, her face pink against a gauzy veil. A bald warrior, his lip covered by a wintry beard. A birdlike hag, a face-painted orc in a feathered hat, a laughing moppet, a swarthy dwarf. The faces grew in number, speeding up, so that she could no longer distinguish one from the next. She glimpsed them in fragments: foreigners, grandees, rustics, laborers, traders, robbers, drunks, magicians, singers, bead-counters, artisans, and whores. The faces flew into her, entered her, lodged in the depths of her memory. With them came a thought, a message from the city: the meaning of this gift would soon become apparent.

Chapter Twenty
Several Taverns

Luma was first to awake. When the others were up, she stuffed her hair under a kerchief. Priza donned a menial's humdrum clothing: beige smock, brown leggings, and a flop-brimmed cap. Thaubnis left herself as she was. The three of them climbed out of the window, on the blind side of Arvensoar Square. As Noole had promised, the few guardsmen milling outside the fortress entrance paid them no heed.

A few streets west, they spotted a work crew whitewashing the side of a bordello. Priza veered toward them, spoke to them for a few minutes, and moved on. The three companions navigated a jagged route through Lowcleft and then Dockway, talking to carpenters, water carriers and dung gatherers. Directed to a Dockway dive, they found a rosy-faced man named Sezlan. Nothing about his appearance marked him as Shoanti. His accent had entirely freed itself of the slurring sibilants she heard in Priza's voice, and from his clanmates at the Varisian encampment.

Sezlan drummed his fingers on the tavern table. "They're trustworthy?" he asked Priza.

"It's for the people," the barbarian answered.

Sezlan addressed Luma. "I'm a scribe at the Pediment. They can't know I'm oldblood."

"They won't find out from us," Luma said.

He leaned in. "They have proof you killed Khonderian."

"Who does?"

"The lord justice. There's a proper warrant out for you now. Whoever brings you in will have you down and square. It'll be straight to the gibbet."

"What proof?"

"A trickbag, which matches the one everybody says you have. I copied down the list but don't remember all of them. Spider bits, a prism . . ."

Luma spoke through gritted teeth. "If everybody says I have it, anybody can duplicate it and plant it."

Sezlan squirmed. "I'm only repeating how the document read."

"And who testified that these were the contents of my spell pouch?"

"The lord-mayor for one, having examined it when he took you. With your brother Arrus as corroborating witness."

"Easy now," said Thaubnis, removing the brandy glass, which Luma was on the verge of breaking, from her grip.

"No one's blaming them for what I supposedly did," Luma said. "What story did Arrus use, to make them think I acted alone?"

"There's an affidavit for that," Sezlan said. "It turns out you were in league with rebellious golems. You killed Khonderian because he was on their trail."

The phrase 'rebellious golems' was a misnomer in at least two ways, but there was no point arguing with the clerk. "And that's why I supposedly died in the golem pit?"

"The golem masters betrayed you, seemed to kill you off."

"Has an explanation been offered for my miraculous return?"

"The affidavit has Arrus saying they have no idea."

"That much is true, then. What about Hellknights? Are they really after me?"

Sezlan scratched at his ear. "It's not in the documents, but I overheard that it's so."

"The lord-mayor hired them?"

"They're after the reward."

"Reward?"

The clerk covered his mouth. "Your family posted it. Twenty thousand."

Luma plucked the brandy glass from Thaubnis' fingers and drank its contents in a single gulp. She banged it down on the table and stood. "Anything else, Sezlan?"

"There was ... Arrus made one other point, but maybe ..."

"Spit it out."

"He said the shock of your revelation as a traitor and a murderer was the final straw that killed your poor sick father."

Luma turned and left; Priza and Thaubnis caught up to her a block away from the tavern.

"If you get what you want," said Priza, "and regain your name, you will see to it that Sezlan is protected."

"I promised him, didn't I? What do you take me for?"

"A Derexhi," Priza said.

She wheeled on him. Thaubnis got between her and the barbarian before sickle or sword could be drawn. Dockway laborers caught scent of a likely dust-up and gathered to watch the action.

"We're here to gather scuttlebutt, not become it," growled the dwarf.

Luma walked away.

Priza and Thaubnis followed her at a remove for several minutes, then closed the distance between them.

"Luma Derexhi . . ." Priza said.

"Let's not talk for a while."

"I spoke dishonorably," Priza persisted, waving her into a quiet laneway. He opened his tunic, laying bare a tightly defined musculature. "My words were unworthy, and did not respect your suffering. In redress, you may strike me once, with weapon blunt or bladed. Through this act, apology will be both extended and accepted."

Luma fumed. "Close your shirt back up."

He opened it further. "You must do it, or we are both dishonored."

"This is ridiculous."

"Show him respect," said Thaubnis, "and quickly, before our audience finds us."

"I choose the weapon?" Luma asked.

Priza braced himself. "That is our law."

"I choose the force with which I wield it?"

"Such is the custom."

She clenched her fist, swung back her arm, and smashed him square in the breastbone. He rocked back on his heels, then recovered his footing. A red circle blushed between his pectorals. "No more need be said?"

"Honor is restored," Priza said, "to both of us."

"Well," said Luma, massaging her hand, "what else have we?"

Priza retied the laces of his workman's tunic. "We have inquired into the part of this conspiracy that concerns you. I accepted this: we must be aware of immediate threats. Now I have a question of my own."

"Go on."

"What of the false emblem? That is what endangers my people."

"What of it?"

"It has been troubling me." He reached into his pack for the plaster cast. "This was made from a mold. The mold would be made from an original model, yes?"

"Right."

"You can see from the carving marks that the original was made from wood, as a real emblem would be. And that the carver was well-practiced. He skillfully cut the clan sigils, but made mistakes. I showed this to the elders, and they thought as I did."

"Which was what?"

"One of ours made the original. The mistakes are not mistakes, but were signs, put there on purpose for those capable of perception. Any oldblood would see that they are wrong."

"As you did, the moment you examined it," said Luma.

Priza nodded. "But you were fooled, as you were meant to be. Who would carve this, betraying us to the weakbloods, while telling himself that he was not?"

"I take it you can answer your own question."

"His name is Dehhak. Finding him will be a task."

"Why?" asked Thaubnis.

"He drowns his misdeeds in wine. And wherever he drinks, he soon wears out his welcome."

"This Dehhak won't be in a Varisian wagontown?" Luma asked.

"The fiddlers have no more use for him than we do," said Priza.

They began walking again. "Tell me of these misdeeds," Thaubnis said.

"It is not a seemly subject."

"Yet may be of use," countered the dwarf.

Priza ran an absent hand over his bruising chest. "Dehhak joined in adultery, with his father's wife. She performed the proper expiation, but he would not, and so was declared an outcast."

"Should I ask what the proper expiation would have been?" Luma said.

"The aggrieved party chooses. Dehhak's father chose an old custom. One enters a pit, unarmed and unclothed, in which a wild boar is trapped."

"You did not throw Dehhak in?"

"Honor cannot be restored by involuntary action."

They headed to Rag's End, where Magnimar's lowest drinking holes clustered. On the way, Luma's vivid dream of the night before returned to waking memory. The faces of each person she passed took on a numinous, otherworldly quality. They cried out from the citysong, their quirks and particularities searing themselves into her. She saw below the surface, through skin to the muscle structures below, and through that again to each individual skull. Some of the faces, she thought, had appeared in the dream, correct to the last line and wrinkle.

As she walked, her awareness of Thaubnis and Priza fell to one side. The faces she saw on the street began to blur and shift. In Lowcleft, they passed a procession of tumbling masquers, their true faces concealed behind visages of painted porcelain. This too resounded with portent, of a connection forged between her and some kind of universal meaning. But the masquers disappeared into a theater, banging drums and blatting on trumpets, and the burgeoning insight dimmed. She tried to recapture it, but it had fled. No matter how she worked to focus on each face as she passed, they blinked back at her from a realm of humdrum reality.

By the time the three of them reached the Founder's Processional and crossed into Rag's End, it was as if nothing out of the ordinary had happened at all.

They toured the district's hardscrabble bars, few of which warranted names. At one place the barman said he'd thrown Dehhak out three months back, after he'd exhausted a purse of coins and assaulted a regular. The victim, a woman named Bissyoni, invited them to cut off his ears when they saw him. She showed them her earlobe, which he'd sliced partially off.

The three trudged along a hovel-lined street. It stank of cabbage and rotting garbage.

"This Dehhak," said Thaubnis, "he's an outcast from a group of outcasts."

"We are the true people of this land, falsely set aside."

"I'm an outcast," said Thaubnis. "One who once belonged somewhere, and now belongs nowhere. Why has Dehhak fallen into dissolution?"

"Because he is scum."

"Because shame has gnawed him from the moment you tossed him out. How do you propose to get him to talk?"

"I will beat him like a dog, until he whines."

"You will go to him, and tell him he has betrayed your people again, and then you will smash him with your fists?"

"He deserves worse."

"And you are considered a hero of your people?" Thaubnis asked.

Priza growled. "You're getting at something, dwarf, but I cannot see what it might be."

"This Dehhak," she said. "I haven't met him, but I understand him. He'll tell you nothing."

"He is a coward and a worm. A few sharp blows and he'll be pleading for his life."

"He'll let you whip him all day long," Thaubnis said. "He'll take it, because he agrees with you."

Priza spat in the road. "Nonsense!"

"He agrees that he deserves it. Mark my words, Shoanti. He might admit what he's done, but not to you."

"You aim to seduce him with pleasing talk?"

"No," said Thaubnis.

At a spot referred to as the Pig, where abattoir workers drank in a condemned former slaughterhouse, they heard that Dehhak now soused himself in a new establishment named for its owner, Feirges.

Feirges's shack looked like it would blow down in a stiff wind. Rats scurried openly across its porch, which had been banged together from salvaged boards.

"Wait here," Thaubnis told Priza. Luma took the plaster emblem from him and followed her in.

Of the four patrons weaving on Feirges's misshapen stools, only one looked Shoanti. He looked up, saw the dwarf and sickle-toting half-elf coming his way, and bolted for a back entrance. Luma picked up a stool and bowled it at him. It rolled under his legs, sending him flying into a stack of barrels. As the other drinkers, and the aproned man who had to be Feirges himself, slunk away, Luma grabbed the Shoanti's collar and shoved him to his knees. Thaubnis dragged a table toward him, then took a series of items from a pouch at her belt, not unlike Luma's trickbag. Like a sleight-of-hand artist performing for Dehhak's benefit, she flourished each of them in turn: a silvery hammer, an assortment of nails, a leather wristlet and five very small straps made of the same material. She displayed and then set aside various other implements: hooks, rasps, and oddly serrated blades.

"Place his arm on the table," Thaubnis said.

"What do you want from me?" Dehhak asked, jowls wobbling. Unkempt hair streamed from his head and dripped into a patchy beard.

Luma followed Thaubnis' instructions, overpowering his attempt to squirm free. The dwarf laid the largest of the straps across his wrist. "Hold this in place," she told Luma. She nailed the strap to the table.

"Who sent you?" Dehhak wailed. "If it's Heiteleyyo, I don't have the money. I don't have the money!"

"We've never heard of Heiteleyyo," said Thaubnis. She splayed out his thumb and forefinger.

"What do you want, then?"

"We hear you made a carving for some weakbloods a while back. You'll tell us who they were."

"A carving? You heard wrong."

Using one of the tiny straps and smaller nails, she fixed his thumb in place.

"What are you going to do to me?" Dehhak asked.

"Depends on how quickly you tell us. They asked you to fashion a war emblem for them. Your people consider those sacred, don't they?"

"Not sacred. A matter of honor. That's why I would never—"

"Honor no longer applies to you, Dehhak. Not since they threw you out." She nailed a strap around his forefinger.

"Oh no—in the name of the Spire, not my hands!"

"Still, you couldn't quite betray the people who despise you, who tossed you aside. You carved a sigil that shouldn't have been there, and incised another of them backward."

"How do you know . . . ?" Dehhak cut himself short.

Thaubnis cupped a gloved hand around the back of his head. "See? You've all but admitted it. Tell us the rest."

"I didn't do anything wrong."

"Who did you make it for?"

"I tell you, it wasn't me!"

Thaubnis picked up the hammer in one hand and one of the curved blades in another, weighing them in her hands. She turned to Luma. "Which do you think? Crushing, or cutting?"

"I made the carving!" Dehhak exclaimed.

"Who for?"

"I only dealt with a servant!"

"Describe his livery," Luma said.

"His what?"

"The colors and decorations of his outfit."

"He didn't wear one. I mean, not a fancy servant's clothes. He dressed like a common drudge. Otherwise he'd have stood out as a mark, here in Rag's End."

"And he came to pick up the carving?"

"No, no. He gave me an address."

They returned to the hideout at the Arvensoar to tell the others.

"The Alabaster District will be well patrolled," said Noole.

"Yes," said Luma. "If it goes awry, I'll need the rest of you to cover my retreat."

"I can throw balls of flame," Hendregan offered.

"Those may be needed," said Luma, "though I hope they won't."

The fire magician's face fell.

"And you've heard of this woman, this Cheiskaia Nirodin?" Melune asked.

"The name's familiar but little else. She's a member of the Council of Ushers—as my father was. As my brother Arrus will be, now."

"I've met her," said Noole. "Fancies herself a patron of the arts. Her taste is frankly wretched, but she doles out the gold to stay in fashion."

"What are her politics?" Thaubnis asked.

"Politics?" said Noole.

"I can't be the only one to see that we deal with a political conspiracy," said the dwarf. "They killed Luma's father to put the brother on the council. And tried to kill her, because they feared she'd catch on. Now we discover that this Cheiskaia Nirodin is assisting with this related scheme to frame the Shoanti for something. Just as the Derexhi have framed Luma for Khonderian's murder. Khonderian, who was looking into the warriors with the fake emblem. Have I missed anything, Luma?"

"We've nothing to link Nirodin to Father's murder."

"That might be a family affair," Thaubnis said, "but we have her on the emblem."

Luma leaned against the wall. "All we can say is that Dehhak's original emblem was delivered to her manor. She could have taken possession of the item as an innocent favor."

"Still," said Thaubnis, "it would be useful to learn what faction she supports. And what they stand to gain from Arrus's elevation."

Noole noticed some dirt on his cloak and brushed it off. "Her factional instincts are as deep as her appreciation for the arts—which is to say not at all. Nirodin's all surfaces and prestige. She used to be glued to Amarai Burda's side. Since she shuffled off the scene, Nirodin's allegiances might go anywhere."

"What gossip surrounds her?" asked Luma.

"A cold fish, I'm afraid. Scarcely an interesting tryst on her resume. She's an abstainer, too." Noole shuddered. "My lady friend Khedre is an intimate, or a rival, depending on what phase the moon is in. Through her, I might be able to secure an invitation."

"Invitation to what?"

"Cheiskaia hosts regular soirees. In the afternoon, of course, so the absence of tipple will not seem so miserly. They talk foolishness about second-rate versifiers and occasionally bring a minstrel in."

"How exclusive are her guest lists? Is it always the same people?" Luma asked.

"Like any good party, there's always a few new lambs to throw to the old lions."

"Where do these lambs come from?"

"Cheiskaia and her lot are vehement snobs," Noole said. "And what's the point of that, with no one to condescend to?"

"So it's not only old families, then."

"What do old families need? Money. So they invite the pretty daughters and stupid sons of gold-burdened merchants, hoping to make lucrative matches for their own useless children."

"That's who I'll be, then," said Luma. "A cluck-headed beauty, reeking of trader coin."

"Who you'll be?" Noole asked.

"A daylight infiltration will teach us more than a burglary. The two of us will attend the next soiree, and see what we see."

"Should it be you who goes?" Melune asked.

"Yes," said Luma.

"I'm off to see Khedre, then," said Noole, moving aside the hideout's false window boards.

"Imposture is no easy matter," said Melune.

"No, I imagine not," said Luma.

"You'll need a way to disguise yourself." Melune reached up for her leather diadem. "I'll lend you the device I use to change my appearance."

"That will not be necessary, Melune." Luma recalled the dream of faces, and her near-epiphany out on the streets. As she did, a power came from somewhere else to nest in her heart. It convulsed through her, sent her pitching drunkenly. She recovered her balance, steadying herself against a support pillar. The others stared at her as the skin on her face crawled, the muscles writhing beneath it, her skull softening, altering, and hardening again.

She stood before them in the weatherbeaten face of a carter—head bald, brow furrowed, eyes milky.

It was not limited to faces, she realized. Her body trembled, blurred, and transformed: now it was that of a hunched, thick-limbed man, calluses on his hands and moles on his arms.

She changed again, becoming a buxom barmaid, a limber acrobat, a rotund cook, a weathered drudge. She transformed herself into a Shoanti maiden, a dwarf warrior, a gnome scullery maid, a sunburned crone, and an elven mountebank.

Luma had worked out the dream of faces, and what the city meant when it said it was about to give her a gift. The annals were right: a cobblestone druid could wear as many forms as there were people on Magnimar's streets.

Chapter Twenty-One
Fishball Way

Luma first heard the voices while asleep and still dreaming. In the dream she was hungry and seeking food on a street that was and wasn't Fishball Way, in the Bazaar of Sails. The food stalls that lined the real street arrayed themselves before her, but their proprietors had all gone. Smells lingered: of grilled sardines, kelp rolls, ginger soup, mulled wine. Luma lifted pot lids, rummaged under food cart shelves. Of the meals themselves, nothing remained, save for a few pot pie pastry crumbs and a smeared cup of hot sauce.

Then the voices, familiar yet not, from a direction she could not discern. Was it her family, come to get her? At first she caught only disconnected phrases:

"—forgotten what this is like—"

"—is it enough?"

"—watch that you don't—"

"—prying versifiers—"

"—see better—moon passes from behind that cloud."

Luma awoke into the dark of the abandoned barracks. Her stomach panged, explaining the simple meaning of her dream. The hushed voices continued, on just the other side of the garrison wall.

The first speaker was Thaubnis. "If more were left unspoken, the world would be much improved."

Then Noole: "A dwarven sentiment if ever there was one."

"Leave me out of your chronicle, or epic, or whatever you choose to call it."

"Politeness would lead me to comply."

"Meaning," said Thaubnis, her inflection turning inquisitorial, "that you will not."

"A poet's first duty is to the truth."

"Posterity and I want nothing to do with each other."

"I will alter that, never fear. But do you not want your higher truth to be accurately portrayed?"

Thaubnis groaned. "What could be worse?"

"Is it because you once belonged, were cast out, and now belong again? Why, after saying you wouldn't, you've thrown in with—"

"There's light enough now," Thaubnis interrupted. "Let's get this in there, before the soldiers change shift."

The window boards shifted and bumped. Luma rose to help move them from their place. A long rectangular item thrust its way through the opening. Luma grappled with the object, which had been wrapped in a blanket and was nearly three feet wide. As it came through the opening, she saw that it extended to over six feet in length. It ended in a set of wooden legs, stained and finished. Luma placed it upright on these as the dwarf and gnome clambered in through the opening. When he was through, Noole replaced its cover.

Hendregan snored in the corner.

"Where have Priza and Melune got off to?" Noole asked.

"I didn't ask," said Luma. "Priza, to the camp and his wife and people, I guess. As to Melune . . . " she shrugged.

"A shabby lot of comrades we are," the gnome said.

"Only one of us noses in on others' business," said Thaubnis, contemplating the newly introduced object. Loops of twine held its protective blanket in place; she got to work untying the knots. "That makes us as fine a war band as I care to join."

The blanket fell away, revealing a full-length mirror in a once-fine frame.

"In that spirit, I won't ask where you got this," said Luma. "But what's it for?"

Noole reached up and place his hands on Luma's forearms, guiding her, still facing the mirror, to a spot about six feet away from it. "We have some sculpting ahead of us," he said.

Luma moved out of the spot he'd picked for her, to examine her face up close. She was still not used to the scars. How much control did the city's new gift grant?

The thought was all it took: the scars vanished, leaving the rest of her new, hard visage behind. Another act of will, and the scars faded back into sight. Without them, Luma decided, she no longer looked herself.

"Not only the face," said Noole. "The body must transform, too."

Luma stepped back, studying herself from head to toe.

Thaubnis smelled the blanket at the mirror's feet, then picked it up, wrapped it around her shoulders, and propped herself against a far corner.

"I've secured the necessary invitation for myself," Noole said. "Should I bring along a guest, that won't be questioned—provided you seem the right sort. Are you ready for this?"

She glared at the mirror. "Why would I not be?"

"Forgive me for saying so, but you don't seem the sort for soirees."

"I never have been, but I'll do what I must."

With a pensive hand, Noole mussed up his hair. "Even if the one you must become is, ah, plush and winsome?"

"It's a pose. Why would I care?"

"Very well then. Let's start with the . . ." At a loss for words, he held out his hands before him, as if holding a pair of rock melons.

"Right," said Luma. She willed her upper torso to swell. The unaccustomed heaviness pulled down on her, altering her center of gravity.

"Perhaps not so much," said Noole. "We'll get a fine dress for you, and that will do much of the work."

She deflated herself accordingly.

Noole mopped his brow. "This is less enjoyable than one might predict."

"Keep going, Tlanibar," said Luma, alluding to the myth of the sorcerer who gave life to a girl made of straw, and lost his heart to her.

"You will also need, ah, more drama in the hips and undercarriage."

Luma willed her hips to widen, and her posterior to rise.

"But keep the waist as it was."

Her midsection contracted.

"You'll want smaller hands," Noole said.

"What if I have to fight?"

"Then you'll revert entirely to the form you know."

"Good point," said Luma. She shrank her hands, already thin but long of finger, into pretty uselessness. "And the feet?" She kicked off a boot, peeled off its sock, and waved her bare foot in the air.

Noole squinted. "They seem fine. We'll put them in an exaggerated shoe, which will be challenge enough to walk in without changing your balance any more than we already have. A merchant's favorite daughter will have been tutored from childhood to glide about gracefully."

"Perhaps he earned his wealth only recently, giving her little time to practice."

"Yes, adopt that story. But still, leave the feet."

Leaning on the gnome's shoulder, she put her sock and boot back on. "And now the face?"

"You will be a blond, it goes without saying."

Luma's red locks turned bright yellow.

"That would fetch you a fine sum in Lowcleft. For Alabaster, we must moderate."

Her hair lost intensity, but gained an electrum sheen.

"Perfect," said Noole. "Now the face. Can you make it rounder?"

She did.

"Round but not plump."

Her cheeks fell; the bones above them returned to their usual shape.

"Remake the chin, so the face is more of a heart shape."

The chin shrunk to a freakish size, then expanded again until it was right.

"This Melune," Noole said, "she is not in her true shape, either."

Luma regarded her transformation in profile. "Anything else?"

"Almond eyes would complete the effect."

Luma's irises changed from green to brown.

"No, I meant the shape of the eyes."

"I see," said Luma. Her naturally narrow, half-moon eyes widened, attaining a horizontal symmetry. "And the color?"

"When embracing a cliche, embrace the cliche."

"What does that mean?"

"Blue."

The hue of the irises rippled again, acquiring a cerulean paleness.

"Congratulate yourself, my comrade, on becoming the dream of every pedigreed young bravo on the good side of the Seacleft."

"The ones who like girls, that is."

"Those who don't will still want to marry you. More so, perhaps. Speaking of disguises, who is Melune really?"

The unfamiliar face flushed. "You'd best leave her out of your poem, too."

"There's a history between you."

"She's the one who found me and nursed me back to health."

"You wouldn't react so if that was all there was to it."

Luma shifted back into her true form, scarred and looming. "You're inquisitive, Noole."

Noole stood his ground. "The others want to know, too. Even Thaubnis, who so zealously guards her own past. I'm the only one of us bold enough to ask."

Sunlight threaded through gaps in the wall. The hup-hups of drilling soldiers echoed from the base of the Arvensoar, as the predawn shift change commenced. A bumping sound came at the window as its covering was pulled loose. Melune crawled through the window, her body unfolding with the grace of a predatory insect.

"I have the coach arranged," she said.

"In the middle of the night?" asked Noole.

The elf's tone gave nothing away. She nodded at the mirror. "Often the best time to find what you seek."

"Noole wants the characters in his poem to explain themselves," said Luma.

"Is that so," said Melune, without a question mark.

Chapter Twenty-Two
Nirodin House

They left in pairs from the hideout, heading north to a park on Vista's eastern edge, where it abutted the Seacleft. There waited a hired coach and its twin black steeds. Luma paid the driver to while his day in a tavern and say no more of it. Thaubnis and Melune, in servants' livery, clambered onto the driver's bench. Their uniforms matched no actual house, old or parvenu, but this would not arouse any great suspicion. Upstart trading families rose to prominence all the time, giving themselves crests and dressing their household workers in outfits trumpeting their newfound status. No one could keep track of them all.

Trouble would come if a private patrol stopped the coach. There, they would find Hendregan and Priza, and the game would be done. As no change of clothing could render innocuous a Shoanti warrior or a man covered in mystic sigils, they wore their usual war garb.

Priza sat rigidly on the bench opposite Luma, surveying with clear distaste the coach's pillows and curtains. Hendregan gazed dreamily out the window. Luma took his expression for one of childlike innocence, until it occurred to her that he was probably picturing her city in flames.

Noole, beside her, tugged at a freshly bleached pair of cuff-ruffles. For the occasion, he'd taken his best doublet out of hock, the transaction funded by Melune's coins.

She'd also paid for the peacockish gown currently binding Luma. Slashed and brocaded sleeves impeded the movement of her arms, while a pearled corset constricted her ribs. A pleated skirt, puffed out by voluminous bloomers, kept her legs uncomfortably angled in her seat. Wings of stiffened lace rose from her collar, forming a V to point at her magically boosted decolletage. Atop her head of side-swept hair perched a steeply raked feathered bonnet. Luma had further altered her form, an inch here, a tuck there, to fit inside the already completed gown. For a bespoke outfit, they would have waited weeks. Still, she could not find a position where it did not dig into her somewhere.

Cued by a sharp crack of Melune's whip, the carriage rolled through Lowcleft to the eastern spur of the Avenue of Sails. The dray-horses strained their way up the steep incline to the top of the Seacleft. Melune stuck to the great avenues, taking the Way of Arches up to the Boulevard of Messengers.

To the east, the vast hippodrome structure called Serpent's Run towered over the villas and manors of the Alabaster District. Afternoon sun highlighted the scaled segments of the stadium's namesake, the stone snake encircling its rim.

In time they reached the gates separating the Stylobate, the most exclusive neighborhood in the already exclusive Alabaster District, from the rest of the city. Derexhi sentinels manned the gate. She recognized them all, and could name both the stout squadman, Huseith, and his hawk-faced adjutant, Maraskol.

Nearby gathered a group of Hellknights. From their armor, Luma could identify them, as well: Maralictor Perest Sere Maximete and subordinates. It was not the habit of Hellknights to reinforce Derexhi guardsmen, or anyone else. Nor was it their business to checkpoint traffic in or out of any neighborhood, not even this one.

Luma told the others.

"There's something your family doesn't want you seeing," said Noole.

"Or they've baited a trap," Luma responded.

They heard the voices of Melune and the squadman. Footsteps came their way.

Hendregan murmured in anticipation.

In answer to a knock at the carriage door, Noole parted its window blind. Priza pressed himself against his seat, to remove himself from the eyeline of the sentinels. With a stiff arm, he moved Hendregan back, too. Luma tensed, half-expecting the fire magician to erupt. Instead he took it in apparent good stride.

"How can I help you, my good fellows?" Noole's vowels oozed hereditary condescension.

"What business brings you to the Stylobate today?"

Noole puffed out his collar. "Why, I am sufficiently fortunate as to be attending the soiree of Madame Cheiskaia Nirodin."

"Have you an invitation?"

Luma readied herself for a transformation back into her true body. Her armor and weapons were stashed in a compartment under the seat.

Noole handed the squadman a sheet of vellum, which a scribe's hand had teased into a display of calligraphic excess. He glanced at it—Luma doubted that Huseith could read—and handed it back.

"There isn't some nastiness afoot, is there?" Noole asked.

Huseith's forehead wrinkled. "Why do you ask that, sir?"

"Those Hellknights over there, looking over your shoulders."

Huseith frowned in exasperation. "Swaggering whoresons, each and every one."

"I couldn't agree more," said Noole. "Dreadful creatures."

The squadman handed the invitation back. "If there's a reason for them being here, they don't tell the likes of me."

Noole slipped him a silver coin, which he palmed in expert fashion. He waved Melune on and the carriage trundled through the gate.

"So," Noole asked Luma, "if you win Derexhi House, do you fire him for graft and incompetence, or wreathe him in laurels?"

She did not reply.

The main gate of Nirodin House asserted lordly rank over its manorial neighbors. A marble archway, carved with heroic figures, dwarfed the coaches trundling through it. Only on a close glance did she note that the strong-jawed warriors and purposeful wizard queens depicted on the archway were attended by small, discreet imps and other stylized angels. The subtle flourish marked the family—at the time of the piece's commissioning, at any rate—as upholders of imperial tradition.

"You didn't tell me she was old guard," Luma said to Noole.

"The architecture predates her," Noole shrugged.

"Still," said Luma, "it runs in families."

Coaches, some gilded, others tasteful, overflowed the greensward. A chauffeur appeared to tell Melune to drop off her passengers and wait along the roadside near its vast garden wall. Luma reached for the door, provoking a teasing finger-wag from Noole. He waited for Thaubnis to climb down and open the door. She held out an awkward arm to steady Luma onto the step. Noole followed her onto the grass, then crooked his arm around hers. His short stature rendered the gesture stiff, adding to Luma's challenge as she tried to seem adept in her ridiculous footwear. By the time she reached the grand front steps, she had nearly mastered the required rhythm. They discreetly disengaged arms for the trying stairway ascent, then resumed the connection to proceed through the manor's two-story doorway.

Guests bottlenecked in the foyer, waiting to be introduced so they could then go into the ballroom, which had been filled with stuffed chairs and low tables.

Luma whispered at Noole: "Introductions? At an afternoon soiree?"

"At Nirodin House, if a thing is worth doing, it is worth overdoing." The poet spoke two degrees above *sotto voce*, eliciting scandalized titters from the brocade-wrapped matrons ahead of him.

The ladies turned his way. "Will you be gracing us with a recitation today?" said the larger of the two, whose white, high-piled coiffure was stained a delicate violet.

Noole bowed, flourishing his collar-ruffle. "I am not on the program, but I might declaim impromptu, should demand mount."

The slimmer matron locked Luma in a frankly appraising, all-over gaze. "And whom do you bring with you, today, good laureate?"

"I have the pleasure to escort Laryss Isulede Zaillo," said Noole.

Luma succeeded in curtsying, in accordance with Noole's coaching. As a Derexhi city-warrior, the gesture had never been expected of her. Were she here as herself, she would extend her hand for a curt shake, in the way of any other armswoman.

"Laryss," said Noole, indicating first the heavy and then the lean, "allow me to introduce the Ladies Sutia Tortala Turos and Sonthia Fosveni Ceilitha."

"Your family won success in trade?" Sutia asked.

"My father is in furs," Luma said.

Sonthia chortled. "Yet you come elegantly dressed today!" She clapped her hands at her own witticism.

Feeling an anger on behalf of this imaginary person, Laryss Isulede Zaillo, Luma reminded herself that the character she played today desired nothing more than to be one of these people, and would not only tolerate whatever indignities they chose to dish out, but paint them over in a rosy sheen. She heard Laryss' words come out of her mouth: "Such a delightful jest!"

The weighty lady hooked her arm around Luma's. "Oh, you are a rare peach!"

"How refreshing," said her companion. "So often the girls who come up here from below appear lovely enough, yet prove balky know-nothings after the simplest exchange of repartee."

"I've never seen a grander place," Luma gawked.

Taking her other arm, Sutia dropped into an exaggerated whisper. "Oh, we'll show you much grander, dear. There is a pleasure in ostentation, to be sure, but where true taste reigns one finds an extraordinary simplicity."

This provoked a pronounced huff from a matron standing behind Noole. Sutia and Sonthia puffed themselves up in response. Luma realized that they'd seized on Laryss as a prop, and that the two staged this scene as a sally at the women in back of them.

Sonthia rattled her fan for emphasis. "When you come to my salon next week, my dear, you'll see a manor appointed in the subtler New Varisian fashion."

From their preference in decor, Luma could deduce their sympathies. They thought of themselves as Magnimarian, of the Chelish Empire as a justly faded relic, and of Korvosa as a bitter rival. This likely placed them at odds with the lady of the house, who would regard herself as a Chelishwoman settled in Varisia, of the empire as a glorious past in need of revival, and of Korvosa as a needed ally to this end. In only a few moments, then, Luma had fallen into the clutches of the wrong crowd. Not because their views were more tedious than any other's, but because she'd come here to sniff around the rival side. It would be hard enough without these two anchored to her. She had to ditch them, posthaste.

The women came to the head of the line, disengaging from Luma to present their invitations to the herald. He called their names, and they glided in, as if basking in nonexistent applause.

Noole passed his invitation to the servant, who accepted it with a pronounced sniff. He squinted at the bottom, where the gnome had carefully inscribed Luma's false name. "The poet Noole and Laryss Isulede Zillo," he declared. Luma assumed that he'd purposefully mispronounced her: again she reminded herself not to take offense.

"You wish this was a problem you could solve with a sickle, or a rain of gravel," said Noole.

"I am aware that it is not," Luma answered. Sonthia and Sutia, she saw, had been intercepted by a gaunt man sporting a sequined doublet. Daring a quick move in her encumbering heels, she darted into an anteroom, where several dozen grandees grazed from a mountain of cheese and grapes. Those few who glanced at her at all assessed her, dismissed her, and returned to their conversations. As long as she seemed interested in the food, Luma found that they paid her no mind when she sidled close enough to eavesdrop. Here, an unranked social position granted an invisibility as reliable as any magic ring.

A gravel-voiced matron wore a high steepled hood, adding precious inches to a diminutive frame. "He'll never be dislodged," she barked.

Her debating partner, a balding, middle-aged fellow, bore the permanent, woebegone look of a hunting hound. "Surely the wretch is not unassailable."

"Haldemeer Grobaras," the matron intoned, "will remain the lord-mayor for decades. He's run rings round the lot of you."

"You say this as if he's a king," said the hound-like man. "His initiatives are often checked."

"That this is all we aspire to—to now and then block him—proves that he has mastered us. To him, ancient prerogative means nothing. Families of lineage are but one faction, to play off against the others."

"There are too many councilors," said a third man, a bland-featured dandy whose off-gray hose precisely matched the hue of his doublet.

"There are too many of the wrong sort of councilor," said the woman.

"What remedy do you propose, then, Histia?" asked the hound-faced man, exasperation showing.

"There is none," said Histia. "With that man in office, our aspirations will forever go unmet. We may not call ourselves true nobles. Without that distinction, we are merely rich. And that is nothing. What separates us from people like that mooncalf there?" Her stabbing finger pointed at Luma.

Coloring slightly, the two men bowed to her.

"Pardon us, young lady," said the hound-faced man.

"Yes, indeed," mumbled his gray-clad friend.

"Pff," said Histia.

"Politics is an awful bother," said Luma, letting all comprehension drain from her face. She grabbed up a morsel of applecheese. "Or so my father tells me."

"Pfft," said Histia, with greater emphasis.

"Grobaras knows too many secrets." Hound-Face continued as if the social waters remained unrippled. "If it weren't for that, there are factions we could band with to drive him out."

"If trout had feet they could walk on land," Histia scoffed.

A new arrival joined the debate: a tall, smooth-chinned man who tossed ash-brown locks from side to side. He pushed toward the cheese table, sticking out the hip with a rapier dangling from it. This one, Luma had met before. He was Bonto Geirbelyn Feste, a friend of Ontor's. Once, when he had polished off most of a brandy bottle, she had seen him attempt to paw Ulisa, of all people. He'd skidded thirty feet across the ballroom floor before coming to a halt. "What rot!" he laughed. "You loathe the lord-mayor, but not so much that you'll skip his grand rededication ceremony this afternoon, hah? We either are or are not genuine aristocrats, but nonetheless must see and be seen."

"We are here to steel ourselves first," said the gray-clad man.

Bonto snatched a glass of sweet hillside wine from a servant's tray. "As am I, my friends."

"Pfft," said Histia.

The wine contradicted another piece of Noole's intelligence. If the typical afternoon soiree at Nirodin House was a dry affair, she had certainly suspended the rule for this occasion. The guests today were being cozened, to one end or another. Most wore the signs of overindulgence on reddened, bleary faces.

"Pfft indeed," said Bonto. "Let us say that a roc carried off Grobaras tomorrow. You'd still be impotently scheming. Who would you use to take the lord-mayor's seat? Pallegin here?" He waved a grape bunch at the hound-faced man. "No offense, good fellow, but you've the personal magnetism of a squid laid out on the fishmonger's table."

"None taken," mumbled Pallegin.

"Nemlezen wouldn't be any better, with his temper. Dolocium's a decade past his prime. To make us true rulers, you'll need to find someone who can induce the rabble to love us. A formidable remit, you must agree."

Luma spotted a familiar face. Urtilia Scarnetti, who had saved her from Grobaras and the Hells, hovered on the threshold between ballroom and antechamber, intent on Bonto's words.

"But here is a creature who is surely love embodied," said Bonto, turning to Luma. "Who might you be?"

Luma's hand went unbidden to the secret fold at the back of her corset, where a small dagger was sewn. "Laryss," she said. She clasped her hands in front of her. It would suit her imposture to appear flattered, if she could manage such a feat.

"Laryss who?" said Bonto.

"Laryss Isulede Zaillo."

He encroached on her position. "You lack the patina of cynicism encrusting this place. Should I presume that your family hails from Grand Arch?"

I smell to you of money, Luma thought. Feste House had fallen on rocky times, and was rumored to be selling off the furniture.

Bonto took her hand in his, bowed, and kissed her fingers. Luma turned her revulsion into an empty-headed yip of surprise.

"This chamber devotes itself to the contemplation of impossibilities," Bonto said. "Shall we seek sweeter environs, Laryss Isulede Zaillo?"

Luma played at nervousness. "I don't know if . . ."

Urtilia Scarnetti came up behind Bonto. "You harbor a form of cleverness, Bonto Feste. You should consider putting it to use."

Bonto performed a mocking, low bow. "Lady Scarnetti, your kind intervention is most . . . appreciated. Laryss, would you like to meet—" His smile collapsed as he watched Luma already slipping from the room.

The last snippet of political talk she heard on the way out was Scarnetti's: "Perhaps I can provide a synthesis of views—" There was more, but Luma had heard enough.

She found Noole in the main salon, watching its small stage, where a woman in a sapphire gown issued instructions to the leader of a lute quartet.

"How do you fare?" Noole asked.

"Eavesdropping will only get me so far. I need to scout where the guests aren't."

"I managed to have myself volunteered for a recitation. I'll hold them in rapt attention while you rummage the silverware drawers."

"How long will that last?"

"It's an epic of the founding, in which all their ancestors appear. My guaranteed salon piece. You'll have three quarters of an hour, if all goes well."

The hostess banged a brass hand-gong. "By special request," she announced, "a recitation by the acclaimed laureate of Magnimar, Noole. He will perform for us his much-admired *Indros against the Vydrarch Dragon*."

Battling her skirt, Luma bustled through a hallway. Hearing the sound of approaching maids, she ducked into an empty library until they had passed. Its windows faced the manor's back garden. Off to one side, partially obscured by a stand of rare, translucent flute trees, she noted a stone guest house. Reflected sunlight glinted briefly from its open doorway. As Luma adjusted her angle for a clearer view, the door swung shut.

Exiting the library, she found the entrance to the back promenade. Painted statues stood at even intervals beside its marble railing. Mindful of the sightline between herself and the guest house, she darted from one statue to the other, then down a set of scalloped steps.

Hunching low, she kept the marble garden wall between herself and her target. She scuttled as close as she could without exposing her position, then peered around a corner near the flute trees.

Behind her, a maid and a butler had ventured onto the promenade. The woman wrapped the man in an embrace and tried to kiss him; he tried nervously to keep her at bay. Finally she pulled him back into the manor.

A bent-over sprint took Luma to the side of the guest house and around its corner, where she wouldn't be seen from the promenade. She crouched below a shuttered, glassless window and listened. "Don't leave anything behind," she heard. The voice was a woman's—hard, low, and Korvosan-accented.

"When does this fool party end?" another voice asked—this one male, its consonants also rolling together as they did in Korvosa.

"Just be ready," said the first voice.

"Something's the matter," hissed a third voice—Korvosan again.

"What?" The first voice.

"My glass eye's acting up."

Luma heard the door bang open. If she made a dash for the garden, she'd be giving herself away. She stayed put.

A hirsute man wearing quilted under-padding turned the corner. He carried a spiked mace and kept an array of knives strapped to his leg. The glass eye he'd referred to was an emerald orb occupying his left socket. He tapped the socket's outer edge, as if prompting its magic to kick in.

Luma stuck a finger to her lips. "Sssh."

"Who the hell are you?" the shaggy man said.

Others appeared behind him, two women and three men, muscled and poised. She'd caught them in the midst of preparation; they had their weapons, but not their armor. From their accoutrements, Luma guessed their specialties: three bruisers, a devil-priestess, a backstabber, and a spell-tosser of some kind. They were proudly unkempt: the men, bearded or half-shaven; the women wreathed in matted hair. One, some, or all of them could have done with a bath.

The woman she'd heard giving the orders inside carried twin swords in an X across her back. She bent down, hands on knees, and spoke through a small, crooked mouth. "Answer his question, you ripe little doxy."

"Sshhh!" Luma insisted. "I'm drunk!"

"It's an idiot from the party," said the other woman. A silver pentagram, symbol of devotion to the devil prince Asmodeus, swung from her neck.

"I'm here with my aunt and I'm not supposed to drink," Luma said. "Can I sit here until I get better? I've never been drunk this bad before."

"These nobles are too stupid to live," said the priestess.

The one-eyed fighter reached under his padding to scratch an itch. "She might be important, though."

The backstabber drew a four-inch blade. "We were told not to be seen."

"And what did you do?" said the priestess. "You got yourself seen."

A V-shaped vein pulsed across the backstabber's forehead. "I've had about enough out of you."

Luma readied herself to grab the knife sewn next to her spine. When the backstabber reached out to slash her throat, she'd open his wrist instead. She'd kick off the shoes and dive for the garden wall. Were she lucky enough to make it over before they downed her, she would scramble off in the form of a giant centipede, wait them out, and escape later.

"Do you work for my aunt?" she asked.

The backstabber stopped short.

"What's your aunt's name?" said the leader.

"Cheiskaia. Cheiskaia Nirodin," said Luma. The lie was a gamble. It would sink her if they took her into the house. They were supposed to be hiding from the guests, and likely wouldn't risk that. Or so Luma hoped.

The priestess swore; Luma recognized it as one of the numberless obscenities of the diabolic tongue, spoken in Hell and by its acolytes. In Korvosa, as in the old Chelish empire, these had made their way into the speech of the common man. "She's the client's niece, you nitwit."

The backstabber wheeled on her, knife outstretched. "I'll slice you next, devil whore."

The leader caught his wrist and twisted the weapon out of it. She pulled the arm behind his back and slammed him into the wall. Then she bit his ear. "You've gone coop-mad, darling."

He hung his head; she slapped him. She bent over Luma again. "What are we going to do with you?"

Luma blinked. "If you don't tell her I got drunk, I won't tell her . . . what is it I'm not supposed to tell her?"

The leader hissed into her ear. "Don't tell her nothing. You didn't get drunk. You weren't out here, to get into more trouble." Her breath reeked of sardine. "You're not stupid, are you, girl? What's your name then?"

"Laryss," Luma slurred.

"I want to let you go. But you have to convince me it's the smart play, don't you?"

"I don't see what you're . . ." Luma let her sentence trail drunkenly off.

"It surprises you, does it, that your aunt keeps the likes of us stashed in her guest house?"

"No."

"No?"

Luma put her finger to her lips. "Auntie's in politics."

"Is she now?"

"That means all sorts of things you're not supposed to talk about. First thing you learn in Nirodin House. Laryss, you didn't see this. Laryss, you didn't see that. I only want somebody to like me."

"So we made a mistake, and you made a mistake, and no one will be the wiser. Yes?"

"Good," said Luma, teetering to her feet. The leader steadied her.

"Now go on back to the house and sober up somewhere else." The swordswoman swatted at her rump, hitting only fabric.

Luma walked an unsteady path back to the promenade, then eased inside.

Chapter Twenty-Three
Inside and Out

As Luma pressed shut the door from the promenade into the manor's back corridor, a voice cut through her: Iskola was near. She placed an ear to the corridor wall; her sister had to be on the other side. The muffled words carried a current of controlled menace, one Luma immediately recognized. Iskola spoke like this when conducting interrogations.

She tested the floorboard beneath her toe; it made no sound. In her left hand she still carried the foolish shoes. She set them down and edged to the library door. Finding it closed but unlocked, she judged the seal between door and frame. The sliver of light shining through it meant a loose seal. It might pull open without making a noise—unless the hinges squeaked.

Deciding to chance it, Luma inched the latch down. She eased the door an inch ajar. As the citysong had promised, the door kept its equilibrium and swung no further.

She heard Iskola: "If you want me to believe it's a coincidence, you'll have to do better than that."

The second voice was Noole's. "You and I travel in similar circles. The surprise is that we have not met before."

"Magnimar is smaller than it looks. But certain coincidences seem less random than others."

"I have had several drams of claret and may be confused," said Noole. "What am I supposed to be explaining, again?"

"Why you, whom our half-sister saw speaking with Khonderian before she murdered him, should happen to show up here?"

"Then, yes, without doubt, you have confused me," Noole said. "What is the coincidence I'm being called to account for, precisely? What does Khonderian—or, come to think of it, *you*—have to do with this place?"

"Have you seen her?"

"Who? Cheiskaia Nirodin? This is far from my first time at her salon."

"The ignorant jester pose ill becomes you, poet."

"In the interest of amity, I'll take that as a compliment to my intelligence."

"Luma. You're in league with her, aren't you?"

"In cahoots with the woman who slit the throat of my good friend Khonderian?"

"That is not an answer."

"If I were, what would I stand to gain by coming here? Aside from the free food and drink."

"At present, we are speaking together politely. Do not force me to expand my inquiries."

Luma weighed options. Had she her sickle, she could burst in and, with luck, close the distance before her sister could loose her lightning strike. With only the reach afforded her by a small knife, the need for luck trebled. Everything depended on Iskola's position in the room. Luma risked peering into the gap between door and frame. It was no good: Iskola, at the library's far end, faced the doorway. Noole sat in a wooden chair, his back to Luma. Beside Iskola stood a broad-shouldered Derexhi sentinel Luma had never seen before—a recent hire, then. His presence foreclosed any attempt at a charge. He would step into Luma's path, protecting her sister as she intoned and gesticulated the lightning into being.

"You're not proposing to harm me, are you?" Noole asked. "Me, a noted fixture of the arts? With Cheiskaia's salon in full swing? I think not."

"We can transport you elsewhere, to quiz you at fuller leisure."

"On what grounds? Unless I missed a political development, you aren't the city guards."

She reached into the sleeve of her robe, withdrawing an embroidered scarf, and advanced on Noole.

Luma burst through the door. "Uncle Noole!"

Noole jumped up from the chair and headed toward her. "Laryss. I lost track of you."

"I got so nervous with all these snobs looking me over that I had to find a place to hide. Who is this?" she said, regarding Iskola and the sentinel as if for the first time.

"This is Iskola, of the Derexhi family. You've heard of them, yes? Iskola, meet my charge for the day. Laryss Isulede Zaillo. The Zaillos are in furs. I owe her father a favor, so I thought I'd bring her along and ease her way into society."

Iskola frowned, but made no move to stop him.

Luma tugged on Noole's doublet. "Can we go? I'm tired."

"What did I tell you about comportment, dear?" Noole left the room with her. "Where are your shoes?"

Luma pointed at them. "They hurt."

Iskola came out into the corridor. "This isn't the end of our discussion, gnome."

Noole bustled down the hallway to grab the shoes. "Laryss, I told your father you weren't ready for this. Put them on."

Her fake face sulking, Luma slipped into the shoes.

Noole turned to the wizard. "What else can I tell you? I met your half-sister but once. I found the experience unpleasant, and her arrogant and threatening. Now I see that both traits run in the family."

Iskola arched her brows, as she did when momentarily stymied.

Luma waved at her. "Pleasure meeting you."

Noole took her by the arm and hauled her down the hallway toward the buzzing of the soiree guests.

Iskola's boot-heels clicked after them.

Noole reached the antechamber, where the sapphire-clad Cheiskaia Nirodin waited, arms crossed, narrow foot tapping. "A misunderstanding," Noole said. "Shall I commence the recitation now?"

"You needn't," said Cheiskaia.

"Are you certain? There seemed some enthusiasm for it." As he offered, he attempted to steer Laryss around her. Nirodin moved to block her.

"I place a high premium on the reputation of those who address my salon. Had I known you were mixed up in Khonderian's murder—"

"Fortunately for the both of us, I am not. That is the aforementioned misunderstanding."

"You were not even a listed item on the program," said Cheiskaia.

Iskola clamped her hand on Luma's shoulder. As Lady Nirodin scolded the gnome, she spoke in a voice inaudible to the crush of chatting partygoers. "You've done it, haven't you?"

"Pardon me?"

"Learned the secret of the thousand faces."

Luma kept up the pretense. "I don't understand, ma'am."

"There's a knife sewn into your corset. And despite those shoes, Luma, your gait remains distinctive. I hoped you'd spare us all a dilemma, and leave the city."

"You hoped wrongly," said Luma, dropping the assumed voice.

"You thought you could stop us, mouseling?"

"From doing what?"

"How droll of you to ask. Come along."

Luma stayed where she was. Cheiskaia Nirodin had finished berating Noole, and now, shifting her weight from side to side, directed a concerned gaze at Iskola.

"You won't try anything here."

"I won't?"

Luma broke from her half-sister, sashayed to the table, and took up a handful of grapes. Falling back into the role of Laryss, she spoke at the volume of ordinary conversation. "Some of the people here like you, but others you only *want* to like you." She shaped her mouth into an O and popped a grape into it.

Iskola addressed Noole. "You choose your friends poorly."

Noole went to Luma's side. "I've heard that about myself."

Guests, detecting the growing tension, edged away from them.

Lady Nirodin brought a false smile to her face. "Shall we all return to the main salon? The lutists are soon to start."

Certain partygoers took this as their cue to withdraw, while others stood transfixed by the prospect of a scene, and the valuable gossip that would issue from it. Among them fidgeted Bonto Feste, a guttural giggle escaping his throat.

"I was sorry to hear about your father," said Luma.

"It has been trying for all of us," replied Iskola. "By the end, he grew terribly weak."

"And your missing sister? She was weak also?"

Iskola's upper lip curled, revealing her teeth. "One might say that."

"I imagine you have much to talk about with the other guests."

Composure returned to the wizard's features. "But it is so lovely to make new acquaintances."

"Nonetheless, we won't detain you further."

Iskola bowed.

"Though we invite you to follow us, if you so desire."

"I was considering it," said Iskola, "until you made the offer."

"Oh?"

"Now I question its sincerity."

Luma essayed an ironic curtsey, her best one yet. "A pity." She turned to depart, Noole at her side. When she reached the stone walkway at the bottom of the manor steps, she tossed the shoes away, letting them sail behind a row of diligently tended bushes.

Melune jolted from readiness as they ran for the coach. She and Thaubnis climbed onto the driver's seat, urging the horses into motion. Priza held the carriage door open. Noole climbed in, and then Luma. Melune's whip cracked in the air, speeding the steeds. Her bonnet already discarded, Luma shifted to her true form and wriggled her rangy body free of the bodice, farthingale, and skirt. As she shucked the disguise of Laryss Isulede Zaillo, she told Priza and Hendregan what she'd seen at Nirodin House. When she was ready for them, Priza passed her armor pieces, and Noole helped strap her into them.

"Do we go back and set them on fire?" Hendregan asked.

"No," said Luma.

"As tempting as that may sound," Noole added.

Luma adjusted her breastplate. "There's six of the Korvosans plus Iskola, undoubtedly others who can handle themselves in a scrap, and dozens of noncombatants to get in the way. And we still can't prove that they're up to anything. If we attacked now, it's we who'd be the criminals."

The coach roared through the neighborhood, past manses and their gardens. As they turned, skidding, onto a road leading to a gate in the wall, Melune cried out from the driver's seat. "Trouble!"

Luma opened the coach door and leaned out. The Hellknight squad stood in the road, just south of the intersection.

"Run them down!" Luma shouted.

Melune cracked the reins, wringing further speed from the horses.

The Hellknights formed a line, setting their pikes. One stood ahead of the others, his head thrown back, feet spread apart, and clawed hands held at his side. A flare of fiery light, shaped like a devil's leering face, appeared before the horse nearest him.

Braying in terror, the animal reared. The careening carriage struck it, and the horse toppled sideways into its partner. Legs tangled, both horses fell into the roadway, dropping under the wheels of the still-careening coach. Its axles struck them, sending the coach pitching up and over. Luma and the other three inside bounced in the tumbling coach like dice in a cup. It impacted the road for the last time, landing on its roof. After a long slide along the cobbled street, the coach veered into a ditch, then tumbled some more. Finally it struck a garden wall, falling to pieces.

Dazed, Luma freed herself from the wreckage. Blood streamed from a head wound, sticking her hair to her scalp. Staggering toward the Hellknights, she called on the city for protection. She asked it for a gravel storm, as she'd used against Noole back at the Triodea. Pebbles swirled from the street and roadside, rising in a spiral column, then flung themselves at her advancing enemies. Stones pankled off armor plates; one of the knights dropped to his knees. Luma ripped the leather protector from the blade of her sickle and looked back to lead the others on.

They were gone.

The Hellknights raised crossbows and fired. She ran, the volley of bolts landing at her heels. Reaching the remains of the coach, she searched for signs of the others, and found none.

Of course. They'd fled, abandoning her. Why had she trusted that it would go any other way, under the heat of combat? They'd never drilled together. Their reasons for joining her ranged from slim to ambiguous. If she couldn't rely on her family, how had she been so thick-headed as to believe in them?

Crossbow bolts thunked into the shattered coach. Luma grabbed a detached door by the handle and held it up, using it as an improvised shield. Bolts pierced its side, stopping short of her throat. Hefting her sickle, she sprinted at the Hellknights. Death by combat would at least be quick.

As she neared them, they grouped themselves into a tight formation. An instant later, a bright pea of red light arced into their midst. A conflagration blossomed around them, enveloping all five of the knights. She brought up the door-shield to protect herself from its heat and brightness. A knight fell on all fours, crawling from the flames, his ornate helmet dampening his screams. Arrows struck him, finding the spaces between his smoldering armor. He slumped on the roadside, vegetation cooking as it came into contact with his hot metal shell.

Smoke cleared, revealing Maralictor Perest Sere Maximete and the remainder of his men stumbling in disarray. A distressing seared-meat aroma filled the air. The maralictor swung his blackened longsword and thudded at Luma.

A yowl rose from behind the manor wall as Priza launched himself into view, swinging his axe above his head. Thaubnis and Noole followed him into the fray.

Luma let Maximete swing his sword into the coach door. It cut easily into the wood, allowing her next trick: she twisted it, pulling his weapon from his grasp. Letting the sword fall away, she brought her sickle down on the back of his neck. Blade rang on gorget, and he spun to the ground, helplessly panting. Hendregan's fireball had scorched his lungs. Luma slashed down at him; he plucked up his sword and managed to deflect the blow.

"You were put up to this by my family?" Luma asked.

He answered by hauling himself up and swinging his sword at her. As she leapt out of range, she caught a split-second flash of the melee on the road behind her. Priza's axe smashed a foe. Thaubnis held a knight at bay with her mace. Noole teased his opponent off balance with a strange flourish of his rapier. Out in the open, the knights faced arrows and bursts of flame from the garden wall.

Maximete lunged at her; in return, she smashed her sickle down on his helmet. The Hellknight's legs buckled. With her off-hand, she tore the helmet from his head, exposing a charred visage. "You fought with fervor," said Luma. "Now yield."

He feebly raised his sword. "A Hellknight does not surrender," he said, sinking to a prone position.

Luma turned to see all but one of the Hellknights prostrated in the road. Priza swung back his axe, ready to behead the last man on his feet.

"Hold," Luma called.

Priza stayed his hand.

"Do you not surrender, either?" Luma asked the remaining Hellknight. A divine symbol swung from his belt. To her surprise, Luma saw that it was the key of Abadar, the deity her own family worshiped.

The Hellknight made no reply.

"He wants to slay you now," said Luma. "His gang bears a grudge against yours. But that's another fight. My family put you up to this, didn't they, war-priest?"

"I follow orders," he said.

"When all comes out, you will learn that the Hellknights were deceived, and that what you did today served neither justice nor the law. At such time, it will be better for me if the men dying at our feet are spared. So, war-priest, rather than giving the Shoanti what he wants, I suggest you yield, and get to work healing your comrades."

The Hellknight nodded his assent, and knelt to tend his commander.

Priza lowered his axe. "Next time, devil-knight."

"Indeed," said the man he'd spared.

Chapter Twenty-Four
Irespan

Luma and the others staggered down the road. They walked until the Hellknights were out of sight. Thaubnis groaned with each step.

"You're hurt," said Luma.

The dwarf fell into Luma, grabbing her for support. "Took one in the ribs . . ." She passed out. Luma let her down to the street. Priza bent to pick her up.

Luma scanned the nearby manors, noting a guest house not unlike the one at Nirodin House. A nod to Priza set him carrying Thaubnis across the manse's green lawn. As they limped toward it, the thrill of battle gave way to an awareness of pain. Luma's right leg hurt like hell; she looked down to see that her calf had been pierced by a crossbow bolt, just above the ankle. Welts rose on Priza's arms. Hendregan, apparently unharmed, walked backward, talking to himself.

A heavy padlock secured the guest house door. Melune pushed a thin rod into the mechanism, popped it open, and tossed the lock to the ground. After a quick check of the dusty, unfurnished premises, she urged the others in. The squad slumped against marble walls.

Priza leaned Thaubnis against the wall. After dabbing blood from Luma's scalp, Melune slid over to the dwarf. She took a bottle from her pouch, opened its stopper, and held it under Thaubnis' broad nose.

Thaubnis jolted awake. "Where are we?"

"We didn't get far," Luma said.

"Why not?"

"One of us fainted."

Thaubnis snorted and reached for her holy symbol. "Let me fix that leg," she grimaced.

"You first," Luma said. "Worry about me if you have any healing left."

Thaubnis called down the power of her god, laying her hand against her side. The air sweetened; the gentle crackle of reknitting bones issued from her body cavity.

"I thought I'd lost you all," said Luma.

"I expected you to follow us over the wall," replied her mother, handing her a vial of liquid. "But you were too disoriented."

"Then I told them to wait!" said Hendregan. "If this lot went to meet them, the knights would have spread out. With just the one of you advancing on them, they clumped together. Rarely do I get so many standing so close! All five of them, burned *hard*."

"Yes, impressive," Luma allowed.

"We are doing very well!" Hendregan said. "Who's next?"

"Brace yourself," Melune told Luma. Using a pair of tongs, she grabbed the end of the crossbow bolt and pulled it out. Luma restricted her outward agony to a single grunt. Melune pressed a cloth to the wound. Thaubnis performed another healing blessing. The two perforations on the front and back of her leg sighed and closed up.

"They were ready for us," said Melune. "How could they know?"

"Iskola can cast magic that transmits her words to distant ears," said Luma. "On certain operations, we would go in first, and she would use it to direct our squad from afar."

"When you attacked us, for example," said Priza.

Luma massaged her calf; as sometimes happened after a healing blessing, a phantom pain lingered after the wound had vanished. "Exactly so."

"So she was able to issue orders to the Hellknights while still at Nirodin House," said Thaubnis.

"Yes," said Luma. She shook her head. "Which reminds me of a second spell she would employ, in tandem with the distant whispers."

"In order to direct you from another location," said Priza, "she had to be able to see you."

"That's right."

"A spell of scrying," said Thaubnis.

"She can do this at any time?" Noole asked.

"Until this afternoon," said Luma, "she had reason to hope I'd fled the city. Now . . ."

"She could be watching us this very moment," said Thaubnis.

Priza grabbed his axe. "And calling in reinforcements."

They pulled themselves to their feet, save for Hendregan, who had already been excitedly pacing.

"We can't go through the same gate," said Luma. "There's a Derexhi squad there and I don't want to have to hurt them."

"Then we'll cut west to the edge of the bluffs," said Priza, "and go around the wall where it ends."

"With a possible scry on us," said Melune, "there's no returning to the garrison. We'd only reveal our safe house."

"With a scry on us, there's nowhere we can hole up," said Thaubnis.

Priza turned to Hendregan. "You're a magician. Scrying spells can be countered, can't they?"

The tattooed man pursed his lips. "I suppose so."

"You mean," said Thaubnis, "that they can, but not by you."

Hendregan's twitch verged on a shrug. "I might learn to wreathe us in a bubble of flame. That could burn away ethereal watchers. Or not. I am not a scholar of these things."

"Might learn?" Thaubnis asked.

Hendregan scratched his bald head. "With enough time, the working could come."

"So you can't do it," said the dwarf. "Not now, at any rate."

"Never said I could," he said, puzzled.

"There are amulets for this sort of thing," Priza said.

"You say it as if you can lay your hands on one," said Thaubnis. "By Folgrit's teats, is there not a one of you that doesn't talk in hints and riddles?"

"In my line of work, one seeks protection from arcane senses," said Priza. "My contact is not so far west of here."

"Bridgeward?" Luma asked.

"The bridge itself."

Luma and her companions reached the bridge before mid-afternoon. Its bass notes sounded from the very depths of the citysong. Like other Magnimarians, Luma took its existence for granted. Now, shaken and bruised, surveying it for the first time since all of her comfortable assumptions had been torn away from her, she considered it anew. From the depths of her aching skull, an inchoate thought nagged at her, but refused to resolve itself. What was she missing?

Only a fraction of the Irespan had survived the aeons, and this portion was said to be hollow and full of monsters. Six of its basalt pillars remained relatively intact; they reached three hundred feet up to support a section of bridge hundreds of feet long. The stumps of as many more pillars jutted from the sea. Members of the Quarrymen's Guild chipped away at these latter remnants, reaching them by means of wooden boats, which they tied to docking rafts.

By purpose or accident, the Irespan's nigh-forgotten builders had imbued its stone with an inherent magic. Wizardly artificers had found in them an ideal material for the construction of golems, among other arcane devices. On this industry the infant city had grown and thrived. Without it there would be no great families, perhaps no city itself.

Luma and Priza started for the shore.

Melune called softly after her. "Luma?"

She stopped. "Yes?"

"You might use your new gift."

"To remake my face? Because I am looked for?"

"There is a value to deception," said Melune.

"At certain times and places. But not forever." Luma considered for a moment. "I'm tired of hiding." As she and Priza departed, Melune joined the others behind a cantina serving fish cakes and sugary ale.

Priza spotted a Varisian beachcomber and beckoned him over. The two men exchanged casual greetings, referring to each other by name. Luma wondered if the Varisian lived at the camp outside the walls.

Having paid courtesy its due, Priza said, "I'm looking for Veso."

The quarryman gestured to the most westerly of the shattered pillars, out in the bay. Black grit filled the creases of his wind-burned face. "He won't want to see you, I don't imagine."

Priza bristled. "Why not?"

The beachcomber shook his head and headed back toward his pile of flotsam. "Far be it from me to mix myself up in Shoanti business."

Salt-eaten rowboats rested on the rocky shore. A wrinkled oldster, back bent by a lifetime's labor, his quarryman's badge polished to a sheen, guarded them, cane in hand.

"We're taking one of these out to a raft, and quickly back," Priza told him.

"The hell you are," the man croaked.

Luma angled herself so he could see her sickle.

Indignation drained from the graybeard's face. "Normally there is a fee for non-members."

Luma indicated her weapon. "This is my membership badge."

He pulled at the most decrepit of the boats. "Take this one."

Together Luma and Priza hauled it to the water. They rowed, Priza easing off to match Luma's lesser strength. Upon reaching the docking raft, they tied the boat to an iron ring. A bare-chested Shoanti sat with his legs in the water, striking a hammer against a chisel. He was at least as old as the guardian of the rowboats, and considerably haler. A good part of the chunk he worked to separate rested below the waterline. Luma understood the basics of the trade, as bigger stones were subject to rustling, and the Derexhi sometimes engaged to recover them. The larger the piece of Irespan stone, the higher the price per pound.

"Veso!" Priza called.

The quarryman ignored him.

Priza said something terse in Shoanti; it was, Luma guessed, a request for the amulet. She reached into her trickbag for a folded paper. It contained an ounce of soot, scraped from a chimney near the bazaar. As the two men argued, she added salt to the soot and muttered a call to the citysong, which contained and understood all speech spoken within its walls. Understanding dawned; although they spoke in Shoanti, she heard it as if they used the common Taldane they all shared.

"You still speak our language, then?" Veso was saying.

Priza jumped onto the wave-smoothed rock to face him. "You dare challenge me?"

Veso spat into the wind. "How could I challenge one who has deserted us for the weakbloods?"

"Give me the amulet before I break you in two."

"I accuse you of nothing," said Veso. "I merely repeat what I hear."

"And what do you hear, old man?"

Veso moved into him and jutted out a gnarled chin. "Your father would weep, to hear you address an elder so."

"He must do his weeping in Elysium, ever since you got him killed."

"Word is, you have set aside your wife and child to cavort with a weakblood doxy."

"When you were war-leader, you lent scant credence to the hissing of snakes."

"At least then we had a war-leader."

"I am leader by right of challenge. You are not, because I downed you."

"Some whisper that you must be a traitor."

"A traitor?"

"To your people, and to your wife."

"Then we must fight to the death, as you have accused me of a great crime. You are old, so I will give you my axe, and use only my knife to free the blood from your throat." Priza extended the weapon to him.

Neither Shoanti paid Luma heed as she again brought to bear the insight of the citysong.

Veso held up his hands. "I accuse you of nothing."

"You merely repeat the slander of others."

"I tell you for your benefit. He cannot lead who squanders the trust of his clanmates."

"My actions are only for the cause. I would explain why, if I answered to you."

"The people at least deserve to learn where you have hidden yourself. You have deserted the usual places."

"Put anyone against me you dare, Veso. Now hand over the charm; it was given to you for keeping but belongs to the people."

"For the protection of your weakblood harlot?"

Luma stepped up to him. "I allow no one to call me that." She spoke in the local tongue.

Veso flinched. "You understand the true speech? A Derexhi?"

"I understand your thoughts, old man. And while you've been calling Priza a traitor, you've been thinking of how much you hate him, because he is war-leader and your best days are gone. Because you fear he will eclipse your meager deeds."

"Nonsense!"

"You've also been picturing a purse of gold—the purse you'll earn by informing the city watch that Priza was here."

Veso's features spasmed.

"That," Luma continued, "is why you wanted him to tell you where we're hiding."

Veso grasped at empty air. "Priza, the weakblood lies!"

Priza folded his arms. "Then why do I credit her, and not you?"

Luma asked, "What is it the Shoanti do with betrayers?"

"Veso knows what we do."

"Is it the boar pit?"

"No, the boar pit affords at least some chance. A traitor's fate comes faster."

Luma turned back to Veso. "Your thoughts did not tell me who promised you that purse. Was it my family?"

Veso studied her for an instant, as if working out whether she could still see inside his head. "No," he said.

"Who?"

"The city guard. Who else?"

"Old man," said Luma, "you had better hand over that charm. Then you should thank your ancestors that Priza has greater tasks before him today, to shield his people from harm. That will give you time to get out of Magnimar and never come back."

Veso fumbled in his tunic, withdrawing a plain clay rectangle about the size of his thumb, attached as a pendant to a strip of leather. He pulled the strip over his head and handed it to Priza.

"Have you any further questions for him?" Luma asked Priza.

"One does not normally address the dead," he answered.

They stepped onto the raft and into the rowboat, leaving Veso on the basalt.

Priza took an oar and rowed. "You spared his life."

Luma rowed with him, now finding it harder to keep up with his strokes. "You meant to slay him then and there? In front of dozens of his fellow quarrymen?"

"Yes."

When they were nearly to shore, Priza said, "When he said I've lost the trust of my people by joining you. He was lying about that also, yes?"

"I can hear thoughts, sometimes see them too. I can't always tell what's true."

"But you could with Veso."

Luma nodded. "That part was not a lie."

Priza set his mouth in a hard line. "Veso has an ambitious young cousin. In my absence, he scents an opportunity."

They put the boat ashore. "Do you need to go, then, and deal with this?" Luma asked.

"No," said Priza. "A man of honor completes his undertakings."

They returned to the others, sitting down on a lopsided bench. Noole passed them fish cakes on wooden plates. Priza wolfed his down and called for more. Luma ate absently, watching as a crew used a pulley contraption to hoist a basalt block onto the back of a heavy cart. The cart's axles, though shod in iron and doubly reinforced, bowed under the weight. A dandified, wide-bellied fellow in a doublet of furs and silk, a bright yellow pillbox hat raked upon his shaven head, paced and fretted as the laborers eased it into place. The extravagance of his garb identified him as a prosperous magician or arcane artificer; the eccentricity of his violet-dyed handlebar mustache sealed the impression. He fidgeted as the mechanism jammed, sending the slab tilting out of the cart. As the workmen ran to place themselves under it, muscling it back into place, Luma saw what made it so valuable, assuming it could be transported to the Golemworks in one piece. First, at over ten feet long, six feet wide, and nearly as many feet deep, it would count among the larger chunks of Irespan stone quarried this year. Second, near the top of the slab one could clearly see the outlines of a stony face. Artificers coveted such irregularities; a golem carved from such a slab often manifested prized abilities. The golem-maker feared for the integrity of the block, and the tremendous investment he must have made in it.

That was it. Golem-makers. Golems.

Here was the piece of the puzzle that never fit.

Her mind reeled back to the raid on the golem lair. Her sisters and brothers hadn't undertaken it only to kill her. Yes, they had intended for her to die, in a way they could explain to Father and the rest of their circle. They hadn't known about the grinder. Most likely they'd intended to leave her exposed in the course of the fight, so that a golem would fell her, and none of them would bear the responsibility of the final blow. When the fight didn't work as they hoped, the grinder proved a fortuitous back-up plan, and she was thrown in.

But why golems? What did that business have to do with Khonderian, or politics, or Korvosan mercenaries?

The lord-mayor's golem bodyguard. That was the connection.

The soiree had given Luma the last pieces she needed. Iskola and her Korvosan sympathizer friends wanted the city. To control it, they needed the lord-mayor's office. The movement lacked a leader, but could find one in Arrus. Where the faction's old lions were thought of as weary, decadent, unpopular, the Ushers might embrace a man like Arrus: handsome, heroic, with a cocky, bully-boy touch. That he had only just been sworn in as a councilor worked in his favor. It made him a fresh presence other factions might rally around. They could look at him without remembering an old slight or lingering squabble. Behind him, he boasted another, greater asset: Iskola, who understood intrigue. Too forbidding to seek power herself, she would weigh the deals, and let Arrus complete them.

That was the purpose behind Iskola's use of the squad to place other councilors in her debt. Even as Randred still lived, she'd been building the alliances she'd need when he was out of the way, and Arrus in his council seat. As but one faction among one constituency, the imperials could not elevate him. With the right allies, they might pull it off.

But none of this mattered with Haldemeer Grobaras still breathing. All the factions danced to his tune. No one dared make the first move against him. Perhaps a decade from now, his grip would falter, and someone would ease him out. But a decade was a long interval, one in which Arrus would go gray, collect enemies, and become one among many amid the bickering din of the council chamber. By the time Grobaras wore out his welcome, Arrus would be as pale and diminished a figure as any.

So they had to kill the lord-mayor. Her father's murder, and their attempt to kill her, had been necessary preludes. Randred, because Arrus had to take his council seat. She, because she'd been asking too many questions. But the death this all hinged on was Grobaras's.

With him gone, other would-be mayors would suddenly find themselves already running behind. While they had resigned themselves to the long continuance of the Grobaras regime, Iskola had her allies in place, her candidate ready.

There was no guarantee Arrus would win, but the game began with the odds stacked his way.

Provided Haldemeer Grobaras could be assassinated. He held two trumps against this. One, the enchantment that turned back arrows and crossbow bolts. Two, the golem of gears and brass, which would, if defeated, explode in a rain of deadly shrapnel. Since its acquisition, and the spreading word of this capability, not a single close-up attempt had been made on the lord-mayor's life. As hated as he might be, none of his aspiring killers wished to die alongside him. You might hire fools to try it, but fools would fail.

The Korvosans in Cheiskaia Nirodin's guest house had not struck Luma as fools. That had to be why Iskola and her allies had brought them here. That's why they were supposed to stay out of sight, first at the Grand Arch squat, then at the Nirodin manse. They would kill Grobaras and fade away, leaving their patrons to maneuver for his position. But they would research his bodyguard first, discover the golem trick, and decline to strike. Unless their patrons supplied a way around it.

And that's where the golems came in. The raid on the golem workshop was only incidentally about money to spend on political favors. Iskola hadn't been looking for the dampening ring of Laurdin Iket merely to sell it. She'd played it as incidental, a bonus if they should happen to find it, when its recovery was the entire reason for the raid.

Iskola must have been surer of the device's presence in the workshop than she'd let on. Maybe one of the salvagers made the wrong inquiry at the library, and word got back to Iskola through her various arcane contacts. The details of that were immaterial. What mattered was what she intended to do with the artifact now that she had it: to counter, control, or deactivate Haldemeer Grobaras's clockwork golem.

And Khonderian? Iskola feared that he'd stumbled onto the Korvosans. He might have been onto them, or not; it didn't much matter. Iskola decided that he was too dangerous a piece to leave on the board. So one of her siblings—perhaps Ontor, perhaps Ulisa—had killed him. When they found that Luma still lived, they went back to plant evidence, to keep her on the defensive.

Luma reviewed the details, trying to think like her sister. They all fit. It was the sort of plan she'd cook up—calculating, manifold, hinged on an arcane detail, and performed at a remove.

The Korvosans were packing up. They might merely be headed to a third safe house, but she had to assume otherwise. If they were ready to strike, when would it happen?

Of course. The Arvensoar rededication ceremony. To instill maximum shock and dismay, they would have the lord-mayor killed at a public event. Other contenders for the lord-mayor's seat would be unable to openly lobby for it during the period of stunned, reverential mourning that would doubtless ensue. Meanwhile, Iskola would have her factions already lined up, giving Arrus yet another head start.

Was this truth, or conjecture? Attuning to the citysong, Luma heard its keening distress, its drums pounding with portent. An upheaval was imminent, one that would affect Magnimar's every district, from Alabaster to Rag's End.

She leapt from the bench. If they made good speed, they might reach the base of the Arvensoar just in time.

Chapter Twenty-Five
Parade Ground

Luma explained as they ran. There was no time to waste on side streets, or on hiding, so she led them along the widest, most obvious route, the Avenue of Sails. Now she changed herself; to risk being recognized and stopped at this stage would be an unforgivable act of hubris. She reached into the citysong to find its catalog of bodies and faces. It had to be someone who might conceivably rush along in this improbable company. Her perceptions rocketed to the sellsword exchange, a few blocks west in the bazaar. There she found a callow, pox-scarred warrior, his jaw set in a perpetual overbite. She borrowed a semblance of his face, softening its distinctiveness. From the man's lanky companion she modeled her new body, which she grew into as she ran, her limbs growing longer, her hips thinning, her already-modest bosom disappearing.

"Disconcerting!" shouted Noole, struggling to keep up.

Sensing trouble, carters and pedestrians alike moved over to let them pass, clearing a wide swath down the middle of the avenue. An almost visible wave of anxiety coursed ahead of them. A horse reared up, panicked, dislodging its rider from his saddle. Behind it, a carriage painted in the gaudy colors of a rising merchant house backed up into a cart stacked with barrels.

They sprinted along the avenue's sharp turn, from north-south to northeast-southwest. Two urchins pointed at them, staring, until an older orphan pulled them from sight.

At a point parallel to the Arvensoar, they turned to the south. From here, Luma knew, any route would channel them through narrower, crowded streets. She checked the sun's position in the sky. They still stood some chance of reaching the plaza before the ceremony began. All depended on the planned timing of the Korvosan attack.

Whistles shrieked after them. Glancing back, Luma saw guards in Derexhi uniform demanding a halt. Hendregan reversed to face them.

"Don't hurt them," Luma said.

"Hmp," replied Hendregan, loosing a glowing bead. It arced up into the air, seeming to hang in the air over the sentinels' heads for a split second. They scattered. The bead dropped onto empty cobblestones, then effloresced into a wall of flame. Hot stones flew up into the air and pelted back down again. Luma and the others plunged on, the whistles silenced. The family's hirelings had orders to intervene on behalf of public safety, but these only went so far. They were not paid enough to place themselves in the path of a second such spell.

"We may face a fight when we get there," Luma panted. "Hope you're not using up your best magics!"

Hendregan laughed. "That was an illusion only!"

Onlookers pressed themselves into alcoves or hopped up onto stoops as the group barreled past Lowcleft shops. A white-bearded man drew his sword but hugged it close to his chest. Up ahead, a juggler let his clubs fall into the street as he withdrew to the shelter of an alleyway.

The exertion caught up with them as they reached Lantern Row, where the workshops of lampmakers clustered. Luma reached into the citysong, letting its fearful drumbeats fill her. She harmonized her footfalls to their beat, and found the strength to speed up again. The others increased their pace in response: first Melune, then Priza and Thaubnis, with Noole and Hendregan lagging a few steps behind.

Crowds thickened on Hourglass Lane, a few streets away from the parade grounds. Carriages parked on either side reduced the street to a narrow passageway. Hawkers pushing carts stocked with salted nuts, colorful ribbons, or clay statues of the Arvensoar obstructed it further.

"Scatter them!" Luma yelled. She jumped onto a carriage roof, whirling her sickle. Priza copied her, darting along the opposite chain of empty coaches, axe held overhead. Terrified citizens squeezed out of sight, letting the others pass.

Reaching the last of the coaches, Luma vaulted down. A broad-shouldered young man stood blocking her path, dull features arrested in confusion, a mace held at half-alert. She reached into the citysong, drawing forth a remembrance of V'lkta, the lizard-woman stevedore who saw conspiracies around every corner. Green scales covered her skin. Spines jutted from her head as it elongated into a snout filled with reptilian teeth. She opened this freshly formed mouth and hissed, unfurling a long, pink tongue. The dumbfounded man yawped and sank to his knees. With clawed, webbed feet, Luma kicked him aside. Lashing her iguana-like tail, she bounded into the throng, stampeding celebrants left and right.

Hourglass Lane emptied, then filled again, from its opposite end. Panicked people now surged into the street from the Arvensoar end, Luma's destination. A woman in gown and wimple wailed, a crossbow bolt jutting from her hand. Two stumbling porters carried an unconscious grandee, a red blot spreading through his tunic.

The attack had already begun.

Unsure of her coordination in lizard form, Luma allowed it to melt away. A burst of dizzying energy struck her as her body relaxed into its familiar shape. Thrusting her hand into her trickbag, she once again borrowed the innate talent of a scuttling cricket and launched her body onto the wall of the nearest shop. Crawling horizontally from storefront to storefront, she bypassed the press of fleeing celebrants, continuing on to the verge of the Arvensoar parade grounds.

A scene of chaos awaited, bounded by emptied bleachers populated only by a handful of trampled or injured onlookers. Behind the bleachers cowered dozens of spectators too terrified to flee. Among them huddled guests from the Nirodin soiree. Luma spotted Sutia Turos, Bonto Feste, and the skeptical matron Histia. Bonto's nose had been broken; with rapier out, he interposed himself between the ladies and the fray.

Other unfortunates, dead or nearly so, had made it off the bleachers but no further. The majority were ordinary soldiers. The sprawled heaps in which they lay testified to the Korvosans' might.

The lord-mayor and members of his bodyguard sprawled motionless on the cobblestones. Three of their comrades still stood, wounded and weaving, backs against the Seacleft.

Of the Korvosans, one had already fallen. One of the bruisers splayed near the golem, his head pulped.

It steamed and clanked, puffs of green vapor spitting from a tear in its copper breastplate. The spell-tosser darted around it, narrowly evading its flailing metal fists. In her hand she clutched the dampening ring of Laurdin Iket. She ducked and weaved in search of an opening that would allow her to slap it onto the creature. Luma presumed that it had been the dead bruiser's job to draw the golem's attack while the magician attached the ring. If so, he had succeeded only too well.

The golem grabbed the woman, pulling her tight to its chest. A bloody mist sprayed up between them. The woman screamed and jerked, then fell away from the construct. Saw blades, once hidden in its chest, had popped up to shred flesh and bone. The spell-tosser slumped to the square, slain, her ruined chest cavity laid bare for all to see.

The golem stopped moving, its exposed saws whirring to a slow halt. Stuck to its back was the dampening ring. Iskola's recovered item had done its work. The golem was defeated but not destroyed, and so would not be sending its signature rain of lethal shrapnel blasting through the plaza.

The remaining Korvosans advanced on the surviving bodyguards. The two-sworded woman charged them, grabbing a bodyguard by the arm and wheeling him into the fray. The backstabber plunged a blade deep into his spine.

Red-black energy wailed around the devil-priestess's hand. She lunged at a bodyguard. The hellforce screamed like the souls of the damned as it entered his chest. He clutched his heart and sank to his knees.

The hirsute Korvosan swordsman with the emerald orb in his eye socket launched himself upon the third bodyguard, thrusting expertly into the space between his armor's breast- and backplates.

The swordswoman scanned the crowd's edges. Whatever she searched for, she didn't find. Her forehead creased, annoyance shading into fear. Luma didn't have to read her mind to guess what the matter was: they'd been promised a means of escape, and it hadn't arrived.

Haldemeer Grobaras groaned. The shaggy warrior's head pivoted toward him. He limped toward the lord-mayor, sword held for a downstroke. His upraised arm gave Luma a clear view of the Shoanti emblem he wore. The others had them, too.

As he prepared his blow, the shaggy man bellowed a common Shoanti curse, one that had so bled into the local slang that everyone knew it. Others, Luma thought, would not hear Korvosa in its vowels.

Luma had her sling ready, but before she could fire it, arrows pierced the shaggy man's chest. He glared down at them, gasped, and dropped to one knee.

For an instant, Luma assumed that the arrows were Melune's. But the heads protruded through his back, meaning that the shots had come from the parade ground's far side.

From the south and the west, Luma's siblings arrived. Arrus charged the shaggy man, sword held out. Terribly wounded, Shaggy still managed to stand and step away from the lord-mayor, bracing himself. At the last minute, Arrus danced to the side, avoiding the frontal assault his actions had promised. Instead, he dodged behind his opponent, slashing into the man's leg. Grunting, the dying man attempted a counter-strike. Arrus anticipated it, smashing the weapon from his hand. Words died in the Korvosan's open mouth as Arrus chopped at the side of his head. His helmet flew off, releasing his dark mane of hair. Arrus pushed his shield under his enemy's chin, choking him. The hirsute man's legs gave out, and Arrus swung his sword, half-decapitating him. The emerald orb flashed, then turned the color of soot.

A bolt of blue energy heralded Iskola's entrance: it passed through the devil-priestess, throwing her against the cliff side.

To the sound of flapping robes, Ulisa lofted into the fray, her bare, outstretched right foot thudding into the swordswoman's chest. The stone cliff magnified the echoed sound of cracking breastbone.

Luma restrained an ingrained urge to call out as the Korvosan backstabber crept up on Arrus. Her warning proved unneeded: Arrus pivoted, smashing his foe in the face with the butt of his sword.

The devil-priestess, her cloak still smoking, shuddered into the square, pronouncing an invocation to her diabolic masters. Before dread force could coalesce around her hand, a series of darts peppered her.

Ontor, having thrown them, loped into the square, shortsword held low. A length of velvet bunting, meant for the ceremony, curled around his boot.

A Korvosan warrior bulled at him, only to be felled by bursts of invisible power launched at him by Iskola. Good, thought Luma. Let them expend their magic.

Haldemeer Grobaras stirred, moaning incoherently. Eibadon, clutching his golden key of the city god, hustled toward his still-prone form.

Luma grasped the scheme's final twist. Iskola's betrayals didn't end with her and their father. She'd destined the Korvosans for a double-cross as well. In lieu of the promised getaway, the squad had arrived to put them down. Before a stupefied audience of dignitaries, Arrus would drape himself in glory, saving Grobaras from his attacker. To complete the plan, they'd have to see to it that the lord-mayor expired from his injuries—which Eibadon could easily arrange. Witnesses would see him perform a healing blessing. In fact he would secretly reverse the prayer's effect to one of mortal harm.

A faint ripple of divine energy flared around his right hand. With his left, he pulled open the lord-mayor's doublet and tunic.

An arrow struck the backplate of his armor, shattering on impact. With a split-second glance, Luma traced the missile's trajectory: from a perch on a nearby rooftop, Melune was sniping into the fray.

The arrow blow left Eibadon unfazed. His glowing hand rose up, the golden key held like a lightning rod.

Luma placed a stone bullet in her sling and hurled it at him. It struck him in the temple, denting his helmet. He groaned, interrupting the final syllables of his spell. The nimbus of life-taking energy around his hand dissipated.

On the street below, she heard Priza bellow a Shoanti war cry. Behind him ran Noole, with his rapier, and Thaubnis, gripping her warhammer.

With the last twitch of her insect magic, Luma bounded into the fray. Sickle held aloft, she ran straight for Arrus.

The Korvosan backstabber, who stood between them with his back to Luma, saw Arrus tense. After a feint to put Arrus on the defensive, he pivoted to see what was coming his way.

But the feint had not done its work; Arrus butted him in the shoulder, knocking him off balance. Arms in the air, the man wheeled to stay upright, giving Arrus the opening he sought.

Arrus's sword plunged through the hardened padding covering the backstabber's side, stabbing into his liver. His fall to the cobblestones pulled Arrus's sword free.

In a mesmerizing, intersecting pattern, the swordswoman whirled her twinned blades, advancing on Ulisa, who responded by bending herself backward. By a secret of her strange fighting arts, Ulisa kept her footing as her body, from the knees up, unfolded itself like a scroll. As the blades whizzed overhead, she seemed to almost hover, perpendicular to the ground. She let herself fall entirely onto her back, then defied gravity to roll back to her feet. As she did so, she whipped a length of rope from her shoulder. Weighted on the far end, it shot through the air, wrapping around the swordswoman's blades, disrupting their rhythm. They clattered together and bounced into their wielder's face.

The Korvosan elbowed aside the incoming blades, warding off serious injury.

While she was still distracted, Ulisa directed a sharp kick at the side of her knee.

The Korvosan's calf buckled. She dropped to her side, leg shattered.

Meanwhile, Ulisa had retracted her weighted rope, and now threw it again, wrapping it around the Korvosan's neck. Her bare feet scarcely touching the ground, she charged across the square at Luma's companions. By the time she was halfway there, the rope tightened completely, breaking the swordswoman's neck.

The swordswman's demise left only one member of the Korvosan party: the devil-priestess who squared off against Ontor.

Releasing the rope, Ulisa reached Priza, who put all of his strength behind a wide swing of his axe. She barely evaded the blow, then, before he could raise his weapon again, surged at him with reaching hands. Her right hand, palm flattened, tapped the left side of his face, pushing it into a position facing her. As part of the same seamless movement, her left hand, its index and middle fingers pressed together, precisely jabbed his neck, between larynx and carotid.

Priza convulsed, eyes rolling back into his head. He staggered back into the square, juddering toward Ontor and the devil-priestess. He raised his axe as if to strike at one or both, then dropped it. He clutched at his throat, then his chest. His arm went rigid. Unable to cry out, he fell back onto the cobblestones.

Slippers whickering across the plaza, Ulisa followed him, hand contorted into an odd, stabbing shape, ready to strike him again.

There was no need. Priza expired, killed by Ulisa's exotic death-stroke.

Two long arrows sprouted from Ulisa's chest. She fell on top of Priza, two enemies joined together in death.

Across the plaza, Arrus slashed at Luma; she brought up her sickle to parry his blows. She let him tire himself against her, waiting for him to step wrong so she could turn a parry into a hooking scrape of her blade.

"You've grown more skilled, mouseling," Arrus grunted.

"More determined," said Luma, taking her opportunity to rip his helmet from his head with the tip of her sickle. A red line of blood opened on his face, reaching from brow to hairline.

Noole joined the battle between Ontor and the devil-priestess, scrabbling back as she aimed her spiked mace at him. "It's him I'm after, you fool!" he cried.

Ontor drove a dagger into the priestess's back. She staggered at him, pulled onward by the weight of her weapon. He grabbed her and pushed her between himself and the tip of Noole's rapier.

"Who the devil are you people?" Ontor asked him.

"Friends of your sister's," said Noole.

"She doesn't have any friends."

"Palpably untrue," said Noole, threading an unexpected rapier thrust past the devil-priestess and into Ontor's abdomen.

Ontor gritted his teeth, then stepped into the priestess's mace-blow. He skittered around her, grabbing the hilt of the dagger still stuck in her back, and pulled it out, twisting. The priestess crumpled at his feet.

Ontor stepped free of her body. With dagger and sword, he erected a guard against Noole's probing stabs.

Over by the mayor, Eibadon shook off the pain of the slingstone, only to be tackled by Thaubnis. The dwarf hammered at his face and shoulders. He rolled her off him, kicking her in the ribs. Freeing his club from his hip, he made to return the favor, trying to pile onto her. Sacrificing her grip on her own warhammer, she knocked the club from his hands. They grappled, he trying to press his thumbs into her eye sockets, she attempting to throttle him.

Near the bleachers, Iskola sought an angle from which to aim a spell. Arrows veered wildly as they neared her, falling yards short of a hit. Looking to their source, Luma saw Melune free-climbing her way down a storehouse wall.

No longer threatened by sniper fire, Iskola ran toward Melune, preparing a spell. She stepped over a body, barely taking note of his scorched robe and arcane tattoos.

Howling gleefully, Hendregan grabbed her ankle, yanking her off balance, disrupting her gestures and nullifying her spell. "Explain yourself!" she demanded.

"Heh!" he replied, his hand bursting into flame. Smoke poured from her as the flesh of her lower leg blackened. From a fold inside her robe she produced a six-inch blade, which she used to hack at his wrist. Hendregan let go, muttering contentedly in the language of fire. With her good leg, Iskola kicked at his head. He jumped up; she held her knife out to stop him. The fire magician sidled into her, ignoring her slashes, and wrapped her in a bear hug. "You are a sorcerer, too," he giggled.

Iskola, arms trapped, pushed her elbows out, but he was too strong for her. "A wizard," she gasped.

"Are you fireproof, too?" Hendregan asked. As she fought his grasp, he looked down at her burned leg, which now ran red as blood fled the wound. "No, I suppose you're not."

Blue flame whooshed around him, enveloping them both from head to toe. Under its roar, he was saying something about not being human, not entirely. Contrary to his words, his tissue charred as easily as hers, the tattoos vanishing as it was consumed. Iskola's robes ignited; her lacquered hairdo crackled and turned to ash.

Though Hendregan's lips and tongue had seemingly burned away, he remained inexplicably capable of speech. The sounds were formed by the hiss of the flames themselves. "You murdered your father," the fire said. "You tried to murder your sister. We are mad, but we wouldn't do that."

The flames sputtered away. Charred but inexplicably animated, Hendregan sat on the cobblestones, legs crossed, soot clouds billowing from him.

Iskola curled up beside him and, with burned-out lungs, breathed her last.

Across the square, Ontor drove his dagger between Noole's ribs. The gnome fell against the Seacleft wall.

Thaubnis clouted Eibadon on the temple with her warhammer. He slumped into unconsciousness.

The dwarf rose, ready to join Luma against Arrus. She started at a hand placed on her shoulder. She turned, swiping her warhammer.

Melune plucked it casually from her grasp, then held it out to her, handle first. "Go heal Noole, then the lord-mayor. Luma will wish to accomplish this herself."

Thaubnis nodded and crossed to the cliff wall, where Noole, paling, pressed a hand against his injured side.

Arrus, feinting furiously, had Luma on her heels. His face tightened into a humorless grin. "You had me worried for a moment, mouseling," he said. "You opened strongly, but have faded."

"The rest are defeated," said Luma. "Give up."

Arrus snorted. "And go to the gibbet? I am Arrus Derexhi. I do not surrender. You should know that, mouseling." He smacked her sickle, further notching its jagged, scythelike blade.

"Say that again," said Luma.

"What?"

"That name you call me."

Arrus laughed. "Mouseling?"

He came at her. She hooked her sickle around his sword hand and pulled it upward, half-severing his hand at the wrist. He went down screaming, gore pooling around him. Luma placed her foot on his forearm. "You'll need a clean wound for my healer to staunch the bleeding," she said, completing the amputation.

Chapter Twenty-Six
The Past

Thaubnis laid the healing blessing of Magrim upon Noole, and then the lord-mayor. Grobaras insisted on dragging himself to the bleachers, where he sat in a shaken approximation of dignity.

Soldiers had arrived from the Capital District. Luma wondered why those garrisoned in the Arvensoar had not come out to defend the lord-mayor. A pounding emanated from the other side of its great door, which was closed. Grobaras's men tried fruitlessly to open it. Someone—the Korvosan spell-tosser, most likely, or perhaps Iskola—had magicked it shut.

"Can your wizard fix that?" Grobaras asked Luma.

Hendregan still sat cross-legged in the middle of the parade ground. His burned flesh had healed itself. Luma thought that his tattoos had returned in a different pattern than before, but could not remember them with the precision needed to say for sure.

"He does not seem one for fixing things," Luma said.

"Hmp." Grobaras nodded. "Well, this city crawls with magicians. We'll find someone to pry it open." He turned for a better look at Luma. "You're different than I last saw you."

Luma sat down next to him. "When you were set to have me tortured, that is?"

"Ah," he said. "I need brandy to quell my nerves. Yes, that is an action I took. When I was a victim of deception."

"Quite so," said Luma.

"Never let it be said that Haldemeer Grobaras forgets a favor."

"I didn't do it for you."

"Don't swat a man's hand when he holds it out in apology. Of the entire Derexhi clan, it appears that you are the only one who did not mean me harm."

"Nor did my father," said Luma. "That's why they poisoned him."

"Which of the traitors survives?" Grobaras asked.

"My sisters are both dead. My brothers live."

"Bring them before me," the lord-mayor commanded.

A bandage covered the stump where Arrus's hand had been severed. Dark bruises encircled Eibadon's eyes. His hands had been bound behind his back, and a gag placed in his mouth, to stop him from calling down any divine magic.

"Isn't there a third one?" Grobaras asked.

Thaubnis approached, addressing Luma and ignoring the lord-mayor. "We still haven't found Ontor. I talked to some of the onlookers. They said he slipped away after stabbing Noole."

"It is imperative that this third traitor be found," said Grobaras.

"I agree," said Luma.

"I'll detail a unit of the city guard to track him."

"Don't bother," said Luma. "I'll take care of it."

"Your travails have not made you any more politick, I see. Who else should I round up?"

Luma shrugged, as if the question was of negligible interest.

Noole, who had been sitting in the row behind them, piped up. "Cheiskaia Nirodin, for one," he said. "There will be others in her circle. You will have to determine which of their patrons merely wanted you out of office, and which ones helped target you for assassination. Urtilia Scarnetti might or might not be among that number."

Grobaras sweated, as if wound-fever was settling upon him. "Scarnetti? That will be difficult. Too many allies. Nirodin should be easier. Though still not without cost."

"You take an attempt on your life with greater equanimity than I," Luma said.

"Yes, yes, very impolitick indeed. It is a good thing, then, Luma, that you are a bastard, and hence unable to inherit the Derexhi council seat."

Melune, who sat beside Noole, spoke. "She is no bastard."

"Naturally, I mean the word in its legal, descriptive sense," Grobaras squirmed. "No insult was implied or should be inferred."

The rangy elf rose and stepped down one row on the bleachers to sit beside him. The gesture's casualness communicated a subtle menace. "I am Luma's mother, and was married to her father at the time of her birth."

Grobaras coughed into his hand, spattering it with red-flecked spittle. "Personally, I couldn't care two rotten figs for the pretensions of puffed-up pseudo-nobles. But naturally there are those who would expect me to subject to serious scrutiny the convenient statements of mysterious elven snipers."

Melune plucked a pristine rectangle of white linen from an inner fold of her doublet and reached over to dab at the lord-mayor's bloodied chin. He flinched.

"Surely," said Melune, "you have the power to vouch for the veracity of testimony."

"You were truly Randred's wife?" Grobaras asked.

Luma sat motionless, gulping, as if she had stumbled onto the working of a spell, and the slightest twitch on her part might end its magic.

Melune answered Grobaras's question: "I was."

Did the words crack with regret, or was this another pose, drawn from her endless well of false identities?

"Under what circumstances did the two of you come to wed?" Grobaras asked.

"We were young," said Melune. "He was not yet head of his house. I had but freshly embarked on my own vocation."

"And what was that?"

"Let's leave that to inference."

"I cannot vouch for the truth of your words if you say nothing."

"I swear," said Melune, "that whatever facts I conceal, I conceal for your protection."

"A family trade?" Grobaras asked.

"That could be said."

Grobaras took the cloth from her and dabbed his forehead with it. "Might I venture to guess, then, that were it this family that had been engaged to kill me, and not these Korvosans, that I would not now be breathing?"

Melune contemplated before answering. "This family would not have attempted it in public, for one thing."

"They would have come masked in the night, to slash my throat with a sawtoothed blade, so that I might drown in my own blood?"

"That might be their preferred way of doing it."

"I interrupted your tale. If Randred was not yet a councilor, he would have at the time been head of the Derexhi top squad."

"Yes," said Melune.

"So the two of you met as you pursued your respective vocations?"

"You tell the story, lord-mayor. When you guess incorrectly, I shall interrupt."

"Some testimony this is." Grobaras balled up the cloth, which was already soaked with his sweat. "Very well. There was a person whose life your family was engaged to end, and Randred's was engaged to protect."

"Go on," Melune said.

"But this individual's identity is otherwise tangential to the tale?"

Melune nodded.

Grobaras smiled, as if warming to the challenge of the game. "Though, also as a mere point of trivia, it was your family who ultimately succeeded, and his that failed."

"My silence on that point cannot be taken as confirmation."

"Here you will have to help me, sniper. Did Randred know who you were, at first? No, he couldn't have. You were posing as someone else. Are you posing as someone else now?"

"I am Luma's mother."

"So you met Randred in the course of this case. He was unaware of your family connections. You did not tell him. Not until later. You were young. You were drawn to one another, as sometimes happens, the line between enemy and kindred spirit being notoriously thin. You fell into one another's arms. This one here, with the trembling look—she was conceived. You could have, and should have, run away. Your people would scarcely approve of such a union. Of any union, except among its own tight circle. Yes?"

"I have not interrupted you."

"But you didn't run away. You turned your back on everything. Betrayed the edicts of your . . . group. Why?" Grobaras leaned back, then forward. "Oh. Yes. Of course. For the first and only time, you saw another life for yourself. Not with your family, but with his. An old story. And so you married."

"This is more than you need to hear."

"Hear? I'm not hearing anything, aside from the sound of my own voice. Melodious though it may be. To weigh the tale's credibility, I must perceive its full outlines. Randred's father . . ." Grobaras turned to Luma. "He was also called Arrus, was he not?"

"Yes," said Luma.

"Old Arrus would have disapproved of any surprise union. But with one of your background? That he forbade, surely."

"He did," Melune breathed.

"So, one, you eloped, and two, you did not tell him who you were. But by this time Randred did know. When he figured it out—he did figure it out, yes?"

"Continue," said Melune.

"You didn't tell him but he worked it out. Maybe you gave him what he needed to work it out. That bit doesn't matter."

"It does not."

"So," Grobaras went on, "he learned, he was shocked, he pledged to stick by you. But then your family found out. They didn't come to him, or to Old Arrus. Because if they'd threatened the Derexhi, the Derexhi would have got their backs up. Sworn to fight for you, no matter what the cost. Warrior reputation, family honor, sheer cussedness and so on and so forth? Yes, I'm right again."

Melune folded her hands in her lap. "Even those who despise you say you are a clever man, Lord-Mayor."

"Thank you. They didn't come to them. They came to you. Wait, this is where your story fails. The Red—that is, *your family*—they do not forgive. They would not have gone to you and warned you to leave him. This group, they would have slain you without a word, appearing suddenly in their insect masks, erasing you from the world forever. This won't do. Your narrative does not hold."

For the second time a tension pushed through Melune's composure. "This is a story with three fathers in it," she said.

"Ah. Let's see." Grobaras counted on his fingers. "Randred's a father. His father is Old Arrus. And then . . . your father. Yes. He falters. Despite his own vows, he loves you. He can't do it. He commands authority in the group, doesn't he? So he expends it on your behalf. He brokers an arrangement. Your life is to be spared. But you must still pay a price. And so must he, I imagine.

"You're not gainsaying me. I'll go on. The price is this—the marriage must not only end, it must be obliterated, wiped from the record."

"That is *a* price."

"The price is, you lose your daughter, the issue of the loathsome union. You agree to disappear. You leave a note to Randred. He must pretend you never existed, that the marriage never existed. He must never so much as speak your true name." Grobaras turned again to Luma. "Melune, that is not a name you ever heard before. Yes?"

Luma nodded. "I always heard a different name."

"An invented name. Melune the murderess-for-hire could not be the mother of Luma Derexhi. Because if word of this were to circulate, it would be known that the Red Mantis assassin cult exercises mercy when its edicts are disobeyed."

"That can never be said," Melune said.

"This is why I did not say it," said Grobaras. "If you had not gone along, they would have taken your husband's life. And his father's, too. But this is not why you agreed."

"It is, in part, why I agreed," said Melune.

"You agreed because they would have killed the baby."

Melune straightened her spine. "Does the tale hold water, then?"

"You could still be lying about the marriage. That's the important detail to the matter at hand."

"Then you must decide whether you think I am lying."

"You're not lying because you said nothing and I heard nothing and absolutely seek no contact with the people of whom we do not speak. Ergo, you must have been legally married to Randred at the time of Luma's birth, making her clear heir to Derexhi House, its properties, contracts, accounts, and obligations. As I will attest and specify, should any dare challenge her."

"It is not good for me to be here." Melune moved down from the bleachers. She turned back to face Luma. "I am sorry," she said. She strode to the nearest street and then, with an instantaneous change of circumstances that must have been aided by some sort of enchantment, was gone.

"Consider that my reparation," the lord-mayor said to Luma, "for the aforementioned threats of torture, unmerited arrest, and so forth."

"I don't follow you, Grobaras."

A team of city guards ran into the plaza, bearing vials of healing liquor. Grobaras tried to rise, but fell faint. Luma caught him.

"You wouldn't have wrung all that from her on your own," he said.

"I think you're right."

"Should it not go without saying, you are also absolved of Khonderian's murder. It is another crime they shall hang for." He indicated Arrus and Eibadon, of whom the arriving guards now took custody. Grobaras surveyed the tumble of corpses in the square before them. "Be of cheer, if cheer you are capable of. You are alive, and free, and this is done.

"No," said Luma, "it isn't."

Chapter Twenty-Seven
Home

A pair of sentinels Luma did not recognize stood guard at the Derexhi House gate. The two of them, a sharp-jawed woman and a ruddy-faced man, jolted from inattention as they caught sight of her. She pulled a sword; he readied his pike. Luma removed her sickle from the strap at her back, leaving the leather guard on the blade.

"Stand aside," she said.

"You're Luma Derexhi, aren't you?" asked the man.

"Yes, and I've no wish to harm you. You'll lower your weapons."

"We've orders to apprehend you, should you come here."

"You will fail if you try," said Luma. "Moreover, your orders are void. Those who gave them to you are dead or awaiting execution. You answer to me now."

The woman eased back a step. "We do?"

"You do. Try my patience no further."

"Shouldn't we ask for proof of this?" The man directed his question more to his partner than to Luma.

"Your continued employment, not to mention your lives, depends on your immediate obedience," Luma said.

The woman sheathed her sword; the man dropped his pike and opened the wrought-iron gate. Luma stepped through it. "Now pick up that pike and stand like proper guardsmen," she said.

She marched to the front door and hauled it open. The servant Bhax appeared from the ballroom, shoes whiffing across its tiles. He crossed the foyer threshold, holding in one hand a silver candlestick and in the other a polishing rag. Both plummeted to the floor, the candlestick thudding onto the rug.

"Do not cry out," Luma said.

Bhax stammered.

"You will take me to Yandine, doing nothing to alert her to our approach."

He showed no sign of having understood her. "Miss Luma, you must get out of here before they get back."

"They will not be back. I am the heir now."

Bhax paled. "What happened, Miss Luma?"

"You will address me as 'Mistress.' Now do as I say."

"Mistress—that is, Yandine—is poorly this morning. She is in her chamber."

"Take me to her."

Trembling, Bhax crossed to the grand staircase and dawdled his way up it, with Luma behind him. He took her to the door.

"Now you may announce me," Luma said, loud enough to be heard on the other side of the door.

Bhax tapped on the door. "Mil—Mis—Luma is here to see you, milady." He darted away from it, as if shocked by contact with the wood.

"Call the guards!" Yandine shouted.

"There will be none of that," said Luma, thrusting open the door. Yandine sat up in her bed, wearing her nightshift, her hair in disarray. A reddened nose and eyes confirmed her state of ill health.

"What has happened?"

Luma took a spot at the foot of her bed. She still had her sickle out. "Iskola and Ulisa are dead. Arrus and Eibadon have been arrested for treason and will see the gallows. Ontor has fled. I'd ask you if you've seen him, but your shock appears genuine."

"I don't—I don't—Iskola, dead you say? And Ulisa? How?"

"By fire and by arrow, as they tried to murder the lord-mayor. I say tried because Haldemeer Grobaras lives."

"Dead?"

"Get up and make me tea, as you did before."

Tearing at the bedsheets, Yandine wailed out in grief. She threw her head back, weeping, then pitched over, burying her face in the covers.

Luma waited until she had expended herself, and then said, "Get up and make me tea, as you did before."

Yandine blinked at her, uncomprehending.

"I'll not tell you again, Yandine."

Shaking, dull-eyed, snot dripping from her nose, her stepmother freed herself of the coverlet and stumbled to the tea chest. "Why are you asking this of me? Can't you see I'm sick?"

"When you poured tea for me before, you told me that Father was ill and dying. I wish to see if you believed that when you said it, or if you were a party to his murder."

She removed the top from her kettle and reached blindly for the water-jug. "Murder?"

"Was this all your plan, Yandine?" Luma gestured to the heatstone, with its High Chelish provenance, and the kettle, with its decorative devils. "You came to us from Korvosa. Have you not often wished that Magnimar would . . . Let's see, what word would you use for our vassalage? *Ally* with the city of your birth?"

Yandine labored to get the water into the kettle without spilling it all over herself. "Many feel that way," she said.

"And many hope for the ultimate reconstruction of the Chelish Empire."

Seeking composure, Yandine pushed her chin out. "I am not ashamed to count myself among them." Unable to sustain this burst of pride, she let herself fall against the wall. "To tell me that my children are slain, and then accuse me of killing my beloved—you are a cruel, terrible creature, Luma, inhuman and cold!"

"If that is true, I have you and your spawn to thank for it," said Luma. "And I owe them a debt, for their betrayal gave the strength I needed to unmask and destroy them. I am here to determine exactly what sort of debt I owe you, Yandine, and how I might dispatch it."

Yandine balled her fists and beat them against the wallpaper behind her. "If you've come to kill me, then do it. To humiliate me as well . . . it is unforgivable!"

"Did you put them up to it? Was it your idea that Arrus should be lord-mayor?"

Yandine put the kettle on the heatstone and watched as it glowed red.

"And if you're thinking of throwing boiling water at me," said Luma, "I welcome the clarity such an act would bring."

Yandine flung herself in a chair and blew her nose into a soggy handkerchief. "Go ahead and slaughter me, so that I might join my daughters in the existence beyond."

"Only if I conclude that you conspired with them."

"Lord it over me, then. Savor your power over a sick and helpless woman."

"You have a cold, Yandine. Did you tell them to poison Father? To do away with me?"

"No."

"Look at me when you say that."

"No, I did not."

"Say it a third time."

Yandine flushed. She twisted the snot-rag like she was throttling the life from it. "Since they were born I have wanted only the best for my children. If that meant nudging you to the side, then so be it. I desired that Arrus be the greatest man in Magnimar, and that he help restore the lost greatness of our empire. All these things I proudly say. But I loved your father as well as I loved any of them, and would never harm a hair upon his head. Nor would I urge my children to treason and murder. Even if I had, I would not urge them to strike against you. I never considered you consequential enough to stand in our way." Her face shone with defiant fury.

Luma assessed this expression for a good long time. "A prize performance. But I think you are probably lying."

Yandine yanked aside her night-dress, baring her throat to the collarbone. "Then I'll die like a Chelish noble."

Luma opened Yandine's tea-box, transferring a spoonful of Jalmeray Black into an infuser ball, which then dropped into a cup. "I said probably. I can't be sure."

"Read my mind, then."

"I have."

"And?"

"The results are ambiguous. As so much is with you, Yandine. And unless I am certain, I must not slay you. So here is your fate. You have one hour to collect necessaries for your trip from the city. You may take a single trunk and whatever of your personal possessions you can fit into it. These I will inspect, to ensure that you do not rob the house of its treasures."

"I would never stoop to such an act!"

"Gold would ease your journey, and so I deprive you of it. Upon the hour, you will be escorted to the family coach, which will convey you to Dockway. There, Bhax will assist you in procuring the first ship out of the city. Though I expect you will eventually make your way back to Korvosa, you must take the earliest vessel Bhax can find, regardless of its destination or amenities. Should you ever return to Magnimar, rest assured that I will execute you. Also, should I find conclusive proof of your guilt in Father's death, I will hunt you wherever you are in this world, and then you will die, like or unlike a Chelish noble. Have you any questions?"

Yandine jumped to her feet. "You haven't the authority!"

"The lord-mayor has declared me heir. I have that authority and more."

"Until Arrus is executed, he remains lord!"

The kettle whistled; Luma poured tea into her cup. "I'd pour you one as well, but your hour has already begun, and you won't want to tarry. Perhaps you have a technical, legal point in your favor. I invite you to bring it before Grobaras, who is in a hanging mood and looking for imperials he can make examples of without political ramification."

"Even if Arrus was dead, you're still a bastard!"

"Not so, it transpires. Now pack."

Fifty-nine minutes later, Luma found a string of black pearls, two ruby rings, and a shimmering elven mantle in Yandine's trunk. After removing these valuables, she bid the servants convey it to the carriage outside. Yandine stood on the threshold of Derexhi Manor, tears drenching her face and speckling down onto the collar of her traveling cloak, until Luma gestured at her with her sickle. Yandine sucked in a lungfull of air, pointed her nose skyward, and swanned to the coach, which she entered with a queen's hauteur.

Luma watched the carriage until it was out of sight, then felt an emptiness that might have been satisfaction.

Chapter Twenty-Eight
The Basilisk's Eye

Luma went to the Basilisk's Eye, the tavern in Dockway where she'd previously found Thaubnis, and took the corner table. When the barmaid approached, Luma ordered a flagon of ale for appearance's sake, palmed her a gold coin, and said, "See to it we're not bothered." She waited past the tolling of the noon bell and then the one o'clock. Growing uneasy, she waved to the barmaid and requested a mug of water. When it arrived, she muttered the arcane words of a purification spell and drank it down. A balding dockworker smiled at her with fishy lips and rose from his chair, as if to come toward her. With a forbidding grimace, Luma bade him retake his seat. Shortly afterward, he wove up to his feet and fumbled out the door.

The two o'clock bell rang. Luma drummed her fingers along the table, to the rhythm of the prevailing citysong. She got up to use the lavatory. When she returned, Melune was there, having taken the seat she'd vacated, the one with its back against the wall.

Luma sat. "You wished to meet me."

The elf woman paused, as if to listen for threatening sounds, before speaking. "Yes," she said.

"Do you want anything?"

Melune, allowing herself a barely detectable gesture, shook her head.

Luma drank the last of her water. "I thought I might not hear from you again."

Melune took a deep breath. "This is why I asked to see you."

"Yes?"

"I must leave the city. I should have left already. But I did not want to simply disappear. From your point of view, I mean to say. I did not want you to think that I had vanished on you without a thought."

"Should I expect you back?"

Melune's right hand clenched. "That won't be possible."

"For how long?"

"For always," said Melune.

"Do I have to quiz you like Grobaras, to drag the truth from you by guesswork?"

The remark seemed to sting her. "It should be an easy guess," Melune said.

"The Red Mantis have found out. By contacting me, by confirming the marriage to the lord-mayor, you have broken your oath to them."

"I'll not be forgiven twice."

"They've come for you already?"

"I can lose them if I go quickly. There are fewer of them than there are routes out of Magnimar."

"Then you're taking a risk by waiting to talk to me," said Luma. "I must thank you for that."

"I thank you for seeing me."

"How could I not?"

"You scarcely owe me filial duty."

"I am not here out of duty."

"I have not been a mother to you. It was never possible that I could be. For that I am sorry."

Luma shifted in her chair. "I do not ask for your sorrow."

"Yet I regret nonetheless."

"Correct me if I misunderstand the story. You had but two choices. Stay, and be my mother, and get all three of us killed. Or go, so that all of us would be spared. The only way you could have avoided that choice was not to have me at all. For all that has happened, I am grateful for my existence. I am glad to hear that you gave my father happiness, for however short a span. The story explains much. Of my father's sadness. Of his willingness to marry my stepmother, for her money and connections."

"He doubtless hoped she would be good for you."

"We live in a world where hopes oft go unrealized," said Luma.

"Yes," said Melune.

"Were you always in Magnimar? Watching over me?"

"I go where assignments take me. Though I suppose I should say that in past tense, shouldn't I?"

"And whenever Mantis business brought you here, you were that figure, always at the corner of my perceptions."

"A series of foolish chances," said Melune, "that I was compelled to take."

"Did you ever kill someone we were hired to protect?"

Melune smiled. "Some graves are best left undisturbed."

"An assassin's motto if I ever heard one," said Luma. "To whose death do I owe my life?"

"I don't follow you, Luma."

"If you hadn't been watching when my siblings threw me to the golem-grinder, I'd be dead. But you watch me only when a contract brings you to Magnimar. Who died, so that fate could place you there, in a position to spare my life?"

"A man's heart still beats, because I distracted myself helping you."

"That's a consolation."

"Perhaps not," shrugged Melune. "He is quite a terrible fellow."

"Not that the Mantis only kills the terrible."

"They do not discriminate on that basis, no."

"Do you know who hunts you?" Luma asked.

"I can make certain assumptions. They'll be led by . . . well, your grandfather."

"Your father, who must redeem himself after arranging your forgiveness."

Melune's voice wavered. "They may require that he forfeits his life, if he cannot take mine."

"You're not thinking of letting him?"

"I am not."

"Good."

"I would not cause him that anguish. It would be hard enough for him to kill me, but if he suspected I was letting him—already I fear that he might sacrifice himself, for me, and that I cannot permit."

"Will I meet this grandfather?"

"For both your sakes, I pray not." Wincing, Melune touched her hand to her side. Blood had seeped up through her dark-colored tunic.

"You're hurt," Luma said.

"It is nothing," said Melune.

"Then you truly do have to go. But there are so many questions—"

Melune smiled. "Which I ought not answer."

"The story Grobaras got out of you. I can treat that as correct?"

She nodded.

"Then only one question, before you go," said Luma.

"Go ahead," said Melune.

"You use a device that alters your appearance."

"Like your new trick, but not so potent."

"The face you wear now. Is that the real you?"

"There isn't a real me."

"You get what I'm asking."

"There hasn't been a real me since I abandoned you and your father." A tear snaked down Melune's cheek.

"Is this your true face?"

Melune pulled the diadem from her forehead, letting it fall onto the table. Her features blurred. Blond hair turned curly, then the same shade of red as Luma's. It tumbled down in a mad tangle. Luma stared at a version of herself—older, without the scars, but more like her than she'd ever imagined her mother to be.

Luma took her hand.

"My daughter," said Melune. Gritting her teeth, supporting herself on the back of the bench behind her, she rose. She replaced the diadem, transforming into a haggard human woman, her face obscured by wavy chestnut hair. Her doublet, tunic and leggings became a rough shift of sackcloth and linen. The spreading blood, however, remained visible. She brushed Luma on the shoulder and seemed for a moment pulled toward her, perhaps on the brink of an embrace. Then she turned and made quick strides for the tavern's back entrance. Luma watched her go, then unable to resist, hastened to the doorway she'd gone through. It opened onto a deserted back alley.

Chapter Twenty-Nine
Ceremonies

Luma sat at her father's desk, sorting through ledger books. The meaning of the numbers inscribed on their pages—mostly in her father's crabbed scrawl, which near the end gave way to Iskola's tightly controlled hand—eluded her. Written words came naturally to her, but these columns of red and black represented a language she had yet to master. Had she asked her father to teach her, he would have done so. But that was a regret, and thus useless, so she dismissed it. By regarding the ledgers as another puzzle, its massed numerals as reluctant witnesses from whom a story would eventually be extracted, she would work it all out. The dozens of servants, sentinels, and squadders on the Derexhi payroll had not been paid for two weeks, not since the incident at the Arvensoar. So far, they'd shown surprising patience, as much out of shock as anything else. Luma had met with the squad captains, assuring them that the house was not done yet.

They wanted Derexhi to live on as well, and trusted her to see them through. None said aloud that this was in doubt. Yet she'd seen the trepidation on their faces. Rival houses already circled, ready to poach what clients they could. They'd come for the best of the Derexhi forces, too, extending offers to several of the captains. These the captains swore they'd never take. For years, they'd granted allegiance to Randred, and to House Derexhi. In his memory, they would stand by it. Arrus, Iskola, and the rest were traitors not only to the city at large but to them, who'd served so faithfully. They wanted their pride back, to be able to wear Derexhi emblems and stride through Magnimar's streets with heads high. At the meeting, each spoke fervent words about the house and what it had done for them.

Luma, who had thought herself more or less alone, could not show how much these pledges moved her. She spoke to the captains as her father would have: steady, sure, paternal. Odd as it might have been to cast herself as fatherly, the other would have been stranger still. Reaching out into the city's shared consciousness for its history of leaders and heroes, from Alcaydian Indros to Aitin Derexhi to Randred himself, she became what they needed her to be. Because they needed to believe in her, they did.

As she performed this trick, it occurred to her that she would have to make it second nature. It would be needed when she took the family seat at the Council of Ushers. But that horror she could, at least, postpone for later.

The ledgers she would have to crack immediately. Neither loyalty nor fine sentiment could buy a sack of flour or appease a landlord. The men and women who served House Derexhi—who now served *her*—could not go much longer without pay. The difficulty lay in figuring out who was owed what.

Once she set that straight, she had the money to pay them. In fact, as near as she could tell, the family safes bulged with additional coin that could not be accounted for. This could only be payment from the imperial sympathizers who'd joined Iskola's conspiracy. Some of it, perhaps, originated from the official coffers of Korvosa. Luma would use it to protect the house and savor the irony as she did so. Anyone attempting to reclaim the funds would identify himself as a member of the conspiracy, earning a place in the Hells and an early date for execution.

This cushion would only last for so long, through. As Randred had explained, the house sustained itself to a surprising extent on the earnings of its top squad. This might be remedied, by finding efficiencies and raising prices. But the latter could not be accomplished while the shame of the Arvensoar incident still clung to the Derexhi name. Sooner or later, Luma would have no choice but to assemble a new top squad. Of all the tasks awaiting her, finding city warriors to rival her siblings would prove the most daunting.

A tap on the door interrupted her thoughts. Noole entered, followed by Thaubnis. Noole wore a fine, new, and even gaudier doublet. Thaubnis had replaced her drab, threadbare clothing with an equally gloomy outfit straight from the tailor's. She tugged at the collar as if rendered uncomfortable by the extravagance.

"Is it time already?" Luma asked.

"Soon," said Noole. "But there's other business. Panayya Serelem sends word that her sentinel squad failed to meet its morning shift change."

Luma searched for the relevant record book. "Why do we hear from the client, and not the outgoing shift?"

"A reluctance to inform on colleagues, I'd imagine. Frankly, it's a wonder we haven't had more derelictions."

Luma found the roster sheet. "Yelgo Lezen's squad should be on duty. He didn't show for the meeting, did he?"

"You keep asking me these things as if I am some sort of interim factotum," Noole said.

"That's because you are my interim factotum," said Luma.

Thaubnis sat down and began sorting the ledgers into piles.

"You appointed me such," said Noole, "but I do not recall accepting."

"Then clearly you have forgotten."

"Forgotten what?"

"Your implicit agreement to my unstated offer," said Luma.

"Do I hear Luma making a joke?" Noole asked Thaubnis.

"A deadly serious one," said the dwarf, flipping open a ledger. "This system resembles that of the templars of Magrim."

"Magrim?" asked Noole.

"My deity, whom I worship still despite my alleged heresies. Surely I have mentioned his name before."

"It's the first I've heard of it," Noole said. "But to return to the point. Luma, I am no steward or castellan. I am a poet. How am I to write so much as a couplet if I'm spending my days chasing delinquent employees and inventorying the armory?"

"You wanted experience you could write about," said Luma. "What could be more fascinating?"

"Virtually every other activity known to gnomekind. And, not to repeat myself, but I am a poet. Which is to say, an exponent of a notoriously shiftless lot. Why do you trust me?"

"Can I trust you?" Luma asked.

"Absolutely, but that's beside the point!"

Thaubnis built a neat stack of ledgers. "This is not so bad a mess, Luma. It can be sorted."

"Then you're hired."

"I made that assumption."

Luma slid another pile of ledgers toward her. "Father warned me that this was the second worst part of leading House Derexhi."

"The first being politics?"

Luma nodded.

"That road might be smoother than it looks," said Thaubnis. "The lord-mayor's in your debt."

"This afternoon's ceremony expends my last chit with him," said Luma.

"Maybe yes, maybe no. And for every imperial you've terrified—and that's not such an awful thing—there's a fat-purse of the independence faction who credits you with saving his city."

"That is of no consequence," said Luma.

"It will be."

Bhax poked his head in the doorway. "It's time you dressed, milady."

Half an hour later, Luma proceeded down the grand staircase in an unornamented black gown. From a wispy bonnet dropped a sheer veil. Noole and Thaubnis waited for her at the bottom.

"As my master of etiquette," Luma asked Noole, "does this pass muster?"

"You have taken tastefulness to an unnecessary extreme, which is to say, yes. You might fill out the hips."

"With padding?"

Noole's nose wrinkled in annoyance. "No, with your form-changing gift."

"I won't be doing that," said Luma.

"Very well. You are supposed to look a warrior, after all. Do you intend to leave the scars today?"

"Today, more than any other."

They walked three abreast to the carriage house and stepped up into the Derexhi coach, which had been draped in mourning crepe. The chauffeur drove them along the Avenue of Hours, then down the Way of Arches.

For a while they sat in pensive silence. As the coach clattered along, Noole spoke up. "It must be a relief to show your true face without fear."

"Yes," said Luma.

"Not that we'll see a change of expression or anything so extravagant as that."

"I'll be relieved when it's over."

The carriage came to the Cenotaph. From its window Luma beheld an unexampled sight. A mixed group of Shoanti and Varisians gathered in the courtyard surrounding Magnimar's most hallowed monument. Black armbands added a mournful touch to the vivid Varisian outfits. The barbarians stood rigid, decked in their customary funereal gear: armor and weapons for the warriors, and outfits embroidered into stylized semblances of armor for the noncombatants. Furs adorned their shoulders; feathers jutted from the rims of their shields. Their faces they'd painted in ash and blood-red pigment pressed from the bark of the kajan tree.

"When was the last time this happened?" Thaubnis asked.

"Not for generations," answered Noole, "if at all."

Luma remembered to wait until the coachman dismounted from his seat and opened the door for her. Noole hopped out first, followed by a cautious Thaubnis. Luma exited last, performing her best imitation of the grandee she had now become. Back stiff, arms at her sides, she fell into a dignified pace, moving toward the mourners. They milled in two distinct groups: the Magnimarian elite, and the mixed press of Shoanti and Varisians. The latter assessed the former with evident suspicion; the former felt the same but made some effort to pretend otherwise.

Seeing Priza's wife and their children, Luma headed for them, but was intercepted by Urtilia Scarnetti. The matron used a black wimple and dark lace cuffs to render her voluminous crimson gown suitable to the occasion. She took Luma by the arm; Luma inwardly rankled while outwardly allowing her the liberty.

"I thought that I would find you here, my dear," Scarnetti said.

"I would be nowhere else," Luma replied.

Scarnetti leaned in, as if sharing a confidence. "You received my correspondence?"

"I apologize for my delay in replying," said Luma. "The task of putting the house in order . . ."

"Yes, yes, I assumed as much. And I do not wish to add to your burdens. Since we are both here, however, I thought to reiterate: in no way was I aware of the treachery Iskola planned. It was she who sought the connection with me, through the favor of rescuing my nephew. Never would I have sanctioned murder of any kind. Especially not within a house." Scarnetti shuddered. "That way lies madness and disorder. The strength of this city depends on the integrity of its great families. History shows that when noble kin fall to slaying noble kin, disaster attends to all."

"That is my judgment as well, Lady Scarnetti."

"Naturally so, Lu—Lady Derexhi. You bear up well under what must be tremendous sorrow."

"I must, and therefore do."

"I'll not keep you. I simply wanted to say in person that if there is anything I, or those who share my views, can do to assist you in the coming days . . . well, obviously, you need only say so."

"Your good will means much in this city."

"When you are sworn to your usher's seat, many questions will bedevil you. I'll be only too pleased to guide you, to whatever extent you deem fit."

"Your generosity is well appreciated."

"My friends and I consider ourselves above outdated questions of empire or independence. More complex issues face Magnimar in the days ahead. Perhaps you will accept an invitation to attend a less frivolous salon than poor silly Nirodin's, so that you might deepen your learning."

"I look forward to it. When my house affairs have been set right." Luma disengaged from her. "Now if you'll excuse me . . ."

Grobaras, ringed by a new crop of bodyguards, signaled for her attention. The golem was nowhere in sight. Luma wondered if he had bothered to have it repaired. She went to him, the sentinels tensing as she came near.

"When this is done," the lord-mayor said, "the city finally will breathe again." It had been two weeks of ceaseless mourning as the victims of the Arvensoar incident had been laid to rest. Of the dozens of soldiers slain by the Korvosan mercenaries, a single one had been chosen as a representative and interred below the Cenotaph. Beside him had been buried a symbolic exemplar of the many ordinary bystanders killed on the bleachers or while fleeing the battle. Four grandees had been entombed here too, with the rest accorded funerals at simpler gravesites. Shoanti tradition, with its long gap between death and ceremony, had allowed for a convenient span before this last, fraught burial.

The remains of Ulisa and Iskola had been unceremoniously placed in the Derexhi crypt, on the manorial grounds. As for the Korvosans, they'd been thrown into the sea, to be gnawed by fish.

"This better not bite me," said Grobaras. "If it does, I'll know who to blame."

"Then I should see to it that it doesn't," said Luma, making her way at last to Priza's widow. Fidgeting with her black armband, the woman kept a sidelong watch on her children. Dried tears ran down the faces of the two younger children. The eldest, in barbarian gear, set his chin in stoic defiance. The axe he held was too heavy for him, pulling him off balance. From the notches on the grip she suspected it had been Priza's. When Luma bowed to her, Zhaana breathed deep, steeling herself for an unwanted encounter.

"You can see," said Luma, indicating the gathering of grandees, "that they have come, as I said they would."

"A more reluctant lot I've rarely seen," said Zhaana.

"Your husband's folk don't look too happy either."

"This is, they say, but a gesture. Maybe you'd like to talk to one of them, instead."

"Whom do you recommend?"

Zhaana bit her lip. "On second thought, never mind."

Silence hung between them.

Luma finally spoke. "You're right. My people found this a hard gesture to make."

"To inter a common criminal in the great Cenotaph." Zhaana dabbed her tears with a silk handkerchief.

"Gestures, however reluctant, matter. The next one might not be so hard-earned. And then from the one after that, understanding might flow."

"Neither my people nor his want your understanding."

"What you desire is of course up to you. Yet you are here."

"My husband completed his spirit journey. According to his shamans, he now dwells in Elysium. From there he has joined his ancestral moot, and will advise his people, just like the spirits of Shoanti heroes past."

Luma knew better than to ask which afterlife the Varisian thought she was headed for. Would a Varisian wife join a Shoanti husband in the celestial realms, or would they be eternally separated? The complexities of marriage between peoples continued, it would seem, even after death. A flush of compassion for this woman struck her, but she was no longer capable of expressing it. So she held herself erect and hoped the moment would pass. "In other words," Luma asked, "the shamans don't object to his burial here, because the body means nothing to them?"

"So I am told." Zhaana faced the great column of the Cenotaph. "You say that placing him here, among Magnimarian heroes, may start to heal the wounds of resentment between our peoples. For the sake of my children, I hope so."

"Fair enough," said Luma.

Grobaras waved to her.

"They're ready," Luma said, and walked with Zhaana as far as a cart decorated with Axe Clan sigils. She went on to join Grobaras and assorted other dignitaries by an empty bier. Conspicuous by their absence were leaders of the disgraced imperial faction.

An honor guard of armored Shoanti pulled the cart to the bier. Luma and two high officers of the city guard came to relieve certain of the barbarians. Together Shoanti and Chelaxians lifted a pallet, on which rested

Priza's body, which had been preserved by forest magic. Apart from an absence about the face, he might be mistaken for a man deep in restful slumber.

Having performed her part, Luma withdrew to stand beside Noole, Thaubnis, and Hendregan, whom Luma had not seen since the day after the incident.

By prior negotiation, the ceremony mixed Chelish pomp with Shoanti rites. When the psalms were sung, Thaubnis added her own quiet prayer. Her god was a guardian between life and death, and although he typically concerned himself only with dwarves, she commended Priza to him just in case.

Finally, to the tolling of bells and the thumping of hand-drums, Priza was conveyed from the bier and into the catacombs below.

Zhaana and her people would not go past the catacomb door. When it closed, they turned as one and strode from the square. Their rude haste let the grandees make a show of shocked disapproval.

As the crowd broke up, Hendregan took Luma aside. The fire magician held himself with uncharacteristic composure, as he had done throughout the funeral. "Noole says you'll need a new team, to replace the one you were in with your brothers and sisters."

"Yes," said Luma.

He looked down at his toes. "I cannot join it."

"No?"

"Noole reminded me of my purpose in coming here. In the excitement, I had forgotten."

"And what was that, Hendregan?"

"I seek a volcano, who is also my brother."

"There are no volcanoes anywhere around here."

The fire magician shook his head regretfully. "I was misled. Or became confused, which happens sometimes. This is another reason why I cannot join your squad. I am mad. Too mad for this mad place."

"A man who says that is perhaps not as mad as he thinks."

Hendregan snorted gleefully. "I am mad and not mad. Or rather, there are two sides of me, human and not, both of them sane, except when they are combined in one body, as they are."

"So you are leaving Magnimar?"

"To find that volcano. This time I won't be deterred, no matter who I fall in with, or how much fun we are having. We did have fun, didn't we, Luma?"

"Is that what it was?"

Hendregan deflated. "Oh."

"Yes, Hendregan, it was fun that we had. Good luck finding that volcano."

"And the same to you, in finding Ontor." Then he turned and marched away, elbows swung high in the air beside him.

The next morning, Luma and Thaubnis arrived before dawn at the Pediment Building. In its courtyard a crew of carpenters had completed their work and tested the set of wooden stairs leading up the gallows. A light wind blew sawdust and the smell of pine across the square.

A mayoral functionary, whom Luma recognized as one of the men serving Grobaras when he interrogated her, waited to meet her. He escorted the two visitors through the side entrance and down into the Hells. There the citysong screamed, commingling anguish and bloodlust— the conflicting moods of prisoners on an execution morn.

"The lord-mayor reminds you that brevity is a virtue," said the official, before taking them down a dank corridor.

"He needn't," said Luma.

The official took Luma and Thaubnis past a row of empty cells. Only the last one to the right was occupied, by Arrus and Eibadon. They'd been permitted fresh shirts and trousers, which Luma had sent over the day prior. Eibadon had taken on a grayish complexion. He slumped in the back of the cell, on a bench. Stubble dotted his scalp: he was growing out his clerical tonsure. His fellow priests of Abadar had defrocked him. His defense, that the coup would have brought stricter law to a chaotic city, earned him nothing but sneers. The fact that he wasn't bound and gagged indicated that divine favor must have been withdrawn from him, preventing him from calling on even the lowliest spell or blessing.

Arrus, for his part, radiated a defiant health. When he saw Luma, he approached the bars, setting his jaw and squaring his shoulders. He hid the stump of his amputated hand; she peered around him to see that it had healed into a bumpy mass.

Thaubnis hung discreetly back.

"You've come to gloat?" Arrus asked.

"To say goodbye," said Luma. "As is customary, in such circumstances."

"If you've come expecting crying and repentance, you'll get none from us," Arrus said.

"I expect nothing."

"And that's what you'll get," said Arrus.

"What of Mother?" said Eibadon, without stirring. "They won't tell us."

"I sent her away," said Luma.

"To where?"

"To a better place than she deserves, I'd guess. Was she in on it?"

Eibadon straightened up. "Of course not!"

"Then it is good that I exercised mercy," said Luma.

"You aren't fit to say her name," hissed Arrus.

"You'll note that I haven't," said Luma. "I take it you won't be making expressions of remorse on the gallows."

"Gallows? We are of noble blood! We demand beheading, as befits our rank."

"Spoken like a true Korvosan. Your mother will be proud."

"And what of it? Your beloved city, it is a place of lies. Its great families act like nobles yet lack true power. We are Chelish, yet say that we are something different. Had you died, as you were supposed to, Grobaras would be in the Cenotaph and the people would acclaim us. They yearn for a man of ambition to lead them. A warrior, a shaper of visions, not some gluttonous dissembler. Your fat lord-mayor may slay us today, but he will not kill the dream of empire."

"You think that's what the city wants?"

"Sheep love their shepherds, most of all when they must be hard."

"That's why you did it, then. For power, and to please your mother. What boring reasons for such terrible deeds."

"In the end," Eibadon said, "all the goals of man are the same."

Luma made a scoffing sound. "You never regarded me, so it meant nothing to toss me in that grinder. Or to kill the Korvosan dupes, or Khonderian, or see the lives of so many soldiers and spectators snuffed. But patricide?"

"He was sick already," Arrus said.

"History is made by ruthless men," Eibadon added.

"Consider my sisterly duty performed," said Luma. "As to the means of execution, direct all grievances to the man you schemed to assassinate."

As she rejoined Thaubnis, Arrus shouted after her: "If you're counting on a shameful display, there will be none!"

Luma remained silent as they left the Hells and the Pediment Building. The crowd for the hanging trickled, then streamed, into the courtyard. Hawkers sold apples and meat pies. A musician clambered onto a box and tuned his lute. Filches wove through the press of spectators, in search of unprotected purses.

Thaubnis and Noole followed Luma as she headed for a distant vantage, her forbidding presence parting the crowd before her.

She watched as her brothers were transported to the foot of the gallows. "For as long as they could talk, I yearned for their acceptance."

"They were your family," said Thaubnis. "Your people."

"But that's the question, isn't it? If they'd given it to me—what monster might I have gladly become?"

As promised, Arrus and Eibadon confronted their nooses with stoic self-possession. Refusing the hoods they were proffered, they died facing the throng. The executioner dropped the lever, releasing the trapdoor. A prison healer checked their swinging bodies for signs of life. When he found none, they were cut down and loaded onto a cart. The crowd followed it, filling the Avenue of Honors, on its route to the city wall, where both corpses would be loaded into separate gibbets. There they would hang as an object lesson to traitors, until the last morsels from their bones had been stripped away by crows.

Chapter Thirty
Korvosa

Yandine, fine features concealed beneath a ragged kerchief, navigated the narrow streets of Korvosa's slum district, a sack hefted over her shoulder. A choking reek of ordure emanated from the gutters. Teetering tenements leaned out over the laneways. Weird, red-pawed rats leapt like squirrels between their roofs.

A blond, chubby-cheeked halfling observed her from behind a derelict food cart. When Yandine had passed, he ambled after her, following her until she doubled back on him. He tipped his floppy hat as she passed him and kept on going. The halfling ducked through an open tenement door and transformed into a Varisian urchin girl, who then darted into the street to catch up with Yandine.

At length she spied Yandine entering a ramshackle cottage. She hung back, sheltered by a mound of rubble.

It was Luma's first time outside Magnimar. Dissonant and thunderous, Korvosa's citysong differed from home, to be sure. But she could hear it, and despite her loathing for this place—its grim crags, its stink of the diabolic, and the crabbed cruelties of its collective soul—she could still draw magic from it.

She waited until her quarry came back out again, without the bag, and then a few minutes more. Then she circuited the block, coming at the cottage through a rodent-infested back alley.

Ontor hunched over a scuffed table, gobbling a salad of seabeets from a pewter bowl. He looked up as she came in, then kicked the table over and reached for a knife which rested on the mantle of a crumbled fireplace.

"You're barging in on the wrong person," he said.

"Not so," answered Luma, reverting to her true form. She pulled her sickle.

Ontor hung back, dagger outstretched. "Don't make me do this. You're no match for me in close quarters."

"Don't be so sure."

She came at him with the sickle. He tried his usual turn-and-grab move, the one she'd planned for. Luma tilted to the other side, slashing his elbow. While she had leather armor under her outfit, Ontor wore only street clothes. Gasping, he wheeled back.

"You're tougher," he said.

She dove for him. He caught a stool under his foot and kicked it at her. Its edge clipped her on the forehead, opening a wound at her hairline. "But I haven't turned into an idiot, either," Ontor breathed.

Wiping away blood, she picked up the stool and hurled at him. He ducked; it bounced off a wall and into a tile stove, breaking into pieces.

"Be merciful, Luma," said Ontor. "No one wanted this less than I did."

With her free hand, she punched him in the face.

"You want to smack me a bit?" Ontor said. "Go ahead."

She plucked loose the throwing darts strapped to her thigh and hurled them at him. Ontor dove low; they passed harmlessly overhead. She threw a final dart; it sailed into his shoulder, above the collarbone.

He winced. "I did my best, remember? I tried to warn you. It wasn't too late then. And all along I argued against it, even at the last minute."

"And Father?"

"I had no idea, I swear. Only after they'd given him the fatal dose did I put it together. Mother still won't believe that part of it."

"So you say."

"I swear. I swear on anything. Luma, of course you have every right to seek vengeance. I merely ask you to find pity, the pity for both of us, so that I don't have to—"

She bowled into him, throwing him off balance, and swiped the sickle into his ribs. He twisted aside, using the burst of momentum to yank her into the wall. As he did so, he seized the sickle, twisted it from her grip, and threw it across the room. It sailed into the far wall, sinking into the half-rotted timber. She saw that he was ready to go for her if she tried to recover it.

When she stayed where she was, he stepped closer. He reached down to the tear she'd cut into his shirt. She'd carved a long red wound across his ribs. "You can pummel me all you want, Luma, but let's keep weapons out of it."

He was leaving himself open. But it was a trick—when she swung at him, he caught her arm and twisted. "I don't expect forgiveness. But between that and killing, there's such a gulf. Why don't we each let the other go his own way? Walk out that door, Luma."

She wrenched herself free, elbowed him in the chest, and tripped him, sending him tumbling onto his back. Before he could wrench away, Luma landed on him, pressing thumbs into his throat. Bucking to the side, he threw her off; she recovered, rolling into a sitting position.

Ontor's face was red. A loop of drool hung from his lip. "You won't let up, will you? I can't let you go, because you'll never let up. I can leave here, and you'll follow me." He lunged at her, his dagger pointed at the hollow between her clavicles. Luma caught his wrist. Their arms trembled as he forced it slowly down, his strength overcoming hers.

"Swear to me that you'll relent," he said, "and I won't have to do this."

Luma put all of her power into her effort, but still the tip of the dagger dipped by increments toward her.

"Don't make me, Luma!" Ontor shouted.

Just as the blade was about to pierce her, the tension went from his arm. He dropped the blade, letting it clatter to the floor.

He fell onto her, sobbing. "Why won't you believe that I'm sorry?"

"I do believe it," said Luma. Her fingers found the hilt of his dagger.

"Then why are you doing this?" Ontor cried.

Luma plunged the dagger into his back. She felt his jolt of shock and pain and wrapped her free arm around him.

"Because," she said, "of all of them, you're the only one who loved me."

He tried to struggle free. She pulled the blade up, pinning him to her, holding him in place. Her tears now mirroring his, she twisted the blade.

"You loved me," she whispered. "And you killed me anyway."

About the Author

Robin D. Laws's previous Pathfinder Tales stories include the novel *The Worldwound Gambit*, the novellas "Plague of Light" and "The Treasure of Far Thallai," and the short story "The Ironroot Deception." His other fiction includes *Pierced Heart*, *The Rough and the Smooth*, and *New Tales of the Yellow Sign*. Robin designed such roleplaying games as *Ashen Stars*, *The Esoterrorists*, *HeroQuest*, and *Feng Shui*. You can find his blog, a cavalcade of hobby games, film, culture, narrative structure, and gun-toting avians, at **robinlaws.com**.

Glossary

All Pathfinder Tales novels are set in the rich and vibrant world of the Pathfinder campaign setting. Below are explanations of several key terms used in this book. For more information on the world of Golarion and the strange monsters, people, and deities that make it their home, see *The Inner Sea World Guide,* or dive into the game and begin playing your own adventures with the *Pathfinder Roleplaying Game Core Rulebook* or the *Pathfinder Roleplaying Game Beginner Box,* all available at **paizo.com**. In particular, fans of Magnimar may wish to check out the sourcebook *Magnimar, City of Monuments* and the upcoming Shattered Star Adventure Path, a whole campaign of Pathfinder RPG adventures that begins in the city of Magnimar.

Abadar: Master of the First Vault and the god of cities, wealth, merchants, and law.

Absalom: Largest city in the Inner Sea region.

Alabaster District: District housing Magnimar's wealthiest and most influential citizens.

Alcaydian Indros: Heroic founder of Magnimar.

Alchemists: Spellcasters whose magic takes the form of potions, explosives, and strange mutagens that modify their own physiology.

Arcane: Type of magic that does not come from a deity.

Arvensoar: Massive tower that defends Magnimar, manned by the city's military.

Asmodeus: Devil-god of tyranny, slavery, pride, and contracts; lord of Hell and current patron deity of Cheliax.

Battle of Charda: Monument commemorating a great battle against the neighboring city of Riddleport.

Bazaar of Sails: Mercantile district near Magnimar's docks.

Beacon's Point: District in Magnimar devoted to docks and shipping.

Bridgeward: Neighborhood in the Capital District; home to many artisans.

Capital District: District devoted to artisans and government.

Cayden Cailean: God of freedom, ale, wine, and bravery. Was once mortal, but ascended to godhood by passing the Test of the Starstone in Absalom.

Celwynvian Charge: Half-living tree-shaped monument gifted to Magnimar by elves.

Cenotaph: Cylindrical mausoleum monument celebrating Magnimar's founder; the city's most prestigious dead are often interred in the newer catacombs beneath it.

Chelaxian: Someone from Cheliax. Most of Magnimar's elite are ethnic Chelaxians, though not actual citizens of Cheliax.

Cheliax: A devil-worshiping nation in southwestern Avistan.

Chelish: Of or relating to the nation of Cheliax.

Cobblestone Druid: One of many names for the urban magic-users who draw magical power from the innate energy of cities and other urban centers, similar to the way most druids draw power and inspiration from nature.

Council of Ushers: Governing body of Magnimar, consisting of the most influential and experienced people in the city. Characterized—and often crippled—by factionalism and debate, the council is currently hard pressed to exert as much control as the office of the lord-mayor.

Derexhi Family: One of Magnimar's powerful founding families, specializing in providing private security and hired justice for those with means.

Devils: Fiendish occupants of Hell who seek to corrupt mortals in order to claim their souls.

Dockway: Magnimarian district most devoted to trade and imports/exports.

Druid: Someone who reveres nature and draws magical power from the boundless energy of the natural world.

Dwarves: Short, stocky humanoids who excel at physical labor, mining, and craftsmanship.

Elemental Plane: A dimension of pure elemental energy that exists beyond the normal world.

Elves: Race of long-lived, beautiful humanoids.

Elven: Of or pertaining to elves.

First Vault: Vast storehouse on Axis where Abadar keeps a perfect master copy of everything in existence.

Flayleaf: Plant with narcotic leaves.

Gnomes: Small humanoids with strange mindsets, originally from the First World.

Golarion: The planet on which the Pathfinder campaign setting focuses.

Golemworks: Consortium of Magnimarian artificers and construct-crafters who build and sell magical automatons.

Grand Arch: Neighborhood in Magnimar's Naos district, home to middle-class residences, many of which are occupied only part of the time by traveling merchants.

Half-Elves: Of human and elven descent, half-elves are often regarded as having the best qualities of both races, yet still see a certain amount of prejudice, particularly from their pure elven relations.

Halflings: Race of humanoids known for their tiny stature, deft hands, and mischievous personalities.

Half-Orcs: Bred from humans and orcs, members of this race have green or gray skin, brutish appearances, and short tempers, and are mistrusted by many societies.

Hell: Plane of evil and tyrannical order ruled by devils, where many evil souls go after they die.

Hellknights: Organization of hardened law enforcers whose tactics are often seen as harsh and intimidating, and who bind devils to their will. Based in Cheliax.

Hells: Magnimar's notorious prison, positioned beneath the Pediment Building.

Iomedae: Goddess of valor, rulership, justice, and honor.

Irespan: Enormous ruined bridge leading out to sea from Magnimar's upper districts; a relic of a now-forgotten empire.

Irrisen: A realm of permanent winter north of Varisia, claimed by Baba Yaga and ruled by her daughters.

Justice Court: Thirteen judges who compose Magnimar's highest judiciary council.

Keystone: Magnimarian district devoted primarily to temples and the homes of the common people.

Korvosa: Largest city in Varisia and outpost of former Chelish loyalists, now self-governed. For more information, see the Pathfinder Campaign Setting book *Guide to Korvosa*.

Korvosan: Of or from Korvosa; someone from Korvosa. Often viewed with suspicion by Magnimarians.

Kyonin: An elven forest-kingdom in eastern Avistan.

Lizardfolk: Race of reptilian humanoids; often viewed as backward by more "civilized" races.

Lord Justice: The most powerful judge of Magnimar's Justice Court.

Lowcleft: District of Magnimar devoted primarily to arts and entertainment.

Magnimar: Port city in southwestern Varisia, best known for its many monuments, including the enormous bridge called the Irespan. Founded by immigrants fleeing Korvosa and its political ties to the devil-worshiping nation of Cheliax.

Magnimarian: Of or from Magnimar.

Magrim: Lesser-known dwarven deity.

Maralictor: Mid-level Hellknight rank.

Marble District: Neighborhood of the greater Alabaster District in Magnimar, home to many of the manors of the city's elite.

Marches: Residential neighborhood for common folk in Magnimar—part of the larger Keystone district.

Naos: District housing much of the "new money" merchant aristocracy in Magnimar.

Orc: A bestial, warlike race of humanoids from deep underground who now roam the surface in barbaric bands. Universally hated by more civilized races.

Ordellia: District of Magnimar dedicated to housing settled foreigners and dissidents; almost a town in its own right.

Pathfinder Society: Organization of traveling scholars and adventurers who seek to document the world's wonders. Based out of Absalom and run by a mysterious and masked group called the Decemvirate.

Pathfinder: A member of the Pathfinder Society.

Pediment Building: Primary government building of Magnimar.

Pharasma: The goddess of birth, death, and prophecy, who judges mortal souls after their deaths and sends them on to the appropriate afterlife; also known as the Lady of Graves.

Qadira: Desert nation east of the Inner Sea.

Rag's End: Magnimarian slum district.

Rahadoum: Atheist nation where religion is outlawed. Abuts Thuvia's western border.

Red Mantis: Infamous assassin cult, renowned for their efficacy, their red insect-like armor, and their sawtoothed sabers.

Seacleft: The massive cliff which splits Magnimar into two sections: the Summit above, and the Shore below.

Shackles: Pirate isles southwest of the Inner Sea.

Shadow District: Section of Magnimar directly beneath the great bridge of the Irespan, and thus usually in shadow.

Shelyn: The goddess of beauty, art, love, and music.

Shoanti: Indigenous peoples of the Storval Plateau in Varisia.

Shore: Group of districts positioned below the Seacleft; the poorer districts of Magnimar.

Sorcerer: Spellcaster who draws power from a supernatural ancestor or other mysterious source, and does not need to study to cast spells.

Storval Plateau: Harsh uplands of eastern Varisia.

Stylobate: One of the most exclusive neighborhoods in the Alabaster District in Magnimar.

Summit: Group of districts positioned above the Seacleft; the wealthier districts of Magnimar.

Tines: Raised fork on which Chelish criminals are sometimes impaled. Also the name of a rude hand gesture from Cheliax, which suggests that the recipient should be impaled in such a manner.

Triodea: Most prestigious performance hall in Magnimar.

Ustalav: Gothic nation bearing a reputation for strange beasts, ancient secrets, and moral decay.

Varisia: Frontier region at the northwestern edge of the Inner Sea region, of which Korvosa and Magnimar are the two largest cities.

Varisian: Something from Varisia, or else a member of the often maligned Varisian ethnic group, which is known for its music, dance, and traveling caravans.

Venture-Captain: A rank in the Pathfinder Society above that of a standard field agent but below the Decemvirate.

Vista: Neighborhood of Magnimar's Naos district featuring high-class shops and merchants.

Wizard: Someone who casts magical spells through research of arcane secrets and the constant study of spells, which he or she records in a spellbook.

In the forbidding north, the demonic hordes of the magic-twisted hellscape known as the Worldwound encroach upon the southern kingdoms of Golarion. Their latest escalation embroils a preternaturally handsome and coolly charismatic swindler named Gad, who decides to assemble a team of thieves, cutthroats, and con men to take the fight into the demon lands and strike directly at the fiendish leader responsible for the latest raids—the demon Yath, the Shimmering Putrescence. Can Gad hold his team together long enough to pull off the ultimate con, or will trouble from within his own organization lead to an untimely end for them all?

From gaming legend and popular fantasy author Robin D. Laws comes a fantastic new adventure of swords and sorcery, set in the award-winning world of the Pathfinder Roleplaying Game.

The Worldwound Gambit print edition: $9.99
ISBN: 978-1-60125-327-9

The Worldwound Gambit ebook edition:
ISBN: 978-1-60125-334-7

the
WORLDWOUND
Gambit

ROBIN D. LAWS

PATHFINDER
TALES

Once a student of alchemy with the dark scholars of the Technic League, Alaeron fled their arcane order when his conscience got the better of him, taking with him a few strange devices of unknown function. Now in hiding in a distant city, he's happy to use his skills creating minor potions and wonders—at least until the back-alley rescue of an adventurer named Jaya lands him in trouble with a powerful crime lord. In order to keep their heads, Alaeron and Jaya must travel across wide seas and steaming jungles in search of a wrecked flying city and the magical artifacts that can buy their freedom. Yet the Technic League hasn't forgotten Alaeron's betrayal, and an assassin armed with alien weaponry is hot on their trail . . .

From Hugo Award-winning author Tim Pratt comes a new adventure of exploration, revenge, strange technology, and ancient magic, set in the fantastical world of the Pathfinder Roleplaying Game.

City of the Fallen Sky print edition: $9.99
ISBN: 978-1-60125-418-4

City of the Fallen Sky ebook edition:
ISBN: 978-1-60125-419-1

CITY OF THE FALLEN SKY

TIM PRATT

In the grim nation of Nidal, carefully chosen children are trained to practice dark magic, summoning forth creatures of horror and shadow for the greater glory of the Midnight Lord. Isiem is one such student, a promising young shadowcaster whose budding powers are the envy of his peers. Upon coming of age, he's dispatched on a diplomatic mission to the mountains of Devil's Perch, where he's meant to assist the armies of devil-worshiping Cheliax in clearing out a tribe of monstrous winged humanoids. Yet as the body count rises and Isiem comes face to face with the people he's exterminating, lines begin to blur, and the shadowcaster must ask himself who the real monsters are . . .

From Liane Merciel, critically acclaimed author of *The River King's Road* and *Heaven's Needle*, comes a tale of darkness and redemption set in the award-winning world of the Pathfinder Roleplaying Game.

Nightglass print edition: $9.99
ISBN: 978-1-60125-440-5

Nightglass ebook edition:
ISBN: 978-1-60125-441-2

Nightglass

LIANE MERCIEL

In the deep forests of Kyonin, elves live secretively among their own kind, far from the prying eyes of other races. Few of impure blood are allowed beyond the nation's borders, and thus it's a great honor for the half-elven Count Varian Jeggare and his hellspawn bodyguard Radovan to be allowed inside. Yet all is not well in the elven kingdom: demons stir in its depths, and an intricate web of politics seems destined to catch the two travelers in its snares. In the course of tracking down a missing druid, Varian and a team of eccentric elven adventurers will be forced to delve into dark secrets lost for generations—including the mystery of Varian's own past.

From fan favorite Dave Gross, author of *Prince of Wolves* and *Master of Devils*, comes a fantastical new adventure set in the award-winning world of the Pathfinder Roleplaying Game.

Queen of Thorns print edition: $9.99
ISBN: 978-1-60125-463-4

Queen of Thorns ebook edition:
ISBN: 978-1-60125-464-1

Queen of Thorns

Dave Gross

PATHFINDER
TALES

PRINCE of WOLVES
Dave Gross

Winter Witch
Elaine Cunningham

Plague of Shadows
Howard Andrew Jones

the WORLDWOUND Gambit
Robin D. Laws

Master of Devils
Dave Gross

Death's Heretic
James L. Sutter

Subscribe to Pathfinder Tales!

Stay on top of all the pulse-pounding, sword-swinging action of the Pathfinder Tales novels by subscribing online at **paizo.com/pathfindertales**! Each new novel will be sent to you as it releases—roughly one every two months—so you'll never have to worry about missing out. Plus, subscribers will also receive free electronic versions of the novels in both ePub and PDF format. So what are you waiting for? Fiery spells, flashing blades, and strange new monsters await you in the rest of the Pathfinder Tales novels, all set in the fantastical world of the Pathfinder campaign setting!

THE INNER SEA WORLD GUIDE

You've delved into the Pathfinder campaign setting with Pathfinder Tales novels—now take your adventures even further! *The Inner Sea World Guide* is a full-color, 320-page hardcover guide featuring everything you need to know about the exciting world of Pathfinder: overviews of every major nation, religion, race, and adventure location around the Inner Sea, plus a giant poster map! Read it as a travelogue, or use it to flesh out your roleplaying game—it's your world now!

EXPLORE YOUR WORLD!

paizo.com